The Wednesday Club

KJELL WESTÖ

The Wednesday Club

Translated from the Swedish
by Neil Smith

MACLEHOSE PRESS
QUERCUS · LONDON

First published in the Swedish language as *Hägring 38*
by Schildts & Söderströms, Helsingfors, in 2013
First published in Great Britain in 2016 by

MacLehose Press
an imprint of Quercus Editions Ltd
Carmelite House
50 Victoria Embankment
London EC4Y 0DZ

An Hachette UK Company

Co-funded by the
Creative Europe Programme
of the European Union

This work has been published with the financial support of

FILI   FINNISH
         LITERATURE
         EXCHANGE

ISBN (TPB) 978 0 85705 351 0
ISBN (Ebook) 978 1 84866 781 5

1 3 5 7 9 10 8 6 4 2

Designed and typeset in Galliard by Patty Rennie
Printed and bound in Great Britain by Clays Ltd, St Ives plc

The Wednesday Club

Wednesday, 16 November

When Mrs Wiik failed to turn up for work that morning, at first he felt irritated.

Perhaps there was also a remnant of irritation from his failed excursion to Kopparbäck the previous evening. He had kept quiet about his thoughts so as not to upset Jary, then had lain awake all night worrying, before making his way to the office two hours earlier than normal.

He was exhausted, simple as that. The Club meeting that evening felt like a burden, and his work was starting to pile up. Three new clients in two weeks, a difficult case in the City Court, outstanding invoices, lingering formalities as a result of Rolle's departure, letters to be dictated and sent: without Mrs Wiik he was stranded.

He had arrived at the office before half past seven. He was not usually there before nine, he preferred to work late into the evening. But he knew that Mrs Wiik arrived at eight o'clock on the dot, even on Saturdays.

His irritation failed to disperse as he waited for her to appear, and was still gnawing away at him at half past eight, when it occurred to him that perhaps he ought to call her at home to reassure himself that she had not broken her leg, gone down with flu or lost her voice, something like that.

When he dialled the number the first time he was not really concentrating. As he waited for her to answer, he thought about that evening's meeting, and about the things he wanted to speak to the others about in private. He would ask Arelius to stop criticising his political opinions in front of his mother, Esther. And, above all, he wanted to talk to Lindemark about Yogi Jary: there had to be *something* they could do.

When Mrs Wiik didn't answer he assumed she must be on her way to the office. He would hear footsteps on the stairs and her key in the lock any time now.

But she did not come. And when he had rung three times without getting any answer, he began to get worried.

She was punctuality personified. And she always asked for his permission when she wanted to take longer for lunch or arrive late in the morning.

It was not yet nine o'clock, but he decided to travel up to Tölö and knock on her door. Once he had taken the decision he acted quickly. He pulled on his ulster and gloves, took his hat from the shelf, went down the stairs and jogged to the tram stop.

Only when he was sitting on the tram did it occur to him how stupid he had been. The car was standing on Kaserntorget. Why had he not gone down there and then driven straight to Mechelingatan? That would have been much quicker.

1

It was a sleepy sort of morning, misty and wet.

Like a sagging cord, Miss Milja thought, a sodden grey rope carelessly slung up between the dying winter and a still distant spring.

Much later she would remember that she had been day-dreaming about going home early, that she had had a clear plan of how the day would transpire.

The dream: leaving the office at three o'clock and walking the few blocks to the Academic Bookshop in Stockmann's darkly gleaming building. Buying a magazine, preferably the latest issue of *Elokuva-Aitta*, the one with film star Rolf Wanka on the cover. Then trying to get an appointment for a manicure with Mrs Tuomisto at the Salon Roma, even though she hadn't booked in advance.

She had treated herself to a manicure for the very first time the previous summer, in July, when Hoffman & Laurén had given her two weeks' holiday on full pay. Now her hands were looking worn again, her nails chipped and uneven as a consequence of handling all those papers and files for Thune, as well as the housework at home. But what was the point of lying? When little Miss Milja felt uneasy and no-one was looking, she would bite them, that's what made her nails ugly, and then stylish Mrs Wiik would end up embarrassed, and try to hide them as best she could.

Miss Milja bit the tips of her fingers as well, late in the evenings when the curtains were drawn for the night. Then she could lose herself in a book or sink into Milja-thoughts, to the point where she did not notice herself start to chew on the outer layer of skin on her fingertips, nipping it off with her teeth. The skin came off in flakes, and Miss Milja had become accomplished at it over the years, knowing exactly when she should stop pulling, and always managing to bite off the thin layer of skin before the fingertip started to bleed, then spitting the fragment out onto the floor, unless it happened to land beside her in bed.

She had not succumbed to doing that for a while now. Her nails were uneven, but otherwise her hands were in good condition and intact, and she would put them to good use in the salon when she began to read the cinema magazine while Mrs Tuomisto performed the manicure, one hand at a time, allowing her to turn the pages with her free hand. She would pick out one article to read, perhaps the international column with all the gossip from Hollywood and the U.F.A. studios in Berlin. She would look at pictures of stars like Leslie Howard and Cary Grant, and just enjoy herself.

In her purse she had a yellowed cutting of Grant, and Randolph Scott, in bathing trunks, it was three years old and she had never shown it to anyone. She was ashamed. Almost thirty-seven years old, but Miss Milja still idolised American actors with pomaded hair, white teeth and a perfect little dimple in the middle of their chin. *I am a very great lover of your art and I should be the luckiest.* Miss Milja would have liked to write to Grant and Scott and Howard and the others and ask for photographs. She would have liked to write to Rolf Wanka as well – *Ich bin eine grosse Verehrerin*. But so far she had not written to anyone at all.

Santeri Soihtu actually had just as perfect a dimple in his chin as Cary Grant and Rolf Wanka. But that was not the same thing. Santeri Soihtu did not live in a distant, fairy-tale city of cinema, but in a flat in the Tölö district with his wife. You could see him in Helsinki any day of the week, you could see him going into a bank or eating dinner at the Kämp or Monte Carlo or another of the city's finer restaurants. On the screen Soihtu might play a courageous activist fighting against Russian oppression in 1902, or an honest *jaeger* officer from the winter of 1918, but in reality he was not exciting at all.

Unless perhaps he was after all? *Elokuva-Aitta* had printed that Santeri Soihtu was a stage-name, and that the star wanted to keep his real identity secret. So that he was left in peace, it had said. It would not have made the slightest difference to her had she found out that Cary Grant's real name was not Archibald Leach but Bronomir Mankulovsky, or that Leslie Howard had been born Yoram Kardashian rather than Leslie Steiner. But here in Helsinki, Miss Milja wanted to know where people really came from. If no-one knew Santeri Soihtu's real name, then no-one could know what he had been doing twenty years ago, during the Civil War. He must have been a boy then, just a child, but imagine if he had been in one of the camps despite that? Maybe he had been an errand boy, or had polished the soldiers' boots to earn money for food. Things had been chaotic back then, hardship and fear reigned, people did things that they kept quiet about afterwards.

Once the manicure was finished and she had paid Mrs Tuomisto, she would go to a delicatessen. One of the exclusive ones, Klimscheffsky's or Marstio's. She would treat herself to something nice for later on, a tin of peaches preserved in syrup, or a cone of assorted sweets. Or perhaps some Da Capo chocolates, she liked the sunshine-yellow wrappers and the dark chocolate inside.

Then she would take the tram out to Tölö.

The smell of rusting iron, damp clothes and unwashed bodies during the journey.

She would buy groceries from the shop on Caloniusgatan. Make dinner, eat it, do the washing up. Wait until the evening concert began on the radio, turn the volume down slightly, switch on the reading lamp, settle into the red armchair with the pale wooden arms, wrap her shawl around her and read, with the chocolates or a dish of peach halves within easy reach.

She would let herself drift off. To Brentwood and Beverly Hills, to villas with twenty rooms, open-topped luxury cars and swimming pools, to a world of manicured gardens with palm-trees and acacias and bougainvillea, chauffeurs in full-length uniform coats, buxom black housemaids who were always ready with a sharp but comforting remark.

A different world from the blunt, grim, grey one she inhabited.

She would let herself be swallowed up by the articles, only coming round when the national anthem played. Concert over, back to reality. Switch the radio off, turn off the reading lamp, perform her evening ablutions, check the gas stove was off. She was scared of being burned alive, gas explosions were common and the ensuing fires deadly: she checked the stove every time she left the house, and every evening before going to bed.

It would be cold in the bedroom, her little two-room flat was always cold and draughty well into May. The bed would be empty, the way it had been ever since Hannes left her, when he had simply had enough and walked out without a word. She would lay out her clothes, get under the covers, roll onto her side, pull up her legs and curl into a foetal position, maybe put a hand on her stomach between the covers and her nightgown to get more warmth.

She would feel alone, of course, she would feel it deep in her bones.

But she would feel happy as well.

Happy because she had got somewhere. Away from everything that no-one – above all not Claes Thune the lawyer, and his smart clients – would ever imagine when they cast surreptitious glances (or so they thought!) at her simple but well-cut skirt suit and her glossy hair and the slender ankles that stretched up from her high-heeled shoes.

And, as of tomorrow: at her manicured hands, her filed and red-varnished nails.

Yes. Tonight one of those newly smart hands would rest against her stomach for more warmth, and Miss Milja would be nice and quiet and Matilda would fall asleep quickly and carry on dreaming. About something better. Something even better than what she already had.

2

Half an hour after lunch she had typed up the letters, put them in envelopes and franked them. Matilda looked up and gazed out across Kaserntorget. The fog had got thicker: she could only just see the Radio House on the far side of the square.

She got up from her chair, about to go and knock on the lawyer's door and ask if she could leave at three o'clock. Thune had met several clients during the morning, and she had shown them into his room, but had hardly seen him otherwise. He had dictated two letters to her, that was all. The letters had been short and measured in tone, on the verge of terse. Thune had eaten his lunch in his office, liver pâté and pickled gherkin sandwiches wrapped carelessly in greaseproof paper; she had noticed him take them out of his briefcase that morning. The sandwiches had looked dry and curled, and she had wondered silently what he drank with them. A soft drink, perhaps – there was a cold-store in the wall beside the window and she had seen brown bottles inside. She knew Thune had recently separated from his wife: it looked as if he had not yet found a new routine.

The door opened and the lawyer's long, narrow, almost bald head appeared in the opening. Matilda quickly sat down again and waited for him to say something. Thune looked a bit like Stan Laurel; she had noticed that during her job interview. Now, as he leaned one shoulder against the door-frame with his hands in his pockets, he looked almost snake-like. Matilda thought that the resemblance was an illusion, a Milja-thought, just something that had popped into her head. Thune's suit was as ill-fitting as usual, today's colour a badly creased blue.

She quite liked Thune. He could be arrogant sometimes without actually realising it, and he dressed badly and occasionally said strange things. But he was also friendly, and he seemed fair. Intelligent and kind, not a combination to be taken for granted. At least not among the clients who visited Thune's office. Pushy but pretending to be nice, was Matilda's impression. Some of them looked right through her like she wasn't there, while others looked at her in an improper way.

"Mrs Leimu has a bad cold," Thune said, sounding agitated as he went on: "She's at home in bed. I have an appointment with Grönroos in a few minutes, and the Wednesday Club is meeting here at the office this evening. Mrs Wiik, do you think you might be able to go down to the Market Hall to get things for the meeting on my behalf?"

Mrs Leimu was Thune's housekeeper, and his right hand since the separation. Without her, Thune would have been overwhelmed by practical worries. And Leopold Grönroos was one of the members of the Wednesday Club, very possibly the wealthiest. Landlord, rentier, miser, *bon viveur* – all terms Matilda had heard used to describe Grönroos, even though she had only been working for Thune for a month and a half.

Grönroos arrived punctually the same time each week, every Wednesday at half past two. He and Thune would sit down in the innermost room, the Cabinet, and talk at length about Grönroos' investments. Every so often Grönroos would make a gesture of annoyance, drumming his fleshy fingers nervously on the desk. Every time Thune calmly pointed out any risk of a lower dividend, a wrinkle would appear above Grönroos' nose. When the meeting had gone on for an hour or so, Thune would

11

call Matilda and ask her to bring in the port, whisky and appropriate glasses from the drinks cabinet in his room. He would suggest a "cheeky little drink" and Grönroos would decline at first out of consideration for his gout, which was getting worse with each passing year. But then Grönroos would change his mind, and soon he and Thune would be on their second, then third cheeky little drink. By this point they would no longer be talking about money, but would have moved on to long-distance runners and composers, and eventually, by the time they reached the fourth or fifth cheeky little drink, they would be drunk. Matilda had observed all this as she carried files in to them and served their drinks. It was always gloomy in the Cabinet; a fire would be burning in the stove, with just one table-lamp lit. That was how Thune preferred it. But she would have been able to observe them unnoticed even if the lighting had been brighter; they were so absorbed in their discussion they scarcely noticed her coming and going.

She was disappointed at the turn the day had taken, but hid her feelings as best she could. The Wednesday Club was a group of Thune's friends who took it in turns to host drinking sessions on the third Wednesday of each month. Matilda knew little more about the Club than that. But she realised that if Mrs Leimu was ill and the March meeting was going to be held here in the office, she would not be allowed to leave early.

"What would you like me to get from the market, Mr Thune?" she asked.

"Rustic pâté, preferably a strong one," Thune said. "A couple of mature cheeses. Salty biscuits, those British ones. And pitted green olives. Italian, not Spanish. Two tins of those."

Thune pulled his glasses down to the tip of his nose and looked amiably at her: "And I've told you before, you don't have to keep calling me Mr Thune. There's really no need to be so formal."

He took out his wallet from the pocket of his creased jacket, flicked through the notes and pulled out a fifty-mark note. Then he changed his mind, put the fifty back and took out a hundred-mark note instead.

"Could you buy some drink as well? Two bottles of port and two of whisky. Ask for the manager, Lehtonen. He was the one who took my order, they didn't have what I wanted in stock."

Matilda took the note, giving it a quick glance. In the foreground was a group of naked, athletic people, while in the background factory chimneys billowed thick smoke. Had Thune noticed that the woman on the far left had a well-shaped rear? Probably, Matilda thought, silently answering her own question.

She would later recall that the grey mist had a smoky, almost friendly quality that day. Not the usual March greyness, rugged and harsh, with sheets of ice and smaller blocks jostling in the inner harbours where the water was still completely black. Instead it was a milder greyness, a blanket to wrap yourself in. Like September, when the heat was over and the last of the thunderstorms had passed.

An unreal atmosphere had settled over the city. Life as a dream, a shapeless mirage. There was that word again, she wondered why it kept occurring to her, over and over again. Then she suddenly thought of Konni. He had written to her in February, from Åbo, where Arizona had been engaged at the Hamburger Börs all winter. He had told her about the new songs he had written, among them one called just that, "Mirage".

Konni had written that he wanted to record "Mirage" with Arizona, but that he was short of money and was thinking of selling the song to Dallapé or the Ramblers. He had sold songs before, when Arizona's records were not selling. Konni, her beloved little brother. They had not seen each other for almost a year now, and Matilda missed him. They had spent many years living in different places without knowing what was happening to the other, when Matilda was almost grown-up and Konni just a child – he still was a child, really. But they were close nonetheless, and wrote letters when they could not see each other. But Konni rarely wrote anything about his feelings or deeper thoughts. He and Tuulikki had had yet another child in November, the third one, and they had been short of money from the outset. Sometimes Matilda wondered how Konni really was.

She thrust the thought aside and carried out her errands mechanically. She was not upset at having to rethink her plans. That was the way of things: life seldom worked out the way you expected. She was used to fitting in with other people's plans, which was one of the reasons why she was so good at her job. Besides, the evening would not have been as much fun as she had envisaged. Her stomach and thighs had already begun to ache as she hurried across Kaserngatan. She would soon start her period, probably that very evening, and she usually had a stomach ache for the whole of the first day.

It started to rain and suddenly there were queues everywhere, and it took her much longer to buy everything than she had expected. By the time she got back to the office Thune and Grönroos were no longer alone. The Wednesday Club had arrived, she could hear a lively hubbub of animated male voices as she headed up the stairs. The building dated from the turn of the century and had no lift, and she struggled up with Mrs Leimu's woven birch-bark basket in one hand and the string-bag of bottles in the other. She could hear the voices more clearly now, the men were probably crowded inside the vestibule, with the door to the stairwell open. She heard Thune's voice, then Grönroos', and several unfamiliar voices: they were talking loudly, with the exaggerated bonhomie of men who had not seen each other for a while.

She stiffened.

Among the unfamiliar voices was one that she recognised. At first she could not place it, but it made her feel uneasy, and soon she began to get an idea of who the voice belonged to. And when she heard the man say something light-hearted – she could not tell what he was talking about, or who he was addressing – and then laugh at his own words, she was sure. The voice might have been slightly deeper, but the laugh was exactly the same.

The men's voices echoed in the stairwell, pouring over her like an unstoppable torrent. She was transported to another time. An open window. Summer. Outside the window a sandy yard, a wide, sun-drenched, dusty exercise yard. Just one solitary, lofty tree, an old pine, broke the monotony of the yard. She had heard them call it the Sahara. She felt sick, and longed to be outside. Longed to be out there, even though she knew that someone died every day of starvation or exhaustion in the course of their labours. She could hear voices; they were in the same room as her, talking several different languages. Her eyes were stubbornly fixed on the view outside the window. The seat sticking to her thighs. Her feet, cold and bare.

She was standing on the stairs. She heard quick footsteps, then the door above closed. The voices shrank to a low murmur, then grew even fainter as the men left the lobby and went into Thune's office. Matilda stood still as silence settled, mute and deafening. Her whole body was chilled, and her legs felt shaky and weak, as if they would never bear her weight again.

Then she pulled herself together, took a firm grip of the net bag and the basket containing the cheeses and other food, and went up.

3

For a few short moments, before he spoke to her or even came into view, just after he had nudged the door open and saw her standing indecisively in front of the desk in the anteroom, while he was still standing in the semi-darkness, Thune remembered their reserved exchange during the job interview. He had found Mrs Wiik intelligent, but also mysterious. Her typed application had not told him much. She was thirty-six years old, and Thune, who had just turned forty, would rather have employed someone younger. And more beautiful, although he had difficulty admitting this to himself: after all, that was not what having an office clerk was about.

Not that Mrs Wiik was unattractive. Far from it: her features were regular, she dressed simply but neatly, had a fine figure, and looked younger than she was. And her skills were beyond reproach: a certificate from business college, good at typewriting and stenography, excellent Swedish and Finnish, reasonable German, not bad English, and a lengthy period of employment at a well-regarded shipping agency, Hoffman & Laurén. But there was something unsettling about her, something chilly that made Thune cautious and wary during the interview.

He: "Your name is Milja Matilda Aleksandra Wiik?"
She: "Yes."

"But you prefer to be called Matilda."

"Yes, I prefer that."

"Why?"

"I don't know. It just happened. Matilda is a nicer name."

"And you're a Swedish-speaker?"

"My father was. My mother spoke only Finnish and Russian."

"Do you speak Russian?"

"No, I'm afraid not. I can understand perhaps a hundred words. But understanding isn't the same as speaking."

He had smiled at her and said: "And speaking about a subject isn't the same as understanding it."

There had been the very faintest twitch in her mouth when she replied: "No, it isn't."

He: "And your parents . . . ?"

She: "No longer alive."

He had expected her to go on, but nothing came. His curiosity got the better of him:

"What happened to them? If I might be permitted to ask?"

"They died young. Illness. I grew up with . . . relatives. Is it important?"

Thune had been taken aback by her blunt counter-question. He chose to draw a veil over his insensitivity, and asked instead:

"Why did you leave Hoffman & Laurén?"

"I'd rather not talk about that."

"But they've given you a glowing reference. If they had such faith in you, why . . . ?"

She had looked at him with the expression of someone listening to a defiant and rather stupid child. And replied:

"Can't you just choose to believe that everything in the reference is true?"

He had seen it: the loneliness that surrounded her. But there had also been something appealing about her curt, precise answers. He had taken a risk and given her the job, and she had not let him down. She did her job impeccably, he had had no

17

cause to worry about her competence so much as once during the seven weeks that had passed.

That Wednesday Thune saw three clients before lunch. He asked Mrs Wiik to arrange a number of telephone calls to other countries, one of them to the Finnish legation on Stankovich Street in Moscow, another to a bank in Stockholm. He dictated two letters to her. They were tersely phrased, and he saw Mrs Wiik raise her left eyebrow slightly at one particularly sharp formulation. Otherwise everything was much as usual. He made use of her services without sparing a single thought as to who she was and what might be going on inside her.

She was quick-witted.

She was clever.

But she was also staff. She was available, she did things on Thune's behalf, that was the whole point.

When he stood in the doorway and pulled out a hundred-mark note and sent Mrs Wiik off to the Market Hall to buy food and drink, Thune was not thinking about his own duties either. They were simple, routine tasks that he could have done in his sleep.

He was thinking about the fact that the Wednesday Club would be meeting in the Cabinet in just a few hours' time.

And about the fact that before then he would once again have to try to calm Polle Grönroos, and his manic fear that his fortune might stop growing. If Thune had not been so furious with Robert Lindemark, he would have sent Grönroos to see Robi long ago. What Grönroos needed was a nerve specialist, not a financial adviser.

The German march into a jubilant Austria would be that evening's topic of conversation, he had no doubt about that. Several days had passed now, but everyone was still talking about it. As for Thune, he had been sitting by the window of his deserted bedroom thinking about Gabi and listening to the church bells ring for Sunday mass, while the newsreader from the Finnish National News Agency read out Hitler's triumphant words over the radio. A Greater Germany, rightful heir to the Roman Empire, a Global Reich with a thousand glorious years ahead of it. That sort of language was in the spirit of the times: Thune had colleagues who liked to imagine a Greater Finland, with its eastern border set beyond the Urals, as they drank themselves silly during dinners hosted by the Lawyers' Association.

Thune was in the process of re-evaluating his life. Sometimes, such as now, he thought about the six young men who had founded the Wednesday Club, and then the six middle-aged men who remained. The first six were not the same as the latter; two had fallen away as the years passed, and two more had joined.

They had founded the Club in the autumn of '27, just a few months after Thune had married his Gabi, in the middle of the boom years when the city was full of new jazz bars and the dancer Ida Bedrich performed as good as naked at the Lido on Fabiansgatan. They had all left student life behind – all apart from the lazy Guido Röman – and taken employment in solid businesses and institutions. Among the statutes of the Wednesday Club was a statement that its purpose was "to contribute to the maintenance and exploration of political and cultural conversation in the Swedish language in the city of Helsinki", but its true purpose was to afford its members an opportunity to drink. The Club had been very lively until early 1933, when it had dwindled while Thune served at the legations in Stockholm and Moscow, but now the Club had become more active again.

Thune was not a boastful man. He was never aggressive, and seldom chose to lead discussions, and to outsiders he was happy to downplay his role. But he knew he was important to the Wednesday Club.

Poor Bertel Ringwald had fallen victim to the capricious waters of Vidskär Sound in the Åbo archipelago during the summer of '31: he was attempting to sheet a mainsail in heavy weather and fell overboard and drowned. One year later Hugo Ekblad-Schmidt married a Parisian woman and was appointed deputy director of his father-in-law's agency, based in a side-street in Le Marais.

Of the founding members, that left the psychiatrist Robert Lindemark, the journalist Guido Röman, the poet and actor Joachim "Yogi" Jary, and Thune.

Leopold Grönroos, a businessman, and Lorens "Zorro" Arelius, a doctor, had joined the group later on, Arelius as recently as 1936.

A mixed company. But united by strong bonds.

They would not be at full strength this time either.

Robert Lindemark was going to attend, for the first time since the business with Gabi. Lindemark had been invited *pro forma* on the past several occasions, but had declined. No-one knew if he had said no out of consideration for Thune, or out of fear or shame. But there was no doubt that it was because of Gabi.

Gabi and Robi. Gabi and Robi and nice, stupid, blind Claes. Thune could still feel jealousy flash deep inside him, like a glinting steel blade, it happened at least once a week. But he had made up his mind. It was time to be magnanimous. He had telephoned Lindemark and personally invited him. The conversation had been awkward, but Thune had insisted, and a somewhat surprised Robi had accepted the invitation.

As one member returned to the Club, another was unable to attend. Joachim Jary had sent his apologies. Or rather, during the course of the telephone conversation, Dr Lindemark had conveyed Jary's apologies to Thune. Jary had suffered another breakdown and had once again been admitted to hospital in Kopparbäck, north of the city.

*

Thune was thinking about his friendship with Robi Lindemark, he could not help it.

The way they would wander through Brunnsparken and along the seashore towards Sandviken when they were still at school, walking through the white light of spring and long, dark autumn evenings, discussing philosophy and literature. Bergson and Barbusse, Kipling and Tolstoy, Aho and Schildt. Thune was tall and thin and fair, while Lindemark was short, thickset and swarthy. The Crow and the Vulture, Wattle and Daub, Max and Moritz: just a few of the many names the more daring boys, the ones who went ski-jumping in winter and swam out to Rönnskär in summer, would call the pair. But Robi and Claes had not let the mockery trouble them. They had been friends all their lives, they both lived on Parkgatan, and they made sure they sat next to each other in the Lyceum School each year. They were best friends – more than that, blood brothers. The summer of their twelfth year they had performed the ritual, solemnly cutting their thumbs with a penknife and swapping blood.

A sworn pact.

But that was a long time ago.

Thune recalled the blustery Friday eighteen months before, and the way everything had seemed so operatic.

October '36. A few months after Thune and Gabi had returned from Stockholm, and a few weeks before Thune was due to move to Moscow. Gabi had already declared that she wanted to stay in Helsinki, she did not have the energy to live abroad any longer. And she did not trust the Bolsheviks, she said, and particularly not one like Stalin.

About a year earlier Thune had accidentally found the place where Gabi kept her diary. And her short stories, the ones she had started to write without his knowledge.

What he read made him feel nauseous, but to begin with he chose not to suspect anything.

Immediately after their return to Helsinki and the move into the apartment on Högbergsgatan, he had reassured himself that she was still hiding the diary and her writings in the same place. And he had carried on reading them every time he got the chance.

One Thursday in October he had told his staff that he would not be coming to the Ministry the following day: he would be working from home, and did not wish to be disturbed by telephone calls.

At eleven o'clock on the Friday morning he had met Lindemark outside the Broberg School. Thune had got into the psychiatrist's metal-grey Opel Olympia and they had driven off towards Lindemark's pride and joy, the modern new mental hospital in Kopparbäck.

They had not spoken much during the journey. Angry gusts of wind had shaken the little steel car, forcing Lindemark to grip the wheel hard and concentrate on driving. As they passed Tusby and were approaching Kopparbäck from the south, Thune had let out a resigned sigh and, without turning his head, without looking at his friend, he had said:

"Gabi's going to leave me. Apparently she's been having a serious affair."

Lindemark had pulled a sympathetic face, but had kept his eyes on the road. Good thing too, Thune had thought, because the Olympia was shaking alarmingly in the wind.

"That sounds rather dramatic, Claes. Not to mention unlikely. With whom?"

"With you, Robi," Thune had replied in a calm voice. At that moment he had wondered why he did not reach across to his left and grab hold of the wheel; it would have been so easy and the consequences would surely have been terrible at that speed, between 75 and 80 kilometres per hour.

But Thune had merely gone on: "That was what you were planning to tell me over lunch, wasn't it?"

*

A stranger would no doubt have thought it rather comical that they chose to keep their lunch engagement. It was an idea that had occurred to them when life began to pull them in different directions, and which they had turned into a tradition: once a year Lindemark would invite Thune to lunch, and vice versa. When Lindemark became a consultant at Kopparbäck he started to invite Thune to dine out there. When it was Thune's turn he usually booked a table at one of the restaurants in the centre of Helsinki, the Kämp or the Royal, or Monte Carlo.

Naturally the circumstances meant that the meal was a torment for them both. They were unable to find any constructive way to broach the subject of the day. So they sat there in silence. The food was well cooked – soup made from horn-of-plenty mushrooms, braised goose, vanilla pudding, coffee with cognac – but its only accompaniment was the tinkle of cutlery and the discreet but rapid steps of the two servants between the kitchen of Lindemark's official residence and the salon in which the men were sitting.

At one point, just as they had embarked on the soup, Robi raised his glass and exclaimed, "Cheers! Welcome, in spite of everything!" Thune raised his glass in response. Then he drained it in one, held it level with the third button down on his jacket, and let out a loud "Ahhh!" He could not help wondering why he and Robi were suddenly behaving like two cadets from the Naval College in Munksnäs. Neither of them was remotely military, nor had they been when they were just twenty years old and the country was transformed into an inferno in which no-one trusted anyone else.

The sun was shining outside the dining-room window, but the north wind was still blowing just as hard and, in the silence that followed the toast, its whine was clearly audible. Thune listened to the sound as he dreamed of an old-fashioned duel with pistols. Then he was struck by how absurd the thought was. He did not even shoot for pleasure, not with pistol nor rifle, and he did not belong to the Civil Defence Corps, and, as far as he knew, neither did Robi.

But later, as they were attacking the solid white pudding, Thune could not help thinking about Robi's hairy backside thrusting like a piston on top of Gabi, between her spread legs; she might have been naked, unless she had just pulled her night-dress up under her buttocks and over her stomach, the way she usually did with Thune. While Thune grasped his dessert spoon he imagined stabbing his former friend's naked backside over and over with a huge carving knife. But when Lindemark looked Thune in the eye and raised his small glass of sweet Spätlese to the height of the third button on his jacket, Thune maintained his mask and thanked him for lunch, and said in a steady voice that the goose had been a fine dish. He felt like asking Linde-mark what he was thinking about – *A penny for your thoughts* – because he guessed that his host was also thinking about Gabi, in this apparently calm and insignificant moment. Had Gabi actually been out there? Had she and Lindemark been together in his official quarters? Presumably they had. But Thune asked no questions, and Lindemark chose to look out of the window as he tucked into his dessert – his eyes fixed on the big maple in the hospital grounds that had already begun to blaze red and gold, his face a perfect blank.

And now it was a hazy grey Wednesday in March, one and a half years had passed, Gabi was renting a two-room flat at the far end of Albertsgatan but spent considerably more time in Robi's spacious apartment on Villagatan, and Thune and Gabi's divorce proceedings were making slow but steady progress.

Thune had refused to file for divorce on grounds of infidelity, which meant that he and Gabi had to spend two years living at separate addresses before the divorce could be granted.

"I am a modern person, and a modern lawyer," Thune had

snarled at Gabi. "I'm certainly not going to start bandying about Old Testament terms such as whore."

At about half past three there he was, ringing the doorbell out on the landing, the first member of the Wednesday Club to arrive (apart from Grönroos, who was already rather drunk), and the man who had stolen Thune's wife. Thune had to open the door himself seeing as Mrs Wiik had not yet returned.

"My dear Robi, welcome," Thune said curtly, and took several steps back to allow Lindemark to walk in.

"Claes, it's been a long time, thank you for the invitation," Lindemark replied. Thune thought the phrase sounded studied. Lindemark's face expressed sanguine goodwill and great calm, but his hand gestures as he shook the water from his umbrella and left it out on the landing to dry were unusually agitated.

It had gone four o'clock by the time Mrs Wiik got back with the delicacies and bottles. By then Röman and Arelius had also arrived. Mrs Wiik had been caught by surprise by the sleet, her coat was wet and she seemed bothered by the state of her hair. Thune knew that the extra bottles were an excess, purely for emergencies. He had already procured enough wine and spirits, but was unwilling to take any risks – the worst thing that could happen would be for the drink to run out.

Thune presented the members of the Club to her in turn, apart from Grönroos. He introduced Robert Lindemark with the title of consultant, but couldn't help adding "and *Lebemann*". Thune's tone was gently ironic. The other men, aware of the situation, noticed this and exchanged discreet glances. Lindemark maintained his mask, and Mrs Wiik did not appear to notice anything.

Then he presented her to the men, not without a degree of pride: "The admirable new addition to our office. Mrs Wiik has been with us no longer than seven weeks, but she has already made herself indispensable."

Guido Röman let out a short laugh and said: "Why do you talk of *our* and *us*, Claes? Everyone knows it's just you and her here."

"Only temporarily, dear Guido. Rolle will be back this summer."

Thune's nephew, Rolf-Åke Hansell, had managed the practice during the years that Thune was employed by the Ministry. Despite his youth – he was twenty-eight years old – Rolle Hansell was already a better lawyer and financial adviser than his uncle. Rolle was about to submit his doctoral thesis in Uppsala. Thune, who never lied to himself about professional matters, wanted nothing more than for his nephew to return to the firm.

He cast a glance at Mrs Wiik, whose face had remained impassive during the exchange. She had greeted Arelius, Lindemark and Röman in a polite but reserved way, and had curtsied very slightly. Thune thought she looked pale and tired. Was it the fog, the heavy, grey day? Or was he working her too hard? Ought he perhaps to let her leave the office early one day?

4

Thune stayed behind after the others had left.

It was starting to get cold in the room, so he fetched some wood, opened the door of the stove and relit the fire.

Outside the window the fog had taken over, thick and heavy with damp. Kaserntorget lay deserted, a silent underwater world: the street lamps' roundels of light were hazy at the edges, like pale jellyfish.

Thune felt a fool.

He had been anxious before the meeting, and had made a real effort to conjure up the goodwill that he was determined to show Robi Lindemark, in spite of his bitterness and loneliness.

Now he felt miserable and trapped, as if someone had tightened a metal band round his head.

The conversation had revolved around Europe and politics. It had not been pleasant. The food that was intended to counter the effects of the alcohol had been devoured during the first hour. Then the drinking had escalated, but had failed to rekindle old friendships in the way Thune had hoped. Instead intoxication had ignited disagreements that had been smouldering for a long time.

Thune had been sitting opposite Robi Lindemark, feeling ill at ease. He had tried his best not to think about Gabi.

Of course he had thought about Gabi.

He had thought about Gabi all evening.

On a couple of occasions his imprecise contributions to the discussion of the burning issue of Germany had blatantly unmasked him. For the first time in the ten-year history of the Wednesday Club there were signs of disunity so great that it threatened to shake the mutual respect of the members. For the first time the men began to suspect that even the most tightly bound friendships ran the risk of fracturing when politics turned to war. And what does Claes Thune, *juris licentiat*, do?

He sits at the table, present in body but not in mind.

He sits there engrossed in thoughts of his former wife, brooding about her behaviour, her desires.

He thinks about their last summer in Sweden.

July '36. Gabi had gone to the west coast with some Swedish friends. Two weeks of freedom. Sailing off Mariestad, beach life and swimming in the sea at Tylösand, Thune was not really sure. He had remained in Stockholm – he had a number of reports to write. Then he was going to take his own holiday: he and Gabi would travel to Finland, to the villa owned by Gabi's family on Sommaröarna in the Esbo archipelago.

Thune had given their housekeeper, Elsa, some time off, and dined at Sturehof and the Anglais. He kept up with routine work at the Embassy on Strandvägen, which was all but deserted for the summer, he drank beer with journalists at Säcken, secure in and satisfied with the knowledge that he and Gabi were each having a good time. He had spent most of his days in their warm, cramped apartment close to St Johannes Church. The typewriter was set up on the table in the small dining room, and he had gone about in his tennis trousers, shirt-sleeves rolled up, barefoot, working on his reports in a rather dilatory way. He had watered the plants, tidied up the paperwork left after a very busy spring and early summer. He tried to find a misplaced linen jacket to wear to a meeting out at Belmansro, and absent-mindedly opened Gabi's trunk instead of his own.

Gabi was as careless of practical matters as Thune himself was: now she had forgotten to lock her trunk. Thune was already rooting through the contents before he realised his mistake. And the diary and sheaves of paper were already there in front of his eyes. And he was in a flat inside which no-one else would be setting foot before Elsa came to clean on the following Monday.

Temptation got the better of him.

Perhaps it was a lack of self-confidence, perhaps simple, humdrum jealousy.

After three years in Stockholm, Thune still felt uncertain in the city. Gabi found it much easier to make friends than he did, people fell like ninepins for her wit and charm.

A corrosive feeling took hold of him as he read, an impotence that crept through his whole body, a physical weakness that made him think he would never be able to move his limbs again, never take a quick stride, never lay a purposeful hand on the back of a woman's neck and kiss her on the mouth, never again feel the tingling as his member began to swell in his underpants.

He had suddenly remembered that he lived in the district depicted in Hjalmar Söderberg's novels. Out there in the church-yard, Söderberg's tormented Arvid Stjärnblom had stood and stared up at Lydia Stille's window.

A "Serious Game" indeed: on his very first reading Thune had found a long diary entry about the tension that had arisen during a garden party out in Grankulla during their visit to Finland the previous summer. The man in whom Gabi had taken an interest was called R.; she wrote that he was charming, had a gentle manner, and was a good listener. R. was only mentioned once more that year, in passing, in conjunction with a large dinner party in November at the home of Minister Erich.

There were no passionate letters. There were no letters at all. There really were no grounds for suspicion. But Thune recalled that Robi Lindemark had been present at the Embassy dinner in

November, because Robi had been attending a medical conference in Stockholm that week.

Thune was like a different person when Gabi returned home from her summer trip to the west coast. He was moody. He complained about Gabi's untidiness, and about the flat they lived in. He was full of nervous fancies, incomprehensible even to him.

Elsa had covered the furniture with sheets, and Thune and Gabi had flown to Helsinki. They landed on the water at Kronobergsfjärden, just off Skatudden, before continuing to Sommaröarna and the ornate wooden villa with its creaking floors, presided over by Boris Fahlcrantz the patriarch, where Gabriella Borisdotter and her siblings obeyed orders and became little children once more.

There, in the family paradise, an increasingly grouchy Thune had made new demands in the bedroom. One of them had involved a lace glove, but Gabi had refused. The demands were the result of Thune having read her short story "The Silk Cushion", but of course Gabi was hardly to know that.

The offices of Claes Thune's law practice were on the fourth floor, and the innermost room was known as the Cabinet, and on that Wednesday in March 1938, as evening slowly turned to night: division, agitated statements, hard words. But Thune's eyes were focused in the distance, on lost summers, and on Gabi. Only fragments of what was said forced their way into his consciousness, and his own comments were vague and demonstrated allegiance to no-one and nothing. It was already late in the evening when Lorens Arelius addressed a question to him:

"Don't you think, Claes? You know Berlin too, of course, and that's what it was like back then, just as I've been saying, don't you agree?"

Thune looked around, and for a few seconds found himself in the middle of Gallen-Kallela's painting "Symposium". The other men's eyes were as dark and staring as those of Sibelius and Kajanus in the famous picture. Zorro Arelius had a pleasant appearance that inspired confidence in his patients, but now those features were dissolved by drink, the look in his eyes was wild and unfocused, and his mouth was contorted in a self-indulgent and arrogant smirk. Arelius was one year older than Thune, and had acquired his nickname as a student: as a youth he had resembled Douglas Fairbanks, the way he looked when he played Don Diego de la Vega, alias Zorro the Avenger. Now he looked more like some creature from Dr Caligari's cabinet, the sort of man one didn't want to rub up the wrong way, to stop him becoming difficult, so Thune replied noncommittally:

"Well, I don't know . . . Maybe."

On the chair next to Arelius a similarly intoxicated Robi Lindemark shook his head angrily and exclaimed:

"For God's sake, Claes, you can't mean that! Would you say that if Yogi was sitting here?"

Thune felt a pang of longing at the mention of Joachim Jary's name. Jary had been in and out of Lindemark's clinic in recent years, and was becoming increasingly fragile. He had always been a nervy person, a dreamer and fantasist whose bow was stretched so tightly that a strand or two snapped each day. Jary had suffered from stage fright since he was young, and a few years ago it had got so bad that he had to give up the theatre. At the same time his generally over-anxious state deteriorated. He had begun to see anti-Semitism in everyday situations when people were only making innocuous jokes, the sort they might make about any race or nationality.

Thune felt another pang, a pang of conscience at having agreed with Arelius' statement without knowing what the subject was. He realised he ran the risk of looking superficial and stupid, and began to search his memory.

They had been arguing about Germany and Austria and Hitler all evening. Lindemark had given a long monologue about contemporary ideologies, talking about the manipulative nature of their quasi-classicism and fondness for grandiose scenarios and dazzling spectacle. He had declared that Nazism possessed the most evil core of all ideologies: "We let the beast out of its cage many years ago, and now we can't get it back in, it just mocks its tamer, and laughs at any carrot or stick deployed against it."

Arelius and Grönroos, who knew that Lindemark voted for the Social Democrats rather than the Finland-Swedish party, had protested. Arelius accused Lindemark of indulging in cheap rhetoric, and asked him if he was genuinely prepared to excuse a murderous schemer like Stalin while simultaneously condemning a German leader who might well be a little heavy-handed, but who had at least got his country back on its feet.

Thune thought he could detect a degree of passion in Arelius that suggested he would have liked to go further with his attack on Lindemark, and to suggest a different way of looking at the current situation – a pro-German way.

And Lindemark had been equally impassioned. The Austrians were going to be voting on whether or not to join a Greater Germany, and the question that was going to be on the ballot paper had appeared in the newspapers. Lindemark was beside himself with fury:

"*Do you agree with the reunification of Austria with the German Reich that was enacted on 13 March, 1938, and do you vote for the list of our leader Adolf Hitler?* What sort of bloody referendum question is that?! How can it be a free vote with a question like that?"

"It's free because people are allowed to vote no," Arelius had replied drily.

Lindemark: "'Allowed to vote no'! At what cost, Zorro? Someone painting a big black N on the wall of my home? Or spending a year in the work camp at Dachau under the friendly watch of Herr Loritz?"

Guido Röman had tried to defuse the discussion:

"Why are you both getting so worked up? Don't you see that Hitler is a *little* man? Soon enough the emperor will be left standing there with no clothes on, looking pathetic, and then no military adventures or nocturnal spectacles in Nuremberg will help."

Arelius, now in a sharp voice: "I haven't fallen for their parades either. But look at the unemployment figures – it's practically disappeared!"

"And the results for heavy industry are almost beyond belief," Polle Grönroos had agreed.

"How can you reduce Nazism to an economic issue?" Lindemark had declared in a voice trembling with anger. He had cleared his throat, gulping air and making his Adam's apple bob – it looked as if he was quite literally swallowing his fury – then went on: "What the Nazis are doing is only good for industry and the party. The citizens are being given margarine instead of butter, and fake rather than real welfare!"

Grönroos had given a rather crooked smile and said:

"Surely you should be pleased that the people have work, Robi? Have you already forgotten the bad years? Given that millions of young men are left idle and hungry in so many countries, what could be easier than their leaders sending them off to war? The risk of war has diminished since Hitler came to power."

Lindemark had shaken his head again:

"If only that were the case! But there are immense forces in motion. The urge to worship and the urge to hate are among our very strongest instincts."

"I'm not defending persecution!" Arelius had snapped. "And I've got nothing against the Jews. They're arrogant, but with good reason. Our very own dear Yogi is proof that they are an unusual but talented people. But I practised in Berlin when I was younger, and every other teacher and lawyer was Jewish. Not to mention the situation in the universities."

And that was when Arelius had turned to the distracted Thune and asked his question. And once Thune had replied and Lindemark had protested, Polle Grönroos had come to Arelius' defence:

"You're being unfair to our friend Lorens here. He's really only saying that the Jews upset other people because they're a successful race. They're better than the rest of us, that's the truth of the matter. Just look at philosophy, science, the creative arts, at the world of business. Everywhere, Jews! The only area where they're kept remotely in their place is sport."

After that the discussion had turned into an angry shouting match in which various nationalities and groups – Russians, Germans, Jews, Finnish nationalists, Swedish nationalists – were evaluated and criticised. In the end someone, Thune seemed to recall that it was Lindemark, had stood up and announced that he at least had to work the following day, and that it was probably time for him to wend his way home. Soon they were all dressed in their raincoats, scarves tied tight against the raw damp of the fog, weaving down the stairs, then out into the street and off towards the taxi rank by the square.

But before they got that far, and while the others were panting and swearing as they pulled on their galoshes, Robi Lindemark had walked up to Thune and, looking rather awkward in spite of all the drink, said:

"Gabi's book is being published in a few weeks' time. By Schildts."

Thune had stared coldly at him.

"Oh? And what does that have to do with me?"

Lindemark had cleared his throat nervously.

"Well . . . authors are allowed to choose a *nom de plume*, if they like. And Gabi has chosen . . . well, Linde."

Thune had raised his right eyebrow.

"Her *nom de guerre*, surely? Because presumably that implies that you'll be getting married as soon as you can? A way of trying the name on for size, perhaps?"

34

"No, no, we've no plans of that sort," Lindemark had mumbled, his eyes darting about. "Gabi actually asked me to tell you. She thought . . . well, that you might like to know."

"Like hell I do."

Thune had muttered these words quietly to himself, but Lindemark had heard them and was seized by a desire to put things right:

"Claes . . . I can't help it. I fell in love. I lost my heart. It's as simple as that. But your friendship has always meant the world to me. I sincerely hope that one day you might . . ."

The Latin phrase appeared from somewhere deep inside, perhaps from those distant lessons in the Lyceum with the dusty, socialist-inclined Magister Grandell, and Thune interrupted bitterly:

"*Amor vincit omnia*, in other words. Everyone has to love you so much that you can be forgiven anything?"

Lindemark had looked embarrassed, not unlike a stubby-legged dog that had failed to fetch something for its master. He had quickly taken his leave, then hurried out through the door and down the stairs ahead of the others.

Thune remained in the office for a long time.

The fire had burned down. All the lamps were extinguished apart from the small one with the green glass shade on the desk.

One last small whisky, there in the gloom.

He thought about listening to a record. Perhaps something by Mozart? Or something modern. Stravinsky? Ravel, who had just died?

The neighbours might wake up and be angry. He chose silence.

And sat and looked out at the rear courtyard instead.

Darkness in all the windows, curtains closed. Melting piles of snow below in the rectangle of the yard. Thick fog.

Helsinki in March. A city forgotten by the world.

Thune began to see images. Gabi, the year they were married. Himself and Robi Lindemark as children. Yogi Jary as a young man, a master of so many art forms in the early '20s, over fifteen years ago now. Zorro Arelius when he still resembled Douglas Fairbanks. Guido Röman when he got his first temporary position on the sports desk of *Hufvudstadsbladet*. Polle Grönroos during the jazz years when he dominated Helsinki's nightlife, edgy and pale and ugly, but always surrounded by beautiful, bold women.

All those lives.

Then, suddenly, a new image. Of someone he had never before seen in his mind's eye.

Mrs Wiik, the way she looked when she had just put down the string-bag and basket. Mrs Wiik with her hair wet with rain, in a coat that smelled faintly of mothballs, greeting the members of the Wednesday Club. Her friendly, neutral face, but also a second or two when Thune thought he could see something altogether different in her eyes, a flash of will flaring up and then fading away – unless she extinguished it herself? – a moment later.

But that was probably just his imagination.

Because had Mrs Wiik not sat at her desk in the vestibule during the first two hours of the meeting?

"No, it certainly isn't a problem for me to stay, I have any amount of work I can be getting on with!"

And did she not come into the Cabinet later to clear away the plates and cutlery once the Club members had finished eating? Then she quickly and efficiently washed and dried everything in the little kitchen to the right of the entrance.

Mrs Matilda Wiik. Just as quiet, amenable and pleasant six days a week. He wondered what she did on the seventh.

Another life. For him to take into account. To some extent, anyway. Perhaps.

Thune realised that he was extremely drunk, and that it was

36

making him sentimental. And weak. *Das Ewig-Weibliche*. To hell with it! He downed the last drops of whisky, walked out into the hallway, pulled on his galoshes, raincoat and gloves, drew his astrakhan hat down over his forehead and walked home. Home to his empty bed in the flat in which Gabi no longer lived.

5

The way they talked! They certainly did go on!

That was the thought that remained with Matilda afterwards.

Thune had asked her to stay and help serve and clear the food during the first hour, and had promised to pay her extra for it. She had agreed – she needed all the money she could get; if she scraped together enough she would be able to send a little to Konni – and the extra hour had stretched to two and a half.

Long cascades of words from a handful of men with high opinions of themselves. Their voices were loud, and at times they sounded like bad actors giving speeches on a stage. No humility, and any humour was without exception coarse and blunt.

Thune had been quieter and less boastful than the others. She had only rarely heard his voice, and he sounded uninterested and distracted.

But the rest of them! Why didn't they understand that being a good listener was the way to wisdom? Not giving grand speeches and falling in love with the sound of their own voices, repeating things they had thought and believed for a long time.

*

He had been called "the Captain" in the camp. By his own men, but also among the prisoners.

Of course he wasn't a captain, just a corporal, and recently promoted at that. The victors had not paid a great deal of attention to promotions in the period immediately following the war, and would even make jokes about military rank. That changed later; the fatherland was too serious a matter for humour.

He had been very young, and seemed extremely proud of his promotion and the role he was permitted to play. A number of the inmates thought he was decent, one of the most decent.

Miss Matilda had disliked him from the start.

If anyone had asked, she could not have explained why. Perhaps she would have stammered something about people who seem friendly, but you still don't trust them. Because there's just something that isn't right, something that rings false, a discordant note.

Unless it was simply the fact that he had been there right at the start, sitting in the doctor's room that first terrible afternoon.

But no-one asked her. And she probably would not have been able to find the words. She did not have many words during the time in the camp, just mute suspicions and fears.

It had seemed to her that the German soldiers, in particular the officers, occasionally made fun of the Captain. She did not understand their language at the time, she was still only a child, but it was evident in their gestures and tone of voice when they spoke about him – *der Hauptmann*. The Germans came up with the nickname, so she had learned that word.

He did not recognise her now. Not the slightest hint of unease in his eyes. No force or tension in his handshake. Quite the contrary. His handshake had been damp and flaccid, uninterested.

Of course.

Because how could he have recognised her?

She had been just seventeen back then, and barely that. A pale, skinny girl with blank eyes and a swollen, unsettled stomach.

39

Now she was in her thirty-seventh year. A knowledgeable and self-assured professional woman.

Then: a plain, almost empty room, the room with the Chair.

Now: Thune's modern, pleasant office, with typewriters, a wireless, new black Bakelite telephones, and a steel safe for the storage of sensitive and valuable documents.

Then: provisional military uniform. Now: a suit, waistcoat and tie.

A standard-issue tunic. Beneath it, nakedness. Always, always nakedness.

When were human beings themselves? When were they being true to their real nature?

Matilda did not know.

The Captain had never looked at her like an equal. He had barely looked her in the eye once. On a number of occasions she never even saw his face; it was dark in the room and she had been staring into the wall next to her – the mortar had come away at the points where the bunk was fastened – and listened to his breathing get faster and heavier, and then he would be gone.

A piece of bread. An intrusive look. A piece of the other person's soul. A few minutes in the darkness.

What people want from others varies.

Sometimes she is taken aback by her own wickedness.

Miss Milja says: *Do something.*

Anything.

As long as you do something.

6

At last Mrs Ellen Pihl realised – that what she was feeling was burning anticipation. She would certainly have explained the way things were to her husband Erik, if only he had been there. Not lightly, however, but with a heavy heart, because such was the diktat of her conscience. But Erik was working overtime at the Chancellery as usual, so Ellen had to make her confession to God and the great, anonymous mass of mankind. And to herself, of course. She lay down on the chaise longue and pressed the embroidered cushion to her tender parts. This was no longer anticipation. It was desire, pure and simple – a blushing, tickling warmth! She moved the cushion back and forth a number of times, and the tickling sensation grew. How great her desire was, how difficult to contain it unnoticed! She could see Mauritz's powerful frame in her mind's eye. She recalled his twinkling smile – so full of life and savoir faire! *– and moved the little pillow back and forth, faster now. She opened her eyes and looked round, as though she feared that someone might be in the room. Then she closed her eyes once more, pulled off her lace gloves and touched the silken fabric; it felt smooth and cool. She placed the cushion beneath the hem of her petticoat and moved it slowly up*

her right thigh, until . . . Someone knocked at the door.
Ellen opened her eyes. She felt guilty and held her breath
at first.

"Who's there?" she called, after a few seconds of silence.

From "The Silk Cushion"
by GABRIELLA LINDE

The Silk Cushion and Other Stories was published by Holger
Schildt's publishing house in early April. At the same time the
last of the sea ice disappeared. The inlets and harbour were now
open, and direct traffic from Helsinki to Stockholm and Reval
began again. It had been a mild winter.

Thune hurried to the Academic Bookshop one Tuesday
after work. That morning Gabi's debut had been reviewed in
simultaneously admiring and critical terms under the signature
of Walker in *Hufvudstadsbladet*. Thune picked up two copies
and glanced nervously at the table of contents as he was waiting
to pay. "The Silk Cushion", "Sunday Morning", "Bringing to
Book", "Little Miss Forlander" . . . all the stories he had secretly
read and feared would be made public were there.

On the Wednesday morning he went to the Scandinavian
Travel Agency on Mikaelsgatan and bought a return ticket,
Helsinki–Stockholm–Helsinki. He asked the assistant to reserve
a first-class cabin on the S.S. *Archimedes*, and to book a room
with a private bathroom at the exclusive Carlton on Kungsgatan.
The furnishings came from the Nordiska Kompaniet department
store, the rooms had telephones and an electronic signalling
system to the porters' lodge, and there was an international
clock in the foyer – Thune not only needed a change of air, but
felt like treating himself as well.

He wanted to get away from the panoptic claustrophobia of
Swedish Helsinki, where the gossip had long since spread and
where an educated readership could not fail to think of Claes

and Gabi Thune, and of Gabi's lover Robi Lindemark, when they read her stories.

He felt a degree of hesitation at asking Mrs Wiik to take responsibility for the ongoing activities of the firm for a whole week. She was, when it came down to it, still a relative newcomer. But he decided to trust her. Mrs Wiik was not only knowledgeable, but he also had confidence in her *Fingerspitzgefühl* and ability to read people.

Thune was aware that he was hardly fleeing to Timbuktu or Tijuana. He was travelling to a place he knew inside out, to a city full of memories, not least of his and Gabi's years together on the other side of the water. He made up his mind not to visit restaurants and bars they used to frequent, not to go near St Johannes Church where they used to live, and to avoid Humlegården, where Gabi had liked to walk. And he consoled himself in advance by putting together as full a schedule as he could.

Exhibitions, plenty of them.

"Peer Gynt" at the Royal Dramatic Theatre. Thune had dreamed of seeing the great Gösta Ekman on the national stage, but Ekman had died of pneumonia in January, shortly after a tour to Helsinki.

Thune also arranged to have lunch with his nephew, Rolf-Åke. His plan was to offer Rolle part ownership. Rolle would then reject the offers he had received from firms in Uppsala and Stockholm and instead return home to turn Claes Thune's law firm into Thune & Hansell.

Beyond that, Thune had also used his legation contacts to arrange an audience with the new and by all accounts fiery ambassador, Paasikivi. He was going to interview Paasikivi about the European situation for an overview of foreign affairs that had been commissioned for *Svenska Pressen* by Valros, the editor-in-chief.

*

The S.S. *Archimedes* was a ship from the 1890s which the Finnish Steamship Company had bought cheaply from Germany, and which had already been in service on the Stockholm route for more than a decade. The atmosphere on board was old fashioned but appealing, and anyone travelling first class – as Thune always did – experienced the pleasant sensation of a bygone world.

Thune was also used to the trip. He and Gabi had travelled on the *Archimedes* or the S.S. *Oihonna* whenever they could, and only flew when there was a pressing need. But Gabi had loved flying. She worshipped the heroes and heroines of the air: Charles Lindbergh, Howard Hughes, Amelia Earhart and the blonde German, Lottie Preisler, the daring pilots who risked their lives to open new routes and break new records. Thune was the one who was scared of flying. He hated being locked in and strapped to an uncomfortable seat inside a metal contraption high up in the air. The cold, the gloom, the lack of space (he was tall, and there was never enough room for his legs and feet), the roar of the engines, the inexplicable shuddering and vibration in the airframe, the sudden drops in height, the terrifying landings on Kronobergsfjärden or at the new airfield in Bromma. And soon Helsinki would be getting its first proper airfield, on the Helsinge side of the city up in the district of Malm, notorious for its gypsies and Bolsheviks. Flying was frightening and hateful, an activity for birds and angels, not human beings. That was how Thune felt, and he even preferred to take the boat when the sea was rough and more sensitive souls – he himself had a cast iron stomach – lay in their cabins vomiting yellow bile.

Thune abstained from the customary whiskies and socialising in the salon after dinner. He withdrew to his cabin and lay on his bunk, smoking and reading Gabi's stories. The same stories he had read over and over again during the lonely July days of that last summer in the flat in Stockholm. At the time he had been in a state of extreme agitation, as if Söderberg's poor Arvid Stjärnblom had still been standing among the trees in the park, casting a spell on Thune to make him as unhappy as Stjärnblom himself was.

This time Thune read more carefully. To restore his self-confidence, he tried to belittle Gabi's talent. She uses too many exclamation marks, he told himself severely, and her writing is affected. Her style isn't tight enough, he decided, and her language lurches helplessly between the prosaic and an old-fashioned pathos.

But Thune did not manage to fool himself. He could see that Gabi's style of writing had great merit. She could see through people's masks, and painted telling portraits with a few well-chosen phrases. Her observations were sharp and elegant. The reader was drawn into the stories, reading on to find out what happened.

If Thune had not been so jealous and diminished he would have felt genuine admiration. But given the way things were he found himself getting annoyed all over again. With a degree of *Schadenfreude* he recalled Walker's criticisms in *Hufvudstadsbladet*:

"The author's ceaseless feverish descriptions of erotic desire and longing occasionally appear to be ends in themselves. One example hereof is the title story, which is so weighed down by purple prose that it risks becoming pretentious. Older readers will recall the furore surrounding Agnes von Krusenstjerna and her suite of novels, and will doubtless be struck by the suspicion that the otherwise so ambitious Miss Linde is prepared to sacrifice her art for the sake of shocking the bourgeoisie. If the bourgeoisie is prepared to allow itself to be shocked anymore, that is."

Quite. With the exception of "Miss Linde", Thune had read that part of Walker's review with great approval. Why had Gabi chosen to write about the erotic in such a freighted and unadorned way? Had she no decency any longer? *Moved it slowly up along her right thigh, until . . . Someone knocked at the door.*

Those three dots drove Thune mad each time he saw them, they summoned the same rumbling jealousy he had felt that autumn when he had gradually realised that everything he had feared and dreaded was utterly true.

Thune had to leave his cabin and go up on deck. He chose the foredeck, buttoned his raincoat carefully and pulled his hat down as firmly as he could. Before he stepped out into the fresh air he lit another cigarette. He liked the sound of the match striking the box. It gave him a feeling of security, just like the strong smell that was released when he inhaled the first of the smoke.

The boat was forging its way through the open sea. The surface was almost motionless, no swell at all, with just the faintest northerly breeze. The moon was almost full, the night clear and full of stars, and it was already surprisingly light. But it was still cold: the temperature was probably somewhere around zero, Thune estimated.

He was not alone out there. There was a group of men on the foredeck; they had made themselves comfortable on the deck-chairs, a few leaning nonchalantly against the railing, and one was standing some distance away over by the funnel, trying to light his pipe. Thune stopped at a respectful distance and cast furtive glances at the men. They were talking loudly and occasionally one of them would let out a laugh, rough and abrupt. Most of them were smoking, the tips of their cigarettes glowing like fireflies in the night.

The men's faces were indistinct in the gloom, but something in the way they gesticulated and laughed suggested that they were young. They had no overcoats, just jackets, shirts and ties, and a few were standing in just their shirt-sleeves in spite of the cold. One of them was wearing a cap, the others all wore narrow-brimmed hats. Thune found himself thinking of a school excursion: young men who had not yet realised how hard

46

it was to be adrift in the world, and were happy to have given their guardian the slip. Organised workers – the youth section, Thune guessed – on their way to some Nordic union congress. Or medical students or scientists travelling to some big student festivity.

"Good evening, sir. Are you Finnish or Swedish?"

There was certainly something of the student about the question, which was posed in Finnish and came from one of the deckchairs. The tone was cheery, and Thune walked towards his interlocutor.

"Finnish, but of the Swedish variety," Thune replied in Finnish. "Claes Thune, lawyer," he added politely, holding out his hand.

"Konni Ahlbäck, clarinettist and trumpeter," the man replied in Swedish.

They shook hands, and the man in the deckchair went on:

"But currently a simple wanderer beneath a starlit spring sky. Did you hear us play?"

"Sorry?" Thune said, not understanding the question. He looked at Konni Ahlbäck more closely. Not as young as Thune had at first thought. Around thirty, he estimated. The others seemed to be about the same age, the eldest perhaps somewhere close to forty.

"We're Arizona," one of the others said, a slim man with thin hair and a sharp face. "We play for the first-class passengers in the salon."

Their relaxed attire, Thune thought. Their careless, slightly provocative manner. Musicians; he should have guessed.

"I'm sorry, but I haven't had the opportunity to listen to you," he said quickly. "I retired immediately after dinner . . . I had some papers I had to read."

"Now, what could be so important that it must be read in the middle of the night on board a ship?" Ahlbäck wondered.

My errant wife's scandalous short stories, Thune felt like

47

replying. But he restrained himself and said instead: "Nothing exciting, sadly. Just some memoranda for a meeting in Stockholm."

"Memo . . . what?" the sharp-faced man said. "Oh, you lawyers . . . you're very dry."

"This is Henrik Seidenschnur, our xylophone player," Ahlbäck said. "He also plays the accordion, a true virtuoso."

"Most people call me Snurre," the xylophonist said, languidly holding out his right hand. Thune had a strong sense of old traditions being cast aside, and leaned forward, took the hand and shook it.

"And Konni here doesn't just play the clarinet and trumpet," Seidenschnur went on in a measured tone of voice. "If it's called for, he can play the piano, violin and guitar as well. He isn't only our Führer, but a divinely gifted musician too."

Even though the others had remained quiet and unobtrusive, Thune had already realised that the musicians were drunk. Perhaps they were out on deck in the hope that the icy night air would clear their heads, so they could remember where to put their fingers and what line they were meant to be playing when they picked up their instruments again. The band-leader, Ahlbäck, got annoyed with Snurre, the xylophonist:

"If you call me Führer once more you'll get the sack," he snapped, with a slight slur in his voice.

He turned to Thune and went on in a different tone:

"We're actually on our way to Stockholm to record some songs. We're playing here at the captain's suggestion. In exchange for free passage and food."

Thune thought of his spacious first-class cabin and felt a little ashamed. But he said nothing.

"Time to go in, Konni," one of the men over at the railing said in Finnish. "We'll do another ten songs, and that'll have to do. We've got some long days ahead of us."

Ahlbäck nodded, and something about his face made Thune

48

pause. He had a feeling that they had met before, that they knew each other.

"Have you ever played at the Brunn in Helsinki? Or at the Casino in Brändö?"

"No, not that I can remember," Ahlbäck said. "Why?"

"How about the Golf Casino? Out in Munksnäs?"

"Don't think so," Ahlbäck said. "But we did play at Heimola, before it became Rio. And at the Mikado and Lepakko. Come in and listen to us now. You seem rather cold, and a hot-fox and a bit of a swing would do you good."

Thune sat in the salon for an hour, sipping a glass of whisky and listening to the band, Arizona. Out here in international waters their homeland's strict closing time and other restrictions no longer seemed to apply; the drink flowed and the dancing went on, even though it was already late in the night. Arizona played favourites from the standard repertoire, from "Yö Altailla" to "Ain't Misbehavin'", but they did it well. Only the lead singer's voice remained rather spineless and thin, perhaps because he was singing with a microphone and did not want to drown out the band.

Snurre the xylophone player had been telling the truth. Ahlbäck led his band with a firm hand, and between numbers he switched from one instrument to the other: he seemed to play every instrument with great ease. Ahlbäck was also an unusual character. He did not lead his men with solemn, calm authority, but with a restless and uninterrupted, almost hostile, energy. He gesticulated, pointed his fingers and pulled faces, and occasionally he would shout a sharp reminder about a solo to a musician who was standing there dreaming: it sounded like a large dog barking, short and hoarse. Ahlbäck's behaviour roused the interest of the audience and drew people's eyes to the band – he was an accomplished performer, there was no doubt about that

49

– but there was also something threatening about his personality, something that simultaneously repelled and attracted.

Thune ordered another whisky. He let himself be absorbed by the music, so different, so much easier that the symphonies and concerts he usually listened to in the office and at home. Here there was none of the usual progression, none of the cerebral tonal development that demanded such concentration from the listener. It was instead as if someone had started to hum or whistle, and then everyone else joined in, band and audience alike, until they found a rhythm and a melody and were carried away by them.

People started to dance.

Started to live.

It was clearly doing good. It was therapeutic.

Thune cautiously tapped out the beat with his foot, and felt his thoughts get lighter and more diffuse. They were no longer as painful, finally granting him a little peace, or at least resuming their proper proportions, so that Gabi's infamy in leaving him for Robi Lindemark and, on top of that, publishing erotic stories, suddenly seemed like insignificant acts of bad behaviour, events that were no more than microscopic motes of dust out in the great, wide cosmos. Thune drank another whisky, his third, and there in the warmth of the salon, amid the noise of the music, he saw before him the heavens twinkling with stars on that dark spring night out on deck. For the first time in many years he felt free inside. Even so, he refrained from asking any of the single ladies in the salon to dance: he did not warm himself up by having a bit of a swing.

7

On the Monday and Tuesday Matilda had to summon all the courage she had to go to the office.

She did not want to walk up the winding stone staircase in the grey morning light. The idea was so unappealing that she had to grab hold of the smooth, polished wooden handrail and almost pull herself up through the echoing stairwell. Her legs felt reluctant and heavy as lead, dragging behind her.

She barely dared unlock the door. On the Monday morning she kept looking over her shoulder as she did so. As if she were sure there was someone there waiting for her. Lying in wait for her. A man. A stranger, or perhaps someone she knew, someone who was not Thune. Someone who had frightened her, someone she suspected was evil. Or knew was evil.

Leopold Grönroos – she did not like him. But she had no basis for her antipathy. It was no character failing to be rich, and it was hardly Grönroos' fault that he was ugly and lacked charm. It was Miss Milja who spoke to her, warning her about him: *Matilda, keep that man at a distance.*

As if she needed any encouragement.

Hannes – she had sometimes been afraid of him. But only during the last year, when they would spend long evenings without saying a word.

Konni – he had had a terrible temper during his time as a mascot and musical prodigy in the Music Corps. He had really been too young to have anything to do with the military, still more a child than a young man. But when Mrs Reincke and Mr Kilpinen at the children's home discovered how musical Konni was, the army took care of him and he found a way out: he gained both a reputation as a talented musician, and a career. But he became increasingly moody and difficult. Friendly towards Matilda and other people of whom he was fond, but with a darkness under the surface. She had sensed it in him, quite clearly: the desire to lash out. As if he were struggling with an anger so great that he wanted to free himself from it by lashing out blindly around him. Would he have been able to hit . . . her? She did not know, but guessed that the answer was yes. Konni had changed, had become much calmer since he left the army and founded Arizona and met Tuulikki. But sometimes Matilda wondered if the darkness was still there inside him, hidden under the struggle to buy food and everything that formed part of daily life.

And the Captain?

Why should the Captain not have been standing there waiting for her?

Popping up out of nowhere, the way he used to, so long ago, when he was young and in a position of power. Suddenly he would be there without the slightest warning, a weight on the edge of her bunk, a strong hand clamped on hers, breath in the darkness.

Thune ran his legal practice in a very informal way. There were trusted clients who would look in for a short chat with the lawyer without having arranged an appointment beforehand. If Thune happened to be busy they could sit in one of the armchairs in the lobby and wait. Usually they read a newspaper, deeply immersed in the stock market or political news from abroad. But occasionally Matilda would look up from the sheet of paper in her typewriter and discover one of them staring at her. The observer would look away, embarrassed, and go back to his newspaper.

Perhaps the Captain was one of those clients? One who had just not happened to stop by yet.

On both Monday and Tuesday Matilda shook off her fears. That was what she was like: decisive.

Had she always been like that?

She did not know, could not remember.

She just knew that she did not want to step into the office, hang up her coat and hat, sit down at the desk and start typing letters. But she did all of these things. When the telephone rang she jumped as if bitten by a snake, it seemed to make a terrible racket. But she still lifted the receiver and took the call, trying to make her voice sound as calm and reassuring as possible.

It was so much easier in the office when Thune was there. Thune's presence made everything clear. Boundaries. Roles. Divisions. Of responsibility, power, duties, everything.

She felt that was how she wanted it.

During those first days someone spoke to her inside her head, someone whose voice she did not recognise.

The voice said: "Get away from here. You'd be stupid to stay. You'll get another job, you've got good references."

Maybe it was Matilda speaking. Practical, sensible Matilda. Not as unruly as Miss Milja, nor as keen to be amenable to everyone as Mrs Wiik.

But somewhere in there Miss Milja was hiding, watching over her. Speaking quietly, almost whispering: "Stay. Tomorrow he will come. If not tomorrow, then another day, sooner or later.

"And *then* . . . Let things happen. Make a move, wait for a countermove."

On Tuesday afternoon the doorbell rang. When Matilda opened the door she found Leopold Grönroos.

She immediately said that the lawyer was away, but still let the visitor in. Grönroos took the chance to stop and talk to her, about the weather, and the Olympic Stadium which would soon be finished, and about a young pianist he knew who had toured Siberia with the great Chaliapin.

He leaned over Matilda's desk as he talked.

She did not like that.

He did not take off his overcoat, nor his hat, made of pale felt with dark flecks of dirt around the brim.

She did not like that either. Why was he still wearing his hat? Why did he have a dirty hat even though he was so rich?

Grönroos had forgotten that Thune had gone to Sweden. Or so he claimed – he was probably lying. He was an awful man, Grönroos: pale and sallow and fleshy, and when he smiled the smile never reached his eyes. But there was still something about him that reminded her of Hannes. Something in his facial features and gestures, as if Grönroos were a grotesque caricature of her vanished husband.

How many years was it since Hannes had left her? Seven? Eight? She barely remembered anymore, the years had started to merge together.

"Mr Thune will be back early next Monday," she said politely, and tried to smile. Grönroos smiled back. He was standing close to her now and his breath was sickly and sweet, as if he had eaten steak and it had caught between his teeth and gone rotten.

"Then I shall return on Monday. I must say, it's considerably more pleasant visiting dear Claes' premises these days."

*

On Wednesday morning something happened. Matilda's mood changed, but she did not know why. Perhaps it was the spring sunshine: it finally broke through the blanket of cloud and lit up the office, situated at the top of the building as it was. Unless it was simply the fact that everything seemed to go well for her that day.

She negotiated with the landlord's agent, then went to the bank and paid Thune's share of the building's firewood bill. She let in the plumber and supervised his work as he repaired the broken waste-pipe in the kitchen. Thune often swore about the old building and talked of moving the office somewhere else. The landlord's agent had told Matilda that he had proposed a thorough renovation, but that the elderly members of the committee had vetoed his suggestion because it was too expensive.

She took one phone call after the other. One of the calls was from Berlin, a lawyer who wanted to consult Thune. Matilda was able to use the German she had learned at business college. She thought it went reasonably well, and once she had told the lawyer to *nächste Woche wieder anrufen* and hung up, she found herself thinking of Rolf Wanka's dimpled chin and his latest film, "The Summer Cavalier", which was due to premiere at the Roxy soon.

Then one of Thune's clients, the stylish Director Gerasimoff, called in to arrange a meeting. Matilda looked in Thune's appointment diary, and felt that she was already receiving clients with a certain authority and elegance.

The sun was shining into the room and all her fears seemed to have blown away. She would not listen to any more voices. She was not going to leave. She was going to stay at her post and be treated with respect.

On the Thursday sunlight continued to stream in through the window. Just past noon Matilda was sitting at her desk eating lunch. She had prepared it that morning while she was drinking her breakfast coffee. A cheese sandwich, a sliced cold potato, a hard-boiled egg, along with a cup of tea that she made in the little pantry.

If Thune had been there she would never have eaten lunch sitting at her desk, but on her feet in the kitchen. But she was feeling bold, and even left the egg on top of her typewriter before she cracked and peeled it. If anyone were to knock at the door she did not have to answer straight away, after all, and could clear the food away first.

A broad ray of sunshine warmed her chest and stomach as she sat and ate.

Thousands, perhaps millions, of motes of dust were hanging practically motionless in the flood of light, like a dusty Milky Way. At the same time the heat of the sun found its way into Matilda and spread through her body.

She felt like a child again: safe.

That was just how it had felt when the spring sunlight had come through the south-facing window, their only window, when she was a little girl.

The row of wooden houses at the far end of Lappviksgatan. Hundred-mark villas, that was what they were called. The sharp but warming sunshine belonged to April Sundays when they were all gathered together.

Her father would sit in the rocking chair, his hands on the armrests, aged, weather-bitten hands – he was almost fifty years old when she was born. He would stare out of the window, stiff and stern, as if he could barely wait for the last dirty grey drifts of snow to melt away and the remaining ice to break up. Then he would light a thick hand-rolled cigarette, greedily inhale the smoke, and open the newspaper on his lap and read it slowly, for a long time, as if he were spelling his way through the articles. Adolf Ahlbäck was a learned man – that was the long-running joke of the other mechanics in the railway workshop. But he was self-taught. Adolf had only spent a few years at school, but later acquired knowledge of a wealth of subjects with the same patience and thoroughness as he scrutinised *Arbetet* and *Svenska Pressen* on those April Sundays. And as Adolf read, Milja Matilda would lie on the rag-rug in the warm sunlight streaming in through the window. She stretched out and felt like purring like a cat, and in the day-bed at the back of the room little Konni would be having his nap, and the strong smell of tobacco would spread through the rented room, competing with the smells of the crackling wood and the dish of baked herring that her mother, Zaida, was making because it was Easter Sunday, when Adolf deserved to eat his favourite food. Milja Matilda's father had a peculiar way of eating baked herring. Whenever he found a fish bone, no matter how soft, he would not swallow it. Instead he would move it to the corner of his mouth with his tongue, where the bones would gradually build up, forming a little bouquet. Only when there were enough bones – Milja Matilda never did work out how many were "enough" – would he remove the bouquet with his thumb and forefinger and place it neatly on the edge of his plate.

Later in the spring, when the trees and bushes had begun to turn green, the light changed and became milder. Rounder and more yellow during the day, redder and longer in the evening. The miracle happened every year: out of nakedness grew a world in which you could hide again, not buried in winter snow, but wrapped in the foliage of the trees. One year – Konni was still very young, and Adolf had not yet started to take him along on his fishing trips – summer arrived early, at the start of May. Adolf had said that the perch would soon be playing, but that he wanted to catch a few before that, so he had rolled little pieces of dough and taken his fishing rod out of the cupboard on the porch, the one the Ahlbäck family shared with the Lahtinens and Tanners. He was planning to go down to Gräsviken, then on to his favourite place to fish for perch, a deep hole off a cliff not far from Lappviken Hospital. But just as Adolf was about to get his rod and high boots out of the cupboard, Milja Matilda ran in and hid, closing the door behind her. It was a simple wooden door, poorly constructed, there were gaps between the planks and rays of sunlight filtered in, and she stood there perfectly still, soaking up the heat and feeling the security of just standing there waiting, she was ten or eleven years old, and her dad would soon be there, he would find her, and then Adolf's lined face would crack into a smile, revealing his tobacco-yellow teeth, and he would reach out his hand to where she was hiding at the back of the cupboard, and he would tousle her hair and say "Oh, my pretty little girl!" or something like that, and she would feel a warm glow throughout her body, warm and certain that they belonged together and would be together for all eternity, Dad and Mum and her and little Konni, the pelargonium would always stand in its pot on the windowsill and the beds would always be folded out at night, the wedding portrait of Adolf and Zaida would always stand on the little lace doily in the middle of the dresser, and every morning Adolf would mutter that the stove smoked far too much, and life would carry on in the same vein, calm and safe.

As Milja Matilda stood in the cupboard feeling the sun on her body, listening to her father's heavy footsteps coming down the wooden steps, she heard a doorbell ring. Matilda was sitting at her desk with her eyes closed, the memories getting closer to sleep and dream, but then it occurred to her: there had never been a bell on the door of that cramped little house, just an unpainted door-knocker that most people never saw, so visitors usually ended up rapping on the door with their knuckles instead. She had been able to tell from the knock whether the person was powerful or fussy or cautious – Adolf had taught her that before she even started school. He had encouraged her to listen carefully to how different people knocked: when the landlord came to collect the rent he knocked twice as hard as their timid neighbour Mrs Lahtinen when she plucked up the courage to ask if she could borrow some flour or sugar.

Matilda opened her eyes and her heart began to beat hard and fast when she realised that someone had rung the doorbell of the office. She looked around quickly and tried to come back to the world where she was thirty-six years old and was taking care of business in a law practice on Kaserngatan. As she stood up from her chair the memories were still there, and it occurred to her that the man outside – she assumed it was a man, Thune had very few female clients – seemed rather impatient. Perhaps it was the caretaker, Lindroos, bringing wood, she had called him that morning and he had sounded hungover and reluctant. During the thirty seconds it took her to sweep the crumbs from the desk, shake her skirt, adjust her clothing and walk to the door, the impatient man had rung the door again, and now once more, and when the doorbell produced no result he banged on the door twice. Not with his knuckles but with his fist, she could hear that very clearly.

She opened the door before the man had time to pull his fist back after banging on it. As the door opened outward it struck him lightly on the shoulder. He started, and there was something timorous about his eyes.

He was short, dark-haired and thin. He looked her in the eye and she could see the fear disappear, to be replaced by interested curiosity.

"I'm looking for Claes Thune. Who are you?" he asked, his voice not entirely devoid of impudence.

When Matilda replied her tone was abrupt:

"I'm Mrs Wiik, Mr Thune's office clerk. The lawyer isn't receiving clients this week, I'm afraid, he's in Stockholm on business. Might I be so impolite as to ask who *you* are?"

"My apologies, I'm the one being impolite," the skinny man said, sounding genuinely contrite.

Good, Matilda thought. Her measured response had served

59

its purpose. She would deal with this character better than she had dealt with the pushy Leopold Grönroos a couple of days earlier – she had already made up her mind about that.

"I'm not a client," the man went on, "just an old friend of Claes'." He paused for dramatic effect and performed a deep bow – like a circus performer, Matilda thought irritably – then continued:

"My name is Jary. Former actor. Former poet. And, on top of everything else, Jewish."

The man was talking quickly now, he was trying to sound light-hearted but there was something underneath. Matilda kept her features as neutral as she could as she searched her memory. She had heard Thune and Grönroos talk about someone called Jary, one of the times she had carried a tray in to them so that they could have their cheeky little drinks. And she had heard Thune mention Jary on the telephone on one occasion. Something had been wrong, but she had not been able to get a clear idea of what it was. She thought Jary seemed eccentric but harmless. She decided to be amenable.

"I'm afraid I don't have a telephone number where you could reach Mr Thune," she lied. "I'm not even sure if he's staying at a hotel or with friends. But if you'd like to come back next week I can book an appointment for you now. Unless perhaps you'd rather leave him a note? Please, feel free to take off your hat and coat if that's the case."

She gestured towards the hat rack and coat hooks, then moved her arm to indicate the two armchairs for visitors and the low table containing that day's copy of *Hufvudstadsbladet* and a number of journals.

"I'd be more than happy to put paper and pen at your disposal. Or a typewriter, if you'd prefer?"

Jary smiled at her. It was a friendly smile, not unlike the one Thune fired off in his brighter moments. Matilda was seized by sympathy for the strange little man. She waited.

"Yes, perhaps I should write a short note," Jary said, then took off his hat and put it on the rack, and struggled to shrug his coat off. "Pen and notepaper, thank you! One never knows how long my personal physician, the esteemed Dr Lindemark, will let me run loose about the city. As recently as the day before yesterday he was uncertain as to whether or not he was going to discharge me."

He leaned forward towards Matilda, stood on tiptoe and whispered conspiratorially with his mouth close to her ear:

"You see, I really am a madman! But I'm only a danger to myself!"

Matilda jerked back instinctively. She realised that Jary had seen her reaction, but she could hardly help that. He smelled of something stale and enclosed, cigarette smoke and moth-eaten clothes, but something else as well – medication, perhaps? For some peculiar reason she still did not feel frightened, not in the slightest. She smiled towards him.

"Please, go ahead and write. Take all the time you need."

Jary took the sheet of notepaper she handed to him. He declined the fountain pen she offered him and instead pulled a pencil from the rack on her desk. Then he sat down in one of the armchairs and chewed the pencil while Matilda found an envelope. When she took it over to him he was writing frenetically. He did not react to her presence until she carefully cleared her throat and held out the envelope.

"Here."

He glanced up quickly, and for a moment the look in his eyes reverted to how it had been when she opened the door and caught him by surprise: guarded and frightened. But he quickly recovered.

"Thank you."

He took the envelope from her hand, folded the brief note he had written and put it inside.

"You're very kind," he said. "I apologise if I'm being forward, but I have a feeling that you're like me. That you understand people. Do you understand their wickedness and love and pain?"

"No, I'm not sure that I do," Matilda said. "Certainly not."

She felt bewildered at Jary's impulsive behaviour and was unsure how to continue. He came to her rescue:

"I could tell you about being broken." He leaned over the table and scrawled some words on the envelope, then went on: "I've got many stories to tell on that particular subject. But not today. Next time, perhaps. Here!"

He passed her the envelope. On it was written, in ornate handwriting: *To Claes, alias Tipperary-Thune. By hand. Your friend, Yogi.*

Matilda could not restrain her curiosity.

"Why . . . ?" She pointed to the word "Tipperary".

"Oh . . . schoolboy humour. It was a long time ago."

"Tell me. Unless you're in a hurry?"

Jary laughed, but it was not a happy laugh:

"A hurry? Me? Do you know what the poet Wecksell said to his old schoolmate when they met after Wecksell had been in Lappviken madhouse for more than forty years?"

"No. How could I know that?"

"The schoolmate asked: 'But aren't you Wecksell the poet? I thought you'd died long ago.' And Wecksell replied: 'Yes, Wecksell the poet is dead, but he still isn't at peace.'"

A cold shiver ran down Matilda's back. She shook her head to shake off her discomfort and said:

"Please, tell me about Mr Thune instead."

"We were at the same school when the World War broke out," Jary said. "We were in our last years there, and many of us were in favour of war. Not me, though, I had nothing to go to war for. I'm not a Zionist, but I don't feel like a Finn either. But suddenly there were boys who dreamed of travelling to Lockstedt to become *jaeger* officers, then returning home to liberate their mother country. Which is, of course, a terrible phrase. The world and our fellow human beings nurture us, not our country."

Jary fell silent and gave Matilda an evaluating look, as if to assure himself that she was not offended and was still willing to listen. When he went on he sounded more thoughtful.

"Claes wasn't one of them. He read books and journals in several languages, and was the first of us to realise what was going on. How terrible the war was, and how many men were dying on the Western Front every day. He became a pacifist."

"But I still don't understand the nickname . . ." Matilda said.

"I'm getting to that. I remember him coming to one lesson with one of those many journals. We were in our final year then. There was a photograph of a new piece of military machinery, the tank. It was a terrible image. An armoured vehicle balancing on caterpillar tracks on the edge of a trench, and down in the trench stood grey, helmeted soldiers looking up at it in horror. They were completely bewitched by it. Like prey hypnotised by the stare of an immense snake. And beneath the picture it said, I don't remember in which language: 'Is this the beast from the Book of Revelation?'"

"You'll have to forgive me, but I still don't understand."

Matilda was losing patience, and was regretting asking Jary to explain. He was showing no sign of getting to the point, and she had a lot of work to do during the remaining office hours.

Jary did not allow himself to be put off:

"The journal also included an account of the torment suffered by soldiers who die from poison gas. They suffocate. That was new to us all as well. But our classmates didn't like Claes raising issues of that sort. Nor did the teachers, with a few exceptions. The only ones who stood by him were Robi Lindemark and me. From that day on the other boys would whistle 'It's a Long Way to Tipperary' whenever Claes walked past. Occasionally they would whistle 'Our Land' or the 'Björneborg March' instead. And one afternoon he was beaten up by two classmates, both of whose older brothers had travelled to Lockstedt. That was how Claes came to be known as Tipperary-Thune."

"But he must have hated being called that!" Matilda exclaimed. This time her own impulsiveness made her flinch: she felt ashamed and immediately regretted her outburst.

"Yes, you're right. He probably did," Jary conceded.

He looked thoughtfully at the envelope in her hand. Then he snatched it back quick as lightning and opened it with the pencil he was still holding.

"What am I thinking? Please, get me a fresh envelope! I thought that now we're so much older, all of that had turned into amusing old stories. But of course that isn't the case. Thank you for making me see sense!"

"I didn't do anything," Matilda said, and went over to the desk to get another envelope. "I just asked you a question."

When Jary had the new envelope in his hand he quickly wrote Thune's name, then his own – "Joachim Jary" this time – and handed it back to her:

"Thank you for your patience. I have detained you with my nonsense and taken up your valuable time, and now I shall go. But I suppose I always do that. Talk too much, I mean. And go. Of course. Always. Because of course that's what life is, an endless sequence of partings. Next year in Who Knows Where! It's been a pleasure to meet you, Miss . . . ?"

"Wiik," Matilda said. "*Mrs* Wiik."

On Saturday spring came to an abrupt halt. There was a sharp wind from the north and the temperature sank back towards zero. The sun had second thoughts too, and fled behind thick, lead-grey clouds. Early that afternoon it started to snow, small, dry flakes that swirled about the pavements and along the streets and refused to land.

Thune was due back on the *Archimedes* at the South Harbour

on Sunday morning. He had asked Matilda to write a report of the past week and a summary of the coming week's meetings, and told her to send them by courier to his home address on Högbergsgatan. Thune always wanted to be in full command of the situation when he arrived at the office on Monday mornings.

She was busy writing the report when the doorbell rang. It was a different sort of ring to the authoritative sound made by Leopold Grönroos earlier in the week, and different again from Joachim Jary's nervous fusillade.

A modest, yet still distinct and purposeful ring. A single signal, then the caller waited; there was no sound at all from the stairwell, no shoes scraping on the floor, just silent, patient waiting, as if the caller were convinced that someone was there in spite of it being late on Saturday, and were just as certain that this person had heard the bell ring.

She went and opened the door. It was the Captain.

The odd thing was that her fear did not manifest itself at once. As she stood there in the doorway and saw who it was, at first it was almost as though she had been expecting him. She was calm, in command of the situation, her voice friendly and polite when she asked him to come in.

Only when she turned her back on him and was leading the way into the office did the reaction set in. The same chill spread through her body as when she had heard and recognised his voice in the stairwell, and when her fear reached her legs they felt instantly weak and unsteady: for a second or two she feared she was going to collapse.

But she overcame herself. When she turned and gestured towards the armchairs and hat rack, and told the Captain that he was welcome to hang up his coat, her voice was controlled and she could feel that her amiable office assistant's expression was perfectly in place.

*

If that first meeting had been recorded on film, Matilda thought afterwards, the scene would have been discarded during editing as being too dull.

Nothing happened.

The Captain said he wanted to speak to Thune on a personal matter.

When Matilda explained that Thune had spent the week in Stockholm, the Captain said that explained why Thune had not been answering his telephone at home.

Matilda wondered silently why the Captain had not telephoned Thune at the office, because she could not recall having received a call from him. But perhaps he had tried, there had been occasions when she had left the office for an hour or so to perform errands about town. She did not ask.

Instead the Captain asked if Thune was experiencing difficulties, and was perhaps without staff, seeing as he was in the process of getting a divorce, and possibly needed help with his household?

Matilda replied that Mr Thune still had his home help, the widow Leimu, but that Mrs Leimu lived in a small rented property of her own in the next block to Thune's.

There was something hesitant in the Captain's manner, as if he felt lonely and wanted to stay and chat to her. Matilda was convinced he did not recognise her this time either. She did not know why she was so certain. Perhaps it was because she remembered that he lacked any talent for dissemblance: he had looked scared and embarrassed the few times – shortly before she was released – they had caught sight of each other out of doors.

Was she flirting with him now that she had suppressed her fear? Was she casting a line?

Yes, she probably was.

She was talkative, she recalled what Leopold Grönroos had said about work on the Stadium and told the Captain that it would be exciting to see what it looked like inside, because it was due to be inaugurated in June, was it not? And of course it would be quite wonderful if such a small, remote city as Helsinki could get the Olympic Games now that Tokyo might be forced to withdraw? It would be such fun to have so many visitors from distant countries; she had thought that one evening when she was taking a walk and happened to pass the Stadium, which was as good as finished, in all its splendour, now that the scaffolding was being driven away on trucks. Not that she was particularly interested in sport otherwise, she confessed. She preferred music, she liked the Valtonen sisters, for instance, they sang such beautiful harmonies and were going to be performing in Helsinki again that spring.

The Captain was flattered by how talkative she was, and visibly relaxed. Certainly, it was a fascinating thought that the Olympic Games might take place in the city in two years' time, and if he was not mistaken there were going to be a number of inaugural contests held in June. And the Harmony Sisters were indeed delightful, he was hoping to go to Brunnshuset to hear them as soon as he could, it was just that work and social obligations demanded almost all of his time. Did Miss Wiik happen to live in Tölö, if her evening walk had taken her past the Stadium? Or up in Alphyddan, perhaps?

"Mrs," Matilda replied, "*Mrs* Wiik." And yes, she did live in Tölö.

The Captain tried to be amusing: in one of those functionalist buildings, perhaps? Might he enquire as to which street?

Matilda smiled at that and said that a lady who cared for her good name surely ought not to reveal her address to a man who happened to visit her place of work on entirely different business?

The Captain smiled back and asked her to forgive his lack of propriety. He had been properly brought up by his mother and father, he added, but he was, sadly, incorrigible, there was nothing that could be done about his poor manners. But, he went on, he could not resist pointing out that if she had a telephone, then anyone would be able to find her address in the Telephone Corporation's directory.

"I don't have a telephone," Matilda replied in friendly but firm voice. "But I do have a radio."

She felt like biting her tongue. That last remark had come out wrong, and sounded far too intimate, almost inviting.

"I see," the Captain said thoughtfully. "You have no telephone, but you do have a radio."

Then he wished Matilda a good weekend, and left. When he closed the door behind him she heard his heavy steps disappear down the staircase.

Good girl, Miss Milja said to Matilda.

Miss Milja most certainly did not think that the remark about the radio had struck the wrong note.

You've been a very good girl.

8

Thune travelled home with mixed feelings. There was no band by the name of Arizona in the salon of the *Archimedes* this time. No band at all, no beautiful starlit sky, no gently rolling sea. Instead the elderly steamer was struggling against a stiff north-easterly, the silent and frozen passengers sat huddled in their cabins, and there was a wolfish howl to the wind as it turned the freezing rain to needles out on the foredeck. There was plenty of time to reflect on the past week.

He had stuck to his principles and done his best to avoid all the places that had once been his and Gabi's. He was particularly careful to avoid the area around their former home, and the restaurants where he and Gabi had entertained other diplomatic couples.

It was easier to go to the journalists' bars, Säcken and Stopet, and have a beer or two with newspapermen he knew, and nod in recognition to bohemian poets and drunken copy-editors with whom he had shared tables over the years. But Thune was no heavy drinker, and had moderated his consumption over the years. He knew it made sense: in his youth drink had made him gloomy and moody.

On his second evening in Stockholm he had met the Finnish journalist Calle Nykopp, who had written a novel about football and would shortly be travelling to France for the World Cup.

Thune and Nykopp sat in Säcken drinking beer and eating smoked sausage, talking about the events of seven years ago. Nykopp had worked on the sports desk of *Hufvudstadsbladet* at the start of the decade. He had been the one who – out of carelessness – had revealed to the Swedes that Nurmi and Iso-Hollo and other Finnish athletic stars had been receiving money in brown envelopes before their races. As a result Nurmi had been declared professional and not allowed to crown his career at the Olympic Games in Los Angeles. Calle Nykopp was so hated in Helsinki that he had been forced to emigrate to Sweden. Thune and Nykopp's mutual friend, Guido Röman, was short, dark-haired and moustachioed, just like Nykopp, and had taken over Nykopp's job when he left the country. Röman's first job had been to cover an athletics competition at the Djurgården sports stadium in Helsinki. There a regional shot-put champion and heavyweight boxer by the name of Yli-Mäntylä had mistaken Röman for Nykopp and beaten him to the ground. "Fucking bastard!" Yli-Mäntylä had shouted as he kicked the semi-conscious Röman as he lay curled up on the ground.

"How is dear Guido? Is he still at *Hufvudstadsbladet*?" Nykopp asked.

"Oh yes," Thune replied. "They tried to move him to general reporting, but he wanted to get back to sport."

"And his terrifying appendage is intact?" Nykopp grinned.

"Yes, as far as I know." Thune smiled back, slightly strained. He had never felt comfortable with that sort of humour.

"What about you, Claes? Why did you leave the Ministry?"

"Oh, you know . . ." Thune replied vaguely. "They didn't want to give me another post straight away after Moscow. And I don't like not having anything to do. I thought it best to resign and take charge of the firm again."

"But getting a foot inside the Foreign Ministry is quite an achievement. Didn't it bother you . . . ?"

"That's exactly it," Thune interrupted brusquely. "There's a lot of competition for posts. Once you're left without a job, you're more or less outmanoeuvred. That's just the way it is these days."

"Even for someone with as many good contacts as you?"

"Everyone knows that Enckell and Holsti and the others were keen to appoint Finland-Swedes," Thune said. "Particularly to posts here in Stockholm. And you probably know why."

"Because the Finns fall victim to envy and excel at being bad-tempered instead of engaging in diplomacy?" Nykopp ventured.

"Quite," Thune said. "But there's no more favouritism now. Finnish nationalism has been getting stronger and we no longer have the same privileges. I thought it best to resign."

"Are you still managing the firm on your own?" Nykopp asked.

"No, I've employed an office assistant. Mrs Wiik. She's very good. And I'm hoping that Rolle, my nephew, will become a partner once he's finished his doctorate."

"He did a good job while you were away?"

"Yes, he's very talented. But he's still young, like you, and sometimes gets carried away. I'm going to be meeting him for lunch tomorrow."

Nykopp looked thoughtfully at Thune and said: "Don't be cross with me now, but my brother says you hated Moscow."

Nykopp's elder brother, Johan, had been a colleague of Thune's in Moscow, and was still an attaché at the legation there.

Thune shrugged and replied: "Yes, if I'd been happy I don't suppose I would have gone to Yrjö-Koskinen and asked for permission to leave my post early."

"Your post was for a fixed term, though," Nykopp said. "You could have seen out the time and retreated with your honour intact. What happened?"

71

"There wasn't any work to do," Thune said. "All forms of contact had been frozen. No trade, no cultural exchange, no tourism either."

"Is that a good enough reason to leave your post?" Nykopp wondered. "You could have sat it out. Taken your salary, drunk Georgian wine and got a good reference."

"I began to hate the city," Thune admitted. "Well, maybe not the city. But the atmosphere there."

"Explain," Nykopp said. "I've never been to Moscow."

"I don't think I can," Thune said. "You have to experience it for yourself. It's something about the smell. Damp sewers, cheap perfume, rotten clothes and disinfectant. And the people are terrified. No, not terrified. Panic-stricken. No-one talks to foreigners at all. The slightest slip of the tongue can lead to the Lubyanka."

"Those trials . . ." Nykopp said thoughtfully.

"Exactly," Thune said. "But the things you read about, the death sentences, Zinoviev, Kamenev, Bukharin, Yagoda . . . I sometimes thought that had to be the tip of an iceberg. There are rumours of work camps in the very far north-east. Vast camps, on an incomprehensible scale. And there are places . . . if a public official is forced to say their names, a strange look comes into his eyes. Vorkuta, Serpantinka, Magadan."

Nykopp was starting to get curious. "So you're saying that public officials speak freely, but the man in the street doesn't?"

"*Nyet. Molchat.* No-one says a word," Thune said emphatically. "You have to read between the lines, deduce things, try to understand as best you can. And you have to be careful. We had a Russian chauffeur for a few months, after our official driver, Bäckman, was sent home for drunkenness. I don't know who employed the Russian, but his name was Vasily, a big man, pockmarked, his face as lined and unyielding as an old chopping board. We soon realised he was a spy for the Cheka, and understood both Finnish and Swedish."

"Hasn't the Cheka changed its name again?"

"Yes. It's no longer the O.G.P.U., but the N.K.V.D. *Narodnyy Komissariat Vnutrennikh Del*. But it's the same old Cheka."

"Which was the same old Okrana."

"Yes, in many ways. Only worse."

"How did you come to realise the chauffeur understood Finnish and Swedish?"

"We said bad things about him in the back seat. Called him all sorts of terrible things. A pederast, among others. That's the worst thing you can say to a Russian. We saw his face in the rear-view mirror. His facial expression hadn't changed at all. But your brother noticed that the back of his neck had turned bright red."

"Ah," Nykopp said. "Ingenious. But presumably dangerous too?"

"Spring in Moscow is extremely beautiful," Thune said. "You go for walks in the parks, or head out to Uspenskoe or Shchukino and sit on the shore. You take along some tea, honey, dark bread, vodka, maybe a few stuffed dumplings if you've managed to get hold of some wheat flour. The river sparkles like silver. The last of the sunlight colours the cupolas of the churches a fiery red, and dusk is long and cool. When I saw the cupolas ablaze I couldn't help wondering if Stalin loves or hates that. He was going to be a priest when he was younger, after all."

"And the Führer wanted to be an artist," Nykopp pointed out. "If only."

"Even so," Thune went on, "it was springtime when I realised that Moscow really wasn't for me. That I had to go home."

"Even though home was empty? Didn't Gabi move out while you were in Moscow?"

Thune tried to keep up his façade, but knew that he had gasped at the mention of Gabi's name, and that Nykopp had noticed. He recalled how he had stayed in Moscow for Christmas and the New Year even though he could have caught the train home if he had wanted to. At the turn of the year he had preferred the grey, endlessly long days in his meagre room on Stankovich Street to going home to his flat in Helsinki.

"Yes, she moved out in the autumn," he said curtly. "But staying in Moscow . . . I just didn't want that. The Cheka's men often come in the dead of night. Just like the Gestapo. I couldn't bear the thought of people being woken by murderers in leather jackets and taken off to the Lubyanka at dawn, while the birds were singing in the blossoming lilacs and everything was so full of life."

"If you're going to die, it probably doesn't matter what the weather is."

"I'm not so sure about that. There's something special about the light in the north. It's so grotesque to be murdered when everything is bright with the joy of existence. Sometimes I think about our Reds twenty years ago, and the fact that they were put in camps in May and June . . . It would be better to be taken on a foggy night – that would at least be more fitting."

"A great comfort, I'm sure," Nykopp said sarcastically, then went on: "My brother says we're not only on the brink of another major war, but a whole new era. After the next war the little people won't have much of a say about anything. The big boys will decide."

"And who would the big boys be?" Thune wondered.

"The ones who win the war," Nykopp said. "We live in a very peculiar age. Shall we have another beer?"

"Yes, let's," Thune said. "My round. Bloody hell, it's not easy to feel confident about anything. Much easier to turn your back on everything and take up monastic orders."

Thune knew he was lying when he said he'd prefer to enter a monastery. There was nothing he wanted more than a woman. There had been evenings when he would have been prepared to give a Nazi salute if only he could have a woman beside him in bed. The previous evening he had stood in a doorway at the base of the south tower on Kungsgatan watching a young woman who was standing at the base of the north tower smoking a cigarette. He had guessed that she was a prostitute, and was on her way to Blue Heaven at the top of the building. He would have liked to go up to her, but had not dared. In the end another girl in high-heeled shoes and with her hat tipped at an angle had walked up Kungsgatan from Stureplan, and the pair of them had gone inside the north tower arm in arm.

Thune had paid for a woman just once in his life. It had been when he was a young trainee in Berlin. He had gone into a dark bar on Friedrichstrasse, his legs trembling; he had not known if that was from excitement or fear. The woman had taken him to a hostel in a narrow side-street. She had looked a little plump in the gloom of the bar, but when she took off her corset she turned out to be an awful lot plumper than he could have imagined. It was late summer, humid, Thune was sweaty and a bit drunk, and the fat woman had washed his penis in a relatively clean basin, then sucked it to get it hard. She carried on too long, and Thune exploded in her mouth. He did not know if she swallowed his seed or not, she had turned off the light next to the bed when they entered the room and was now little more than a shadow. They had only been in the room for a few minutes, and the shadow said: "*Mein Herr, Sie haben doch für viel mehr Zeit bezahlt. Können Sie noch einmal?*" In his broken German – he knew all the judicial terminology, but this was not the sort of legal transaction he conducted in daylight hours – Thune said: "*Noch nicht, fürchte ich leider.*" He got dressed and left, and felt ashamed at what had happened for years, and was never able to visit a prostitute again.

"The paradox," Nykopp said to Thune as he waved over one of the waitresses to order more beer, "is that the worse the times we live in, the more there is to write about, and the more exciting pictures there are to be taken. I should like to launch a illustrated news magazine here in Sweden. Something like *Life* or *Look*. But more irreverent, with more of a punch."

75

"Do you really think that would work?" Thune wondered. "After all, the market is so much smaller."

"I think so. People of our age want to be addressed directly. And as long as you're honest and courageous, most things turn out alright."

Yes, then you run away and let others take the punishment, Thune thought mischievously, remembering Guido Röman's bruised and limping appearance at the meeting of the Wednesday Club just a few days after he had been beaten by the athlete Yli-Mäntylä.

The day after his meeting with Nykopp Thune had a terrible hangover when he ate lunch with his nephew Rolle in the dining room of the Hotel Continental.

Rolle Hansell was the same as usual, tall and blond and powerful, with a jaw so square it could have been chiselled by Braque or Picasso. A wide, flat nose sat in the middle of his amiable face, and gave Rolle a rustic appearance, rather like a boxer. People sometimes underestimated Rolle, and thought he was going to be easy to outwit because his manner was so unguarded and boyish. His nephew's good-natured appearance was reinforced by his voice, which was keen and bright. Thune had been in meetings where the opposing party had adopted a patronising attitude towards Rolle, and had made mistakes as a result. Rolle had waited for the right moment, then pounced and gained a serious advantage. He had been a recent graduate at the time, just twenty-three years old.

"That was very skilfully done," Thune had said afterwards. "They walked right into the trap."

"Thanks, Uncle Claes," Rolle had replied.

"You're welcome to call me Claes, Rolle," Thune had said, then went on: "I've been asked by the Foreign Ministry if I'd like a post at the legation in Stockholm. I want to try something

76

different, and Gabi would also like to move. Would you care to run the practice for me? Six months' probation, and if it goes well and you're happy, you can carry on. It's not too arduous, you'll be able to continue your studies at the same time."

That was the start of something that over the years had come to resemble true friendship. Thune was surprised at how much he actually liked Rolle. He did not get on particularly well with his elder sister Ulla, who had been at odds with the world ever since the Red prisoners were released and had their rights as citizens restored after the War of Liberation. Sister Ulla had supported the far right Lapua Movement, called Mussolini "a stylish fellow", and also set her faith in Hitler and his Third Reich. And Thune thought even less of his elderly brother-in-law, the honorary industrial counsellor and businessman, Sigurd Hansell. His brother-in-law not only thought the new age and its customs offensive, but was still unhappy that Prince Friedrich Karl of Hesse had never been allowed to reign as King Kaarle I of Finland: Hansell had received a verbal promise from the monarchists that his family home, Villa Ulla on Rehbindervägen, would become a royal palace.

"I assume that your mother and father are delighted with the *Anschluss*," Thune said to Rolle as they dug into the Continental's veal steak, his nephew with a healthy appetite and Thune as a weary and pale shadow of his energetic relative.

"Of course," Rolle said, "but they don't use the word '*Anschluss*'. They prefer the Chancellor's term, '*Heimkehr*'."

"Oh, dear Lord," Thune sighed, suddenly feeling deeply depressed. "I hope you don't feel any conflict of loyalty from my holding a different political opinion to that of your parents," he went on, and added: "Actually, I've never asked before, where do you stand?"

"I don't stand where Mother and Father stand, and they know that," Rolle said. "Hitler has behaved in an extremely arbitrary fashion as far as laws and ordinances are concerned."

Thune maintained a neutral expression and said nothing. Rolle hesitated for a moment, then went on in a sombre voice:

"But I'm also from farming stock. You know, of course, that my paternal grandfather, Zacharias, had a farm in Snappertuna? Father still has it, a steward manages it for him. Father's the son of a farmer, a child of Swedish soil who happened to go far because he has a good head for business. And those of us with farming in our blood prefer things to be neat and tidy."

"Yes," Thune said lamely. "But surely the question of what neat and tidy means is open to interpretation?"

"Of course," Rolle conceded. "And the ends do not justify the means. Rather the means reveal the truth of who you are. Do you remember who wrote that?"

"No," Thune said. "Who was it?"

"You, Uncle. In a book you gave me when I graduated from high school. *Kant. The Old Man of Königsberg. The Categorical Imperative.*"

"Goodness," Thune said. "The things you remember!"

"In contrast to you and the other pessimists, I believe that everything will get better," Rolle said. "The Germans are a cultured people. Just as the Jews are, so things can't go on like this. By the way, I'm going to be spending a few weeks in Germany this summer. A cycling tour with Elin. It's all arranged, formalities, route, lodging. We're going to be staying with Herr and Frau Weitze in Jena, they're old friends of Father's."

"I see. That's not a bad plan," Thune said, trying to sound cheerful. He was actually feeling a little better – his nephew's bright outlook on life was infectious.

"So have you found a new candidate to be your wife, Uncle?" Rolle asked bluntly, chewing absent-mindedly on a toothpick as the waitress cleared the table.

Thune looked into Rolle's young face, so free from calculation, and said slowly: "No, that will just have to take as long as it takes."

He had decided to wait until coffee and dessert before he asked about the practice and a partnership. To his surprise and delight, Rolle did not even ask for time to think about it and said yes at once. Rolle's only stipulation was that he did not want to start until September: his trip to Germany with his fiancée Elin was planned for the start of August, and after that they would be spending a few weeks at Elin's ancestral home up in Roslagen.

Thune could not help thinking of the leaky old Fahlcrantz villa, with all that ornate woodwork, out in the Esbo archipelago, and of his last tense summer with Gabi. But he said nothing, and merely nodded his agreement.

The rest of his week in Stockholm had not been as enjoyable as he had anticipated. The exhibitions had been rather disappointing, as had "Peer Gynt" at the Royal Dramatic Theatre. The lead was certainly no Gösta Ekman, and Thune never ceased to be surprised at how drab and unassuming Sweden's national theatre was inside.

Ambassador Paasikivi had proved to be just as brusque as his reputation suggested. Thune had been shown into Paasikivi's private apartment by his old friend Vagello, the caretaker, but any sense of comfortable familiarity quickly turned out to be transitory. He brought with him greetings from Sigurd and Ulla Hansell and their son Rolf-Åke – "dear, grumpy old Uncle Juho!" Rolle had exclaimed when he found out who Thune was going to interview – but that had done nothing to lighten Paasikivi's mood.

"Oh, the Hansells. Well, it's been a long time," he muttered.

But the hour-long interview in the residence on Strandvägen had not been entirely in vain. For all his grouchiness, Paasikivi had given Thune an honest and informed overview of the troubling European issue, naturally with a strong emphasis on Finland.

"Back home I'm regarded as soft," Paasikivi had snorted rather bitterly. "I'm said to be far too lenient to the Russians." And then he had added: "What everyone ought to understand – even Mannerheim, with his experience of the imperial court – is that the Bolsheviks are *more* conscious of prestige than Tsarist Russia, not less. That's what happens when those in power have their origins in poverty. There's not so much regalia, but they demand clear signals of subservience."

Without beating about the bush, Thune had asked if Paasikivi thought another major war likely.

Paasikivi had grunted and asked Thune if it was likely that a scorpion would sting its neighbour when it estimated that it was itself in danger.

Thune had written down the metaphor, but said that he did not quite understand it.

"Oh, I daresay you do," Paasikivi had said, before going on: "I'll tell you something in confidence. Because you seem to be a decent fellow, and because you're related to my old friends the Hansells. But before I do so, I need your word of honour. You must swear not to mention or allude to what I am about to say in your article, nor to discuss it with anyone."

"You have my word," Thune had assured him.

Paasikivi's eyes bore into him, then he said:

"The day before yesterday the second secretary at the Soviet Embassy in Helsinki, Comrade Yartsev, contacted the Ministry outside all normal diplomatic channels and asked to meet Foreign Minister Holsti. They should be deep in conversation right now, at exactly the same time as we're sitting here."

Thune had squinted towards the large drawing-room window facing Strandvägen and the water. Yellow sunlight was streaming in through the glass. The Djurgården tram rattled past; it was spring in the world outside.

He had not known how to react. Paasikivi was sitting in silence, watching him. Eventually Thune had said:

"That was quick. Considering the difference in rank, I mean."
Paasikivi had nodded.

"I guessed that you'd notice that. But the point is that Comrade Yartsev isn't actually his name. His real name is Rybkin. He's head of the N.K.V.D. in Helsinki, and is said to have received his orders directly from Stalin."

"And what are his orders?" Thune had asked.

"It's perfectly straightforward," Paasikivi had replied. "The Soviet Republic wants a guarantee that we will defend our territory against any conceivable German action in the event of a war in which the Soviet Republic and Germany are on opposite sides. They also want bases along our coast, and are offering weapons and other assistance in return."

Thune had screwed up his eyes towards the window again. The sun was still shining just as strongly, the sound of the street filtered in, and he heard a seagull call. But everyday life had disappeared down into an echoing well.

"Can you recall any event in the past that Stalin might remember and be concerned about?" Paasikivi had asked.

"General von der Goltz and his 10,000 men in Helsinki precisely twenty years ago?" Thune had suggested.

"For instance," Paasikivi had said, looking simultaneously troubled and pleased.

The sea was rough and Thune slept fitfully throughout the night. He woke up at regular intervals and felt his thoughts churning still: he ought not to have run through the events of the week so thoroughly as close to bedtime as he had done. When the milky grey morning light began to penetrate the round porthole he gave up and reached for his wristwatch: half past five. The window was wet with spray, but it seemed to Thune that the boat was rolling less now. He got dressed, picked up his cigarette case – a new purchase, silver, from Nordiska Kompaniet

– and matches from the little bedside table and went out onto the foredeck.

On the port side, barely discernible in the morning fog seeing as the *Archimedes* was following a course far out to sea, lay Porkala's long, curving tongue of land. Thune screwed up his eyes and peered ahead, but visibility was poor and Helsinki was not yet in sight, not even the spires of the Agricola and Johannes churches which, along with the tower of the new Stadium, were the first landmarks that would appear on the horizon.

With an equal measure of anxiety and pleasure, it occurred to him that it would soon be time for the April meeting of the Wednesday Club. He hoped they would manage not to fall out. It was Guido Röman's turn to act as host. Guido lived on Kammiogatan in Tölö, and as usual would probably send his wife Ghita and their four daughters to stay with his mother-in-law in Grankulla.

Thune recalled the evening at Säcken, and Calle Nykopp's remark about Guido Röman's appendage. Even though Thune usually found such jokes childish and beneath him, he could not help smiling. His friend Guido was only 165 centimetres tall, extremely skinny, and had cultivated a black moustache that was so thin and neatly trimmed that it made an almost feminine impression. But Guido also possessed a huge penis, almost unbelievably long and thick even in its resting state.

The first time Thune saw it was when the newly established Wednesday Club held one of its early meetings in the similarly new swimming baths on Georgsgatan. *Mens sana in corpore sano*, a healthy mind in a healthy body, as the more sport-inclined members of the Club, Röman and Ringwald, had declared when they suggested the baths as a venue.

It was a Wednesday in December, just before closing time. The baths were as good as empty, just the Club members and a few law students whom Thune knew vaguely, former Lyceum pupils who nodded to him as they passed on the way from the

82

pool to the shower room. Then the youths caught sight of movement from the corner of their eyes, turned their heads as if on command, and saw Guido standing there naked, legs wide apart, drying his back with a large white towel. The young men froze. Ten years later, Thune could still recall their blank, confused faces. Faces from which all self-confidence had been erased in less than a second, to be replaced by a peculiar mix of feelings: respect, envy and fear.

Respect for nature's capacity to create aberrations.

Envy, for obvious reasons.

And fear, because their thoughts veered towards the possibility that the unknown man in the shower might be a homosexual.

Thune had already noticed Röman's penis earlier that evening. But the youthful Thune had a realistic view of himself and seldom felt threatened by other men's physical attributes. By that time, towards the end of the twenties, Thune was married to Gabi and they had slept together countless times. And he had had other women before Gabi. He knew that his penis was small in both its resting and aroused states, and he also suspected that he lacked passion and endurance. His only chance of impressing women was through his intellect, and by being a good listener. Only when he failed at this and lost Gabi to a professional listener, Robi Lindemark, did he feel real jealousy for the first time in his life.

Thune shook his head impatiently to get rid of the image of Gabi and Robi that had come into his mind. He had other things to think about.

The previous meeting of the Wednesday Club, for the first time in the Club's history, had come close to descending into an open row. Thune asked himself why.

In earlier years they had discussed the new marriage law, the stock market crash, the Lapua Movement, women's emancipation and Ivar Kreuger. The conversations had been heated and sowed division, but they had never lost respect for one another.

83

Not when Hugo Ekblad-Schmidt, a practising Catholic, had expressed his loathing of contemporary marriage legislation in company consisting mostly of agnostics and atheists. Nor when dear departed Bertel Ringwald exhibited certain sympathies with the Lapua Movement among men who, with the exception of Ekblad-Schmidt and Ringwald, were all liberals or out-and-out leftists, like Joachim Jary, who also happened to be Jewish.

In the spring of 1932, shortly after the Mäntsälä Rebellion, Leopold Grönroos had been accepted as a new member. Polle Grönroos hated Bolshevism, and in him the Wednesday Club acquired a new right-wing member to replace the deceased Ringwald, and Ekblad-Schmidt, who had moved to Paris. Grönroos had said he understood the attempted coup by the desperate men of Mäntsälä. But the other members had taken this expression of sympathy calmly. Even Guido Röman, who in his youth had praised the Soviet Union's New Economic Policy and had painted his rented room red and black, all to upset his father Eugen, who was a director of Nordiska Föreningsbanken, had smiled amiably and contented himself with a comment that Polle could only speak from his own experience.

Naturally there had also been plenty of issues on which the Wednesday Club had been 100 per cent unanimous.

They had raised a toast and sung drinking songs on the April day when the state-run alcohol stores opened and the era of prohibition was finally dead and buried.

And, seeing as they were all Swedish-speakers, they all believed that the language dispute was the fault of the Karelia Society and other Fennomaniacs. When the Club discussed the language question there were moments when Thune heard and saw – with a sharpness that he also directed towards himself – how patronising their attitude to the Finnish-speaking majority of the population was.

Things became more heated when Lorens Arelius joined the group in the spring of 1936. The Club had been a dwindling force for several years, but with Arelius as a new member and Thune on his way home from Stockholm, it became more vital once again. Polle Grönroos gained an ally in Arelius, and the balance of strength was restored to what it had been when the Club was founded: four liberals and two conservatives.

Zorro Arelius was a successful private doctor of classic right-wing persuasions. His scepticism towards liberalism and democracy was based on profound personal conviction, whereas Grönroos tended to be sceptical about anything that was likely to make his wallet lighter. Arelius had even belonged to the Student Activists' Association, but had withdrawn from the right-wing group because of personal differences with the other members.

Tension arose the first time Arelius hosted the Wednesday Club. The meeting took place in his newly built villa out in Westend during the summer of '36, a few months before the German reoccupation of the Rhineland. Thune happened to be in Finland on business, and for once was able to attend. The Club debated Hitler's aggression and France's supine response, and the evening also featured a sharp exchange about the impending Olympic Games in Berlin. Arelius and Grönroos thought that sportsmen's achievements reflected their nation's vitality in a very tangible way. Guido Röman expressed no firm opinion, as usual, even though sport was his area, but Thune and Lindemark thought that athletes should be freed from their national flags and allowed to compete as individuals.

Once again, Arelius pushed his political thesis. He claimed that the architects of the Versailles Treaty bore all the responsibility for the unstable situation, that the terms of the peace had been a grotesque error on the part of Lloyd George and Clemenceau, and a disgrace for the whole of Europe, and that it ought not to be too difficult to understand that a revived Germany wanted to break out of the bear-trap in which the toothless Weimar Republic had spent its entire existence.

85

When Thune looked back now, he could see that the spirit of the Club had changed the moment Zorro Arelius became a member.

It struck Thune that he might not have wanted to see that this was the case, that the Wednesday Club had become so important to him that he had closed his eyes to the obvious and clung to the idea that the Club was a refuge in an unquiet age, an idyllic haven in which politics might well be discussed, but where the threatening clamour of the world found little purchase.

The year before Arelius became a member the Club had unanimously condemned the Nazis' Nuremburg Laws. No-one, not even the pro-German and always business-minded Polle Grönroos, had said a single word in defence of the race decrees. Naturally, they had all felt a strong sense of loyalty towards their Jewish colleague Jary, but there was more to it than that: the very idea of racist legislation struck them as outrageous.

Arelius, on the other hand, often vacillated on the Jewish question. Like the others, he had been a childhood friend of Yogi Jary and had no desire to upset his friend, so he always tempered his remarks when Jary was present. He was happy to praise Jewish artists – he liked Mendelssohn's music – and scientists, but he made no secret of the fact that much of the Jewish mentality was alien to him.

Like all the business with money and the obsession with buying and selling and lending. Or harping on about ancient traditions the way the more orthodox Jews did.

On those occasions Jary usually replied that Jews had founded clothing stores and lent money because those were among the few things they were permitted to do: they had been prohibited from practising various professions and subject to other restrictions in countless countries in the course of their history. And as far as ancient practices were concerned, he would go on, the veneration of tradition was the only way to preserve a culture that lacked a geographical home, a country of its own. Even

86

he, Joachim Jary, understood that, despite the fact that he was assimilated and godless – in the rabbis' eyes he was no longer a *mensch*, but merely a lost soul.

In the early summer of 1936 Jary was admitted to Kopparbäck for the first time: he did not attend the meeting in Arelius' home. The mild June evening and the pastoral setting lured them all to drink more than they usually did, including the host.

Without warning Arelius began to attack the French prime minister, Léon Blum. No-one was surprised that Arelius was critical towards Blum, but they were shocked at his tone. Arelius, who travelled to Paris as least once a year, mocked Blum's feminine weakness and poured out a torrent of invective about the leader of the Popular Front's squeaky voice and accursed intellectualism and big, flat Jewish feet. Arelius claimed that Blum received visitors while lying on a divan, drenched in *eau de Lubin* and dressed in purple pyjamas and a silk dressing gown, even if it was three o'clock in the afternoon.

The description was positively dripping with anti-Semitism, and the situation was made no less embarrassing by the fact that they were in Arelius' home. Thune knew he ought to say something, but remained silent. Robi Lindemark was more courageous, unless he was merely unable to contain himself. He told Arelius in a stern voice that hatred of Jews and other racist views had never formed part of the Wednesday Club's programme, and that he hoped this would continue to be the case. Otherwise he would have to resign his membership.

Arelius' face had betrayed contradictory emotions on that occasion, both regret at having gone too far, and fury at being corrected in his own home. But he had restrained himself, mumbled an apology and said that he was not anti-Semitic, but just happened to dislike Léon Blum. And then he had promised that it would not happen again.

But the atmosphere had remained strained for the remainder of the evening, and in spite of Arelius' promise, the meetings of the Wednesday Club were never again as relaxed as they had once been.

The S.S. *Archimedes* was getting close to Helsinki. Thune tossed his cigarette into the sea and tried to brush his anxious thoughts from his mind and enjoy the sight of the approaching city.

He failed. A storm was gathering, and the wind was getting stronger as heavy, lead-grey clouds gathered above the cathedral and city centre, and Thune could not avoid seeing the symbolism in the tumbling mass of cloud.

Calle Nykopp had hit the nail on the head as they were sitting in Säcken drinking one last glass of beer.

They were living in a remarkable time. War and conflicts were flaring up, illegal Communists made secret plans, scaring people like Thune's elder sister Ulla and her Sigurd, and a few weeks ago Thune had seen four young men in long black coats perform the Hitler salute one morning outside the New Student House.

There were days when it felt as if the spring light were disappearing, as if humanity would not be granted any more summers. On days like those Thune felt dispiritingly useless, like Chaplin's tramp in "Modern Times", or as if he had tumbled into a Jules Verne contraption that had carried him off to some age in which he did not belong, to an era in which nothing but physical might mattered. An age that demanded unthinking courage from absolutely everyone.

Courage had never been Thune's strong point. His specialities were analysis and reflection.

The question was whether anyone wanted those anymore.

The present was giving off an ancient stench, and Thune suspected that it was the stench of future sacrifice.

When he was young and studying law, there had been a growing belief that people who had once been mere serfs were on their way to becoming valued citizens. "At last," people said to each other, and that feeling had been common to most of Europe, it was part of the new objectivity, of the weariness that followed the great human slaughter.

War was no longer trusted as a solution. Instead people chose to believe that humanity could change.

But now, once again, seething hatred towards real and imagined enemies was demanded.

As was unconditional love for a mythical, feminised mother country, a love as blind and hopeless as a mole's to his hole in the ground.

The Finnish Maiden. Mother Svea. The Nazis' slogans about women as the most important custodians of the German birth-right. And who was that behind Stalin's demands for realism in art and heroic industrial endeavour, if not the Mother Russia whom Lenin had sought to bury?

What else could this mean but that the corpses of millions of young men would once more be buried beneath the ground close to battlefields, so near to the surface that the sites would reek of death for decades after? The only question was when and where the sacrifice would start.

But Thune had no thoughts of giving up. Broad-mindedness was oxygen to him, a way of looking at the world that he had developed over many long years, and he would defend it by peaceful means as long as he lived.

And soon it would be summer again, in spite of everything, with sea and archipelago and rest: he needed to arrange some-thing, to conjure up some sort of surrogate for the Fahlcrantz villa. Because he knew that if he could just sit on some sun-warmed rocks in his bathing trunks, or row a tar-scented boat across still water, then everything would feel a good deal better.

The *Archimedes* was approaching Gustavssvärd, and, beyond the bastion of Sveaborg, the market square and south harbour were just visible. It was starting to snow: wet, restlessly swirling flakes. Thune thought of Mrs Wiik. How had she coped that week? And would she have remembered to send the report and plan for the week ahead by courier, as they had agreed?

9

As spring progressed and the buds began to open, the German chancellor disappeared from the headlines. The newspapers were now writing more about the Spanish Civil War and the Sino-Japanese War than Germany and Austria. Matilda was relieved. Throughout March and April Hitler had featured on the front pages every day and it had annoyed her: she hated the fact that the ugly chancellor had the same first name as her dead father.

Thune seemed revitalised and happy after his week in Stockholm. He had also been pleased with the way Matilda had managed the office. He had paid her 400 marks extra in her wages for the second half of April, and said that from now on he knew he could go away and leave the ongoing activities of the office in her capable hands.

They were alone in the office most of the time; Thune had at most one meeting with a client each day. Thune would sit in his room, and Matilda out in the lobby, but they often met and conferred. They exchanged friendly but brief remarks when he gave her new tasks, and they saw each other when she went into his room to take dictation or leave copies of typed letters.

They saw each other when she made him his tea and carried in the tray bearing the steaming drink and the hard British biscuits with raisins in, made by Ryker's – Thune loved them, and it was one of Matilda's duties to see that supplies never ran out – and put it down on his desk. They saw each other when Thune put on his hat and coat and left for lunch at the Kämp or the Royal or Monte Carlo, and they saw each other when he came back: when lunch took a long while he might return intoxicated, and was then particularly distracted.

Sometimes she had a feeling that Thune was building up to saying something to her. Not something ordinary, like when he joked about the government or remarked upon the fine weather or passed comment on a client who had just left the office. Something more important, something he had been thinking about for a while.

Some days were so quiet and uneventful that it would have been no more than natural for them to talk to one another a little more. But seeing as Thune never got the words out, Matilda never found out whether or not he really had been thinking about something. Thune preferred to stick to banal subjects. Apart from the very few occasions when an apparently light-hearted comment on some current event might contain a deeper, often ironic edge.

Those were the times she liked him best of all. Like the occasion when he asked her for her reaction to the fact that 99.73 per cent of people had voted for the same thing in Germany and Austria.

"My main reaction is one of fear," Matilda had replied.

"*Genau*," Thune had said, with a sad smile, and then dropped the subject.

Perhaps he is just shy, she thought. She wondered if Thune had already met a new woman since his separation. She did not think he had: he seemed quite a lonely person. She had seen no sign of him socialising privately with anyone but the members of the Wednesday Club, the exiled Russian businessman Gerasi-moff, and a couple of other clients.

Only men.

What if Thune doesn't like women at all? The thought struck her one afternoon when he returned from lunch with Gerasimoff and Grönroos and was even more vague and distant than he usually was, almost brusque. What if he secretly prefers caressing men, and that's why his marriage came to an end?

Matilda spent the latter part of April and more than half of May on tenterhooks.

She was waiting for something to happen, but was gradually starting to lose hope. Everyone who had looked in or been in touch while Thune was in Sweden came to see him during the following weeks. Leopold Grönroos, Gerasimoff, the peculiar little Jew, Jary, and plenty more.

But not the Captain.

Until one rainy afternoon towards the end of May.

Then the letter arrived.

It came in a small, delicate envelope, addressed to *Miss Wiik, c/o Claes Thune Legal Services, Kaserngatan, Helsinki.*

The Captain had his own notepaper; his name was printed in nice modern capital letters at the top left corner. She felt no discomfort as she looked at his name, she was in control of her feelings now.

It was a long letter. He wrote that he had been thinking about her since their short meeting in the office, and that he had realised, to his own surprise, that he would like to continue the conversation. During those brief minutes he imagined he had seen a similarity in their way of looking at life and the world. He had a feeling that they could become friends, even though they probably came from rather different worlds, and it was this possibility that he now humbly asked her to explore together with him. Would Miss Wiik be prepared to meet him one day after work, perhaps for afternoon coffee and something sweet, at the Mississippi or Nya Fiskartorpet, or perhaps even an early dinner at some suitable establishment? Perhaps a *chambre séparée* at the Golf Casino? That would allow them to talk undisturbed. Or the buffet at the restaurant next to the new bathing area in Westend, which was so beautiful at this time of year?

Naturally, his car was at her disposal should it be required, he added.

Matilda smiled at the Captain's faith in his own cunning. He called her *Miss* even though she had made it very clear to him that she was Mrs. And all the cafés and restaurants he had suggested were far out in the suburbs, with little risk of anyone seeing them and spreading gossip. If he had suggested dinner at Klippan or the Savoy, the risk of discovery would have been considerable, and if they were seen there would doubtless be an immediate scandal: he wore no ring, but she had a feeling that the Captain was spoken for.

She waited until Saturday afternoon. Then she wrote a short note in reply, put it in an envelope, wrote the address by hand, making an effort to make her handwriting look attractive, franked it and added the letter to the outgoing post.

He would not receive her reply before Monday at the earliest. But that did not matter, he could wait.

She declined his offer, and did so without hesitation.

Miss Milja had told her that was what she must do. The Captain would not give up, Miss Milja assured her. On the contrary, a no would only make him more eager, and whet his appetite.

Matilda walked all the way home to Mechelingatan after work. She ate some leftovers out of the refrigerator and then took the tram to Berghäll: the Bio Fenix on Andra linjen was holding a Gary Cooper week. She liked visiting her old stamping ground.

It was lovely to go back when she knew that the reunion would be short.

Afterwards she did not feel remotely hungry. She got off the tram early and slipped into the Astra to see the late evening screening. Greta Garbo as Mata Hari. She had seen the film twice before. But that did not matter, she was happy to watch it any number of times. She loved it, loved everything about it except the ending.

When she unlocked the door and stepped into her home she felt satisfied with the day. She still did not feel at all hungry. She drank a glass of water, undressed, performed her evening ablutions, pulled on her nightdress and dressing gown, hung her work blouse and skirt in the wardrobe and closed the wardrobe door.

The street outside was quiet. The trams had stopped running, there were no cars about, no footsteps or voices. Mrs Wiik had been left at the office, her clothes in the wardrobe. Even Miss Milja was being nice and quiet. Matilda felt calm. As she turned back the bedspread and slipped under the covers she made up her mind to forget the whole thing. Everything would be as it had been before she heard the Captain's voice echoing in the stairwell on Kaserngatan. She wanted peace and quiet, nothing else. If the Captain wrote to her again, her reply would be unambiguous and abundantly clear: it was not possible for them to meet, not under any circumstances.

But that night the images forced themselves upon her for the first time in a very long while.

She dreamed about the night when the first women were taken from the starvation camp to the other camp east of Helsinki. And when she woke from the dream, sweaty and frightened, her thoughts would not stop as the memories flickered past.

She had been in the first transport. But she no longer knew if she remembered everything the way it had been in reality. In

95

her memories were people and moments that she sometimes thought Miss Milja had made up.

That month of June, so long ago.

The summer heat arrived, the sun beat down without mercy, day after day, and the food ration in the camp out to the west grew smaller and smaller, worse and worse.

That was when the prisoners had their breakfast ration reduced from a whole herring to half of one, when the sun was high in the sky almost twenty-four hours a day.

That was when the flour began to run short and they had to eat barbed wire bread instead of normal bread. They called it "barbed wire bread" because it was full of oat chaff that caught in your mouth and then – if you made the mistake of swallowing it – cut like knives in your throat and stomach.

That was when they began to be given watery soup made of dried cod that was rarely cooked properly: the little pieces of cod remained raw, and most prisoners threw the soup up at once.

The number of deaths from sickness – those who were shot were accounted for separately, but there were few of them, only one or two each day – began to rise, and soon reached more than a hundred dead each day.

What was called "sickness" was nothing more than starvation. And it was the men who died. They actually did die like flies, while the women remained alive, as long as they avoided being shot.

Milja Matilda did not know why the female prisoners were so much more tenacious than the men.

Certainly, the women had their own secure barracks, and the guards did not hit them with batons and electric cables as often as they hit the men. And most of the women had only been taken captive at the end of the war: she herself was one of them. The women had had more to eat during the winter; they had not been freezing and hungry off at the front like the men.

But that was probably not the whole truth.

There was something else too, something she could not put words to, not at the time, nor later.

There was something extinguished, dead in the eyes of many of the men. As if they had sunk into a despair so deep that they no longer wanted to live.

But the women's eyes were still ablaze. She saw a lust for life flash in their eyes in the gloom of the barrack, she heard them say goodnight to each other in unbroken voices before they lay down and tried to get some sleep on the rough asphalt floor. Some of them were burning with hatred for the Whites, others were supported by the simple dream of one day being able to walk out of the camp and back to their lives.

Perhaps it was the case, Matilda thought later when she had had time to read books and also got to know Hannes, that men always expected too much. Of themselves, of life, of the revolution. Whereas women – working-class women, anyway – did not expect anything at all, at least not anything good.

As a result the women were like tightly twined rope: unyielding and equipped for endless wear and tear.

But perhaps – and this thought only came to her many years later when she had more knowledge – the truth was far more banal than that. Perhaps the women merely had more fat reserves to live on, not only in their breasts, but other places too.

At the time, during that hot, sticky summer after the war, Milja Matilda did not think anything at all. She just did the same as everyone else, she tried to survive.

The food situation quickly got worse.

The men started to catch frogs at dusk. They lived in the clump of trees that separated the camp from the shore. The barbed wire fence was only some fifty metres from the water. It was a beautiful inlet, the prisoners could see the source of cool comfort but were not allowed to experience it: inside the camp there was a severe shortage of water.

The frogs were boiled or grilled – the guards allowed the

prisoners to have open fires in the camp, but it was hard to find anything to burn – and then the meaty thighs were torn off and eaten. If the frog had been properly cooked it would stay down, but when the men were too eager and ate the thighs half raw, they suffered terrible stomach cramps, and their vomit had the force of a mountain spring. Several of them died.

Men and women tore bark from the trees with bleeding fingernails, and ate it raw or grilled, trying to suck up the sap from the fleshy innards.

One morning – they later found out it was a mistake and not an attempt to kill the weakest of them – the prisoners were served rotten cheese. It was hard to get it down, most of them threw up at the smell alone. But some ate it, and that afternoon a dozen men were found dead in various parts of the camp. They were leaning against trees or lying on the sand, or on the floor inside the barrack, all with half-chewed cheese between their teeth and mouldy remnants in their hands.

Someone – Milja Matilda guessed it was the camp doctor – was so alarmed at this that he decided that all the women should be moved. To a camp where there was not such an extreme shortage of food, and where their eventual death would be someone else's problem.

The first transport took place in the middle of the night. But it was almost light then anyway, a sort of prolonged twilight.

They were taken in the prison camp's two trucks to a train that was not standing at a station, but out in the middle of the forest. The drive took half an hour or so. The women were on the back of the trucks with their legs tied together, with the guards in smaller vehicles right behind them. The road was badly rutted and the trucks' tyres thin, it was impossible to brace against the jolts. Gloom, people as flickering shadows, a crescent moon in the clear sky, the swearing of the guards above the sound of the engines, Loviisa, another prisoner, vomiting bile next to her, and the constant ache in her own stomach.

In the past three days she had eaten just a few small pieces of bread and a bit of watery soup. She had not passed anything for she did not know how long, weeks, probably. Her stomach was a hard, tense knot; she would go to the stinking latrine and try to push but nothing came out. She had not had her monthly bleeding since early May when she was taken captive, and it was almost July now. She had turned seventeen just a few days ago. She had not told anyone it was her birthday, not even Loviisa, her closest friend in the camp. She knew she was not pregnant. No-one had interfered with her, not in that way. Her body had simply begun to stop working, and was gradually shutting down.

Even though her legs were shaking and trembling on the back of the truck she had turned round, but then one of the guards hit her with the butt of his rifle and she ended up sitting down. The last images had etched themselves into her memory: the dark, brooding brick barracks, the trees, pale and damaged at the bottom where the bark had been hungrily removed, the little mound of earth marking the latest bodies to have been buried in the long mass grave a short distance from the gate.

They were herded into two goods wagons. Cramped, no benches, no matting, no straw, not a drop of water. Just their shadowy figures filling the wagons, and the cloying, rank air as more and more of them broke wind in their anxiety and fear at what was to come.

No-one had said a word to them all night about where they were going. They had heard rumours that small groups of prisoners who had been told they were going home had disappeared without a trace; there had been similar instances in different parts of the country.

She tried to think that there were probably too many of them now, that the Whites would be taking too great a risk if they killed this many prisoners in one go.

It was almost dawn before they set off. The wagons had no

99

windows, but the growing light filtered in through the cracks in the doors.

The train rattled and jolted as it slowly began to move. The guards sat leaning against the barred doors, their rifles aimed at the prisoners throughout the journey. As if any of them would have had the strength to revolt, jump up and throw themselves at the guards – they were all men – and start fighting. Their combined strength would barely have been enough to open the door, they were so undernourished.

When they reached Helsinki they switched transport again, this time to horse and cart. On the back of the cart, bound together now. Milja Matilda's throat was tight with thirst, she would have done anything for a gulp of water. She did not feel hungry, not anymore. It was morning and there were a lot of people about, but a prisoner transport did not attract as much attention as you might have thought. Two upper-class women and a gentleman with a walking stick and a silver goatee beard spat vile words at them, *Time to reap what you sowed, you bitches*, that was all. Children just stared at the prisoners, wide-eyed, without a word.

That was what had happened the day they came to pick her up. The children in the block had stood and watched in silence.

Children rarely said anything unkind, only if they had been taught unkind phrases. They kept quiet instead, in their eyes an unspoken question about what sort of place the world really was.

In Matilda's dream the prisoners were moved to the new camp instantly. One moment the silver-haired man was waving his walking stick at them outside the railway station, and the next the carts rolled in through the camp gates and Milja Matilda's swollen eyes watered as she squinted against the sharp June light.

In reality the journey had taken one and a half hours, and they did not arrive until lunchtime.

The sandy yard, as dusty and wide as in the old camp. Soldiers – boys, really, not much older than her – being drilled by sergeants and corporals who were no older than their subordinates. The big pine tree out in the yard, its top surprisingly sparse, gave little shadow. The long brick barracks, dark and gloomy, just like in the starvation camp, even in the middle of the day in the month of June, in the brightest sunlight.

A group of prisoners was engaged in some sort of work at one corner of the yard next to one of the barracks. Some were digging with shovels, others were pushing large wheelbarrows with wooden wheels that dug stubbornly into the sand. A tall, grey-haired man had collapsed on top of his barrow and lay there catching his breath with his head resting on one of the handles, drenched in sweat, thin as a rake.

He's dying, Milja Matilda thought. Then she saw his face and recognised it.

Her father was lying on his side, his cheek against the handle of the barrow, staring in her direction with empty eyes, not recognising her, not seeing her.

A few metres from Adolf a woman was sitting down, leaning against the wall of the barracks.

Zaida. Her eyes black and empty, like dried-out wells.

Even before she woke up Matilda knew she was dreaming, that it couldn't be real – neither of them was still alive, neither her father nor her mother.

Yet she still shouted out when she woke up. Or at least she had a feeling that she had shouted out. It was always hard to know if you had shouted in the real world or just in the dream.

No-one banged on the wall or stamped on the floor in annoyance, the building was completely silent. Perhaps she had only shouted internally.

The room was cool but she was wet with sweat. She went over to the window, pulled the curtain back, opened the window and let the outside air stream in. She leaned out. It was already morning, the sun was on its way up over the rooftops. A newspaper boy was pushing his clattering cart along Caloniusgatan, and two workers were waiting for the tram that would take them to the factories in Gräsviken. She went back inside her room and looked at her alarm clock: twenty past six.

Sometimes when she thought about the past she tried to convince herself that it had all been a bad dream, that none of it had ever happened, that she was just mad, seeing things that weren't real, that she had had a different life, one that she had somehow forgotten, and because of her amnesia she dreamed these terrible dreams instead, but one day her real memories would come back and fill her with comforting, bright images.

A place where she was not Milja Matilda, not the reserved Mrs Wiik, not Miss Milja, and not timid, film-loving Matilda.

A place where she was someone completely different.

10

The early part of the summer had been chilly, and the Wednesday before Midsummer was no exception. Thune was sitting in the north end of the Stadium, freezing, and cursing the fact that he had let himself be persuaded to attend a sporting event for the second time in less than two weeks.

But had he really had any choice? Ought he not to be cursing the fact that he was so ensconced in the city's most prestigious social circles that he knew the influential men who ordered sports arenas to be built and gave lofty speeches when the facilities were inaugurated?

First the chairman of the Stadium Foundation, the cosmopolitan acting city manager Erik von Frenckell, had sent a large number of tickets to the inauguration to the Bar Association. This was the same von Frenckell who had turned Helsinki into a viable candidate for the Olympic Games by giving the city's application speech to the International Olympic Committee in five different languages.

Thune, who was on the board of the Bar Association, but intended to step down at that autumn's annual meeting because he found the association's activities imbecilic, had done his best to find an excuse that would prevent him from attending. But he had failed to find one. Von Frenckell was an intimidating man, renowned for ruining anyone who provoked his displeasure, and Thune had felt he had no option but to sit through the entire opening ceremony as it progressed at a snail's pace – it had started at two o'clock one Sunday afternoon, and the national anthem was not sung until a few minutes past nine. Thune wondered what the reaction would have been if he had told the truth to von Frenckell and the chairman of the Bar Association: that running races, javelin throwing, girls' gymnastics, patriotic poetry readings and patriotic speeches bored him almost to death.

One week later Polle Grönroos, who had business dealings with von Frenckell and had donated a large amount of money to the Stadium Foundation, came up with the idea of linking the June meeting of the Wednesday Club with the international athletics competition in the Stadium just before Midsummer. It was to be the Club's last meeting before a lengthy summer break, and because Grönroos was on the best of terms with von Frenckell it had been a simple matter for him to get hold of tickets. Thune ground his teeth but was unable to do anything.

For the first time in several years the Club was at full strength. Guido Röman sat in the press section while the competition was taking place: he had been sent by *Hufvudstadsbladet* to cover the event, but would join them later. The others were sitting at the north end – Grönroos, the host, Arelius, Lindemark, Jary and Thune.

Robi Lindemark was unusually quiet; there was something almost humble about his behaviour that evening. A few weeks before, on one of the first days of June, Lindemark had been rather more effusive. Thune had gone to Brunnshuset for a *souper dansant* and to listen to the Harmony Sisters. He was there alone, and was given a small corner table at a comforting distance from the restaurant's *clou*, the terrible mirror ball that rotated in the ceiling above the dance floor, casting angry reflections around the darkened room. Thune had been happy with everything: his plan was to eat a portion of *poulet à la Turenne*, drink two glasses of Burgundy, listen to the music and then go home. But at one of the other tables sat Arelius, Röman and Lindemark. They were already somewhat over-refreshed, and were utterly enchanted by the singing Valtonen sisters. Thune had huddled in his corner as best he could, but of course his fellow Club members had caught sight of him and insisted he join them when he had finished eating. Lindemark in particular had been extremely jolly: talkative and arrogant, and so delighted by the blondest of the sisters, Vera, that he took the lily-of-the-valley out of the vase on the table and lurched up to the stage, where he tried to press the flower into the hand of the poor singer while the trio were in the middle of singing the very catchy "Harbour Lights".

"And where's Gabi this evening?" Thune could not help asking when the giddy Lindemark returned. Thune had asked the question as sarcastically as he could, and his wry tone had not escaped either Arelius or Röman, who quickly looked down at the table.

But Robi Lindemark had been happy and stupid that evening, and he had failed to detect any subtext in Thune's question.

"Oh, she's just got a bit of a headache," he had said.

Thune: "A headache? Ah, she gets those sometimes, when it suits her."

Röman and Arelius had trouble keeping a straight face. But Lindemark did not seem to be paying attention to the conversation, and his eyes were firmly fixed on Vera once again.

As Thune walked home that night he felt lonely and out of sorts. It was past midnight, but the sky was perfectly light. Everything seemed to be blossoming at the same time: the last of the hawthorns were still white, the first lilacs were out, and the buds of the chestnut trees were ready to burst.

He could not help it: the whole city smelled of Gabi.

Helsinki smelled of and echoed with Gabi, while in Brunnshuset sat the man who had stolen her and was now letting himself be enchanted by twenty-year-old girls singing catchy ditties.

As he sat in the Stadium in the pouring rain three weeks later, Thune thought with a degree of *Schadenfreude* that Lindemark, now so meek, might have had time to read the various reviews of *The Silk Cushion* since the evening at Brunnshuset. Perhaps Robi had, in spite of everything, been a little offended that Gabi's book had received such a colourful reception? *The Silk Cushion* had been received overwhelmingly positively by the regional press and literary journals as well, but there had been plenty of ambiguous comments about – and a fair amount of criticism of – the stories' openly erotic content. Thune allowed himself briefly to ponder which role was heavier, that of betrayed husband or that of current lover of the "new high priestess of literary sensualism", which was one of the labels the critics had given Gabi. But he dropped the thought at once, the way you let a really hot potato fall back in the pot.

He would rather think about something else. For instance, the fact that Yogi Jary was back at last.

Robi Lindemark had discharged Jary from hospital in Kopparbäck in April, while Thune was in Sweden. His stay in hospital had been short this time, and Thune had no idea how it had been. Jary had never liked talking about his illness and the periods of hospitalisation it occasioned. In the past Lindemark used to keep Thune updated about Jary's health, as much as his oath of confidentiality permitted, but he no longer did that.

Jary had not attended the April meeting, nor the one in May. He was a fragile individual even when he was at his strongest, and had perhaps decided to avoid the strong emotions that their heated discussions could easily give rise to. He need not have worried: Zorro Arelius had had a brief outburst, but otherwise the two spring meetings had been calm and apolitical. And on that point, Thune thought, the Club was in tune with the spirit of the times – all of Europe was pausing for breath that spring, relieved that the union of Germany and Austria had not led to an international catastrophe.

But Joachim Jary was the sort of man who never felt calm. He had visited Thune in his office one sunny day in May, gesticulating as anxiously and intensely as ever. He had asked Thune all about his trip to Stockholm, was curious about which plays and exhibitions he had seen. Thune had dutifully told him, including "Peer Gynt" at the Royal Dramatic Theatre, and how he imagined that the tragically deceased Gösta Ekman would have played the role much better.

"I saw Gösta when he was performing in Helsinki in December," Jary had said solemnly. "I knew he was going to die soon."

"Now you're talking nonsense again, Yogi," Thune had replied in a friendly voice. "How can you see someone on stage and know that they're going to die?"

Jary, deadly serious: "Not on stage, Claes. It was when I was crossing the Esplanade Park. I was on my way to Bronda. I saw him get out of a cab near the theatre. I was going to say hello – he was here plenty of times, of course, and we had met more than once. But I didn't dare. Gösta had no make-up on, and death was written on his face."

"The worse for wear?" Thune had asked.

The great actor's alcohol and cocaine abuse had been a poorly guarded secret for years. Even so, the first five rows of the stalls in the Swedish Theatre were filled by Helsinki's female student population during this most recent tour, just as they had been on each previous occasion. Thune's niece, Marie-Louise, had managed to pester her way to an interview with the great man for the girls' high school magazine, and had written elegiacally about Ekman's luminous, almost unearthly beauty, which was only made more profound by the fact that the years had left furrows on his face.

"More than the worse for wear," Jary had said, before going on: "Gösta was broken. People can be tormented by afflictions, but as long as they don't break the defeat is never definitive. Brokenness is the measure of everything. Once you are broken, death can take you."

Thune had shrugged and replied: "That sounds like some divine statement, and I don't believe in those. I believe in reason and common sense. And the fact that people and their fates must be judged case by case."

At those words Jary's face had broken into a brief smile, simultaneously ironic and sad, and he asked: "Claes, don't you believe in evil? That it actually exists?"

Thune had taken his time before he eventually replied: "No, not in the biblical or any other metaphysical sense."

Jary had then pulled out a photograph and offered it to Thune.

Thune had taken the photograph from Jary's outstretched hand and studied it.

It was a poor photograph, taken by an amateur. Blurred and out of focus, a careless snapshot of a group of people in a village or small town. The fact that the picture was blurred gave the impression that it had been taken in haste, possibly even surreptitiously.

Four men and one woman were kneeling on all fours in a cobbled street. They were busy doing something but you could not see what, their figures were blurred and their faces were turned towards the cobbles, it was not possible to see how they looked, only that the men were wearing jackets and trousers, and the woman a coat and skirt.

Because the figures on their knees were out of focus, Thune's attention moved on to the other people in the picture. There were plenty of them, everyone in the village seemed to have gone out onto the streets. Old men, young men, women of various ages, children. Close to the kneeling figures stood a group of large men, a dozen of them. They differed from everyone else in the picture in that they were in uniform.

"What's this?" Thune had asked.

"Jews scrubbing a village street with toothbrushes," Jary had replied.

"What's the name of the village? Where is it?"

"That doesn't matter. That village is every village. And every village is that village. But it happens to be in Austria."

"How did you get hold of the picture?"

"A distant relative of my sister-in-law took it. He made copies and has been sending them to everyone he knows."

"What for?"

"So that people will finally begin to understand."

"What is it that people will finally begin to understand? That evil exists?"

"Look at the faces," Jary had said. "Not the Jews', because you can't see theirs. The others'."

Thune had looked, and had seen what Jary wanted him to see. Most of the people were laughing, openly and coarsely and scornfully. The old men and youths. Old and young women alike. Even many of the children, although others looked thoughtful and sad.

A beautiful young woman in a spring coat and scarf had lifted her little daughter onto her shoulders so that she could see the spectacle better. The woman was looking up to one side, at her daughter's pointing finger, and the look in her eyes was full of love.

Thune looked at the men in uniform. Ten men in brown shirts, all wearing armbands with the swastika on. Two men in long black leather coats and black military caps. The men with armbands were laughing, but the two officers looked serious and focused, as if they were conducting a secret mission.

"I'm sorry, Yogi, I'm so terribly sorry," Thune had said, suddenly feeling very helpless.

*

Now they were sitting in the Stadium in the chill June evening, two months had passed, and Thune sneaked a glance at Jary beside him. He was engaged in a discussion with Robi Lindemark, a conversation in which an agitated Jary was discoursing and Lindemark was doing little more than listening.

It pleased Thune immensely that Jary was back in the group. But Thune had known Yogi from the early days of their youth and had followed the progress of his illness from the start, progress which had wrenched Jary from a position as one of the city's most talented artistic figures and turned him into someone who increasingly resembled a shadow of the man he had been. Thune had watched as Jary slowly succumbed to his tightly strung psyche and his ever more vivid imagination – what had once been one of his strengths as an artist had gradually become the Achilles heel of his private life – and his trained eye could see that it would soon be time for another hospitalisation. Because Jary was once again going at top speed, and for a short time everything would be dynamic and energetic and fine. Jary was still a wonderful person when he livened up, with a seemingly endless supply of stories and anecdotes that were more dramatic and entertaining than anyone else's. But the periods of liveliness always ended with a profound breathlessness of the soul, in vague and imprecise fears and obsessions that were both cruel and persistent. And every time it ended with Lindemark admitting Jary to his clinic again to give him Luminol and other anti-anxiety medication as he tried to get Jary to calm down through the use of in-depth counselling and therapies of the most modern variety.

Throughout the years Thune and Jary had been united by a shared hatred of all forms of competitive sport. The other members of the Wednesday Club were all interested in sport. For some of them, Guido Röman, for instance, it was less an interest than a passion. For others, like Robi Lindemark, this interest had arisen later and was at most tepid, but it was there nonetheless. The others sometimes made fun of Thune and Jary's dislike of sport, calling them "the Club's sewing circle ladies".

Now Jary had surprised them all by looking forward keenly to that evening's competition. During the pre-season his young nephew Salomon had emerged as one of the country's most promising sprinters, and was one of the favourites for the 100-metre race. The starting line-up was strictly domestic, but it was still impressive. All the top Finnish names were there, Ruikka from Viborg, Marttinen from Savolax, Tallberg from Sports Club '32. And Salomon Jary.

Just before the starter fired his pistol Yogi Jary's slender body tensed. For a few moments he resembled a cat, a skinny stray, ready to pounce, just like the runners down on the track.

Some eleven seconds later Jary relaxed, a relieved and proud man. It had been a splendid, exciting race. The roar of the crowd settled into an even murmur, and a few seconds later the announcer confirmed over the loudspeakers what everyone had just seen: the race had been won by Salomon Jary in the outside lane, just ahead of Ruikka, Marttinen and Tallberg.

For several joyous minutes the other members of the Wednesday Club took turns slapping the delighted Yogi on the back. Their happiness was genuine; only Zorro Arelius seemed less than enthusiastic. Then their attention turned to the evening's main event, the 5,000-metre race in which the impressive Swede, Jonsson, was up against the Finnish hope, Mäki, and there had been speculation in advance that a new national record would be set on the Stadium's fast cinder track.

The race had already started – Mäki was leading the field ahead of Jonsson, who was running with a featherlike stride and sphinx-like calm – when the announcer delivered the final result of the 100-metre race.

First, Marttinen, second, Ruikka, third, Tallberg, and fourth, Jary, all with the same time, eleven seconds precisely.

A surprised murmur ran through the crowd. But at the same time Jonsson made his move, and Mäki grimaced and seemed to have trouble keeping pace with the Swede. All attention was focused on the race taking place down on the track, and any surprise at the result of the 100-metres died away in a collective shrug.

Thune glanced at Jary and saw that he had gone quite white. His mouth was moving but no words came out – his throat was not making any sound at all.

From the corner of his eye Thune saw Robi Lindemark trying to catch his gaze. Thune turned his head and let it happen, and the former friends' eyes met, each shaking his head sombrely. Lindemark pursed his lips in an expression of incredulity.

Grönroos and Arelius were absorbed by Mäki and Jonsson's battle and did not appear to have noticed anything.

"Claes," Jary said in an unsteady voice. "What did they just say over the speakers? I must have misheard."

Thune and Lindemark exchanged another glance. Both hesitated, and the moment of silence grew longer and longer until it became embarrassing.

It was Thune who broke the silence.

"No, Yogi," he said slowly. "You heard right. They've put Salomon in fourth place."

"But they can't do that," Jary said, his voice thin and slight. "Schlomo won, after all. Everyone saw that. They said so over the speakers when they crossed the line. And they haven't got the others in the right order either. Ruikka was ahead of Marttinen; everyone saw that as well."

"I'm very sorry, Yogi," Thune said.

He had an uncomfortable feeling that he was experiencing something he had experienced before, and that he knew what was going to be said before it was spoken. He shook off his discomfort and added optimistically:

"But they're bound to correct it."

He looked over at the finishing line where the officials were preparing for the last race of the evening, the 400-metre hurdles. There were twelve adjudicators, all dressed in light grey summer suits and pale hats. They look like penguins that have lost their colour, Thune thought. Like a directionless flock of birds.

"But this is . . . this is an absolute travesty," Jary stammered. "Tallberg was several metres behind! How can they have him in third place? And the same time for all of them! Claes . . ."

"Yes?"

"What's going on? Why are they doing this?"

"I don't know, Jary. I really don't know."

The 5,000-metres finished with a crazy sprint duel between Jonsson and Mäki. Jonsson won in a new Swedish record time. There was no correction of the erroneous result for the 100-metres. When it was time for the medal ceremony, Marttinen, Ruikka and Tallberg mounted the podium. There was no sign of Salomon Jary.

The incident spoiled the Wednesday Club's Midsummer meal in Polle Grönroos' palatial villa on Ekallén in Munksnäs. An unhappy Yogi Jary could not let it go, and raised the subject time and time again during the rest of the evening and night, calling it a "miscarriage of justice", and encouraging Grönroos and Röman, who had contacts in the sporting world, to intervene.

Thune was Jary's closest friend in the Club. He also brought a sober legal view to the matter. A wrong had been committed, and wrongs ought – as far as was possible – to be put right. Even so, Thune found himself getting irritated by Jary's unwillingness to drop the subject, but did his best not to let it show. Lindemark, in turn, hid behind his role as Jary's doctor and asked him to calm down for his own sake.

Grönroos and Arelius made no attempt to hide their annoyance, least of all later that night once the alcohol had taken effect. Grönroos snapped at Jary, saying that he had no intention of going to the mighty von Frenckell with such an absurd Jewish issue: it would not do any good, and he, Grönroos, would end up making a fool of himself into the bargain.

Guido Röman, on the other hand, listened politely and said he would do what he could. Röman had already mentioned the inaccurate result in his report of the competition. He had called the error "incomprehensible" and had included a photograph of the four runners at the finishing line, and another of the judges, grey and anonymous, standing at their places with stopwatches in their hands. He promised Jary that he would raise the matter at the paper again, before Midsummer: he would ask his bosses if they thought the scandal worthy of a follow-up article.

11

Matilda had been sitting inside the Stadium that Wednesday evening too. For that reason she was not taken aback when, on the Monday following Midsummer, Thune started to talk about the competition and the scandal surrounding the sprint.

Matilda had only a vague appreciation of the scandal itself. She had noticed the odd response of the crowd when the result of the 100-metre race was announced, and she remembered that there had been whistling when the prizes were handed out. But she knew little about sport, she was not accustomed to following the activity down on the track, and she had spent the greater part of the evening concentrating on her brother Konni and what he had to tell her.

She and Konni had talked about everything that had happened during the year or so that had passed since they last met. Matilda, true to form, had been very quiet, giving him the impression that she was still following the same lonely but relatively secure path as before. But if she was quiet, Konni seemed distracted and distant. Sometimes Matilda felt hurt that he asked so little, that he was so uninterested in her life.

Konni had never asked her why Hannes had disappeared – which she was certainly glad about – and now he was not asking anything about her new job, what branch she was in, or even what the firm's name was. She decided not to volunteer the information either. Not much happened in her life, she had told Konni as they sat in the Stadium, but the job was relatively pleasant and her new employer seemed a decent man, the salary was good and she had slightly greater financial freedom than before.

"Do you still spend half your wages at the cinema?" Konni had teased, and she had to admit that was the case. Then she had quickly changed the subject and asked Konni about his life.

At first Konni had been reluctant, and she had to prise the words out of him. Gradually he had thawed out. But he spoke in clipped, staccato sentences, with rather a forced masculine tone of voice.

The main thing is that he's talking, Matilda thought. That he's not keeping quiet and bottling up all his worries inside, the way he used to when he was younger.

Konni talked, and Matilda listened, and the races down on the cinder track below them assumed their correct proportions, becoming an insignificant trifle in the great river of life. Konni was sitting to Matilda's right, and from the left corner of his mouth he portioned out angular, granite-hard words about the everyday trials afflicting his and Tuulikki's lives, about how much he missed Helsinki, and the constant rows in the band. He said that Arizona was earning money, but that the band was very expensive to run: there were wages to pay, instruments and music to buy, songs to be arranged, the band's daily expenses and transport cost a lot of money, and so on.

"If we had our own premises, and could give lessons to anyone wanting to learn," Konni muttered, "like Dallapé have got, then we'd really be in the money!"

Matilda had been given the tickets by the Captain.

Several more letters had arrived at the office during the spring, small envelopes addressed to Mrs Wiik – he remembered

116

her marital status now – with suggestions of lunch at restaurants close to the sea, or a *souper dansant* at various establishments, all of them off the beaten track. Matilda had not ignored the letters, but declined all the offers, without exception.

In June, when she had politely but firmly rejected several more invitations, she had received an envelope containing two tickets to the athletics competition.

Unfortunately I was unable to acquire tickets to the inauguration, the Captain wrote, then went on in a slightly teasing tone: *but perhaps these might serve as some small recompense? I myself am obliged to watch the same competition in tedious male company, but am sending you two tickets in the hope that you might find the time to go with someone of your choosing. Because did you not say during our regrettably short meeting that you should like to see our Stadium from the inside while it was still shiny and new?*

She had realised at once that the contest was being held on her birthday. At first she had thought of giving the second ticket to Fanny, a fellow student at business college with whom she sometimes went to the cinema. But then Konni had written to tell her that he was coming to Helsinki – Arizona had been offered an engagement at the Mikado from the start of July. Tuulikki and the children would be staying in Åbo, but Konni would be arriving in the capital in the middle of June to make preparations. Amongst other things, he needed to rent a room – close to the centre, and ideally as cheap as possible – for the duration of the engagement.

Matilda had replied to him, suggesting that they go to the contest at the Stadium together. She had also offered Konni the use of her living room on Mechelingatan. *I can get a camp bed for you, I really have far more space than I need*, she had written.

Konni had not answered her letter, and simply turned up in Helsinki and rang her doorbell one June evening. He had a parcel with him that he held out to her as he entered the porch:

"It is your birthday soon, isn't it?" She had asked if she could open it immediately, and Konni had nodded.

A fountain pen in a beautiful case, and a bar of chocolate.

"But this is a Mont Blanc," she had said, pointing at the case. "You've got to learn to hold on to your money, Konni!"

"It's not a Meisterstück," he had replied, "it's a much cheaper model."

She had squeezed his arm impulsively, and repeated her offer of the living room and camp bed. But Konni had smiled rather wryly and said a cup of tea and a sandwich, and that contest at the Stadium she had mentioned, would be enough. As an office worker with regular hours, she probably wouldn't like to share her home with a dance musician, not even for a month or two, and not even if the musician in question was her brother. Besides, he had already arranged terms for a room in the Imatra youth hostel on Berggatan, he said. But then he added: "Thank you, dear Milja. You're the best sister a man could have."

I love you, little Konni, she had thought, but please don't call me Milja.

To him she merely said: "Don't call me Milja, Konni. Matilda."

Konni was in one of his dark moods again. He was friendly, almost unnaturally kind towards Matilda, but she could still tell: he was restless and unhappy inside, almost like before. The unsettled, angry look was back in his eyes.

At the Stadium it turned out that she and Konni were sitting just a couple of sections away from Thune and his company. Fortunately she and Konni were sitting much higher up, on the last but one row. But it was her time of the month and she had had to go to the ladies' room, and on the way back she had seen them at fairly close quarters out in the corridor: Thune, the Captain, and the others. She had turned on her heel and hurried away. She knew she was not thinking very logically, but she could not help thinking that if she were forced to meet the

Captain together with Thune, everything would become much more difficult.

And if the Captain were one day to be so conceited and stupid that he revealed to Thune that he had been courting his office assistant – well, then everything would be over before it had even begun.

Thune was in a terrible mood when he returned to the office on the Monday after Midsummer.

He had spent the holiday with his sister Ulla and her husband Sigurd, as a guest at their large summer-house in Kallvik, east of the city. It had rained a lot, and the house had been cold and damp. Rolle was still in Sweden with Elin, so hadn't been there to cheer his uncle up. Instead Thune had been obliged to listen to Rolle's younger sister Marie-Louise and three of her friends from the girls' high school. They had spent the entire weekend talking about film stars, horse-riding lessons and the boys at the Blue & White Lawn Tennis Club. They had eaten American Kellogg's cornflakes with milk for breakfast and lunch, and feigned dismay when Sunday came and the cereal box was empty: what were they going to do now. Porridge was so disgusting, not to mention Ovomaltine! Thune could not stand the girls' spoilt, drawling tone of voice, still less their attacks of the giggles.

Thune and Ulla's mother, the almost eighty-year-old widow Esther Thune, had also been there. Esther, her back as straight as a poker, had arrived in Sigurd Hansell's shiny black Packard, driven by their faithful servant and chauffeur, Vaattovaara. She and her only marginally younger son-in-law had at once settled into their usual lament over the moral decline of the younger generation, and devoted hours to remembering the constitutional struggle and the heroes of the turn of the century. Esther was well equipped for remembering: she was a good friend of

119

the artist Sigrid Schauman, whose heroic brother Eugen had first shot Bobrikoff, the wicked Russian Governor General, and then himself.

Thune was inclined to believe that any age that needed heroes armed with pistols was a bad age. Thune had also heard that Eugen Schauman wanted to die because he had been rejected by the woman he loved, and merely took the opportunity to take Bobrikoff with him. But Thune avoided getting involved in his mother's discussions with Sigurd Hansell. He knew that Esther Thune was not only unhappy with the direction things had taken in the twentieth century, but also disappointed in her only son, and that disappointment had only grown in recent years.

The Claes Thune law practice did not bring in any great sums of money, and Esther had still not got back the 26,000 marks she had lent him as starting capital almost ten years ago. Esther Thune had also been responsible for recruiting most of the firm's clients – friends and the children of friends of his deceased father, Thorolf Thune, a porcelain manufacturer – and she never missed an opportunity to remind her son of this. Esther had also been less than impressed by his modest postings as an attaché to two legations (Thune guessed that nothing but ambassador would have been good enough), and he regularly came up short when he tried to defend his liberal attitude to life to his mother. But Esther did not regard him as useless. It was worse than that. She regarded her son Claes as a diligent and conscientious boy who always did his best, but whose intellectual abilities were somewhat lacking. The fact that he had lost Gabi, who had been an excellent match – the Fahlcrantz family was not only rich, but also had a finer pedigree than the relatively modest commercial background of the Thunes – had only made Esther even more disillusioned.

For his part, Thune often reflected upon his mother's ability to use stubbornness and malevolence as fuel for a long life. Esther had already outlived her husband by almost twenty years; she was seventy-eight years old but wiry and strong as a mountain, with the health of a sixty-year-old. Thune had often thought that it was her fury and bitterness at everything that had gone wrong in her life that made her heart beat so remorselessly and powerfully.

On Midsummer's Day, when it had already been raining more or less without interruption for two days, the sea had risen so high that the meadows along the shore below the Hansells' villa in Kallvik flooded. Large schools of bream, orfe and perch lost their way and found themselves trapped on the meadows when the rain stopped and the water began its rapid retreat. Sigurd Hansell put together a team of fishermen consisting of himself, a few neighbours, and Thune. The fish had found their way up to the meadows via a ditch that drained into the sea, and Hansell decided to block their retreat with a fine-meshed net, after which the men settled down, lit their pipes and waited for the slaughter to begin. Then they waded about all evening and half the night, in a splashing inferno of half-dead fish that they clubbed and beat to death on the rocks. Next they gutted them, and a delighted Hansell was able to count almost a thousand fish. Mother Esther and sister Ulla were similarly pleased, and began talking about former catches back when Ulla and Claes were children, and then they remembered the elk hunting of which their father Thorolf had been so fond, particularly the moment when the hunt was over and the hunters had a drink or two as they dismembered, gutted and skinned the strung-up elk, whose heart still twitched and spasmed if you threw salt at it, and whose innards steamed and stank in such a wonderful musty way.

By this point Thune was already longing desperately to get back to his apartment in the city. But another twenty-four hours of torment remained. On the Sunday morning he finally had cause to visit the outdoor privy. Thune always suffered constipation when he visited Ulla and Sigurd in Kallvik; he guessed it was because he had to hide his political beliefs from them: intellectual constipation gave rise to the physical manifestation. This Sunday he discovered that the south wall of the outhouse had a new adornment, a fresh idolatrous portrait of Mussolini. In the picture Il Duce was wearing what looked like a Scout's leisure uniform, complete with some sort of Tyrolean hat with feathers in it. The leader's square, rock-like jaw jutted out as defiantly and imperiously as it always did, and his eyes were fixed on the sky above like an eagle's. In case anyone managed to miss the symbolism, the photographer had placed Mussolini beside a stuffed eagle posed in the act of landing: the bird's wings were spread and its talons embedded in a white marble plinth of prodigious size. On the plinth were engraved the words *Due Aquile*, "Two Eagles", and, in order to enhance the effect, someone – probably his sister Ulla – had contributed a generously proportioned gilded frame. With an audible groan Thune managed to squeeze a hard and far too small lump of excrement from his bowels, as he stared at the portrait and tried to work out which eagle looked more stuffed, the one in the Tyrolean hat or the other. Simultaneously he swore that this would be his first and last Midsummer in Kallvik. He had loathed the enforced socialising and reactionary behaviour in the Fahlcrantz villa in Esbo as well. But there he had at least been able to row out into the bay and hide on one of the skerries and cobs off to the south, and take a refreshing dip in the sea. There was no rowing-boat in Kallvik, and thus no possibility of escape.

Thune took all of these experiences, as well as the three latest Helsinki editions of *Hufvudstadsbladet*, with him to the office on the morning of Monday, 27 June, and, taken together, they gave him a gnawing sense that the times, the world, and he himself were out of joint.

"Would you mind waiting a moment? There's something I'd

122

like to show you," he said to Mrs Wiik when they were planning the week ahead, which promised to be relatively quiet.

He went into his room and fetched one of the papers – the Thursday edition, the one with Guido Röman's article and the results of the athletics competition in the Stadium – and held the paper out in front of her. It was open at the sports pages, and he held up the lower half, showing a picture of Marttinen, Ruikka, Tallberg and Salomon Jary at the finishing line.

"Tell me, Mrs Wiik," Thune said. "Which of these men won the race?"

Mrs Wiik looked at the picture with interest, then let her eyes roam up the page to look at the date at the top of the paper.

"Last Wednesday?" she asked. "I was actually there. But I wasn't paying that much attention to the races."

"Why not?" Thune wondered. "Seeing as you were there?"

"I was talking to my brother; it was the first time I'd seen him in a year," Mrs Wiik replied. "It also happened to be my birthday."

Thune looked down at the floor.

"I'm sorry," he said unhappily. "Obviously, I should have . . . permit me to offer my very best wishes, albeit somewhat belatedly."

"Thank you. But please, don't reproach yourself. How should you have remembered something like that?" Mrs Wiik said lightly as she pointed at the picture, then went on: "You can see who's won. The one closest to the camera. He's already crossing the line, and the others aren't there yet."

"Yes," Thune said. "You'd think so, wouldn't you?"

He could hear how strange his voice sounded, annoyed and triumphant at the same time. So he tried to control himself as he went on:

"But according to the official results, he finished fourth. The one on the inside lane won."

"The one on the far side?" Mrs Wiik sounded surprised now.

"Was that why the spectators whistled when they got their medals? He isn't even second. He's third."

"Not according to them," Thune said, pointing at the grey-clad, bird-like line-judges in the picture next to the one of the runners.

"Are they the ones who decide who the winner is?" Mrs Wiik wondered.

"Yes. Well, no! They're really only supposed to record the times. After all, the one who reaches the line first is supposed to be the winner," Thune said, feeling momentarily dizzy.

"Sport's strange," Mrs Wiik said, then smiled. "I've never understood it. I don't usually go. I was given the tickets by . . . an acquaintance."

Thune could feel his internal unsteadiness growing. There was a transparent, brittle sharpness – like ice that had formed overnight – to Mrs Wiik's way of choosing her words. Usually Thune liked that sharpness, but there were times when she made him feel confused.

"There's not usually any doubt about who's won," he explained. "Not even in the hundred metres, actually. And in really difficult instances you can actually let two athletes share the victory."

"Yes," Mrs Wiik said, "but there are four here. Should they have let that many win?"

Thune's confusion grew.

"I'm not sure," he said. "But I don't think that would work."

"Mind you," Mrs Wiik said, pointing at Tallberg, "this one's several metres behind the others. So there can't be any good reason for him to share the victory, can there?"

"No," Thune said, feeling very tired all of a sudden. "There can't."

He turned his back on her and looked out of the window. Kaserntorget was bathed in strong sunshine, and the sharp light made him squint. His thermometer had read nineteen degrees early that morning, so perhaps summer had arrived at last?

He was longing to take a few weeks off – he could feel it as a physical ache. He shook his head firmly and turned back to Mrs Wiik again.

"You remember the Wednesday Club, the group of my friends that met here in the office one evening in March?"

"Yes," Mrs Wiik said, "I remember them. You and four others, is that right?"

"There are six of us really," Thune said. "The one who wasn't here in March is a close relative of the runner who won but was demoted. His uncle, to be precise."

Mrs Wiik looked at the picture of the runners again, and read the caption.

"Jary," she said calmly. "I remember him too. He tried to see you while you were in Stockholm. That note, if you remember – the one that was left for you."

"Of course," Thune said, "now I remember." He looked at her apologetically and went on: "I forgot to ask . . . was he much of an inconvenience?"

"Not at all," Mrs Wiik replied. "He was very friendly. Talkative, but friendly."

"He was at the athletics as well," Thune said. "And he's been doing his best to put things right. He went to see Kolehmainen and demand justice for his nephew."

"Sorry, but who's Kolehmainen?" Mrs Wiik wondered.

"You don't know?"

Thune felt exhilarated. He was used to everyone, both women and men, knowing more about sport and sportsmen than him.

"Excuse my ignorance," Mrs Wiik said, "but I really don't know."

"Kolehmainen is in the inner circle of the Kisa-Veikot sports club," Thune said. He could hear how smug he sounded as he went on: "Kisa-Veikot were one of the organisers of the competition, along with the police. Kolehmainen has a sports shop on Kajsaniemigatan, but he's also one of our sporting heroes. He took Finland's first gold medal for running in 1912."

"Oh, *that* Kolehmainen. But he couldn't help?"

"No," Thune replied. "Unless he just didn't want to. According to Yogi . . . Jary, the uncle, Kolehmainen said that what had happened didn't matter."

"So there was nothing more to be done?"

"Oh no, Jary didn't give up. He tried to get an audience with von Frenckell."

"The city manager?" Mrs Wiik wondered, sounding reluctantly impressed. "Did he succeed?"

"No. Von Frenckell had already left for Midsummer, but sent a message saying that the published result would stand. And when Guido Röman . . . he's another member of the Club . . ."

". . . as well as being one of your clients," Mrs Wiik interrupted. "He comes here occasionally. He's the small man, the one with the neat moustache and nice jacket and shoes, but with the awfully baggy trousers."

Thune wondered where Mrs Wiik had picked up the habit of interrupting her superiors. She didn't do it often, but once was more than enough. Perhaps it was Mrs Wiik's lack of respect that had contributed to her leaving – or being obliged to leave? – the shipping agency, Hoffman & Laurén. Thune made a mental note to ask at Handelsgillet and the Swedish Club. Discreetly, of course.

He felt his cheeks burn. He knew why his friend Guido favoured baggy trousers, and even though Mrs Wiik's comment had been innocent, he still felt embarrassed. For at least the thousandth time in his life, he cursed the lack of *savoir faire* that Gabi had so often teased him about. He fumbled in desperation for the thought that had led to the conversation about Guido, and eventually found it:

"Guido Röman," he said, "tried to persuade his bosses that

126

the Stadium scandal was worth following up. He promised to take care of everything himself, and put in as much overtime as was required. But both the sports editor and the editor-in-chief said enough was enough, and that the newspaper had already pointed out that a mistake had been made, and that would have to do."

Thune rapped his knuckles on the windowsill and went on irritably:

"The thing is, not everyone thinks that this is a scandal. People don't see that it's about justice, they just see Jews whining. And they ignore the fact that there were German dignitaries among the spectators. That they were the ones everyone wanted to please."

Mrs Wiik was looking at him intently. Thune noted, not without surprise, that there was something hard in her eyes.

"I hope you don't mind me saying," she said, "but it surprises me that you think justice should be obvious. Getting justice is a privilege. And Jary clearly isn't privileged. Neither the runner nor his uncle."

Thune looked at her in astonishment. She had never spoken to him as sharply as *that* before. Mrs Wiik evidently realised as much herself, because she added in an abashed tone:

"I'm sorry, I shouldn't have . . ."

"Not at all," Thune hurriedly reassured her. "Besides, you're quite right."

He looked her in the eye and went on:

"Once upon a time Jary *was* actually privileged, more than most people. Not because he was a Jew, of course. But because he was so talented."

He shook himself again, determined finally to leave this uncomfortable matter behind him.

"Well," he said. "It may be summer, but we've still got work to do. Grönroos is coming in today, and Gerasimoff. Could you get their files out, please? And by the way, I was thinking of letting you have three weeks off, on full pay. When would you like to take them?"

He could see that Mrs Wiik was surprised. When she seemed unable to speak he went on:

"Would Saturday, 16 July to Monday, 8 August suit you?"

"Of course," Mrs Wiik said, looking almost shocked. "But, how were you thinking of . . . ?"

"I'll be closing the office for those weeks. I'm going to be moving, amongst other things."

"Congratulations!"

Thune didn't answer. Instead he looked out of the window and tried to appear manly and decisive, so that it wouldn't show that he had suddenly been seized with melancholy. Out of the corner of his eye he could see that Mrs Wiik had realised her mistake, and actually appeared to be blushing at her own impulsiveness. After a few moments of silence, she attempted to regain her composure:

"Might I ask where you . . . ?"

"Out to Munksnäs," Thune said. "Borgvägen."

"Oh, then you'll still be living close to the water," Mrs Wiik said.

"You're familiar with Munksnäs? Do you know where Borgvägen is?"

Thune sounded surprised.

"I can't claim to be familiar with it," Mrs Wiik said. "But I know where Borgvägen is. I've been for Sunday walks out to Fiskartorpet. It's very beautiful out there."

12

Matilda knew that she had been playing cat and mouse with Thune that Monday when he showed her the picture in the newspaper and was so perturbed by the result of the 100-metre race.

She felt a little ashamed. Mrs Wiik could react sharply at times, but was generally fairly timid. Now she had gone further than she usually did.

She had not dissembled *that* much, but certainly a little. A woman could always play ignorant about a subject, and thereby prompt even the most dilettantish man to give a lecture.

But Thune had withstood the test well. He had not lectured her at all, but let Matilda know that he was also fairly ignorant. And he had not made any secret of his confusion in those moments when she managed to unbalance him.

She had thought it before, and now did so again: she rather liked Thune, precisely because he sometimes showed himself to be human. Whether it was the case that his weapon was inadequate and that he would have preferred a better one, or whether he simply did not care about power, nor about being the object of others' admiration, Matilda was so far unaware.

But what she did know very well, on the other hand, was that four runners would never be allowed to share the victory in a race, and that even sharing it between two was unusual.

She understood why Thune had been surprised by the fact that she knew of Borgvägen. Only well-off people lived there, close to the shore, and obviously he was working from the assumption that she was poor. In recent years the Munksnäs Company had built large rental blocks further inland, along Stora Allén and Grundvägen. The people who owned villas close to the sea had written angry letters to the newspapers, they were scared that the suburb would become a slum and the value of their villas fall. In spring last year Matilda had seen Errol Flynn as Captain Blood at the Bio Rita on Grundvägen, just when the trees were coming into leaf, and she had thought that the entire suburb – including the rental blocks along Allén – was astonishingly beautiful.

She would always remember the occasion when she and Thune the lawyer talked, properly talked to each other for the first time: the sunny summer morning immediately after Midsummer, when the Jewish runner's victory had been stolen from him, and she dared to tell Thune that justice was a privilege.

Summer had taken its time arriving, but when it finally arrived it did so with a vengeance. Right after Midsummer the mercury began to rise towards twenty-five degrees each day, and some afternoons it carried on and came close to thirty. Down by Sandudd, just a stone's throw or two from where Matilda lived, the beach was covered with half-naked people lying on blankets or on the warm sand, listening to dance tunes from small portable gramophones and browning themselves in the sun. The evenings were warm as well, and Matilda's two-room flat up on the sixth floor was hot and stuffy all day and night: the sun shone straight into her rooms from early afternoon until shortly before dusk.

Sometimes she reflected upon the fact that it was almost ten years since she and Hannes had moved in. The building was new then, and they had been married little more than a year. She had just got a job at Hoffman & Laurén, and Hannes worked at Maskin & Bro, the rent was high but they had decided to take the risk.

In those days the city stopped at the corner of Mechelingatan and Caloniusgatan. There were more rented flats – also new – in the block down towards Museigatan, but beyond them the landscape opened up, rocks and meadows and forest took over. Julius Nissen ran a coffee merchants in the ground floor of their building, but apart from that there were no shops. The tram route along Mechelingatan, leading to the Maria Hospital and on towards Gräsviken, was still under construction, the streets were not tarmacked and puddles could hide holes so deep a child could drown in them, and the scrawny saplings that the city had planted in the hope that they would grow into sturdy, shade-giving trees all died.

In one of the other stairwells lived a woman by the name of Mrs Craucher. Men of all sorts, uniformed and civilian, would visit Mrs Craucher's apartment at the most unusual hours. Young girls also came to the flat, and the gossip was that they stayed a long time, sometimes several days. The girls had heavily painted lips and showy hats, they talked in loud voices, and occasionally Matilda heard them laughing out in the street in front of the building. The men who visited Mrs Craucher tried never to look the other occupants of the house in the eye, and would often have pulled their hat or uniform cap down so that the brim or peak covered half their face. Even so, Matilda and Hannes recognised faces they had seen pictures of in the newspapers and appointment notices.

Both Matilda and Hannes had realised that it was wisest not to pay too much attention to the visitors, and not to think too much about what happened inside Mrs Craucher's home.

Even so, Matilda had been surprised one late winter morning when she came home from work and found the building full of police officers.

131

It was the year after Hannes had given up and moved out: he had got up from his reading chair one summer's evening and put his paper down, then said he was going out to buy some tobacco, and when he came back he had filled his pipe and lit it, but he did not start to make their evening tea as he usually did. Instead he had got out a rucksack, their biggest, and without a word began to fill it with his clothes and books.

Matilda remembered how abandoned she had felt the evening after Mrs Craucher's murder. The sense of loneliness had been suffocating, even though it had already been eight months since Hannes disappeared. She remembered the gloomy, slushy road, the greasy light from the street lamps, and the constables standing guard out in the street in front of the stairwell in which Mrs Craucher had lived. Matilda had simply been scared, scared of the evil of mankind. The man who shot her was evidently a feeble, lost wretch. But Mrs Craucher had had influential contacts, particularly in the most patriotic circles, and in the weeks and months following the murder there had been a great deal of talk throughout the city.

Matilda tried to do the usual things, as if everything were the same as before.

In the evenings she went to the cinema and watched a film or two. Sometimes she stayed at home instead, sitting in her armchair reading a ten-mark novel and listening to the evening popular music concert on the radio.

But she was sitting by an open window – necessitated by the heat – and the summer was so oppressive outside. The warm evening air embraced her, there was a smell of fried food from the restaurants over on Runebergsgatan, a tram rattled past, and the sound of people drinking or walking past, some talking in soft voices, others harsh and shrill, found its way up the building and into the flat.

She missed Fanny, her only friend. One afternoon she took the tram to Sörnäs after work, went to Fanny's flat in one of the stone buildings on Tavastvägen and rang the bell. Fanny was not at home, and Matilda wrote a short note in pencil and pushed it through the letterbox. A few days later she received a postcard from Fanny, saying: *Dear Matilda. I am looking after children at the public health camp for a few weeks. My niece is watering the plants and found your note. We must meet when I get back! Sincerely, Fanny. P.S. Aren't you going to get a telephone soon, so we can call each other?*

She missed Konni. But he was probably busy with his own concerns, playing with Arizona at the Mikado half the night, and sleeping in his room on Berggatan long into the day. She had not yet heard Arizona. Konni kept pleading with her to go, and she certainly wanted to, but she had no gentleman friend to go with. The Mikado was not only a dance restaurant, but also a place where both staff and the male clientele would quickly draw conclusions when they saw an unaccompanied woman trying to get in.

She made a mental note to contact Konni as soon as possible. She also made a note to buy into the Telephone Corporation. She could afford it now. She had given Konni some money after their evening at the Stadium, but she still had savings.

One evening she found herself actually missing Hannes, even though it had been many years since he had taken his bulging rucksack, stepped into the lift and gone off down the street, never to be seen again.

They had never talked much, she and Hannes. She had not said anything then either, had not cried, had not begged him to stay, had not even said goodbye. She had just stood there silent and immobile in the opening to the living room and watched him put on his shoes and jacket, getting ready to go. When he opened the door their eyes had met and he had nodded in farewell, his eyes sad. She had nodded back.

133

She had been alone since then. How could she have been so alone for so long?

Because she had to admit it – that was what she was, deeply and undeniably alone, there was no point thinking otherwise.

All she could do was pretend that the loneliness was not painful at all, and that she liked it.

She did all she could to find peace.

She bought a wavelength chart from a radio shop on Henriksgatan and studied it in the hope of finding a solution to the interference during the evening concerts that were broadcast from Lahti.

She went out to Munksnäs one evening and watched the Mayerling film at the Bio Rita, with Charles Boyer as Prince Rudolf of Austria and Danielle Darrieux as the young Marie Vetsera. After the film she felt restless and out of sorts. She did not feel like catching the M-tram back into the city, and instead wandered through the leafy, sleepy suburb towards the water. When she reached Borgvägen she walked from the Cadet School all the way to the rocks above Fiskartorpet, and tried to guess which building Thune's new flat was in, the one he was going to be moving into in a few weeks' time.

Another evening she walked through Tölö and across Alphyddan, all the way to Sturegatan, where "Hulda from Juurakko" was still showing at the Bio Louhi.

It was the third time Matilda had seen the film: once again, the cinema was full. There were women of various ages, with just the occasional man – presumably dragged along – sitting beside his wife or fiancée.

The Louhi was off to the north, a few blocks from where the inner city came to an end. It was a poor district, and that showed in the audience. They were factory workers and shopgirls – the secretaries and students who filled the cinemas in Tölö

134

were noticeable by their absence. The men puffed on cigarettes throughout the course of the film, as did some of the girls, blue veils of smoke curling up towards the ceiling, and there was a strong smell of tobacco and sweat and far too sweet perfume. She was the one who stood out, Matilda, with her smart, dark blue blouse and her polished shoes and painted nails.

And that, she thought, was rather ironic.

The first two occasions she had liked the film, but this time she got almost angry. Nothing seemed to affect the central character, no setbacks, no lack of faith, no gossip. Hulda from Juurakko remained strong and robust as a prize sow, apparently prepared to move mountains to get what she wanted.

Fanny had told Matilda that there were upper-class families who had tried to forbid their maids from seeing the film, because the ladies and gentlemen were worried that their staff might get ideas in their heads after watching Irma Seikkula's triumphant turn as Hulda. Matilda could not understand what they were worried about, she thought Seikkula was overdoing it, and that Tauno Palo as Judge Soratie was overacting as well.

On the way home she got off the tram at the sugar factory, skirted round some noisy drunks who were sitting by the shore of Tölö Bay, and strolled home through Hesperia Park.

Unsettled in both body and mind.

She had finally said yes, she had met the Captain.

And she knew that she would meet him again.

When Matilda acted naïve towards Thune on the Monday after Midsummer, she already knew that she was going to meet the Captain.

She was going to take the first step, but she could still back out afterwards.

That was what she was thinking before the meeting. And for a few moments – when there had been a glimpse of a wordless, almost humorous understanding between her and Thune – she had actually felt an impulse to confide in the lawyer, and tell him. Not everything, but some of it. For instance, who she was and where she was from. Not everything she had been through, but enough to make Thune understand why things had turned out the way they had.

The impulse had vanished as quickly as it appeared.

Which was just as well.

Because after the meeting, when she had sat opposite the Captain and looked him in the eye and listened to him speak, she had known. She would go on, she would play the game: fate's will be done, on earth as it is in heaven.

She and the Captain had drunk a cup of tea and eaten a sandwich in the Café Mississippi in the Mejlans district.

Up on the hill, at sunset, just before closing time, with a view of Fölisöfjärden and Drumsö.

The sea had been still, the landscape had been steaming with heat, and the leaves on the trees were not moving at all: not even the aspens.

The last rays of sunlight had sought their way in through the leaded windows of the wooden villa, colouring the floorboards a gentle red.

It could have been beautiful, romantic. If only she had been sitting there with someone else. Hannes, for instance, the way he was during the early years.

There was not much to say about the meeting itself.

They had talked.

He had been very polite, asking her how she had come to work for Thune, and where she had worked previously.

She had replied just as politely, but rather vaguely. But she had still told him that her previous place of work had been Hoffman & Laurén.

The Captain had nodded and replied that he used to know Risto Laurén, he had been a good fellow, such a shame that he should have died so young.

He had asked if she had used the Stadium tickets and, if so, who had received the other ticket. She had thanked him warmly – it had been a real experience to see the great edifice from the inside! – and told him that she had gone with her brother, who was a musician, actually a band leader.

"A famous dance band, by any chance?" the Captain had asked.

"Not as famous as Rytmi-Pojat or Dallapé. But they've recorded a lot of songs. Their name's Arizona. They're playing at the Mikado this summer."

"Imagine the pair of us going there and dancing!" the Captain had said, with boyish eagerness in his voice.

Matilda had smiled dispiritingly.

"That probably wouldn't be appropriate, I'm afraid. As you can no doubt appreciate."

The Captain had of course raised the issue of the 100-metre race and the penalisation of Salomon Jary. Matilda had not told the Captain that she already knew everything from Thune, and therefore had to listen to the whole thing again: how upset Joachim Jary had been, how he had approached both Kolehmainen and von Frenckell on his nephew's behalf, and so on.

The Captain preferred to see the event as a meaningless trifle. He had nothing against Jews, it wasn't that, they were a talented if somewhat peculiar people. It was more that poor Yogi Jary had sadly had problems in recent years.

"Problems with himself, with his nerves, to be blunt about it," the Captain had added.

Matilda had asked about the Captain's work, asked whether private practice was more profitable than being an employee, and had enquired about the heavy responsibility and long days and so on. She had also simultaneously tried to steer the conversation so that she would find out more about his private life. She did not want to appear too curious, but was there someone, a former wife, a lover, children?

She had not succeeded terribly well. At times the conversation resembled a fencing match. Or shadow boxing.

Because that was what they were, of course. Shadows from each other's past.

Even if the Captain did not remember and did not understand.

"Why did you really want to meet me?" she had asked, just before they parted.

"I'm not sure I can put it into words," the Captain had said. "But it's as if something happened to me when I saw you in the office back in the spring."

He had looked at her rather uncertainly, as if to see if she was offended by what he had said, then went on:

"Something that made me realise that I should like to get to know you. Because I believe that we could truly appreciate each other. And understand each other."

"Surely you appreciate . . ." Matilda had said, stopping herself at exactly the right moment. She had looked calmly into his eyes and clarified: "People talk, and I don't want them to. Not about me."

"I understand," the Captain had said. "But I assure you, I only want to get to know you. I have no improper intentions, I . . ."

"And what might those improper attentions have been . . . ?" Matilda had interrupted, smiling at him in as warm and teasing a way as she could manage.

The Captain had looked away. He had not managed to maintain his composure, and picked up his teacup and drank the dregs so quickly that he made a slurping sound.

"Pardon me," he had mumbled. And then, in a voice which had suddenly assumed a sharper edge, a tone that had not been there before:

"I'm sorry that I'm behaving like a clumsy youth. I simply want an opportunity to see you again. I'm not asking for more than that."

13

Lorens Arelius called to invite Thune to a sauna with sausages cooked over an open fire down at Löknässtranden, and drinks on the veranda.

The phone-call came a few days into July, when the heat had settled like a saucepan lid over the city. The newspaper deliverers did their work in short trousers and sleeveless vests, dripping with sweat as they dragged their unruly carts behind them through the light summer nights. Even early in the morning the air was sticky and stagnant in the narrow shafts of the streets. An invisible smell of smoked pork and slaughterhouse waste, simultaneously appetite-whetting and noxious, spread south and west from the sausage factories in Sumparn, the smell of coffee and iron spread from the roasting houses and workshops in Vallgård, and a thick aroma of malt crept along the Boulevard from the brewery down by Sandvikens torg. A heavy stench of waste settled upon the many hundreds of backyards in the city, not that this appeared to bother the thousands of dirty, barefoot children in the slightest, they just went on playing the way they always did. At the kiosks of Magi and the other ice-cream manufacturers, the ice cream melted and ran down into the wafer cones and along the customers' fingers no matter how quickly they tried to lick up the delicacy. Even the seagulls no longer had the energy to shriek and cackle, and wandered silently and irresolutely around the market square and the harbours, picking at any remnants they could find.

For Thune, who had nowhere to go during his approaching summer holiday, an evening in Arelius' white stone villa out on Löknäset ought to have been a heaven-sent chance to escape the quivering heat of the city.

But the invitation came at short notice. The evening in the sauna was due to take place in just a couple of days' time, and Thune's first reaction – and one which surprised even him – was that he would rather not go.

He did not want to admit it to himself, but the fact was that his feelings for Arelius had changed. And presumably vice versa: their warm friendship was no longer there.

Robi Lindemark had been Thune's best friend throughout his childhood. But Lorens Arelius came along not too long after Robi. The three of them had attended the Lyceum together, they lived in the same block, and during certain periods of their youth they had been very close friends.

Lorre, as he was known then, had been best at everything. Arelius was the oldest and most courageous of them, good at all sports and utterly fearless in all games. When he was fifteen his friends gave him the nickname "Thorpe", after the American Indian who had won everything he possibly could at the Olympic Games in Stockholm. But Arelius had not liked the name, and threatened to hit anyone who used it. The threat was not meant seriously, and was presented with a smile, but the others still obeyed him.

Lorre Arelius was a good fighter: when the Swedish-speaking boys from Brunnsparken fought the Finnish and Russian gangs, the Swedes won every time Lorre was with them. Boys like that tended to be ruffians, with no intellectual ambitions, but young Arelius had many interests. He did sport because he thought it was fun to win, and he fought because he was bound to defend his own and his friends' honour. But he was at least as happy with his nose in a book, or discussing the predicament of modern man with swots like Robi Lindemark and Claes Thune.

Very occasionally Arelius could be a little hot-headed and flare up, even then, but when it happened he would soon calm down. During the past ten years his attitudes had gradually hardened, until eventually Thune had been forced to admit that his much admired childhood friend had turned into an argumentative sceptic. Sometimes Thune thought he had had his eyes closed to the obvious all along: Arelius had been invited to join the Wednesday Club when it was first founded, but had declined and joined a right-wing club instead.

Zorro Arelius' opinions on political and ideological issues were becoming more and more reminiscent of Ulla and Sigurd Hansell's, and even if Arelius was far too intelligent to fall for uncritical hero-worship, Thune often felt ill at ease in his company. The change was most noticeable in Arelius' attitude to Jews, Finns and various other ethnic groups. After his first indiscretion – his invective against Léon Blum, when Robi Lindemark had threatened to resign from the Club – Arelius had controlled himself, but even so the Club's discussions occasionally got out of hand because of him.

At the meeting hosted by Guido Röman in April, when a whole year had passed since Guernica and it was clear to everyone that the nationalist rebels would sooner or later win the Spanish Civil War, Arelius, to everyone's surprise, had voiced the suspicion that General Franco was Jewish. Franco's high-pitched voice and feminine gestures suggested Jewish ancestry, Arelius had claimed. Thune, Lindemark and their host Röman had entered a pact in advance of the April meeting, a pact to the effect that the March row would not be repeated, and that their meetings should be as apolitical as possible. They therefore declined to pick up the gauntlet Arelius had thrown down, and instead began to joke about the mollycoddled kingdom of

Sweden, where all corporal punishment in prisons had recently been forbidden, and where a woman had actually been employed to read the news on the radio.

In spite of his doubts, Thune had accepted the invitation. His life was governed by soporific routine, he was longing for change, and the temptation of a cooling evening out in Westend was too great to resist. Besides, he had given Mrs Leimu some time off: she was visiting her sister in Idensalmi, and Thune had been living off boiled eggs and macaroni on the evenings he did not go to restaurants.

And Sergey Gerasimoff was going to be there.

"Gera" Gerasimoff had been forced to flee his beloved Petrograd in the winter of 1918. He loathed the Bolsheviks, refused to utter the name Leningrad, and was far to the right on a lot of issues, just like Arelius. But Gera was a genial, sociable person who disliked argument and conflict, and would surely back Thune up if Arelius started anything.

Thune finished work early that afternoon. When he mumbled "Good afternoon" to Mrs Wiik as she sat there straight-backed, typing out the letter he had dictated, she barely seemed to notice that he was leaving.

Mrs Wiik was wearing a short-sleeved, polka-dot dress in the heat, and Thune could not help glancing at her forearms, where small muscles tensed as she tapped at the keys. He noted with approval that her hands were slender and well cared for, that her fingernails shimmered bright red with fresh varnish, and that her arms were very white even though it was summer, and the middle of a heat-wave. Thune did not like women sunbathing too much. Gabi had loved sunbathing, and he had always thought that her suntanned skin became harder and more leathery the longer summer went on.

*

Thune went home and showered, then put on a pair of white trousers, a shirt with a piqué collar and a thin summer jacket. He ordered a cab, and during a long detour to the north he asked the driver to drive through Munksnäs and then turn down to the shore: Thune wanted to take a walk through the streets around Borgvägen.

He stood for a while looking at the stone steps and beautifully ornate door leading to the apartment that would soon be his.

The building had been designed by the great Eliel Saarinen, which was no mean thing.

But it still struck him that he might have taken a decision that would involve too much change for a city boy like him.

He was worried about what his new life would be like. There had been a lot of newspaper articles about Munksnäs in recent days. The district was suffering a water shortage, the pumping station at Långängen was inadequate, and the inhabitants of the rental blocks were unable to shower, and sometimes could not even get water for coffee from their taps.

Thune went back to the car and told the driver to leave his post and seek some respite from the heat by the water. Then Thune walked over the hill and down to Fiskartorpsstranden.

He and Robi Lindemark often used to cycle or walk to the old cottage café, they got into the habit when they were at school and continued as university students. They would make themselves comfortable at one of the café's wobbly outside tables, then sit there with a cup of tea or glass of lemonade and discuss books and life.

And girls. Desirable, unobtainable girls.

Suddenly Thune recalled Mrs Wiik saying that she often took Sunday walks out there.

Smart, respectable Mrs Wiik. He tried to imagine her in sporty leisurewear, but it was impossible.

Thune had not visited Fiskartorpet for many years. The leaky

144

old cottage had been replaced by a modern brick building, with both a dining room and a café. Construction work was still going on: they were laying the foundations for another building, to house a circular banqueting hall where dignitaries from the whole world could eat and drink and have a good time if Helsinki was actually given the chance to host the Olympic Games.

Thune breathed in the scent of the pine forest, and the more pungent smell of washed-up seaweed down on the shore, and persuaded himself that he would probably be very happy there in the suburbs when it came down to it.

But more than anything else he was longing for a holiday, for the chance to sit in a deckchair so close to the shore that he could dip his toes in the warm water while he smoked a cigarette and read a novel. He made a note to ask Arelius and Gerasimoff if they knew anyone who had a house to rent for a few weeks in July. A simple cottage would do, small and easy to look after, within comfortable distance from Helsinki by bus.

He thought about his many summers at the Fahlcrantz villa in the archipelago further to the west, and how he both missed them and was relieved to be free of them. And he thought how nice it would be to empty the flat on Högbergsgatan and leave behind all its memories, all the sights and echoes and smells that reminded him of Gabi.

They found themselves talking about excess that evening, Arelius, Gera Gerasimoff, and Thune.

The subject had been raised by Gerasimoff.

They were sitting on the veranda of the villa at the time, on white-painted cane armchairs which, to the guests' surprise, turned out to be comfortable. Their light summer jackets were draped over the backs of the chairs, their shirt-sleeves were rolled up, top buttons undone: Gerasimoff had unbuttoned two. Before them on the glass top of the cane table stood three

145

misted glasses, and in the middle of the table was a beautiful dish made by Arabia, containing spiced chargrilled sausages – they had already eaten most of them – from the Marschan factory in Sörnäs. They had bathed in the sauna, the dust of the office was washed away, their skin prickled and tingled, and beneath it the blood was racing around, oxygenated by blows from scented bundles of birch twigs, cooled by dips in the sea, and warmed up once again by a flaming sunset and large quantities of alcohol.

"When I read biographies and memoirs, I'm always struck by the fact that our excesses reveal our true selves," Gerasimoff said. "The grotesque things we do just because we can and we feel like it, without sparing a thought for their morality."

"What exactly do you mean by that, Gera?" Thune wondered. He was already feeling rather drunk, in a bright, light-headed way. He was usually careful with drink, but this evening they had drunk a welcome toast with champagne, then Thune downed three bottles of beer while they were in the sauna and grilling sausages, and since then he had drunk two thirst-quenching gin and tonics. At sunset Arelius gave the maid leave to withdraw, after which their host excused himself, spent a few minutes clattering about in the kitchen, then returned with three tall glasses on a tray: a new drink that was said to be all the rage in Hollywood, and which Arelius wanted his friends to try.

"Liberating someone from the chains of decency and plausibility is a dangerous experiment," Gerasimoff explained. "Our ideals and our uninhibited actions do not always match. Whisper to someone that no-one will dare judge them no matter what they do: history shows that most of us would then succumb to excess. And those excesses show us as we truly are. *Mon cœur mis à nu*, as the poet says."

It struck Thune that Gerasimoff spoke without any trace of an accent. Gera had learned fluent Swedish during his first years in Helsinki, but it had taken him almost twenty years to get rid of his Russian accent.

146

"Give us an example!" Arelius demanded.

"Take Catherine the Great's journey of 1787," Gerasimoff said. "When she makes her triumphal progress through the lands around the Crimea, conquered on her behalf by her lover Potemkin."

Gerasimoff raised his glass, swallowed a mouthful, pulled a face and asked:

"What on *earth* have you put in this drink?"

"Mexican spirits, orange juice and grenadine," Arelius replied, looking very cheerful as he went on. "Isn't it terrible?"

"That's far too weak a word," Gerasimoff said, and continued:

"Catherine's journey begins in January, and crosses the Russian steppes. First go fourteen huge sledges, constructed like houses. Then one hundred and sixty-four ordinary sledges, carrying the household troops. Great bonfires light up the snowy wastes so that Catherine can travel at night, and at each resting place there are six hundred fresh horses waiting to take the caravan further. When they reach Kiev it is already the start of spring, and a fleet of galleys carries them down the Dnieper. The first seven galleys are colossal fairy-tale vessels painted red and gold: these carry Catherine and her entourage. Next come seventy-three smaller vessels carrying the court and household staff, all in all three thousand people. The Empress' galley contains bedrooms, dining rooms, drawing rooms and a library, and there is also a concert hall with enough room for a symphony orchestra and seating for the entire court. There Giuseppe Sarti conducts his orchestra and the Queen applauds as the eighty vessels glide slowly down the river. But gradually the diplomats in the company start to become concerned. There is something wrong with the flourishing landscape on show, the beautiful shoreline looks like painted scenery. Several of the emissaries report home that they are extras in a theatrical performance, and that the well-fed peasants waving to them from the shores are probably hired players."

"You're in the company of educated men, Gera," Arelius muttered. "Claes and I both know what Potemkin villages are."

"If only I could show you the Tauride Palace in Piter!" Gerasimoff exclaimed. "Then you would understand how rich Catherine made Potemkin as thanks for his services, both physical and non-physical. Unbelievably, excessively rich! But I daresay the Communists have plundered the palace and there isn't as much as a single piece of the original furnishings left."

Gerasimoff looked miserable at the thought, then shrugged.

"There are other examples. About a hundred years ago one of my compatriots, I believe it was the young Count Kushelev-Bezborodko, ordered all of the champagne that was available here in your city. It was a fine summer's evening, much like this one, and the Count wanted to spoil his friends. He managed to buy so much of it that he and his company were incapable of drinking it all, not by a long shot. So he poured the rest into the gutter, hundreds of bottles of champagne, while the city's poor looked on with their fists clenched in their pockets."

"Gera, if we're going to have a competition in the lunacy of kings and emperors, I've got the best example of them all," Thune said in a thick voice. "The Sun King, our old favourite Louis XIV. Before Louis pulled down his trousers and sat on the toilet he would let his courtiers draw lots to the spectacle. Admittance to the performance, so to speak. A crap audience in the true sense of the word. Five courtiers at a time were granted the honour of attending, and of noting the smell, colour and consistency of the royal excrement. Need I say that the courtiers never neglected to admire his majesty's performance?"

"Now you're just being tawdry, Claes," Arelius said irritably. "Not that one should expect much from an embittered Jacobin and Menshevik like you, but that was beneath your dignity."

"I believe that dear Claes has enjoyed a few drinks this evening," Gerasimoff said. His tone was amused but still gentle, as if he wanted to tease Thune a bit, but still keep Arelius calm. He added, in an even more friendly tone of voice:

"We're not used to that, you're usually so careful. Is it Gabi? Does the divorce still bother you?"

"No, I never think of her these days," Thune lied. "Robi's very welcome to her!"

It was a still and warm summer's night, of the most beautiful, lightest sort, and Gabi had been there like an ache inside Thune all evening. Only with a great effort of will had he succeeded in stopping the ache from turning into memories and thoughts. Now Gabi was nagging at him again, and he tried to find a way to steer the conversation back to the historical events Gerasimoff had been talking about just a few moments earlier. He did not have to look for long. Drink made him bold, and something unusual happened: for once, Thune did not hold back and said what he thought.

"Don't you ever get fed up of those damned stories about the excesses and decadence of kings and empresses?" he asked crossly. "Why are our anecdotes so often about them? Why aren't we interested in how ordinary people live? Why don't we care about the poor, but pretend they never existed?"

"Don't get upset, Claes," Arelius said in a surprisingly conciliatory tone. "Gera wasn't trying to provoke you. I'm guessing that his stories form the foundation for some point he hasn't yet made. And there's probably nothing you can do about the fact that biographies get written about rulers and artists who have been elevated after their deaths."

"But that's precisely what's so bloody wrong about it!" Thune muttered. "As long as stories about corrupt kings keep being written, their excesses will take up far too much space. They warp our picture of humanity. And humanity can actually be changed!"

"I wonder," Gerasimoff said quietly. "Time passes and different epochs replace one another, but how much do we change?

149

Technology improves our general lot, but deep down we remain the same as we have always been."

Arelius said in a dry voice: "I can't help sitting here and wondering what dear Polle would say if he were with us. He'd probably tell us that any attempt to limit human excess is an example of the insipid tyranny of the mediocre."

"Then he would be wrong," Gerasimoff said. "Our sense of what is decent and acceptable is dependent upon there being some resistance somewhere. When no-one questions us, we lose our inhibitions. Once again: *notre cœur mis à nu*. The heart of an intelligent but aggressive ape, who loathes his own vulnerability more than anything else."

Thune got up from his cane armchair and left the veranda. After urinating behind a clump of lilacs that had finished flowering, he walked the fifty metres down to the shore. He took off his shoes and socks, rolled up his trouser-legs and walked unsteadily out on to the rickety jetty, to the far end where the water was already quite deep. He sat down and rested his feet on one of the steps of the ladder for swimmers. The step felt slippery and slimy beneath his soles, the water was lukewarm and quite still in the light night, like a dish of tarnished silver with tiny flecks of copper in it.

The conversation had left Thune agitated, but he could not put his finger on why he felt so unsettled. Perhaps he was simply out of sorts: he really did need his holiday this year, he was longing to spend a few weeks with his books and music, and his own company. He took some deep breaths, inhaling the smell of seaweed and decay, and tried not to think about Gabi. Tried not to think about anything at all.

He did not succeed. For some reason he found himself recalling an April day more than twenty years earlier, a damp, cold afternoon of heavy rain and fog. It was a few days after von der Goltz's troops had taken the city. The last of the Reds' snipers had capitulated and emerged from Smolna and from Bergström's tobacco factory with their hands in the air, and once the inner city was secure the Germans decided to stage an improvised victory parade. A number of lesser officers rode slowly down the North Esplanade on their famous horses, and along the side of the carriageway closest to the park rolled a long series of open vehicles: first a small troupe of musicians, trumpeting out marches, then the senior officers in their luxurious carriages, then truck after truck after truck of common soldiers.

Lorre Arelius, Robi Lindemark, Yogi Jary and Thune had joined the procession of right-wing-inclined Helsinki residents that followed the German parade. They kept pace with the officers on horseback and the slowly rolling vehicles all the way from the burned-out Åbo barracks, round the corner by Wulff's paper merchants and along the North Esplanade.

It was a quiet parade. Hardly anyone smiled, hardly anyone said anything, the dark-clad Helsinki residents walked with sombre faces, keeping close to the edge of the pavement, so close to the Germans that they could have reached out their hands and touched the riders' spurs or the horses' flanks if they had wanted to. And just five metres away rolled the vehicles in which the German infantry sat and stared curiously at the buildings and citizens of the city they had just conquered. They looked so young, the soldiers, a lot of them were just as young as Lorre and Robi and Yogi and Thune. Perhaps that was why they were all so quiet – being young in a time of war is a serious business. And perhaps the weather also contributed – the thick fog and the jagged, naked branches of the trees in the parks lent Helsinki a grey, autumnal feel even though it was the middle of April and the days had already grown long.

Unless it was death, Thune thought now, on that summer's night. Perhaps it was the majesty of death that made the people of Helsinki remain silent on that occasion, the majesty of death

151

and vengeance? Plenty of people had already lost their lives on both sides, everyone knew that. But what they did not know – but possibly suspected – was that many of those who lost the war would have to die, and many of the victors would be transformed into executioners before life could settle back onto a more peaceful path again.

He remembered that dark April day so clearly, he remembered their young faces with terrible clarity. Lorre Arelius' stately profile and powerful chin, his slightly sceptical smile and the blue gaze that was usually friendly in those days. The sinewy but lively Yogi Jary in the raincoat that was slightly too big for him, and in a hat that was far too large, borrowed in haste from Thune. Jary had a typical Jewish appearance even as a young man: curly black hair, a sharp nose, full lips. Even Robi Lindemark looked slightly foreign with his squat frame, brown eyes and dark hair. But Lindemark's hair had often been badly cut when he was young, and he did not yet have the easy manner that he acquired later. Robi had not been the sort of boy at whom girls smiled, the way they smiled at Lorre Arelius and Yogi Jary. He had shared that fate with the gangly, blushing and insecure Thune.

The German parade had turned in to Unionsgatan and carried on towards Stortorget, where the city's elite were waiting to honour their saviours. The four friends had left at that point, having no desire to listen to the military music and lofty speeches, and instead walked down to the market square. The rain had got heavier and they only had two umbrellas between them, Thune's and Arelius', so they had huddled beneath them as best they could. They had sought shelter in the Hotel Kleineh, settling down in the shabby dining room and ordering soft drinks and sandwiches. Arelius had shared out some cigars he had been given by his surgeon father "in honour of the liberation". They were studying at university back then, in their first or second years. Arelius and Lindemark were in the medical faculty, Thune the legal one, and Jary was studying history of art and literature. They had talked about what they were going to do next, about the fact that they wanted nothing more than to return to normality, to the hard work of studying the subjects they had chosen. The only one who had not said anything – for some reason Thune remembered this clearly – was Arelius, who had merely puffed deeply on his Cuban cigar, looking serious and thoughtful.

Where had all those years gone? How quickly and jerkily life passed!

All of a sudden Thune recalled the first time he saw Gabi. The pain brought him up sharp as the image appeared out of nowhere, lit up by lightning, it was as if someone had stuck a knife between his ribs.

A couple of years into the '20s – 1922, possibly 1923. She had been walking towards him in the crowd during an interval at the Swedish Theatre – they had been performing an operetta that evening, he could not remember which one. She had been wearing a turquoise dress that clung to her body, and black high-heeled shoes with buckles, and he had thought, *Here comes a beautiful girl*, but had adopted a neutral expression. Their paths were about to cross and he had stepped aside politely to let the girl pass, when at that precise moment Yogi Jary appeared behind her back.

That was how it had started. Gabi, a talented performer, had played soubrette roles in the theatre in her early twenties. She and Yogi Jary had become friends – purely platonic – which was how he came to introduce Thune and Gabi to each other, right there and then, in the theatre.

She had smiled to him as she held her hand out in greeting.

"They're putting on a good show this evening," Thune had said when Jary left them alone to fetch drinks.

There had been something inquisitive and slightly sharp in Gabi's eyes. Thune had felt insecure and added:

"On stage, I mean."

"Yes, I realised that," she had replied. "But it's rather a conventional piece, don't you think?"

Those were the first things they said to each other, and perhaps the seed was sown even then.

He took things as they were, Gabi was not happy with half-measures.

Obviously the longing and bitterness were still there, he had to admit that now, as he sat there on the jetty that night, splashing the calm, silvery water with his feet.

Gabi had been inside him all evening, she had been there even though eighteen months had passed since their separation, and even though to the best of his knowledge she had never visited Arelius' villa in Löknäs. (Obviously she could have gone there with Robi, Thune realised now: Arelius and Lindemark were both members of the Finnish Medics' Association and socialised outside the frame of the Wednesday Club.)

Gabi was present even though she was not, even though she was somewhere else altogether, possibly in the arms of the unscrupulous Dr Lindemark, or perhaps putting together another scandalous short story.

Thune tried to think about his holiday instead, and the fact that he only had two more days at work to go. He let his thoughts drift to his impending move, and also to the monotonous but pleasant daily grind at the office. He thought about the peaceful days when he had no meetings with clients, about the modest pleasure he took in ticking off task after task, in going through different cases and then calling Mrs Wiik, who would come into his office at once and take care of the paperwork and type everything up and punch holes in the documents and file them in the correct folders, which she would then put in the archive cabinet, where everything was scrupulously organised. He thought about how restful it was, the industrious silence that filled the office, and he thought about his tentative exchange of thoughts with Mrs Wiik. It was hardly confidential, but had it not assumed a friendlier note during the early summer, possibly even a degree of trust? He felt a quiet joy that he would be seeing Mrs Wiik tomorrow and on Saturday, before he locked the office door and they went their separate ways for three long weeks.

But these mental exercises did not help: Gabi's image was still there, and it still hurt.

He clambered to his feet and then walked up and down the jetty until his feet and calves had dried. He pulled on his socks and shoes, rolled his trousers down and went up to the others.

Thune had sobered up down on the jetty, but on the veranda they had carried on drinking. He looked at Arelius' flushed face, then at Gerasimoff, whose features were still sharp and handsome, even though he was practically cross-eyed by now.

"Time to think about making a move," Thune said. "It'll be time to go to work in a few hours. Is it possible to get a cab out here, Zorro?"

He found his glass, raised it to his lips and took a large gulp. The mixture of strong spirits and orange juice was tepid now, and tasted revolting.

"This really is a terrible cocktail," he said. "It should never have been allowed to leave California."

"You're right there," Arelius agreed, and tried to get out of his chair. "But it works well. I'd be happy to drive you in to the city, but I'm in no state to get behind the wheel. I'll go and call for a cab."

Thune remembered a thought that had struck him when he first arrived at the party, and said: "By the way . . . if you chance upon anyone wanting to rent out a cottage for a few weeks, feel free to let me know. I'm going to be moving house during the holiday, so something close to the city would be best. Any suggestions would be gratefully received."

"I'm renting the old Russian Villa out on Söderskär from Saturday," Arelius said. "Living the hearty, invigorating life of a lighthouse-keeper out on the very edge of the sea for four weeks. Come and visit, Claes. There's no need to bring a Höganäs pot like that fellow of Mr Strindberg's – just come as you are. And you can bring your legalistic tomes if you want to work."

Arelius had got up from his chair as he spoke, and was now on his way into the house.

"I'll let you know if I hear of a cottage," Gerasimoff said. "I assume there's no point putting an advertisement in *Hufvud-stadsbladet* now?"

"No," Thune said, "it's probably too late for that. Actually, I'd like to ask one more favour."

"Is there no end to the things you want help with?" Arelius said, turning at the door and clinging on to the post to hold himself upright. "What is it?"

"You may have noticed that I have been lucky enough to get hold of a quite excellent office assistant," Thune said. "But Mrs Wiik isn't particularly talkative. She gave me a splendid reference from Hoffman & Laurén, but wasn't at all keen to go into why she left their employment. She didn't even want to say whether she resigned or was dismissed, and skirted the issue very elegantly. You know the Laurén family, don't you, Zorro? And you, Gera, you see the Hoffmans socially? Would you mind asking a couple of discreet questions?"

14

The change of life is a critical period for men, when all manner of ailments make themselves known and masculine strength, so essential to the conduct of life, inevitably dwindles. Certain sexual functions, in particular, make themselves felt, as a result of a noticeable diminution of the potency of the pubertal glands. Do not neglect this vital and sensitive issue, and be sure to make use of the latest excellent scientific advances. "Dr Weiss' VIRILIN" is sold without prescription by chemists in bottles of 40 and 100 tablets. Ask your doctor or visit Dr Weiss' clinic at Mikaelsgatan 8 for a free brochure.

Advertisement in *Hufvudstadsbladet*,
Saturday, 16 July, 1938

Matilda was as good as teetotal. She would drink a small glass of sherry or red wine if someone insisted, but she never touched beer or strong spirits. But she was not unaware of the effect that alcohol could have on the human mind and body. She knew Konni had periods when he drank: she had never seen her brother properly intoxicated, but from Tuulikki and others she had heard that he could become difficult when he took to the bottle.

During the last years before he disappeared, Hannes would sometimes come home with a bottle or flask. That was back in the days of prohibition, and the bottles and flasks contained smuggled vodka or poor quality contraband whisky. Hannes had not been easy to deal with on the Saturdays when he drank. Drink made him stubborn and depressed, and he would curse the world – he was a socialist, and did not believe in a god – for giving him such a poor lot, and so few reasons for joy.

Matilda had found it very difficult to defend herself from Hannes when he was drunk. On some Saturday evenings the passion of their early days was rekindled in him and he wanted her again, the way he had back at the start. But in those last years Matilda could no longer do it, she had not been able to for a long while, but she could not even stretch to do what had saved their life together for several years. When making love began to feel repellent to her, she had got into the habit of taking hold of his eagerly fumbling hands and whispering that sadly it was that time again and she was bleeding so heavily, or felt a little feverish and feared that she was susceptible, and of course they had discussed the fact that they could not afford to have children yet, had they not? In which case Hannes would want Matilda to reach out her hand in the darkness and take hold of his member and touch it, it usually only took a minute or two, she always wanted to go to the bathroom and wash her hand afterwards, before it dried and turned to glue, but she did not feel able to, at least not until Hannes had fallen asleep.

In the final years she had not even felt able to do that. Hannes was not a violent man, he was never brutal, and eventually he stopped insisting. Instead he started to drink more, sometimes much more. On those occasions he looked a terrible sight when he woke up on Sunday morning, lying as far away from her as possible in the not particularly wide bed. Then he would sit at the kitchen table with his cup of coffee and stare down at the deserted Mechelingatan without bestowing so much as a

158

glance or a single word on her. His eyes would be bloodshot and narrow, and the stale smell of drink would spread from his lips and permeate the whole of the little flat. And it was that memory of Hannes – the very worst she had of him – that made Matilda realise the situation when Thune fumbled with his keys out in the stairwell and then tumbled into the office on Friday, almost an hour later than usual.

Thune's eyes were red-rimmed and swollen, just like Hannes' Sunday eyes used to be. He had made an attempt to comb his hair, presumably with water, but it had not been a success: spiky tufts stuck out at the back of his head, as if he had slept on top of a powerful magnet. His tie was sloppily knotted and Matilda could detect an acrid smell from several metres away. He greeted her with a quiet and indistinct "Good morning", looking down at the floor shamefacedly as he did so. Matilda returned his greeting in a friendly but neutral voice, at which point Thune appeared to remember something. He stopped on the way to his door, took a few steps towards her desk, and said:

"I'm sorry I'm so late, I do hope I haven't missed any clients?"

Matilda assured him – feeling oddly superior at that moment, like a big sister whose younger brother had grazed his knee and was crying and needed comforting – that no damage had been done. Director Stjernschantz was due to come at half past eleven, and Consul Gadd at three o'clock, they were the only clients that day. She had to make a real effort not to turn her head away as Thune stood beside her, the stench of stale alcohol was so strong. And it was not merely the drink, there was something else too, something that made the smell of drink stronger and even more disgusting: a fruity but unpleasant smell, like mouldy berries or rotting oranges.

Thune gave a confused bow and went into his room. After a while the sound of music began to filter out: he had put on a gramophone record. It was something Thune played a lot, a long orchestral piece that repeated the same strict melody the whole time, louder and louder, with more and more instruments, so that in the end the noise became quite deafening. Konni was bound to have known what it was, Matilda thought, he liked all sorts of music, he would know who had written it and what it was called.

She did not see much of Thune that Friday. At four o'clock, when all her work was done and she was longing to leave, she knocked cautiously on his door and asked if there was anything he wanted her to do. The music had fallen silent many hours before, and both Director Stjernschantz and Consul Gadd had been to see Thune and then left. There was no sound from within, and she was about to knock again when Thune finally answered. He sounded like he had just woken up, and Matilda guessed that he had been sitting asleep at his desk, or in one of the armchairs in the Cabinet.

"Nothing else today, thank you. You can go."

And, content with his answer, she left.

But when Thune demonstrated the same red-rimmed eyes and mournful expression – albeit without the attendant smell of alcohol – on Saturday morning, Matilda was seized by anxiety and sympathy.

It was the last working day before the holiday. How lonely was he? How bad a state was he really in?

Thune obviously had infinitely more money at his disposal than her. A large apartment that he no doubt owned, and now he was going to move he simply had to sell the old one and buy another with the money. And he had nice furniture, and exclusive if rather tragically ill-fitting suits, and expensive *eau de cologne* and gentleman's scent that hid the smell of sorrow and loneliness.

But he was lonely. And as the summer drew on, the more lonely she had watched him become. Thune's loneliness was like a small cloud above his head, and the cloud was getting greyer and darker with each passing day. Matilda was good at spotting loneliness: she had also seen it in the Captain, she had spotted it on their very first meeting.

And perhaps it was this, the fact that she could see Thune's loneliness so clearly, that meant that she dared to ask such an inappropriate question that afternoon. And not just one, but two.

Thune slept badly on Friday night, sweating and kicking off his sheet in the heat, unbuttoning his pyjama top and thinking miserable thoughts about men who get hangovers when they are past forty.

Towards dawn he opened the window and let the night air stream in. Then he pulled the new volume of Gullberg's poetry off the shelf, plumped up his pillows and lay there looking through the book, without really being taken by any of the melodic verses. He remembered how he and Gabi had wrapped themselves in blankets and read out loud to each other from *Love in the Twentieth Century* during their first winter in Stockholm. He still knew some of the lines off by heart.

> *Tristan, Isolde, Romeo, Juliet,*
> *Were more to our grandparents' taste.*
> *We've packed off love to an oubliette,*
> *Let boudoirs gone stale with light be braced!*

And:

161

We do not kneel for any priest.
We give no vows of being true.
Thus runs the oath at our wedding feast:
I love you, for as long as I care to.

When the collection had only just been published Thune had known more of the poems by heart – recitation, often with a splash of irony, had been his party piece when he was younger – but most of the stanzas had faded and vanished from his memory.

Gabi and he had liked the directness of the young Gullberg's poems. There had been no jealousy between them in those days, nor any weariness. Thune had been proud to be the husband of beautiful Gabi. And perhaps Gabi had been a little proud of him too, in spite of everything.

Those first years in Stockholm were among Thune's best years as a grown man. Perhaps they had been good years for Hjalmar Gullberg as well. Be that as it may, the poet had not achieved anything as powerful and precise since then.

One thing Thune did know for certain was that Gullberg had inspired a certain female novelist who would debut five years later, and that awareness made it no easier for him to sleep. But in the end he dozed off anyway and slept for a few fitful hours, an anxious sort of sleep that was somewhere between sleep and waking, perforated by vaguely threatening dreams that all tended towards the absurd.

In his agitated state, Thune was even more touched by Mrs Wiik's concern than he would otherwise have been.

Just before lunchtime she had gone out and bought two warm wheat loaves from the bakery on the other side of the square, then went on to the Market Hall where she bought freshly churned butter, Seville orange marmalade and a large piece of Seeck's smoked *mettwurst*. And Ryker's raisin biscuits,

162

of course: the large tin was almost empty. She bought most of this on the company's account, but she paid for the loaves of bread from her own purse, which Thune categorically refused to allow.

Then Mrs Wiik had brewed some tea, sliced one of the loaves and made sandwiches, half filled with sausage, half with marmalade, and put everything on a tray before carefully knocking on Thune's door and asking if she could offer him a simple lunch in honour of their impending holiday. And, if so, where would he prefer to eat: in his room, or perhaps in the pantry or vestibule?

Thune replied that he would be happy to eat in his room – or why not the Cabinet? – but only on the condition that Mrs Wiik keep him company. She agreed to this without objection, and carried the tray into the Cabinet where she put it down on the table with the tubular steel legs, then brushed some dust from the seat of one of the leather armchairs.

When she had fetched the teapot and her own cup, and had served Thune, she did not sit down in the free armchair but on one of the simpler chairs further away from him. They ate with a healthy appetite, in a silence that was only interrupted at first by Thune's admiring praise of her sandwiches.

"I daresay you read the newspaper this morning?" Thune asked, when he thought that the silence had become rather too oppressive. "It's settled now."

"No, I went for a walk instead of reading," Mrs Wiik said. "What is it that's settled?"

"The Japanese have got their hands full with their war, Tokyo has had to withdraw from hosting the Games. Helsinki will be an Olympic city two summers from now."

"Oh," Mrs Wiik said, not sounding particularly interested. "Well, I suppose it's good that the Stadium's going to be used now that we've built it."

Thune felt a wave of relief course through his body.

"To be perfectly honest, I'm not terribly interested in sport

163

myself," he admitted. He thought he could see a glint of amusement in her eyes as he said this, and searched frantically for a subject with which to continue the conversation.

"You live in Inner Tölö, don't you? Do you walk to work every morning?"

"It's probably closer to Outer Tölö," Mrs Wiik said. "I live down on Mechelingatan. Number twenty-three."

"But number twenty-three, isn't that . . . ?" Thune began.

Mrs Wiik pre-empted him:

"Yes, the building where Mrs Craucher died. We . . . I was actually living there at the time. But in answer to your question: it's no fun walking in winter, which makes the pleasure all the greater now. I usually walk along the shore every morning before I come to the office. It's so hard to sleep in this heat."

"Yes, it is . . ." Thune agreed, and was about to go on, but an image of Mrs Wiik in a nightdress having difficulty sleeping passed through his mind. She was twisting and turning on her bed impatiently, just like he usually did, and had kicked off her sheet and bedspread, her slender calves glowed white, her face glistened with night-cream in the first light of dawn. He knew that Mrs Wiik could have no idea of the images in his mind, but embarrassment caused him to abandon the sentence halfway through. Not that it made any difference: he had already forgotten what he had intended to say.

"Yesterday morning I got up early," Mrs Wiik said instead. "It couldn't have been much past six o'clock when I left home. And can you imagine, down at Edesviken they were filming already! With real film stars!"

"Perhaps to take advantage of the cooler temperature?" Thune suggested. "Their make-up must run in this hot weather. Who were they, then?"

"They had put up a kiosk in the park," Mrs Wiik said in a dreamy tone of voice. "One of those old wooden kiosks, you know, somewhere where there isn't really one. And they were

164

all there! Palo and Soihtu and Kalske. Ikonen and Seikkula and Linnanheimo. It will be the biggest film ever when it reaches the cinemas!"

Thune had never heard Mrs Wiik so excited.

"Did you get any idea of what the film might be about?" he asked.

"I think it was a musical," Mrs Wiik said hesitantly. Her face was quite soft now, and for the first time Thune had an impression of what she would have looked like as a young girl. She went on:

"Ansa Ikonen was standing inside the kiosk – she must be playing the sales assistant. And Santeri Soihtu was standing outside, he was leaning in towards her and she leaned out and tilted her head to look up at the sky, and then they sang together. But you couldn't hear what they were singing, they were singing so quietly. Unless they weren't singing at all, just moving their lips? They looked like they were in love. And all the others were standing round the kiosk watching them as they sang."

"Do you have a favourite film star?" Thune wondered.

"Oh," Mrs Wiik said, batting the question aside with a look of embarrassment. "If I'm honest, the films from Hollywood and Paris and Berlin are much better. But I do like Santeri Soihtu. People always talk about Palo and Kalske, but forget about Soihtu. And I don't like Seikkula at all, Ikonen looks much better on the screen."

Thune could not hide a slight smile. She was talking quickly, almost breathlessly, and had very firm opinions. Finally, a little crack in Mrs Wiik's perfect professional façade.

She must have noticed his smile, because she stopped immediately, raised her teacup and took a silent sip. Then she said:

"I'm running on . . . sorry, I don't know what got into me."

"Please, don't apologise," Thune said, cursing himself for smiling at what she said. "It's nice sitting here and chatting. I like going to see films myself. But I don't get a lot of time these

165

days – you know, work, so much to do. The last one I saw was 'The Soldier's Bride', and . . ."

His explanation tailed off into helpless silence. He guessed that Mrs Wiik had a good idea of the true state of things: that it had been Gabi who had dragged him to the cinema, and since she left him he never quite got round to it anymore.

"I haven't seen that one," Mrs Wiik said, in an almost apologetic tone of voice. Then she grew bolder once more.

"The light was so lovely in the park by the shore yesterday morning. And so many beautiful people too, the whole world was radiant, it was impossible to imagine that there's so much murder and war . . ."

Her voice had shrunk to a distracted whisper, her face soft and dreaming again. Thune was still trying to think of something to say when she went on:

"But there is one thing I've been wondering about. They used lamps and arc-lights, and big screens to direct the light. Is that really necessary, on a morning that was as beautiful as yesterday?"

Thune could see the scene before him, and for some reason it made him feel sad.

"Perhaps that's one of the shortfalls of reality," he said. "That we have to improve it even when it is at its most beautiful."

He thought for a few seconds, then added:

"Unless the shortfall isn't in reality, but us? Perhaps we never quite dare to trust that beauty exists, and will last?"

"Like Garbo, perhaps," Mrs Wiik suggested. "The whole world admires her perfect profile, but all she can think about are her big feet."

They sat in the Cabinet for a long time. There was hardly any work to do. Mrs Wiik told Thune that she had two letters to frank and post, but that was all. Thune had been thinking of

166

preparing a paternity case that would be going to court after his holiday. He was representing an engineer called Wilhelmsson who had misbehaved and was now trying to shirk his responsibilities. But he felt no enthusiasm for the Wilhelmsson case; it was as if his holiday had already begun.

Mrs Wiik went out into the pantry to slice the other loaf and make more sandwiches. "Marmalade in mine, please!" Thune called after her as she went. While she was gone he smoked a Chesterfield and ate two raisin biscuits.

When Mrs Wiik returned she served more tea, then became more talkative again. She talked about her brother Konni, who played half a dozen different instruments and was the leader of the band Arizona, who had been engaged at the Mikado. Mrs Wiik had been wanting to go and listen to Konni's band for a long while, and now her friend Fanny had come back to the city and their evening at the restaurant was finally going to happen. Konni's wife Tuulikki had come by train from Åbo and was going to go with them. The Mikado, Mrs Wiik stressed, was no place for three women to go on their own, but Fanny's brother Reinhard and Tuulikki's cousin Heikki had promised to accompany them.

Thune listened politely and even managed to ask Mrs Wiik if she liked dancing – "I don't know, I really haven't danced very often," she replied – before an image from the foredeck of the S.S. *Archimedes* came into his mind and he began to connect her words with his own memories.

"Wait a moment!" he said so abruptly that she started. "What did you say your brother's band was called?"

"Arizona," Mrs Wiik replied.

"And your brother is Konni . . . Ahlberg?"

"Not Ahlberg," she said. "Ahlbäck. So you already know of him?"

She sounded surprised but happy as she asked.

"Not really," Thune said, then went on to tell the story of

the voyage in April and the meeting on the foredeck and how he had sat in the first-class salon drinking whisky and listening to Arizona, but had not managed to pluck up the courage to ask any of the ladies to dance.

"I'm not exactly Fred Astaire," he added, in case she was wondering.

Mrs Wiik had listened to his story with twinkling eyes – it was obvious that she was proud of her brother – but now she asked:

"Yes, I remember that they were supposed to go to Sweden to record some songs. I hope he wasn't unfriendly towards you?"

"No, how so?" Thune asked in surprise. "He was friendliness personified."

"Konni's really very sweet," Mrs Wiik said. "But he can be a little unruly at times."

"I couldn't help noticing that he'd had a couple of drinks," Thune said. "But they all had, the whole of Arizona. But they were as pleasant as could be."

He fell silent for a moment, then said:

"So your maiden name was Ahlbäck?"

"Yes," Mrs Wiik said, with some reluctance. "That was my name."

Thune was expecting her to say something more, perhaps talk about her and Konni's mother and father, where she had grown up, and so on. But after confirming her name she clammed up again.

He felt a little hurt that Mrs Wiik's brother evidently hadn't mentioned him afterwards. It was clear that the siblings were in relatively close contact, and one would have thought that Konni would have told his sister that he had played the hot-fox and tango for her employer, given that it really was quite a coincidence.

Thune mentioned his surprise to Mrs Wiik, but tried to hide the fact that he felt hurt.

She gave a resigned smile and said: "If you knew what Konni

was like, you wouldn't be surprised. Nor offended. He hasn't asked me anything about you. He doesn't know your name, he doesn't even know that I work for a lawyer. That's just how Konni is: he lives for his music and his children. And Tuulikki. He barely notices the rest of us."

Thune raised his hands to fend off her explanation, as if to indicate that it had not been his intention to broach a sensitive subject. He felt like giving some sort of apology, but words failed him: he was starting to think that was happening more often than it used to.

Mrs Wiik appeared to notice his predicament, because she said:

"But he's a talented musician, no doubt about that. And he writes good songs as well, he's sold several to Dallapé, and to the films."

Suddenly her face brightened and it suddenly poured out of her, eagerly and impulsively, and so emphatically that it almost made Thune duck in his chair:

"But why don't you come? We're one gentleman short, Konni will be playing the whole time so he won't be able to sit at the table with us or dance with Tuulikki. You live close to the Mikado, so you can always go home if it gets boring!"

Thune said nothing at first. He could feel himself starting to sweat, but did not know if it was because of the sultry air, the many cups of tea, or her uncomfortable question. Mrs Wiik seemed to notice his discomfort, because she quickly tried to retract the suggestion and smooth things over:

"Sorry, Mr Thune, I don't know what's come over me today. I'm behaving inappropriately the whole time. Of course you wouldn't . . ."

"No, no, Mrs Wiik, it's not that!" Thune interrupted. "There was nothing wrong with your suggestion. I was just a little surprised."

"I understand what you must be thinking," Mrs Wiik said.

"But Fanny's a proper lady. If I didn't know better, I'd never guess that she was the daughter of a longshoreman in Åbo docks."

She fell silent – Thune thought she might be regretting those last words – but then added rather helplessly:

"And Tuulikki's a very nice girl as well."

Thune raised his hands again.

"Please, Mrs Wiik, I really don't look down on the working class. Many . . . many thanks for your invitation. I should very much like to come. As long . . . as long as you're quite sure that Mr Wiik won't have anything against it?"

Mrs Wiik smiled, but the smile quickly faded. Then she said, in a tone of voice that Thune just then found unnecessarily curt:

"I can assure you, Mr Wiik has absolutely nothing against it."

As soon as Thune had said yes, he wished he could take back his words. But he was a man of principle, and he was also (as he admitted to himself, but never to others) vain and naïve in his liberalism. He had always voted for bourgeois parties, but liked the idea that he was the loyal friend and confidant of the little people. As a result, he was unable to back down from his promise once it had been given.

An awkward silence settled in the Cabinet. A spontaneous exchange had led to something that until very recently would have been utterly unthinkable – that they would spend an evening together – and even Mrs Wiik seemed paralysed by what had happened. An outsider would probably guess that they both regretted it, Thune thought, as he searched desperately for something to say.

But once again it was Mrs Wiik who recovered first, and so thoroughly that she managed to push the arrangement a step further.

"We're going to meet at Fanny's before we go to the Mikado.

170

Well, not Konni, of course, but the rest of us. Just to drink a simple toast to the summer."

She hesitated for a moment, then went on:

"Fanny lives in Sörnäs, on Tavastvägen. I don't suppose you . . . ?"

And Thune, still bewildered at the turn the conversation had taken, to his horror found himself saying:

"Yes . . . I think I might. Thank you, I shall be there."

As Thune was standing in his bedroom picking out clothes from his wardrobe – he was unsure: summer suit and tie, or smoking jacket and cobalt blue bow tie? – he wanted nothing more than to call Mrs Wiik and say he could not go.

It was seven o'clock, and the rays of sunlight hitting the building on the other side of Högbergsgatan shimmered red and mournful in a way that made him remember the June evening when he had wandered home from Brunnshuset through a city that smelled of Gabi.

He found himself wondering why he should go out on the town and make a fool of himself. And why should he pretend that he was capable of having fun in the usual way? He was not.

Mrs Wiik had recently bought shares in the Telephone Corporation, and had written her number in the book containing the firm's important contact details, in very neat handwriting. Not only that, she had also brought a folded note to Thune's room, saying that the Telephone Corporation's directory for 1938 had unfortunately been printed before she joined, but here was her number, for his personal use: he was welcome to consult her or call her in to work whenever necessary, even on Saturday evenings or during public holidays.

Now Thune was standing half dressed in his hall, looking at Mrs Wiik's note, which had been lying on his telephone table for more than a week: he had not got round to writing it in his personal notebook. The urge to call was almost irresistibly strong, his lips moved as he rehearsed the phrases he would utter. He would say he was unwell, or had to pay an unexpected visit to his ailing mother. He just wanted to avoid the whole thing, avoid being introduced to people he did not know and in all likelihood were of a sort he was not used to, he wanted to give in to his pettiness and social prejudices, simply call and say he was unable to go, and get it over and done with, then sit down on his sofa with a book and perhaps a refreshing glass of beer. All he had to do was pick up the receiver and turn the dial, and pull himself together. These days there was no need to inform an inquisitive telephonist of the number you required, which had been such a torment for shy young men when he was growing up, now all he had to do was call and give a reasonable excuse, the sort that Mrs Wiik would hardly doubt, but which she would not be able to disprove or reject even if she did not believe him.

But Thune did not telephone.

Instead he finished dressing – he chose the more discreet option, a white shirt, thin grey summer suit, patterned tie – and then held two fingers to the top of the bottle of *eau de cologne* and turned it upside down. He patted the scent onto his cheeks, then pulled on his shoes, opened the door, stepped out into the deserted stairwell, called the lift and made his way to Skillnaden where he got into a cab – he rarely used the tram, and had no knowledge of the lines that ran north to Sörnäs.

It was a few minutes past seven and Matilda was sitting on the tram on her way to Fanny's, she had called to say that she would be a little late. She was clutching the bag containing her dancing shoes, purse, lipstick and other bits and pieces on her lap. Her dark blue summer dress with the white spots was four years old, but it suited her, she knew that: she was slim and fairly tall, and still looked good in a dress. Even now, in the tram, one of the

172

male passengers was looking at her, but she ignored him, not even deigning to look at him.

She was fretting about what had happened in the office earlier that day.

Thune had been shocked, and little wonder: she had been surprised herself, and she had been the one who started the whole thing, and then went on to make it even worse.

Her interaction with Thune was strictly professional. Yet more and more often she found herself breaking the rules she had set for herself. She was becoming talkative and careless in a way that she could not remember being before, apart from the first years with Hannes. Unless perhaps she had on some occasion been open and unguarded with Fanny, when they had gone back to whoever's home was closest to drink a few glasses of port and talk about the film they had just seen? She was not sure.

Why was she so chatty in Thune's company?

She felt a degree of sympathy for him, certainly, but that did not usually make her talkative.

Either way, it was risky. Not because she was in any danger of saying something indiscreet about her plans, because there were none. She still did not know what she was going to do about the situation that had arisen, she merely suspected that it was too late to back out now.

But there was so much that she did not want Thune to find out about. And the more she talked, the greater the risk that she might let slip something that would put him on her trail.

She was annoyed with herself about various things she had said over lunch. What she had told him about the film she saw being made down at Edesviken had been silly and nonsensical and was bound to have made Thune smile at her, even if he had managed to keep a straight face and ask polite questions.

But what she had said about Fanny's father and his job in Åbo had been worse.

Fanny had talked about her father being a longshoreman

in the strictest confidence: how could Matilda Wiik, daughter of mechanic and railway worker Adolf Ahlbäck and his Zaida, betray a friend's trust in that way?

The fateful questions she had asked Thune did not trouble her to the same extent. They had simply slipped out of her.

The first about the Mikado, when she had noticed his face assuming that puppyish, sad expression again.

And the second, asking if he would like to toast the summer in Fanny's flat.

That was probably Miss Milja's work. Miss Milja, showing her naughtiest side.

Anyway, who could have guessed that Thune would answer yes to both questions?

When there were only a few stops left before Aspnäs, where she would be getting off, the thought struck her that she might be behaving the way she was because she suspected that she had already lost, one way or another.

It occurred to her that her openness, with all those words pouring out of her before she could stop them, was a form of nonchalance, a conscious carelessness: as if she *wanted* to be found out. She recalled a phrase from Master Strang's English lessons at business college:

Catch me if you can.

A phrase for Miss Milja, not for cautious Mrs Wiik.

It was that business with her former employer, Director Hoffman.

Someone who knew the whole of Helsinki but did not really belong anywhere, someone who climbed to the top of the Stadium tower and looked out across Tölö and the southern districts of the city, then the centre and on towards Sörnäs and Berghäll and the other working-class areas to the north, and new suburbs like Kottby, and self-sufficient villa communities like Brändö and Munksnäs, would be tempted to see a large, modern city of several hundred thousand inhabitants, a city where both terrible and wonderful things happened under the guise of anonymity.

Matilda was part of the big, bustling city. In her city people were strangers to each other. A place where Someone moved aside so that No-one would have room beside them on the seat in the tram.

But she also knew that there was another city, one for the initiated, a very small city. That city lay largely to the south of the centre, with outposts in Inner Tölö and Munksnäs, and on islands like Drumsö and Brändö. In that city the Swedish language still reigned unchallenged, spoken both at home and at work, people kept a careful eye on one another, and their curiosity was both a comfort and a burden. And that little city was also mostly a city of men: at its core were the Swedish Club, the Merchants' Guild, the Bar Association and a number of other gentlemen's societies.

In spite of his loneliness, that was the city to which Thune belonged. Matilda had realised that on the March day when she heard the members of the Wednesday Club talking loudly in the vestibule – in *her* room! – and it had been confirmed to her many times since then. Thune was part of that little city, even if it was obvious that he was uncomfortable with it. And in that city people talked, all the time, without thinking. Sooner or later someone would tell Thune about the circumstances that had forced her to leave Hoffman & Laurén.

And then there was the Captain.

He was away for the time being, and would not be returning to Helsinki until August.

But before he left they had met for a second time. At the English Tea-Room, on Unionsgatan, close to the Edlund corner.

Right in the middle of the bourgeoisie's favourite promenade: that was how bold he had been.

She guessed that the Captain's boldness had its roots in the fact that his fiancée wasn't in the city – maybe she had already gone off on holiday. Matilda had worked out by then that there was a fiancée or beloved of some sort. She had no clue as to who it might be, but little slips of the tongue from the Captain had convinced her that there was another woman.

She knew she would meet the Captain again, if not straight away in August, then later. She could feel how she was being torn apart inside, the feeling was almost painfully tangible, but it was as if she could not pull away.

Their meetings were associated with fear. And not only because of the risk of gossip. Matilda did not know whether to be horrified or relieved that the Captain had distorted his own story so much that he did not recognise her, did not realise who she was. But sooner or later she would give herself away, something would slip out and the Captain would begin to realise who she was. Or else he would see her from a different angle, maybe see her face in profile, close up, and the sight would activate an old, forgotten memory, and then a cruel, dark light would dawn on the Captain.

The day when she and the Captain had met at the English Tea-Room a sudden area of low pressure had swept in over the city from the north-west. It had happened overnight, it had rained hard all morning and the temperature had dropped almost fifteen degrees. Afterwards the heat returned as quickly as it had disappeared, but that afternoon had been raw and chilly, almost autumnal.

The Captain had been wearing gloves, black leather gloves.

They had sat at the back, in the darkest corner of the tea-room, with the rain tipping down outside. Matilda had jumped at a sudden flash of lightning and crack of thunder, when the storm was immediately above them. The Captain gave a slightly crooked smile and said: "That one probably hit the cathedral."

Matilda's hands had lain still on the table while they talked about this and that, she remembered that her hands had been clasped – not that it meant anything, she was not religious, she just liked sitting with her hands like that. The Captain had talked about a scientist, Fleming, who had discovered a wonderful medicine almost ten years ago: now people were dreaming of mass-producing it. Matilda had asked if Fleming's medicine worked on tuberculosis as well, and had parted her hands and put them on the table on either side of the steaming cup of tea, and that was when the great crack of thunder had come. The Captain had broken off in the middle of his reply and quickly reached out his gloved left hand and placed it firmly on the back of her hand, her right hand. She had twitched slightly, but she did not think he had noticed.

The Captain had left his hand there for a good while, looked her in the eye and smiled, saying: "Don't worry, when there's thunder, there's no safer place to be than inside a solid building in a big city." She had felt almost paralysed, unable to pull her hand away, but when she eventually did so he had not protested or persisted, nor had he made any further attempts.

The night after the second meeting with the Captain she had lain awake.

She had tried not to scratch, even though it felt as if her whole body were itching, and tried to thrust the memories away, tried to conjure up other images instead, images of Cary Grant and Greta Garbo and Santeri Soihtu and other film stars she liked.

It did not work.

The examination, the first one, the one that took place immediately after her arrival at the camp.

They had been shown to a barrack at once, one that already
contained women who had been moved there from prison in
Tavastehus. They had been left to sort themselves out and find
a place to sleep: that was what had happened in the first camp
whenever new groups of prisoners arrived.

When one of them, Lea, who was pregnant, told the guards
it was getting too crowded and that there was not room for
everyone in the same barrack, an officer appeared and gathered
up thirty of them and took them off to another building. Milja
Matilda and Lea were among the thirty. In the other barrack
there were male prisoners too, but the women were given their
own room and another smaller room alongside, and the officer
assured them that their quarters would be guarded.

In the new camp there were not only soldiers from the White
side, but also German officers and soldiers: the Germans had
smart uniforms, and all their soldiers wore helmets.

The surveillance was stricter and the discipline harsher here
than in the first camp. There, away to the west, the prisoners
had lived almost in a separate society of their own, except when
food was distributed and when they were summoned to work
or herded off to Ekenäs to be put before a court. It had been
relatively easy to escape, at least it was if you were a male prisoner
entrusted with specific duties, and none of the camp's leaders
had seemed to know how many prisoners there were in the
camp, nor where they came from nor what their names were.
So the inmates had appointed their own Minister of Death.
That was not his official title, just a nickname he ended up with.
The Minister of Death was an inmate who checked anyone who
was sick and worked out which ones were in a particularly bad
way. Then he would find out the dying inmate's name and place
of residence while they were still able to speak, and report the
details to the management of the camp.

In the new camp there seemed to be fewer inmates, and they were better monitored. There were, however, more women than in the last camp. There were a number of fixed bunks and rickety beds in the barrack, so not everyone had to sleep on the floor. But people seemed to be starving here too: when they moved into the first barrack, Milja Matilda had watched through a window as two emaciated inmates collapsed in the heat, one man slumping unconscious over his spade while the other fell head first over a barrow.

A few hours later three officers came to prepare them for a medical inspection. The women in Milja Matilda's room were divided into two groups, and the group she was in was ordered to make its way to a hut on the other side of the yard. They were told to leave all headscarves, shawls, cardigans, pinafores and other unnecessary garments in the dormitory.

The first to be called in was a pale, black-haired girl. The others sat in silence in the waiting room, guarded by two young boys who stood either side of the door with bayonets on their rifles.

Anxiety spread through the room when they heard the girl crying inside the examination room. They met each other's gaze, some scared, some defiant, but no-one dared say anything.

The anxiety grew when the next patient was called in without the black-haired girl coming out. The tall, heavily pregnant Lea stood up from her place on the bench, stared at the two boys by the door, and looked as if she was about to say something. The boys, their faces expressionless, raised their rifles so that the barrels and bayonets were pointing straight at the women. The woman next to Lea tugged at her sleeve in terror, and Lea sat down again. When a handful of women had been called in without anyone coming out again, the others realised that the examination room had two doors and that they were not meant to find out what went on in there until everyone in the group had been examined.

When Lea was called in, the remaining women got an idea of what was going on. Milja Matilda did not know Lea well, but knew she had a fiery temper. In the first camp she had snapped at one of the guards while she was queuing for food, which led to him hitting Lea on the head with the butt of his rifle. He had struck her so hard she fell to the ground like a clubbed heifer and lay there unconscious for a couple of minutes before coming round.

When they heard her voice from inside the examination room, it was hoarse and croaking, more a hiss than a scream.

"You monsters!"

And a few seconds later, after they had heard low male voices laughing in there:

"You're not men, you're devils."

Milja Matilda was called in last of all. She was unbearably thirsty now, her throat so dry and tight it felt like she might throw up at any moment. The ache in her stomach was worse than ever, simultaneously rumbling and stabbing. She did not know if it was because of hunger, exhaustion or terror. Probably all three.

It did not really matter anymore, all she wanted was to lie down on the floor or a bunk and just let herself drift away.

Sleep.

Sleep for a long time, a long, long time, maybe die.

There was a man sitting behind a desk. He was wearing a white coat, but had uniform trousers and boots on under it. Just behind him, leaning against the wall, stood a German officer; he looked fairly old and had a greedy, proud expression on his furrowed face.

There were two more men in the room, Finnish soldiers or officers. She could not work out their rank at first, exhaustion and fear meant she was not thinking as clearly as she usually did. But she could see that they were both callow youths. They were sitting on a pair of simple wooden chairs further into the room, some distance from the Chair.

That was what she called it, "The Chair", even though it was something between a chair and an examination table.

"Would you get undressed, please," the man in the white coat said from the desk.

Milja Matilda did not move from the floor in front of the desk. Stock-still. She made no attempt to obey the doctor's order.

She turned her head and looked out through the window. It was already late in the afternoon, but the sunlight was still white and merciless. On the far side of the exercise yard – it felt like the world outside was impossibly distant – there were trees and bushes and even flowerbeds, and a little gravel path that wound off towards some yellow-plastered buildings that looked nice: she guessed that was where the officers' mess was, maybe the senior officers' lodgings as well.

"Get on with it!" the doctor snarled.

She did not want to. She was incredibly tired of being punished so relentlessly and harshly even though she had not committed any crime, just tried to scrape together money for food and lodging after being left alone with Konni.

She looked outside again. The sunlight was playing on a tall birch that stood at the start of the gravel path, the path that led away from there, the path to freedom, and she looked at the slender white trunk of the birch and at the path winding off towards the nice yellow buildings, she was walking there, she was walking free, she was wearing a thin skirt and the breeze was warm against her bare legs and the gravel crunched beneath the soles of her shoes. It was beautiful. Summer was beautiful. The sun was beautiful. The trees, the blue sky, it was all so beautiful. And at the same time, so devoid of meaning.

From the corner of her eye she saw the German lean over the doctor's shoulder and mutter something.

"What's your name? Quick!"

181

The doctor's voice was like the crack of a whip, and she felt terror grab hold of her again.

"Milja . . . Milja Matilda . . . Ahlbäck," she stammered.

"I must ask you to stop wasting time, please," the doctor said, his voice still sharp. "If you don't take your own clothes off, *we* will have to do it."

"Why should I take my clothes off?"

One of the boys laughed and gave her a mocking look.

She too was wondering where she had found the courage to ask the question.

Sleep. Sleep until she was allowed to die.

"We merely wish to rule out certain venereal diseases," the doctor said.

She did not know what the word meant, but guessed.

"But I can't . . . I haven't . . ."

Objections were flying through her head, but she had no more energy: she could not say another word. She fumbled with the buttons and catch, and slowly began to take off her dirty, frayed skirt, trying to imagine herself walking along the gravel path once more.

It was impossible. The image was gone and she did not dare look out of the window again – she was scared of antagonising the men.

Blouse. Stockings. The stone floor was cold in spite of the heat outside, she could feel the chill work its way through her feet and up into her body. She had started to shiver now, the right hand that was holding the blouse and stockings was shaking, her legs were shaking, and she knew the men could see it. She could not help thinking about her stomach, which she had not managed to void for several weeks, and about the pain and how tight her abdomen felt, but the only thing that occasionally escaped was air. All of a sudden she felt scared that something embarrassing might happen to her, and the thought alone was enough to make her wish the floor would swallow her up.

"Well, then," the doctor said in a neutral voice, gesturing impatiently towards the Chair. "Underwear as well. Then would you please get into position."

She let her clothes fall from her right hand, removed her last item of clothing and stood naked before them.

The doctor took out a pair of pale protective gloves. They were thin, his bare white fingers were clearly visible inside them. She looked at the Chair and could not understand what it was doing there, in a military camp. When she sat down the leather stuck at once to her back and thighs. The footrest was metal and felt as cold against the soles of her feet as the floor had done. Her stomach was rumbling with fear, and then there was a whistling sound, coming from her guts. The noise lasted several seconds, and was clearly audible in the silence of the room. Then it rose in pitch and disappeared.

"Right," the doctor said. "Let's take a look."

Matilda snapped her eyes open and looked around the tram, confused. There was a heavy, cold lump in her stomach, and she felt sick in the stifling heat. She carefully raised one hand to her forehead. It was wet with sweat.

It was Saturday evening and the tram was full of happy, eager people absorbed in their own affairs. The only person looking at her curiously was the man who had given her an appreciative look when she got on.

She looked out of the window and saw that they were already far out in Vallgård. She had missed her stop, and another two besides.

There was no point waiting for a tram heading in the other direction: if she walked quickly she could be at Fanny's in ten minutes. And the walk would help clear her head. She had been looking forward to this evening for so long, and was happy it was finally going to happen.

15

Thune knew that he had been somewhat subdued at Miss Fanny Ålander's.

He had lost his nerve the moment he rang the bell and Miss Ålander opened the door and he held out his flowers and walked in. The flat was so small that there was no entrance hall, and he saw at once that Mrs Wiik was not there.

Miss Ålander had of course been warned that Thune would be coming; she curtsied deeply and said it was an honour for her to have the lawyer visit her home. She added shyly that Tilda had called just after half past six to say that she would be late. At first Thune had not understood who Miss Ålander was talking about, but at the same moment as she began to blush and stammer "Well, of course to you she is . . ." he realised that his hostess had been referring to Mrs Wiik.

Mrs Wiik was always at the office in good time in the morning (it was Thune, not she, who had trouble with punctuality), and he was annoyed with himself that it had not occurred to him that she might be seriously delayed. If he had considered the possibility, he would have made sure to be significantly later than the ten minutes – it was twelve minutes past seven when he rang on Miss Ålander's door – he had allowed to pass after paying for the cab and watching it drive off.

He had walked one block along one of the streets known as "the Lines", passed through a doorway and stood in a courtyard smoking first one cigarette, then another. The windows of the surrounding buildings had been open in the heat. Somewhere someone was playing a guitar, and a male voice was singing "Kostervalsen" in Finnish, the sound came from one of the upper storeys and the music echoed around the stone walls. Otherwise the courtyard had been deserted, in contrast to the steep street outside, where a number of Saturday drunks were already standing on the pavement muttering at passers-by, or arguing noisily amongst themselves.

Where there were no other men around, there was no chance of being beaten up: that was Thune's philosophy.

His mood sank still further as he stepped into the room and shook hands with the others. Tuulikki Ahlbäck, the musician's wife, was a plump woman with a large bosom and a wide and generous mouth. It did not take Thune many minutes to realise that Mrs Ahlbäck's mouth was also generous insofar as she liked talking a great deal. He pondered – not without some surprise – the fact that she was the sister-in-law of the strict and reserved Mrs Wiik, and wondered what sort of temperament Konni Ahlbäck had. During their short encounter on the S.S. *Archimedes* Ahlbäck had talked both more, and more quickly than his sister usually did, but he had been intoxicated at the time.

It was not Mrs Ahlbäck who made Thune's mood sink, but Heikki Puttonen and Reinhard Ålander, the former Mrs Ahlbäck's cousin, the latter Miss Ålander's brother. They were both proper men's men: strong, muscular, sporty types, the same sort as Zorro Arelius and Rolle Hansell, but in working-class form. They were neatly dressed in jackets, shirts, ties and pale promenade shoes, and their light summer hats were perched on the shelf by the door. They both had friendly, open faces, Thune could see that when the men spoke to Mrs Ahlbäck or Miss Ålander. But when they had to turn in his direction – Miss Ålander made valiant attempts to draw him into the conversation – suspicion crept into their eyes and around their mouths: even when they introduced themselves they practically spat their names at him.

Fortunately Mrs Wiik arrived a quarter of an hour after Thune. She was wearing a blue dress with white polka dots, neatly cut, which did justice to both her waist and legs. It did not take long for Thune to realise that Mrs Wiik was also something of an outsider in this company. Not to the same extent as him, of course, because she knew both Mrs Ahlbäck and Miss Ålander. But she was very quiet, particularly when Puttonen and Reinhard Ålander turned the conversation towards politics: she remained silent and looked down into her glass or at the wall hangings and photographs in Miss Ålander's neat little room.

They spent an hour and a half at Miss Ålander's.

Thune did not say much, but drank several glasses of the cheap *Sekt* offered by their hostess. He also took a large, bitter swig from the hipflask Reinhard Ålander held out to him without a word just as they were about to leave, after Thune had given Ålander and his sister a Chesterfield each.

As they strolled towards the centre of the city Thune realised that he had drunk far too much, too quickly. In the middle of the Long Bridge he could feel the tarmac swaying beneath him, and for a few dizzy moments it felt as if the bridge were going to collapse: then he realised that the world was standing perfectly firmly, and that any giddiness was inside his own head.

He had been surprised by how nice and clean Miss Ålander's home was. The little flat was scrubbed and swept. The furniture, hangings, glasses, the dishes she served the sandwiches on – everything was rustic, but tasteful in an unassuming way. The thin tulle curtains smelled fresh, the pelargonium on the windowsill and the pansies on the telephone table looked well cared for.

186

That sense of surprise and wellbeing stayed with Thune as they walked the few blocks down Tavastvägen and across Hagnäs torg, back to the landscape that was his. In films and books the working-class areas of Helsinki were still depicted as gloomy and run-down. The flats were sooty hovels, the dark backyards and narrow alleyways were full of thieves and fallen women, factory whistles blared as chimneys spewed out their black smoke, unruly gangs of boys roamed the streets looking for people to rob or assault, and drunken, angry voices emerged from bushes as a vicious *puukko* was drawn back and thrust into someone's guts as easily as a knife going through summer-warm butter.

Thune had friends, not least in the Wednesday Club, who swallowed those images hook, line and sinker, and who had never set foot north of the Long Bridge. He remembered his years as a student in the early '20s, when he, Yogi Jary and Robi Lindemark would break the unwritten social rules of the city and occasionally attend dances in Sörnäs. They had discussed the matter, telling each other that it was the fault of the war that the chasm between peoples and classes had grown so deep, and agreed to do all they could to make their city a better place to live. But they never felt welcome at those dances beyond the Long Bridge – as Thune recalled, Robi Lindemark had felt particularly uncomfortable and sometimes did not come – and after one evening when a shoemaker's apprentice and promising boxer for Jyry sports club had beaten both Robi and Yogi to the ground, their excursions had come to an end. And now, as Thune acknowledged his own surprise at Miss Fanny Ålander's neat little rented rooms, and at the *joie de vivre* he had heard echoing from the windows of the apartment blocks on the Lines, and the good humour he had seen on the streets during their walk towards the centre, he realised: he had turned into a narrow-minded worrier, one of the prejudiced fools he had despised so deeply when he was younger.

They headed south down Unionsgatan. It was almost half

187

past nine but the air was warm and soft as balsam, and Thune experienced flashbacks to summers abroad.

Last year, his only summer in Moscow, the final weeks before he moved back home to Helsinki, the terrible heat, the smell of smoke, the white poplar pollen that lay like sticky snow after the trees had finished flowering.

And another summer, half a decade ago, a summer in Stockholm when the right-wing legation secretary Snellman had tried to smoke out the envoy, Erich – who was of Jewish extraction – using a spy scandal as an excuse. One evening Thune got fed up with all the scheming and intrigue and took Gabi to the Cecil restaurant where they drank champagne and danced all evening. He could still remember the last dance: the band was the Erik Nilsson Octet, the song "Stardust".

And he remembered the way Gabi's hips and waist had felt beneath his fingers through her thin summer dress as they walked home to their apartment up near St Johannes Church.

Thune started when he noticed that the others had been talking about "The Soldier's Bride" while he was immersed in thought. Reinhard Ålander was upset about the film, and declared that Hitler's Germany clearly was not the only place where the propaganda machine was reaching new heights in its attempts to pull the wool over people's eyes. Heikki Puttonen agreed, while Mrs Ahlbäck laughed and said that "The Soldier's Bride" might not be the best film in the world, but Kullervo Kalske certainly looked very stylish in his role. Miss Ålander asked Mrs Wiik what she thought, and Mrs Wiik replied quietly that she had not yet seen the film.

"Really? When you go to the pictures all the time!" Miss Ålander and Mrs Ahlbäck exclaimed in unison.

Mrs Wiik looked uncomfortable and said: "Yes, but I actually prefer foreign films."

"Nonsense!" Mrs Ahlbäck huffed. "You've seen both 'Hulda from Juurakko' and 'The Women of Niskavuori' several times!"

"I know, but I still prefer . . ." Mrs Wiik began lamely, but abandoned her protest.

Thune had seen neither "Hulda from Juurakko" nor "The Women of Niskavuori". But he had seen "The Soldier's Bride" only a few weeks ago. Alone at the Kino-Palats, just after Midsummer.

He had not liked the film. But he still thought Ålander's anger exaggerated. Historical films always had a patriotic sense of morality, it was like that everywhere, so why should Finland be an exception? What Thune remembered best was a scene in which one of the Finnish soldiers – he could not remember which one, he had found the plot complicated and confusing – kicked a spy and hissed "Jewish bastard!" Thune had seen the film just a week after the athletics contest in the Stadium, and his thoughts had been drawn to Yogi Jary and Yogi's hopeless attempts to get justice for his nephew.

They went round the Edlund corner, crossed the North Esplanade and walked slowly through the park towards Runeberg's statue and the Swedish Theatre. Thune looked around nervously, he could not help it, he was worried that some fellow lawyer or old friend would see him and make a big deal of the fact that he was spending Saturday evening with the hoi polloi. Now it was Puttonen's turn to offer a hipflask as he glanced furtively at the women, who were walking a few paces ahead of them. At first Thune shook his head: the very idea, in the middle of the Esplanade Park, drinking stinking *fusel* straight from a flask! Besides, his instinct for self-preservation was telling him not to drink any more, at least not yet. But then he changed his mind, grasped the flask, closed his eyes so no-one would see them watering from the alcohol, and took a deep swig. When he opened his eyes his gaze landed on the outdoor terrace of the theatre restaurant, up on the first floor. That was where Yogi Jary and Robi Lindemark and Polle Grönroos and Gabi and he and hundreds more had danced to the Aurora Premier Brass Band in the summers of

'26 and '27, and some evenings he had drunk too much smuggled whisky and got cross and jealous of Gabi when she danced with other men.

The women had moved on to another subject now, and were talking about the news that had been in all the newspapers that morning.

The German aviatrix Lottie Preisler had begun a week-long visit to Helsinki, she was going to give lectures at a civil guard party, to the students at the reserve officers' college, and in various other colleges and schools.

Reinhard Ålander flared up again, saying that Miss Preisler might have bedroom eyes and a fine profile, but she was still a Nazi.

Miss Fanny got angry in turn and snapped at her brother, telling him he was a donkey for dragging politics into everything. And "bedroom eyes", what was that supposed to mean? Surely everyone had those when the time was right!

Reinhard Ålander looked hurt and glanced at Heikki Puttonen for support, but Puttonen just stared at the ground and said nothing. Mrs Ahlbäck tried to smooth things over and said that Lottie Preisler might not be entirely faultless, but she was nevertheless a pioneer of flight, and a courageous woman, just like poor Amelia Earhart.

Thune found himself thinking about Gabi again, as he remembered her admiration for pilots. But the thought of pilots and planes also aroused his fear of flying, and he was deluged with memories of awful flights from Helsinki to Stockholm and from Stockholm to Reval and Leningrad. He felt sick, and his resolve not to drink any more alcohol that evening was strengthened. He tried to suppress the nausea by thinking of the picture of Lottie Preisler that had been printed in *Hufvudstadsbladet* that morning.

Lottie Preisler had been sitting in a flower meadow in Gumtäkt, surrounded by admiring schoolchildren. According to the caption, she was telling the children "about her adventures in the skies above four continents, and about the newfound passion of German youth for exciting adventures and healthy games". Miss Preisler was wearing a tight pullover, long, narrow-waisted trousers and a pair of sports shoes. Her long blonde hair was loose, and the photograph, showing her in profile, did her full justice. Miss Preisler's bust jutted out in a very eye-catching manner under her pullover, and Thune had got an erection as he sat alone at his breakfast table, thinking that he really did need to sleep with a woman soon, otherwise he would go mad. He had been struck by the same reaction in the darkness of the cinema during one of the advertisements before "The Soldier's Bride": on that occasion the object of his desire had been a young blonde mother in a tight petticoat nursing her baby.

He thrust aside his thoughts of Miss Preisler, increased the length of his stride slightly, and then walked next to Mrs Wiik for a while, without actually thinking of anything to say.

As they crossed Henriksgatan to get to the Mikado, Puttonen pulled out a bottle of Vademecum and he and Reinhard Ålander gargled with the mouthwash so that their breath would not smell of alcohol.

I'm not drinking another drop, Thune thought. I shall dance and be talkative and charming. The others might think me boring, but Mrs Wiik knows that I'm not.

Matilda did not sleep a wink that night.

She got home shortly after two, when the doctor who had been called had managed to stem the flow of blood and patch Thune up, and had given him some pain-killing tablets just to be on the safe side.

A bank of cloud had swept in from the sea and the night had suddenly become pitch black: it was that melancholy week when the night sky was still light when the weather was clear, but when summer is preparing to change form and starts to meander stormily towards darkness and autumn.

She was awake when dawn came, lying in bed but unable to relax. Anxiety was gnawing away at her from different directions and doing countless different things, and to make a bad situation worse Miss Milja was talking to her non-stop, and she was at her very worst, whispering that now Matilda was going to lose Fanny the way she had lost all her previous friends, and then wondering if Matilda might not be a little infatuated with Thune, which would be odd considering that Thune was utterly devoid of sex appeal, and anyway, he was bound to find out about Director Hoffman soon, and it was probably the case that Konni and Matilda were each as mad as the other, that they both suffered from the same sickness of the soul, it just hadn't burst into full view in Matilda yet: that was how Miss Milja went on, and once she had got going she refused to let herself be silenced.

Everyone had gone home after the scene, some silent and sad, others upset or angry. Matilda could not understand how an evening that had started so well could have ended so badly. Of course she had noticed that Reinhard and Heikki did not like Thune. But that really had nothing to do with Thune as a person: they did not like having a person of Thune's type and class sitting among them on a Saturday night – it upset the balance. When they had been sitting in Fanny's home Matilda had regretted her decision to invite Thune, and regretted even more the fact that she had pestered a reluctant Fanny – the dear, sweet thing! – until she agreed. And Matilda herself had struggled to shake off what had happened during the tram ride. It was as if she were still in the camp, or with the Captain in the English Tea-Room. The Captain's gloved hand on her bare one, the harshness of his grip even though he probably thought he was providing gentle comfort. Only when they arrived at the Mikado and heard the music and saw Konni and his musicians sitting behind their stands did she forget the visions and come back to life.

It got better after that, much better, to start with.

Reinhard and Heikki forgot their mistrust of Thune and offered him some of the drink they had brought with them in the gentlemen's lavatory and out in the vestibule when the doorman was otherwise occupied. Konni came over and greeted them all warmly, then had a drink and smoked some cigarettes at their table during both the first and second breaks. Konni had not recognised Thune at first: Thune had to remind him of their meeting on the foredeck of the *Archimedes*. Tuulikki was in her element as usual, dancing and talking and laughing and drinking. Matilda had noticed Konni's mood darkening slightly, but had not paid it much attention. Fanny was sweet as an angel, and a little squiffy from the *Sekt*, all the men wanted to dance with her. Matilda presumed that some of them asked where the young lady lived and if they could escort her home. But Matilda was not worried – she knew Fanny could take care of herself.

Matilda danced with them all as well – with Reinhard, with Heikki, with Thune, and even with a few strangers. But she was unable to forget the Captain completely even at the Mikado. When one of the strangers took too firm a grip of her hand during a dance, she saw the table at the English Tea-Room again, the lightning and rain outside, herself and the Captain, his hand on hers.

Thune was a terrible dancer, uncertain, with no sense of rhythm, he had no idea about how to lead, his tall, thin body tottered back and forth across the Mikado's dance floor like a ship abandoned in an autumn gale, and Matilda had just tried to follow as best she could. When Thune asked her to dance a third time she declined, saying she had to visit the ladies' room – by that point she had already understood that her employer had drunk far too much.

Her declining to dance was unfortunate, because from then on Thune devoted all his attention to Tuulikki.

There was really nothing remarkable about that. Thune had already danced with Tuulikki earlier in the evening, and had even managed to get a dance with the very popular Fanny, despite his being such a hopeless dancer. In all other respects he behaved with complete propriety, asking the ladies to dance according to the customary etiquette and escorting them back to their table afterwards, and his hands – so far as Matilda could judge – did nothing untoward during the dances.

But he must have done or said something, because after the last dance of the evening Konni appeared at their table, and he was furious. Matilda had seen Heikki go over to the band's podium and say something to Konni, but she was still completely unprepared for what was to come. Just as Thune escorted Tuulikki back to the table and pulled her chair out for her, Konni rushed over and punched Thune.

Only once, but right on the nose, and hard, so that the lawyer's nose started to gush blood.

Thune lay on the floor for a good while, dazed but conscious, while the caretaker called for a doctor. Fanny and Matilda fetched water and towels for Thune, and an angry Tuulikki dragged Konni aside to give him a scolding.

The doctor came quickly, and once Thune had received first aid there followed a negotiation between him, the maître d', the caretaker and Konni. The maître d', a man called Granqvist, wanted to call the police. The Mikado was no place for ruffians, he said sourly, and as soon as he had told the proprietor, Director Norkko, about the incident, the ruffian dance band Arizona would have to start looking for a new engagement. Konni looked at Thune with desperation in his eyes. Thune looked away but said he did not want to call the police, he just wanted to go home and go to bed, and draw a line under the whole business.

*

194

Matilda did not know what worried and upset her most.

Of course she was concerned about how Thune would behave towards her from now on – she was scared of losing her job.

She was both worried about and angry with Konni. She had seen it happen before. His sudden jealousy, his way of behaving aggressively whenever he was in mixed company. His motiveless anxiety about Tuulikki's honour: Konni's wife could appear flirtatious, but beneath her cheery exterior she was a faithful soul and would never betray her husband; Matilda knew that, and Konni probably did as well.

Warrior-Konni. A contrast to the artist who could play so many instruments beautifully on stage, to the generous man who bought expensive gifts that he could not really afford, to the man who was not merely jealous of his beautiful Tuulikki, but told her that she was his queen, the best thing that had ever happened to him.

Last but not least, Matilda was also angry with herself.

She had not only danced, she had drunk two glasses of *Sekt* at Fanny's. And at the Mikado she had allowed Thune to buy her a terrible cocktail that tasted of fruit.

She never usually drank, and she never talked out of turn.

And now she had done both.

The music had made her feel happy and carefree, the alcohol had made her giddy, and before she knew it she had revealed something to Thune. Something that Konni and Fanny knew about, but no-one else.

Thune had escorted her back to the table after their second dance, and Matilda felt like being funny and smart, and made a comment about a question Thune had asked when they were eating lunch in the Cabinet, and which she had really already answered.

As soon as she said it she regretted it, so deeply that she felt like biting her tongue.

But it was too late for that. What was done was done, and

195

she could only hope that Thune had been sufficiently drunk that he would wake up next morning with a thundering headache and no memory of any conversation from the previous evening before the moment when Konni's clenched fist hit him on the nose.

16

The engine puttered gently as the fisherman – who had introduced himself as Kvickström – steered the boat away from the jetty. Arelius' Studebaker, which was parked next to the general store, grew smaller and smaller: the car looked incongruous in the rural setting. It was August now but the heat was still holding. "It was already twenty-six degrees at ten this morning," Kvickström called from his cramped wheelhouse. Thune nodded, turned his face to the sun, closed his eyes and relaxed.

He had called Arelius the day after the incident at the Mikado. He was acting in haste, more in hope than expectation. Thune wanted to get away from Helsinki, but had not expected anyone to answer in the house out in Westend, seeing as Arelius had said he would be renting the cabin on Söderskär from the Saturday.

To Thune's relief, Arelius had answered. He had been obliged to postpone his departure by a few days: a number of his oldest and most important patients were suffering badly from the heat. One of them was Thune's mother, Esther, and Thune made a mental note to call her as soon as he could. Arelius had not had the heart to abandon his patients, so had decided to open his surgery on Monday and Tuesday.

Thune had asked whether the offer of a few days in the Russian Villa was still open. Arelius had hesitated a fraction of a second too long, then replied that of course Thune was welcome whenever he wanted to come, for a few days or longer.

"I don't want to be any trouble, Zorro," Thune had said. "I can book into a boarding house for a few days. Or take a trip to Stockholm."

"You won't be any trouble at all," Arelius had assured him. "I just hope you won't mind if my fiancée happens to be there when you come. Astrid – Miss Segersven, I mean – has promised to spend a week or two out there with me. But the cabin has room for three. And if you want more space for yourself we can always make up a bed in the kitchen."

"Well, congratulations!" Thune had said, to which Arelius replied:

"To be strictly accurate, Astrid and I aren't engaged yet. But it's only a matter of time before we are. Listen, if you can make your way to Borgå, and from there to Tolkis, I'll sort out the rest of the transport. Do you already know when you're likely to come?"

"It probably won't be for a week or two yet," Thune had replied. "I need to sort out the move first."

The move to Munksnäs had gone smoothly, and Thune even managed to fit in a visit to see his mother on Parkgatan. In the middle of the move Thune had tried to contact Arelius by calling the lighthouse-keeper out on Söderskär. When he failed to get any answer he sent a postcard: *Coming in three days' time*. He had hoped that the postal service would live up to its reputation and that Arelius – and possibly Miss Segersven – would be forewarned of his arrival.

All he had done in the house on Borgvägen was unpack a few clothes and make sure his office was in order and that the files he would need after his holiday were laid out in readiness. He had fewer rooms than he and Gabi had at their disposal on

Högbergsgatan, but that was balanced by the fact that all the available rooms were his, and his alone: he was still not used to the feeling.

In his briefcase he found the notes from his interview with Paasikivi, the envoy in Stockholm, from April. He had put off work on his article on foreign affairs all spring and half the summer now, and had put any writing on ice so many times that he no longer felt any guilt at his negligence. He decided to take all his notes with him to Söderskär, along with a recently published book, *Quo Vadis, Europe?* Perhaps the open water would open his mind and he would finally be able to come up with a plan for the article.

As far as the kitchen was concerned, he set his faith in Mrs Leimu. He had carried two sealed boxes labelled *Kitchen Equipment* from the hall to the kitchen, but that was the extent of his contribution. After Mrs Leimu sorted everything out in there, she had made his bed and hung the unpacked clothes in the wardrobe, and dusted the furniture in the living room. Then she had laid out the carpets and prepared an excellent sausage stroganoff. Mrs Leimu had promised to carry on working for Thune until he found a new help: she was already old, she had told him, and in the long term would not be able to make her way out to Munksnäs every morning, and then back in to the city each evening. Thune had said he understood, and found her a new position – starting in October – with a fellow lawyer, Wuorimaa, a member of the Supreme Court.

Thune was determined to put down roots out in the suburb. But that would have to wait until later in the summer, possibly even September. Then the schools would open once more and life in Munksnäs would get back to normal. At present the district lay drowsy and lethargic in the heat. Borgvägen and the other streets close to the shore seemed particularly deserted. The affluent families were all hidden away at their summerhouses, the only life to be found was in the rental blocks along Stora

Allén and Grundvägen. That was where the tram and cycle routes taking people to work each morning ran, that was where people gathered outside the Bio Rita in the evenings. But by the time the trams reached the Cadet School and the residential blocks close to the shore, they were quite empty.

Kvickström the fisherman was heading south across a mirror-like sea, and Thune took out the morning paper that he had begun to read on the bus.

It was the usual concoction of large and small: Franco's planes were bombing Barcelona, ice-cream sales in Finland had hit a new record in July, Jewish homes in Nuremburg were going to be pulled down, despite protests, and lovely Dorothy Lamour had fallen in the water while filming in Alaska.

Thune read on, and found an article about another cultural visitor from Germany.

No sooner has the courageous and much admired Lottie Preisler left Helsinki, than another beauteous Valkyrie arrives. The Third Reich's glorious dictator of film is here to attend the premiere of her film about the Berlin Games of 1936.

According to the newspaper's reporter, Leni Riefenstahl was "one of the most enchanting and charming people one could ever meet, slender, delightful, always girlish and pretty with her flaming red hair and her soft, low voice which has a rare suggestive tenor."

Thune felt weary down to his very marrow: he despaired of his ability to write any political analysis that could do justice to the chaos in Europe. He put the newspaper down, turned his head so that the warm breeze hit his left cheek, closed his eyes again and began to think about Mrs Wiik.

She had called him immediately after the Mikado catastrophe, the same Sunday afternoon he had called Arelius. She called first, but it had not changed Thune's decision to leave Helsinki as soon as he possibly could.

She had sounded anxious. Presumably she was worried about her job, but had not dared raise the subject. Thune had been calm as he spoke to her, but had refrained from saying straight out that he had no intention of dismissing her simply because her brother happened to be an idiot and a violent ruffian.

There had also been a hint of inquisitiveness about her, but she had made no attempt to sate her curiosity: she did not venture to ask if Thune had said or done anything inappropriate while he was dancing, something Heikki Puttonen had seen or heard and then relayed to Konni Ahlbäck.

Thune, of course, knew the truth.

He had complimented Mrs Ahlbäck on her dancing, and added that her forthright, open manner reminded him of his wife, who had left him for another man.

Heikki Puttonen had been dancing alongside them with a stranger, and had heard what Thune said. What Puttonen went on to tell Konni Ahlbäck, Thune did not know, nor was he particularly interested in finding out. For him the whole affair was over the moment he left the Mikado, and he had made that clear to Mrs Wiik when she nervously enquired after his health:

"Under the circumstances, I am very well, there's no cause for concern."

"I really am most terribly sorry about Konni. He's . . ." she had begun, but lost her train of thought and fell silent for a few seconds, before concluding:

"He's done this sort of thing before. I don't know what's wrong with him."

"I can assure you, it's alright," Thune had said. "Really quite alright."

He had hesitated, but then went on:

"This is for your ears only, Mrs Wiik, but I often used to get upset and angry when I was younger and drank more than I do now."

When she did not respond he continued:

"And I used to get jealous as well. So, while I don't want to say that I condone what your brother did, I can understand the thinking behind it, even though he had no cause for concern."

"You were jealous . . . of your wife?"

Once again Mrs Wiik had crossed the invisible boundary. This time she had not interrupted him. But she had asked a question that broke the tacit understanding between employer and employee, between boss and subordinate. She had broken the unwritten rules governing who could say what to whom. Thune had replied irritably:

"Yes. Of Gabi, my former wife."

Then he had changed the subject, and asked:

"And the band, Arizona, are they going to continue their engagement?"

"Yes," Mrs Wiik had replied. "Granqvist hasn't said anything."

"Granqvist?" Thune had wondered.

"The maître d'," she had said. "The man who said he was going to report to Director Norkko. He's promised not to."

"You have a good memory for names," Thune said. "Would I be mistaken if I were to say that you have a good memory in general?"

"No, you wouldn't. Not entirely, anyway."

Her voice had sounded happy, relieved, and she had even let out a small laugh. Then she had become serious again:

"But having a good memory isn't always a good thing to have. Don't you think?"

Thune had not answered her question. Instead he wished Mrs Wiik a very pleasant holiday, she reciprocated and asked about his impending move, Thune had answered, and they had hung up.

They had not spoken about the rest of Saturday evening, nor about their long lunch earlier that day. They had not returned to anything that had been said in the Cabinet or in Fanny's flat or at the Mikado. But one thing in particular had stuck in Thune's mind. Mrs Wiik had said something very strange during their second dance, which turned out to be their last. He wondered if she remembered saying it afterwards, or if she too had been a little befuddled.

Perhaps it was that remark which lay behind her restrained curiosity during their telephone conversation the following day? Perhaps she was not at all curious about what Thune had whispered to Mrs Ahlbäck on the dance floor, perhaps she was simply worried that Thune remembered what she had said.

"You asked if I was sure that Mr Wiik would have nothing against your joining us. The last time I heard any opinion from Mr Wiik was in the summer of '31."

Thune was dragged from his thoughts by a change in the sound of the engine as the boat slowed down. He turned and saw the lighthouse rising up high above the sea. Below the lighthouse lay four small red wooden houses spread out on the grass-covered skerry. The air was thick with the sound of calling terns, and there were bare rocky outcrops in every direction. On a neighbouring skerry Arelius was standing with his hand raised in greeting, and beside Arelius stood a large man in a peaked cap. There was a red house on that island as well, and Thune presumed that must be the Russian Villa. He saw Arelius run nimbly down to the rocky shore where a rowing-boat lay moored: even though the sound was no wider than forty metres, there was no bridge between the two skerries.

Thune was relieved to find Arelius alone out there. Miss Segersven had spent a little over a week in the Russian Villa, but had gone home a few days earlier.

203

He had been wrong about the house on the other skerry. It was not the Russian Villa but the pilot's cottage. Arelius had been sitting there talking to the pilots while he waited for Kvickström to bring Thune out. The Russian Villa was a much smaller house on the main island, close to the lighthouse and lighthouse-men's cottages.

"Over there is where the pilots live, it's known as Bastulandet, sauna island," Arelius said. "But there's no sauna on Bastulandet. That's on Mattlandet. But there's a shithouse on both of them."

Thune thought Arelius had changed in the two weeks he had been on the island. He had adopted the simple, hardy life out at the very fringe of the sea, and had regained a little of the sinuous muscle and indomitability that had been so much a part of his youth, when he had been invincible at sport.

"This is how we ought to live," Arelius said that first afternoon. "Living off our instincts. Without having to make allowances for what we like to call *civilisation*."

He said that last word with contempt, as if he were spitting at a snake, and added:

"Culture spoils us, Claes. It makes us confused and weak."

Miss Segersven's presence could still be felt in the Russian Villa. There was a faint smell in the air, an odd mixture of violets and pine detergent and iron. And when Thune admired the exemplary organisation of the kitchen cupboards, Arelius said simply: "Astrid."

The kitchen was small and dark and smelled of dirty water. Thune was glad he was not going to have to sleep there. The remainder of the villa consisted of one single but generously proportioned room. There were bunk beds fixed to two of the walls. Arelius slept in one of the lower bunks, and obviously Thune chose the other one. The bunks were narrow and hard, and Thune could not help wondering how Arelius and his Astrid had spent their week together.

Presumably they had been occupied with love, Thune

thought. The setting was practically made for it. This was a place where two human beings could stand naked, hand in hand, in the face of the sea, exploring the most sensuous side of life, particularly as neither the family of lighthouse-master Jonasson nor those of lighthouse-keepers Karlsson and Huhta seemed remotely interested in what the visitors from Helsinki got up to.

Thune could not help wondering what Miss Astrid Segersven looked like.

In his imagination Miss Segersven had Mrs Ahlbäck's wide mouth and happy laugh. She had Miss Ålander's soft cheeks and blue eyes. She had Mrs Wiik's slender, shapely ankles and her chestnut brown hair, and she had the bust that had jutted out so visibly beneath Miss Preisler's pullover. But Thune gave her none of Gabi's features – that still hurt far too much. He did not want to think of Gabi that way.

Thune's vision evaporated into nothing on the second evening. Arelius took out a framed photograph from his rucksack. The picture showed a dark, fairly plain woman staring into the camera. Thune thought her eyes looked stern. Perhaps she just did not like being photographed. Arelius said:

"Astrid."

That same evening Thune asked if Arelius had found out anything about Mrs Wiik's employment at Hoffman & Laurén, and, more specifically, about the termination of that employment.

Arelius shook his head.

"No, I'm afraid not. I did ask when I had lunch with young Antti Laurén last week. Only in passing – I'm sure he didn't realise why I was asking. But he didn't know anything. He didn't even remember her. Mind you, Antti is pretty hopeless, only interested in sailing and rich girls. I don't think he's terribly aware of what goes on in the business."

They were sitting on some rocks below the sauna, and had just taken a cooling dip in the sea. Arelius jumped straight off the jetty each time, like another Johnny Weissmuller. Thune chose to slide down on his backside, feet first. The slippery seaweed tickled his testicles, and the sensation was not wholly unpleasant. He was longing for a bottle of beer, but there was none. Arelius only drank rainwater out there, and Thune was too shy to go and ask the lighthouse-men.

Water, potatoes, carrots and boiled, freshly caught cod – that was what Arelius could offer, meal after meal. Thune dreamed of a portion of veal *à la Oscar*; he could see before him the moist steak, smell the time-honoured aroma of meat that had been seared over an open fire, he could see the tender asparagus and the thick red Choron sauce and the salty, firm prawns, and his stomach rumbled.

Arelius looked towards the setting sun and said in a light tone of voice:

"By the way, I've read Gabi's book out here. Well, not all of it, I've still got a couple of stories left."

Thune waited nervously for the *coup de grâce*. That was what Arelius was like, had always been like, even when they were children: beneath that pleasant exterior he was playing a Machiavellian game with his friends. Only someone with no experience of Arelius relaxed in his company, because he was fond of sticking the knife in just when his opponent felt most secure in the warm embrace of male friendship. Now Arelius nodded towards the red sky to the west and said:

"Piquant. Not the view, I mean. The book."

"How do you mean, piquant?" Thune asked, resigned to his fate.

"She's not without talent, our dear Gabi," Arelius said in an amused tone of voice. "Every so often one almost feels like that silk cushion while one is reading."

Thune made up his mind to ignore Arelius' provocations. It was not difficult, he just had to act distracted, a method he had developed and refined when they were growing up together: he pretended he could not hear, and Arelius would soon get tired of teasing. Apart from that, Thune soon settled in, and kept congratulating himself on his decision to come out to Söderskär instead of sorting out his new home on Borgvägen.

He and Arelius spent the greater part of the days apart. Arelius lived the active life, swimming each morning and evening out to one of the rocky islands that lay half a kilometre or more from their island he practised shooting with Pilot Fagerberg's rifle, even though it was not the hunting season, and went off several times a day to go fishing or set out lines with the lighthouse-men.

Thune swam occasionally, but had never enjoyed either hunting or fishing. Fishing involved far too much slime, wriggling and death for him – he preferred his fish on a plate with nice names like *sandre Walewska* and *sole meunière*. Out on Söderskär the presentation left something to be desired, but Thune was happy to eat the catch, which was landed daily and consisted of cod and the occasional pike.

He wandered about the island on his own, lay in the crevasses between rocks, dozing and reading. But all the lighthouse-men were married and had children, so the island could get rather lively during the day. When that happened Thune would take one of the rowing-boats and head over to Bastulandet, or to Synnerstlandet, away to the south-east. There he would read his notes or *Quo Vadis, Europe?* by the French philosopher Alois Hummelschmitt, a pan-Europeanist and adherent of Count Coudenhove-Kalergi's already tragically forgotten vision. And out there on Synnerstlandet, with the rocks and rolling swell of the sea to question and challenge him, the idea of an article finally began to form in his mind.

It was just that whenever Thune's thoughts started to meander to and fro across Europe, they inevitably settled on cities he had visited and cities where he had lived.

He remembered the summers of his youth as a trainee law student in Berlin, he remembered the last summer when the zeroes on the banknotes of the Weimar Republic were already breeding like fat flies.

He remembered his honeymoon with Gabi, and their later amorous trips together. The intoxicating summers of the late '20s, he and Gabi in Paris, he and Gabi in Venice, he and Gabi in Rome, he and Gabi in Naples and on Capri. But he also remembered that it was during that last summer trip, when the '20s had become the '30s and the Depression had already struck, that they began to suspect that they might not be able to have children together. They had spent three happy weeks in a *pensione* on Lake Garda, making love like they had not done since they were newly engaged. But nothing happened. And it was probably Thune who took the lack of any pregnancy hardest. He thought it was, anyway.

He remembered the years in Stockholm, and how he and Gabi slowly and imperceptibly began to move apart, how she sought solace in socialising and he in his work, how in the end they were like two strangers at the breakfast table, reading separate newspapers. But they had had good times in Stockholm as well, especially during the first year. So good, in fact, that when Thune found Gabi's short stories and diaries several years later and realised that she had had lovers, he was shocked.

The lonely year in Moscow. Barely ten months, to be precise, but that had felt like years.

Was it because he was grieving for Gabi, because his humiliation was so fresh, that he was so unhappy in the capital city of Communism? Thune had always believed himself to be something of a connoisseur of big cities – if he could, he preferred to travel to cities larger than Helsinki, and his dream was to spend a period of time in New York. Moscow was the first – and so far only – big city to have roused terror and revulsion in him.

The suspicious glances people gave one another as they passed on the muddy, poorly lit side streets. The churches – the few that were open – full of muttering old women, where the Komsomol youths still conducted violent raids. The old-fashioned European luxury of the Hotel Metropol ballroom, champagne and lobster for the initiated in a city where people wore rags and the shelves in the shops gaped empty. The loudspeakers set up on the squares, the crackling, metallic voices babbling quick, excited Russian. The car that followed at a discreet distance every time Thune, trade attaché Nykopp or one of the others decided to go on an excursion to a riverbank or to somewhere outside the city. The cramped and ramshackle premises of the Finnish legation, crawling with mice and cockroaches: everyone was waiting for the new building on Kropotkinskiy pereulok to be finished, but the work was dragging because the builders did nothing but drink and shirk their duties.

And the hub of the city, the secretive Kremlin, the bells ringing, the red flag flapping in the wind.

Thune remembered a parade that took place one week after he arrived. The city had been preparing for the big event all week. The red flags, made of thin, cloth-covered pieces of wood, covering entire ten-storey buildings. The equally vast heroic portraits of Stalin and Lenin, so big that they had to be lifted into place by an army of cranes. The red banners on every building, streamers with slogans like *Long live October 16!* Red, red, red everywhere, and all the floodlights glaring across the broad main streets and deserted squares, across the schoolchildren and students marching in strict formation with flags in their hands.

That morning in early November, when the march set off towards Red Square, it was a little past nine o'clock. The weather was cold and windy, freezing rain pricking your cheeks like nails. The long detour along the river, the young militia soldiers leading the diplomats up onto the roof of Lenin's mausoleum. There they stood with their backs to the wall of the Kremlin, and just to their right stood Stalin and little Yezhov and the others who made up the leader's inner circle, or what was left of it.

First came the soldiers' cheers for Stalin, set off in stages, rolling back and forth across the square like a huge wave. Then the "Internationale", and then a salute – 101 guns – which took several minutes and made the ground shake and the windows in the city centre rattle. Only when the salute was over did the parade begin. Infantry corps, military bands, an elite company, a women's company, tanks, convoys of vehicles, the air force with shiny steel planes on vast trucks, more elite troops, more tanks, and everywhere those red flags and banners with revolutionary slogans . . . the parade never seemed to end, and went on for several hours.

That evening Thune and Nykopp walked back in to the centre; it took them a quarter of an hour to get from Stankovich Street to the river below the Kremlin. The festivities of the parade day were still going on, demonstrators pouring down the streets, people of all ages, but mostly young, carrying flags and portraits of Stalin and Lenin and those party ideologists who had not yet been discredited and shot, shouting out slogans in praise of the revolution and condemning bourgeois imperialism and the oppression of the world's impoverished colonies.

It was still cold, but the rain had stopped and there was no wind at all, it was as if the city had frozen to ice. But Thune could see that the big red flag was still fluttering above the Kremlin as if in a gale. That morning he had stared at the gilded Romanov eagles that shimmered from the parapet. For some reason the Communists had let them remain there, and Thune had not been able to help thinking: *It's always eagles.* Now he pointed to draw Nykopp's attention to the fluttering flag. Nykopp smiled wryly and said:

"It's a wind machine. The revolution never rests – its great wind blows all day and all night."

Thune stared at the illuminated, restlessly billowing flag. In

210

the autumn evening it looked oddly dark, like a pool of blood spreading this way and that across the backdrop of the night sky.

He opened his eyes where he was lying among the rocks of Synnerstlandet, and for a few seconds the shimmering blue surface of the sea looked like a mirage: he was still caught in the November chill of Moscow even though the sun was caressing and burning him.

Quo Vadis, Europe? lay open, upside down, on a tuft of grass to his left. A white patch with irregular black streaks blemished the cover, right where the publishers had listed the awards and honorary doctorates Alois Hummelschmitt had received after he published his magnum opus. Thune could not recall having seen the mark before, and leaned over to scrape it off. The consistency was still fairly soft: a bird had dropped its excrement on the book without his noticing. He could not summon up the energy to feel cross, and was merely relieved that he himself had been spared.

Trickles of sweat were running down his chest, taking little detours when his sparse body hair got in the way. His forehead felt hot and wet, and there were big pink patches on his arms and stomach. Thune had fair, freckly skin, and knew he had burned himself badly. Even his hands were sweating, as were his feet and calves, although he had rolled his thin linen trousers up above his knees to keep them cool.

He felt slightly nauseous and suspected he had sunstroke. With a decisive gesture he stood up and took off his trousers and underpants, sat down on the rock, hesitated for a moment, then slid into the water. He took a few strokes, ducked his head under the surface and felt better at once: his bad memories faded away.

He did not want to remember Moscow. He did not want to

211

think about Moscow at all: he wanted to erase the city from his life, deny that he had ever spent any time there.

It suddenly struck him that perhaps he was not a big city person after all.

Perhaps Arelius was right.

Urban civilisation ruined people, made them not only stressed and irritable, but also weak and spoilt. City culture took them away from their original existence where they lived in small groups and affirmed their physicality and uninhibited instincts.

It was not a year in New York or a return to Stockholm that Thune needed to make him happy again.

He needed somewhere like Söderskär, a refuge where he could spend the summer.

Not too far out to sea, though. Somewhere in the archipelago. Thune was no sea-dog. After just two days he was already so sick of the sight of cod that he felt like grabbing the ugly fish by the whiskers on their chins and throwing them at the wall.

What he was missing was somewhere like Estherdal, the Thune family's former summer villa in Jollas, just east of Helsinki.

He had once been a happy child of the summer there. And he had never got over the fact that they had been forced to sell Estherdal when he was in high school, after Thorolf Thune's porcelain factory went bankrupt.

His father, Thorolf, died of a heart attack a few years later, after many vain attempts to get back on his feet again. The apartment in the city was still there, and his mother, Esther, had been in a position to lend her son money to set up his law practice. The family had not been ruined, but was poorer than before. Only Thune's sister Ulla was able to carry on living the high life thanks to her marriage to Sigurd Hansell.

Thune splashed about in the cool water off Synnerstlandet for a good while. As he lay there he formulated a plan.

He would work harder than before. He would get more clients and take on spectacular judicial cases, and with the help of his nephew Rolf-Åke and clever Mrs Wiik he would make Thune & Hansell Legal Services the finest law firm in the city. He would repay the bank loan he had taken out to buy the apartment on Borgvägen. He would become a rich man, and when he was rich he would get a summer place of his own, maybe not as fine and showy as Estherdal had been, but close to it.

When Thune swam back to shore and with some effort managed to clamber up onto the rocks, he saw a small black dot far out to sea, to the east of Söderskär.

He thought no more about it, and lay down naked to rest in the crevasse between the rocks, letting his inflamed belly dry in the sun. An ant slowly made its way across his left ankle. His penis, still shrunken from the cold water, nestled by the side of his right testicle. The cold drops of water on his stomach and chest were evaporating in the sun, and beads of sweat were beginning to appear once more.

When he looked up a while later the dot was no longer a dot, but a rowing-boat that was approaching the archipelago. Thune assumed that the lone rower was on his way to the main island, perhaps a friend of the lighthouse-master or one of the others. He felt embarrassed at his nakedness and quickly pulled on his underpants and trousers. Just to be on the safe side he pulled on his shirt as well, but left it unbuttoned.

He made himself comfortable again, picked up *Quo Vadis, Europe?* and started to read.

Five minutes passed, perhaps ten. He never heard the splash of oars, she must have been rowing very quietly and skilfully, because he only reacted when a voice said:

"Hello."

He looked up and saw a sturdy rowing-boat bobbing in the water right next to the rocks. The rower was wearing short trousers and a grey working shirt, and was anything but robust: a thin little creature with slender legs and short, sun-bleached hair.

Thune felt shy, as if he had been caught out, but did not understand why. The boat had been far out to sea when he was lying there naked, so far out that not even a telescope would have revealed any closer details. And now he was respectably dressed, considerably more respectably than her.

"Hello," Thune said, then added foolishly: "I saw you earlier. But I assumed you were heading for the main island."

"That's exactly what I was doing," the rower said. "But then I caught sight of you and thought . . . well, I didn't really think much. I was just curious. Are you a lighthouse-man?"

"No," Thune said. "A summer visitor from the city. Or rather, I'm visiting a summer visitor. I . . ."

"No need to explain," the woman in the boat said amiably. "On days like this no-one should have to explain themselves, or introduce themselves. You'll notice that I haven't said who I am either."

"Of course," Thune said. "That suits me fine."

He had been studying her as she spoke, and found her hard to place. She was fairly young, he could see that much, but could just as easily have been thirty as twenty. When she spoke she seemed almost boyish: perhaps it was the short trousers, suntan and short hair.

Most of all she resembled a faun. Or some timid animal, one of the last survivors of some rare species.

"I've been here before," she said. "I like lighthouses."

"You've come a long way," Thune said, making a feeble gesture out to sea.

Off to the east lay Pellinge, he knew that. But he was taken aback that she should be so far out at sea, alone, in an unwieldy tarred rowing-boat: he could smell the pungent tang.

"The boat isn't as heavy as it looks," she said breezily. "And I'm used to rowing. As long as you wear gloves it's fine, other-wise you get blisters."

214

It was as if the woman could read his thoughts, and Thune began to think her rather peculiar, almost a little spooky. Then she bent over a rucksack that lay between her feet on the bottom of the boat, loosened the straps and took out a Thermos flask and packet of sandwiches. She unfolded the paper, took out a sandwich and playfully pretended to throw it to Thune:

"Would you like one? I've got strawberry juice as well."

Dark bread, slices of hard-boiled egg and finely chopped chives. Nothing special, but Thune thought of the boiled cod he would probably be served that evening and nodded:

"Yes, please. But I don't need any juice, I've got my own water. You'll probably need the juice for the journey back."

The boat lay motionless in the water some distance from him, where the rocks were steep and slippery. He made his way down towards her and leaned out as far as he dared. He came close to losing his balance and sliding into the water, but managed to straighten up and take the sandwich from her outstretched hand. He brushed her hand as he took the sandwich: her skin was warm and dry.

"You were reading," she said as Thune began to eat the sandwich: he had never tasted such wonderful boiled eggs before.

"You're a journalist, perhaps?" she went on. "Or a writer?"

"No," Thune said. "A lawyer. A fairly unsuccessful one."

He had no idea what got into him, but before he had time to change his mind and swallow the words, he continued: "And a fairly unsuccessful man."

The woman looked at him calmly, then said:

"I'm a painter. And I draw. I like observing people. And I don't believe that you're unsuccessful. Perhaps you've just been trying to solve your problems the wrong way?"

Thune looked at her in surprise.

"What makes you say that?"

"It shows. Mind you, you're right, I don't really know

215

anything. But I think you should trust your instincts a little more. And worry a bit less."

She smiled at him, a fleeting smile that was quickly replaced by a look of well-meaning seriousness.

"It was very nice talking to you, but now I'm going to look at the lighthouse. I've got a long way to row before it gets dark."

She grasped the oars and took a few strokes that quickly carried the boat away from the rocks where Thune was standing. Her neatly shaped calves made him think of the humid summer days in the office before the holiday, and he suddenly realised that he missed Mrs Wiik a little.

"Thank you for the sandwich," he called. But he was not sure if she heard him.

Thune stayed at Söderskär for five days, until Saturday, 6 August. He would have liked to stay longer, because the heat and stagnant air showed no sign of ending. It was as if time were standing quite still, and he liked that feeling.

But he could not stay. Because off to the north-west where the sun went down, there was the city. Out of sight beyond inlets and islands and skerries, but there nonetheless. Nagging. Demanding. There, at one corner of Kaserntorget, lay the building on whose top floor a moderately successful law firm was based, and Thune and Mrs Wiik would be opening that law firm to its clients once again on Monday morning. In just a month's time the talented Rolle would enter the firm's service again, equipped with a legal doctorate from Sweden and armed with new skills to put at the disposal of the firm's clients. And out in the suburb of Munksnäs an apartment was waiting to be sorted out and inhabited, and in Thune's bag was the outline of an article on foreign affairs, an outline which Thune – without a trace of modesty – found both simple and ingenious.

It was time to carry on the struggle.

Time to change from carefree grasshopper to industrious ant once more.

Time to let the autumn come.

On the last evening Thune and Arelius sat on the southernmost point of the island and talked.

Thune was drinking beer: he had finally plucked up the courage to beg a few bottles from lighthouse-man Huhta's store. Arelius feigned disinterest when Thune offered him the bottle each time he took a swig. Arelius had some rainwater in a water-bottle, and to start with he performed sit-ups and other exercises as they talked. But in the end, once he had lectured Thune and found his own words profoundly moving, he fell into line and took deep, thirsty gulps each time Thune offered him the beer bottle.

They ended up talking about politics, in such a way that Arelius got angry.

It all started with Thune's article, so long dreamed of but as yet unwritten. Thune knew what Arelius thought, and he was both too diplomatic by nature and too cunning to go into the details of his idea. He was even more cautious when it came to the liberal – not to say left-wing – analysis he was considering. He knew that certain points of view and certain politicians were like red rags to Arelius, and he did not want to annoy his friend unnecessarily.

Because Thune had begun to worry about Arelius' mental health.

Now almost forty-two years old, Zorro was on his way to becoming a prime example of a man defying his biological age. The sea air, lack of alcohol, strict diet and hard exercise were making him more sinuous and muscular with each passing day: his biceps and calf muscles looked like bundles of wire beneath his suntanned skin.

But the isolation, exercise and strict diet seemed to be having a very different effect on Arelius' mind.

Afterwards Thune would have difficulty remembering at what point Arelius became so angry. It might have been his remark suggesting that neither Blum's Popular Front government nor the Weimar Republic had been given the chances they deserved: in Thune's opinion, the chaotic situation in Europe had made sensible reforming policies impossible at the very moment when there was actually a desire for them.

"You incorrigible democrat!" Arelius snarled. "Let's be honest with each other, Claes. People who get posts in the diplomatic service are usually reckoned among the best in the country. But I can no longer see why. You've worked in two of our embassies, but you have absolutely no understanding of either politics or history. Not Finland's, and not Europe's. No understanding at all!"

"That's putting it a bit strongly," Thune said gently. "I . . ."

"You're defending Weimar!" Arelius interrupted. "Weimar was a cancer on the history of Germany! Thank God it's gone now, and thank God it didn't have time to spread. Berlin in those days . . . Don't you remember? It must have been the most depraved city since Gomorrah! It's not that I want to defend Hitler – he says a lot of foolish things. But he was right when he said that Berlin was the capital of cultural Bolshevism and racial mixing. And the economic policies, Brüning and those other cretins! There's no water in the taps, and what do their leaders do? Tighten the taps still further while simultaneously encouraging their citizens to drink!"

He paused for breath, as the veins stood out like crooked rivers on his suntanned temples, and before Thune managed to say anything he concluded:

"Idiots, the lot of them! But then Hitler came along and saved the German economy several times over, you can't deny that."

"Please, Zorro," Thune said. "Your analysis is one-sided. Forgive me, but I hesitate even to call it an analysis. On one side you see nothing but failings, and on the other nothing but virtues. Isn't that a little . . . emotional? How can you have fallen so completely for the coarse rhetoric of a charismatic politician?"

Thune had sat down on a rock, and as he spoke he looked up at Arelius. Arelius was standing upright, making tiny movements the whole time, as if he did not have the patience to listen. As soon as Thune fell silent he took over:

"You liberals don't see that the struggle has already started. You stand there like donkeys in no-man's-land, trying to look in every direction at once, and your gaze is so blurred that all you see are haystacks of slightly different sizes and shades. Maybe a little more evil here, a little more goodness there, but it's all just grey to you. But other people see much more clearly, Claes! The new war started a long time ago. It's only the final battle that's starting now, don't think otherwise."

The war to end all wars . . . Thune thought, and opened his mouth to disagree. But Arelius went on:

"No sentimentality, no protracted agonising! When we feel scared, we need to put our foot down and make the engine roar; when we feel doubt, we thrust it aside with a forceful swerve. That's how we shall find the force to defend all that is holy!"

Thune was struck by a thought that had never occurred to him before: that volubility and vehemence were in some strange way two sides of the same coin, that they were like siblings. And that as a result irony and self-awareness were among humanity's most important weapons. A sort of antidote that wise people could use when more emotional souls got caught up in unsustainable arguments about dirt and purity.

Always this same dream of purity.

Suddenly he remembered.

One summer in the early '20s.

Berlin. Working as a trainee for the firm of Kirella, Reichenberg & Töttges, the whore in the bar on Friedrichstrasse. He had been brilliant that day, dominating the whole office with his sharp wit and inventive solutions to a variety of different problems. He had been praised by the most senior boss, Dr Töttges, in front of the rest of the firm's staff. Dr Töttges had said that Thune not only had a good legal mind, but also possessed a good deal of wisdom for one so young. When Thune left the office at eight o'clock that evening he had felt so happy and full of life that he had almost been shaking. He had felt invincible. But at the same time he was on his own, all alone in the stifling August heat of a big city. How many minutes had passed since he had found the paragraph that would almost certainly bring victory to engineer Schorrle, and Kirella, Reichenberg & Töttges, in the engineer's inheritance case, when Dr Töttges had put his arm round Thune's shoulders and held him up as an example to the other young lawyers, to the moment when he helplessly shot his seed in the fat prostitute's relentlessly sucking mouth?

A hour at most, possibly just thirty minutes. The journey from the loftiest heights, from the fruits of years of hard work, to a moment of utter bestiality took no longer than that. And what reason did he have to believe that other men – or women, for that matter – were any different from him, deep down?

"You're not even listening!" he suddenly heard Arelius complain. "Christ, I don't want to stand here making speeches to myself!"

So at least you realise that you're making speeches, Thune thought sharply. But he suppressed the witticism and said instead:

"Sorry, I didn't mean to. I just lost my concentration. What were you saying?"

"Only that no age is as unique as it would like to think. The times may always be new, but they also borrow features from former eras."

Arelius gestured towards Bastulandet and went on:

220

"State-employed pilots have pushed their boats out from shore here since the time of Gustav Vasa. *Swedish* pilots. Tradition and continuity. Surely you must understand that those are important values?"

Manliness, mettle and muscular men, Thune thought sarcastically, remembering the patriotic Swedish song. But he stayed silent, because there had been a beseeching tone to Arelius' voice, and Thune really did not want to upset his host again.

He was still trying to think of something suitable to say when Arelius took a few steps towards the very edge of the skerry, pointed south-east across the Bay of Finland, and said:

"That's where they'll come from. When it's time."

"Who?" Thune asked wearily: he knew the answer, of course.

"The Vandals," Arelius said. "Stalin's terrible, discordant orchestra."

17

Last time they had suffered a seasonal quirk of the weather, an autumn day that had gone astray in the middle of a heatwave in early July.

It had been almost two months since then, and according to the calendar it was now autumn. But the quirks continued: it was hot enough to be summer, and it had not rained for weeks. As they walked down the woodland path leading to the shore there was a dry smell of pine needles and heather and herbs, and Matilda felt she was about to break into a sweat even though she was wearing a thin summer skirt and a short-sleeved chequered blouse.

The Captain walked ahead of her, dressed in a white shirt and navy blue trousers. He had canvas shoes on his feet, as if to underline how sporty and informal their meeting was. He was carrying his jacket nonchalantly slung over his shoulder, his shirt-sleeves were rolled up and he was bare-headed, just like Matilda. He looked healthy after the summer, he had a suntan and his stride was nimble.

A short while ago, when they turned off onto the woodland path and he felt sure that no-one could hear them, he had said he had thought about her every day during the summer, wondering how she was and what she was doing.

Matilda did not believe him.

*

The Captain had presented the idea of a walk and lunch by the sea back in the spring, but she had refused at the time. He had suggested Westend, but now that it was happening they had ended up in Munksnäs.

They had driven out in his car and parked it close to the Golf Casino, and then walked along the shore. The path was well maintained, beautiful, and the sandy beach that opened up at the end of the path was magnificent, with its diving platforms and jetties and its confusion of changing rooms up at the edge of the woods.

When they walked out onto one of the jetties and each put a hand in the water, it still felt warm enough to swim in. A few weeks earlier there must have been crowds of people there, the air full of children shouting and boys laughing loudly, their voices on the brink of breaking, and office workers like Matilda would have sat on blankets drinking coffee and lemonade and eating Marie biscuits and gossiping about film stars and friends who were not present. But now the schools had started again and everyone was back working hard in their offices: there was no-one on the beach but the Captain and her.

It was Tuesday, a little before one o'clock, and Matilda had asked for some time off between twelve and three: she had a lot of work to do that day, and had promised to stay in the office until eight o'clock to make up for it. Thune had nodded his consent, but lawyer Hansell – who happened to be seeing Thune at the time – had pursed his lips.

She had told Thune she was going to have lunch with Fanny, and then she and Fanny would be going to Tempo to buy a new bedspread and some household accoutrements for Fanny and Reinhard's elderly mother.

In a way everything was easier now that Thune had met Fanny

223

and Konni and Tuulikki and seen with his own eyes that Matilda actually had a life outside the office. The fact that his meeting with Konni had ended the way it had was unfortunate, but all the evidence suggested that Thune had drawn a line under that evening at the Mikado: he had not said so much as a word about it after the holiday.

Lying had its risks, of course. Only when Matilda had left the office and was on her way down to the harbour where the Captain would be waiting in his car did it occur to her that Fanny might try to call her at work, which would ruin her alibi. But on the other hand, Fanny had never called her at work. And neither Thune nor Hansell usually answered the telephone when Matilda was out, so the risk was extremely small.

The first month after the summer break had been full of work. The holiday and house-move had worked wonders on Thune, who returned to the office cheerful and full of energy, almost like a new person. Matilda had also felt rejuvenated. She had used her weeks off to read and listen to the radio, and go to the cinema, sometimes with Fanny but most often on her own. She had spent a few days with Tuulikki and the children in Konni's little house on the outskirts of Åbo, and Konni had come by train from Helsinki one day when the Mikado was closed. The remainder of the time Matilda had stayed at home.

At the end of August Thune's nephew, Rolf-Åke Hansell, had started work for the firm. There was a lot of fuss about lawyer Hansell and his position in the business at the start. Thune had the Cabinet refurnished for his nephew. He had the ox-blood armchairs removed – to Matilda's relief, because she did not like the colour, and did not like leather – and ordered a new desk for Hansell. A locksmith had cut extra keys, and the janitor had set up brass signs bearing the new name of the firm, both downstairs on the front of the building and on their door.

Thune & Hansell Legal Services. It sounded powerful, it sounded solid. But unfortunately lawyer Hansell and Matilda did not get on very well. Hansell had a patronising attitude towards his office assistant, and addressed her abruptly in a commanding tone of voice. And Matilda responded by becoming more and more taciturn with each passing day.

After a few weeks she had begun to wonder if her boss could really not have noticed the frosty silence that had settled over the office. Hansell was no ordinary employee, he was a junior partner in the firm. But Thune was still the one in charge, he had made that clear to Matilda the week before Hansell arrived. But Thune was so focused on his own affairs, partly his clients and partly an article he was writing – it was for *Svenska Pressen*, and was about "the European situation", he said when Matilda ventured to enquire – that he was practically deaf and blind to the world around him. Matilda missed their open conversations from the spring and early summer. But at the same time she felt relieved. Because the more they talked, the greater the risk that Thune would find out things she would rather he did not know.

Lunch went by the wayside, the café was as deserted as the rest of the beach. The Captain suggested that they walk across the bridges to Tarvaspää and look at the house where the painter Gallen-Kallela had his Helsinki studio. Then they could walk back and have a warm sandwich or a bowl of soup at the Casino. Matilda looked at her watch and replied that they might as well do that.

When they were walking back past the beach again, she decided to let her hair down. It was warmer and sweatier that way, but she had tied it up badly and several curls and strands of hair had already worked their way loose. She stopped on the sand, close to the water, removed her hairclips, put them in her handbag and then shook her head so her hair would hang correctly.

On the woodland path, when the Captain was walking just behind her, without any warning he reached out his hand and stroked her hair. He did it quickly and surreptitiously, but she still shivered and stopped in the middle of the path and looked at him.

Said nothing, just looked.

Immediately before it happened the Captain had been talking for a long time about the Sudetenland, about which there had been a lot of articles in the papers. He had sounded very engaged, but Matilda was not interested in grand politics and had not listened particularly carefully. Afterwards it would dawn on her that she had never really understood if the Captain was on the side of the Czechs or the Sudeten Germans.

Then, suddenly: his hand running through her hair. Impulsively, tenderly.

But also hungrily. She could sense that – it was in his touch.

She had felt proud at how well she had learned to suppress the waves of fear and disgust that welled up inside her when he came too close. She was used to hiding from other people, and she was sure he had never noticed anything, not at the Mississippi, nor at the English Tea-Room: even when he had put his hand on hers she had recovered quickly, smiled at him and left her hand there for a long while.

But this time she could not do it, the touch came so unexpectedly that her mask slipped.

Yet the caress was not unpleasant in and of itself.

But it was him. Him. And, on top of everything else, he had no idea who she was.

Touching her, running his hand through her hair. But he did not know, did not remember.

And the fact that he just happened to be the first person, the first man to touch her in . . . how long had it been?

Seven years, perhaps a little longer.

*

226

There was no hurried lunch at the Casino.

She neither wanted it nor felt capable of it. Not anymore.

When she had torn herself away from that first moment when she was just standing there on the woodland path staring at him, when they had emerged from the trees and were walking along the bright, neat beach promenade again, naturally she attempted to give an explanation.

Even though the Captain was really the one who should have explained his actions. But that did not occur to her until after they had parted.

She said that sadly she was unable to stay as long as they had planned, so they would have to skip lunch and drive back to the city, because she had more work to do at the office than she had anticipated when they had agreed to meet.

Of course the Captain did not believe her.

She saw the surprise and shame in his face and knew that he had realised it was because he had run his hand through her hair. Simply because of that.

In his bewildered expression was a hint of irritation, even rage.

Perhaps the thought: what happened? All I did was stroke her hair, carefully and gently, and this is the third time we've been out together. She must surely have realised, must have understood that I am a man and that we are here because I have . . . interests.

Yes. What she could see in the Captain's eyes was: what sort of woman *is* this?

A question that no doubt aroused a degree of alarm. But perhaps it also contained a certain challenge. An enticement, a temptation.

Possibly even the thought: an office drudge who imagines she actually has some honour to defend.

*

He accepted her explanation without objection, however. He apologised if he had behaved inappropriately: it had not been his intention either to frighten her or to insult her honour. He said he thought he had detected a sign from the god of favourable moments, and had been seized by tenderness and carried away by the moment, that was all.

Then he drove her back.

During the drive to the city they remained mostly silent, but as they were driving along Åbovägen and approaching the exhibition hall and sugar factory, he asked if he could see her again.

In spite of his solecism.

Those were his exact words. "*In spite of my solecism today.*"

That was how they expressed themselves, men like the Captain and Thune.

They used words that forced ordinary people to spend time working out what they had said, and thereby gained – or assumed themselves to have gained – the upper hand.

What they did not know, or perhaps knew but did not care, was that ordinary people laughed at them behind their backs.

She did not answer his question. They drove on in silence, until she asked him not to drive down Henriksgatan but take a detour via the western harbour. She asked to be let out at Sandvikens torg: she wanted to walk through Sinebrychoff Park and Rödbergen and buy a pasty or pie from a bakery on the way. She was not really hungry, she just wanted to be left alone to think for a while.

As she got out of the car the Captain repeated his question. This time it was not as humble, more a combination of a desire and an order.

"Let me see you again. I want to make it up to you. I shall behave like a gentleman, I promise. Tell me you'll see me again."

"I don't know," she replied.

She was pleased her telephone number had not had time to

228

appear in the annual telephone directory. She was certain that he would have started calling her at home by now if it had.

"Could I possibly have your number?" he asked, as if he could read her mind. "Not to the office – I have that, of course. Your home number. You mentioned that you now have a telephone."

"No," she said. "I'm not giving you my number. I'm sure you can find it out, but I'm asking you not to."

And that was that.

But she knew: if the Captain really did want to see her again, she would receive another letter at the office, folded into one of those small envelopes.

"You're back earlier than you said," Thune said in surprise as she was sitting down at her desk when he happened to look out from his office.

"Yes, Fanny and I were quick today," she replied.

Only when she went to the toilet half an hour later did she see that her loose hair was tousled and that there was a flake of pastry – she had bought a meat pasty from a bakery on Vävaregatan – stuck to the corner of her mouth.

Not good, but hardly a disaster. Hansell had already left for the day, and Thune was preoccupied – he had quickly withdrawn his head from the doorway, his door had closed and a short while later she heard the sound of his typewriter. He very rarely used the machine – that was Matilda's job – so she guessed he was working on his article.

After the caress her nights became harder again, and the insomnia returned.

She tried to think of films she had seen, films she was going to see, she tried to think of work she had to do at the office, she tried not to think of anything at all.

But nothing helped: her body remembered.

229

Everything was written on her skin, bubbling up inside her, making her muscles hard and taut.

The first night when he had forced himself upon her.

About a week, ten days, maybe, after she had been moved. New female prisoners arrived daily from the starvation camp, one delivery after the other. Even so, they still had a little more to eat in the new camp, salted herring and proper bread, even if it was mouldy. They had even been given some potatoes, which had also tasted mouldy, but that did not matter, they had at least been boiled.

The women in Matilda's barrack had been allowed to wash that evening, in lukewarm water that had been poured into large wooden containers at the edge of the camp. There had only been a few guards, young boys who were sufficiently well-mannered to look away while the prisoners were naked.

It would have been a lie to say that she felt alright. But it all depended on what you had to compare it with, and she felt less bad than she had done for a long time. She had slept without interruption for several hours during the previous few nights, and one morning her stomach had actually worked. She had to push horribly hard, it was solid as rock and only came halfway out, she had reach back into the latrine hole with her hand to help. But at least her stomach was less painful afterwards.

They had also been permitted to move into the smallest dormitory, Loviisa and Lea and her and five more from the starvation camp. The other women were jealous of them, and Lea, who never minced her words, told it like it was: compared to what they were used to, this was like living in a manor house and having a private bedchamber. There were four bunks fixed to the walls, and a decent amount of floor space. They took turns on the bunks, so that each of them only had to sleep on the floor every other night.

The night after they had eaten mouldy potatoes and herring and had been allowed to wash, Milja Matilda was sleeping in the bunk closest to the door. She woke up in the middle of the night, then lay and listened to the sound of the others breathing as they slept.

The barrack was at the edge of the forest, and it was a cloudy night: the room was dark even though it was only early July. Someone let out a snore, close but still some way away, because although the room was smaller than the others it was still fairly large. It had started to rain heavily, the drops beat against the window and as she listened she could hear it drumming against the roof tiles.

She lay there still, listening, and every now and then she thought she could hear the sound of more rapid, restless breathing among the sleeping prisoners. Perhaps it was Lea. Lea was in her sixth or seventh month and was beginning to have trouble sleeping, the child inside her was kicking and pressing on her bladder, meaning that she had to pee a lot.

Unless it was someone else, someone who was not a prisoner, someone who should not be there? Was that why she had woken with a start in the middle of the night?

Before she had time to decide whether or not to investigate her suspicion and sit up to look around the murkiness of the room, the hand was there. Hard and determined, over her mouth and face, while the other hand locked her hands as his arm pressed her body down on the bunk. As if that were not enough, his thigh was also pressing against her hip, to make absolutely certain that she was pinned down.

In the midst of her terror she could feel that his whole body was trembling as well.

He whispered in her ear: "Don't scream. Don't say anything. Then it will be easier for both of us."

That first time he whispered nothing more. He did not call her Miss Milja, nor anything else either.

The deep breathing coming from other parts of the room, the occasional snore, the rain and the wind outside. Otherwise

231

silence, almost no sound at all from him, he simply pulled back as much fabric as he needed to, fumbling and pulling. All the while with his hand tight across her face, but he had withdrawn his thigh from her hip and now held her legs between his as he searched. He was lying close behind her now, with his head by her shoulder-blades, slightly lower than he had been at first, and he was trembling even more now. Then he parted her buttocks and it was not long before she felt him, estimating and seeking, and he pushed in and it hurt, it hurt so much that she gasped. He was probably expecting her pain, because just at that moment he pressed his hand even more tightly to her mouth, then he let go enough for her to get some air, and he started to breathe more heavily now, first heavily and slowly, then heavily and fast as he moved inside her, until it was over. And even though he was so quiet, and even though she herself made no sound, all the while she knew that others could hear, not all of them of course, because she could still hear even breathing and little snores, but one or more of them: if no-one else, then certainly Lea.

She heard nothing but the slight rustle of clothing. He was probably pulling his trousers up, perhaps tucking his shirt in as well. Then he disappeared as silently as he had come. She lay awake until morning but afterwards had no memory of having wept, of having any feelings at all. In the morning she saw that her guess had been right, in Lea's and the other women's eyes she could see that they knew. But none of them said anything. And so it would remain. He came to her a handful of times that summer, perhaps six times, or seven, she lost count while it was going on, the odd thing was that he came specifically to her in a camp with more than a thousand women, that he had fixed on her even though the only occasion he had to remember her from was while the doctor was examining her, he had seen her at close quarters in daylight just one single time, that first afternoon when he had laughed at her, commenting on her nakedness and the way she looked, but not as roughly as the others, yet despite that he found her time and again even though it was getting close to the end of July and the nights were already black, she changed bunk almost every night but it didn't help, yet at the same time she couldn't be sure, perhaps he slept with other women on the nights when she was left alone and managed to sleep, perhaps it was only an illusion that he always came to her, she didn't know, all she knew was that he found her time and time again, and lay down behind her and clasped his hand tightly over her mouth, once he lay on top of her when she was lying on one of the thin mattresses on the floor, the mattress was stained and full of holes and the straw was sticking out of it, sharp as knives against her back, that time he closed his hands over her throat as if to reassure himself that she wouldn't make a sound, she looked at his face in the weak moonlight from the window, his eyes were clenched shut, his face turned away and hostile, and when the moment came he pressed her throat with such force that for a few moments she thought her time was up, that she was going to be suffocated, that she was finally going to die and that there was no-one in the whole world who could prevent it, she gasped desperately for air and none of the other prisoners did or said anything that time either, she used to think that if the others were awake, they were probably lying there hoping that the man in the room would never go to them.

In the weeks following the unsuccessful meeting with the Captain, Miss Milja came more often, and was more strident than ever before. Usually she stood or squatted behind the red armchair, or sat on the windowsill in the bedroom when Matilda had gone to bed, and looked at her with eyes black as coal. But she also came to the office a few times, and that had not happened before, not in that intrusive and surprising way: all of a sudden she was just there, aiming a torrent of raw and embarrassing words at Mrs Wiik as she sat respectable and defenceless behind her desk.

Most of what Miss Milja said was the sort of thing that Matilda was already used to hearing, and she steeled herself as best she could. But in the evenings and at night Miss Milja was merciless, saying things she had never said before, the most hair-raising things, suggesting that Hannes had not moved out and made a new life for himself far from Helsinki – emigrating to America or Sweden, Matilda usually fantasised – but that Matilda had killed him and then dumped his body in a marsh, unless she had actually dismembered him and thrown the pieces into the sea from the city's bridges? Yes, Miss Milja said, perhaps it was actually the case that some of the human bones that had been found in Tattarmossen belonged to Hannes, surely Matilda remembered that case, in autumn '31, wasn't it, the autumn after Hannes so conveniently disappeared? And how was it again: did Matilda have any sort of alibi for the summer's evening when she claimed that Hannes had packed his things and left without saying a word? People only did that in bad novels. And how come the police never cross-examined Matilda properly when that would seem to be the place they should have *started*, when a man disappeared without trace and then body parts were found at Tattarmossen only months later, body parts that could not be identified?

"Stop, please, stop it," Matilda whispered with tears in her eyes as she lay in bed trying to sleep, or sitting in her armchair trying to listen to that evening's popular music concert on the radio. The broadcasts from Lahti were finally free from interference, but now there was interference in her home instead, because Miss Milja was not the sort of person who stopped when you asked her to. It was merely grist to her mill, and she got more and more excitable, going on and on and inventing increasingly monstrous reasons as to why it simply *must* have been Matilda who killed Hannes. Take that business with Director Hoffman, for instance: if Mrs Wiik was capable of reacting so vehemently to a trifling transgression in the office, why wouldn't Matilda be capable of sticking the bread knife or the kitchen scissors into Hannes when he became difficult?

And it was not only the things that Miss Milja spat out. It was the way she looked these days: her hair messy and unkempt, her eyes wild and staring, and she had started biting her nails and cuticles again.

On one of the difficult evenings Fanny called, wanting to go to the cinema. She thought it was high time that Matilda saw "The Soldier's Bride", because everyone else had already seen it, and Fanny would be more than happy to see it again.

They met at Fazer's café on Glogatan the following evening. They drank coffee and each had a Tosca tart, surrounded by giggling schoolgirls and students from the *gymnasium* with loud voices.

"You look a bit tired," Fanny said sympathetically. "And you were so happy and relaxed after your holiday."

"I'm fine," Matilda said curtly. "I feel absolutely fine."

It was only two blocks to the Kino-Palats, but it was raining: they half ran, the wet tarmac was slippery and shiny, autumn had arrived at last.

She did not like the film. And it was not just that she missed Santeri Soihtu and thought the new star, Kalske, dull. She did not like films with soldiers and uniforms, at least not when the soldiers were at war. She much preferred romantic stories set in the past, the sort in which a low-born hussar or officer of the guard courted a princess or duke's daughter, someone he could never have, until the young couple ran away together and, at the end, before they kissed, had to evade the evil king's soldiers, who chased after them on frothing horses, firing and firing and firing but never hitting their target.

235

When the film was almost over Miss Milja asked in a whisper if Matilda had noticed that one of the *jaeger* officers resembled the young Captain so much that they could be twins.

Matilda had already noticed the resemblance, but when it was pointed out to her like that she began to feel sick. Not that she felt she was actually going to throw up, but her head was spinning and her stomach churning.

In the final scene the men cried out "*Long live a free and independent Finland!*", and then rode off into the chaos of the battlefield swinging their sabres as gunfire echoed around them. Matilda's nausea grew slightly worse, and without thinking she reached out her hand in the darkness and clasped Fanny's, squeezing it tight.

"Yes, isn't it majestic?" Fanny sighed in the darkness. "Reinhard hates this film, but I think it's wonderful."

Matilda was now squeezing Fanny's hand so hard that Fanny flinched:

"Ow, what are you doing? That hurts!"

Unaware of the force of her grip, in the flickering light of the screen Matilda saw from the corner of her eye that Fanny had turned her head to look at her, and that Fanny had realised that she did not think the film was at all wonderful, and that it was something else that had made her grasp hold of Fanny's hand.

"What is it, Tilda?" Fanny asked with amazement in her voice. "What's the matter with you?"

"Just hold my hand, Fanny. Just let me hold your hand for a little while."

Matilda's grasp was less clenched now, and Fanny left her hand there. But something had changed in Fanny. It was as if she were stiffer, more reserved, Matilda felt it quite clearly. When the film was over and the lights started to go up in the auditorium Fanny freed her hand and pulled it away. She did so quickly and firmly, and when they emerged onto the North Esplanade and headed towards the tram stop, she was nothing like her usual cheerful self: she was as quiet and evidently immersed in thought as Matilda.

18

During the eleven-year existence of the Wednesday Club the autumn season had always begun on the third Wednesday in September. The only exception was the autumn of '34, when Thune had been based in Stockholm and the Club's activities had been much curtailed. And once again this autumn the September meeting failed to take place. No-one had time: they each blamed the fact that there was so much to do with business or at their practice or office. It was as if all of them – apart from poor Joachim Jary, who had been admitted to hospital once again – were being forced to work harder and harder with each passing year. Perhaps it was middle age demanding its due, Thune thought, perhaps this was their last desperate blossoming, a few hectic years before they were forced to give up and admit that no matter how hard they exerted themselves, they simply could not keep pace with the youngsters anymore.

The first host of the autumn was Robi Lindemark. He took the decision to call the others and ask if the members were prepared to make an exception and agree that the first autumn meeting be held on the first rather than the third Wednesday in October.

Thune had been dreading the forthcoming meeting in

Lindemark's home. He knew he would be unable to help himself looking for signs of Gabi, and he knew he would find them. Mutual friends had told him that Gabi was still spending more time at Lindemark's – where, according to Thune's sources, she had both her own writing desk and wardrobe – than in the two-room apartment she rented on Albertsgatan.

When Lindemark called Thune to solicit his opinion on the start date for the Club's autumn season, he began by asking if Thune had acclimatised to life out in Munksnäs.

Thune had that very day admitted to himself that he was not at all happy there. The terraced house on Borgvägen was certainly picturesque, and each of the houses had its own garden at the back. But in spite of its two storeys it felt cramped, and the tram journeys into the city each morning and back again in the evening felt unbearably long. The trams were always full, and Thune could only imagine how they would smell when first the rain and then winter set in seriously: unwashed hair, wet woollen gloves, damp dogs.

So he replied to Lindemark by saying that he was very happy indeed, life in Munksnäs was peaceful and the air was clean, the change of environment could not have come at a better time, he really did not miss the pace of city life at all. Before Lindemark had a chance to comment on this, he went on to lament the fact that their friend Jary had suffered another relapse, Yogi's bouts of sickness really were occurring far too regularly these days. Only then did Thune go on a form of counterattack by asking if Lindemark's summer had been pleasant. Presumably they had spent all their free time out at the Fahlcrantz villa in Esbo, he and Gabi? How had that been? Was old Boris Fahlcrantz as misanthropic and reactionary as usual? The old bastard really did have remarkable staying power, didn't he? Lindemark parried elegantly by saying that no, they had only been out to the islands for a few weekends, and had instead undertaken a lengthy tour of Europe, he and Gabi, towards the end of the summer, because of course that's when the south of Europe is at its very best, as Claes would know better than anyone.

And Thune's fragility rose to the surface again. Afterwards he would curse what happened, but by then it was too late. Because precisely there and then, at that moment, he was not tough enough, and asked the question he should not have asked:

"Did you go to Lake Garda as well?"

"No," Lindemark replied in an artless voice, "we didn't have time. Why?"

The meeting at Villagatan was not as painful for Thune as he had feared.

He could certainly see evidence of Gabi, even though their host, Robi, had done his best to hide it. Robi had locked the door to the bedroom, and none of the cupboard doors was open, but the door to the combined library and study was. On the smaller desk over in the corner stood Gabi's Underwood typewriter in its case, and in the bookcase Thune counted no fewer than four copies of *The Silk Cushion*.

Late that evening Thune went into the library on his own and sat down at the desk with the Underwood typewriter and smoked a cigarette. He imagined he could detect a slight fragrance, a trace of Gabi that was lingering in the room, just as he had imagined he could detect a scent of the absent Miss Segersven in the Russian Villa on Söderskär. This time the trace was different, a mixture of Chanel No. 5, dry autumn leaves and the Twenty Gold cigarettes Gabi smoked. Thune was tempted to take the four copies of *The Silk Cushion* down from the shelf to see which one she had dedicated to Robi. But for his own peace of mind he refrained, and instead stubbed out his cigarette and went back to the others.

*

It was the evening of October 5, and Hitler had marched into Bohemia and seized the Sudetenland, to the dismay of the Czechs and jubilation of the Sudeten Germans.

The Wednesday Club discussed the Munich Conference. Robi Lindemark was naturally disappointed and called Chamberlain and Daladier naïve fools who had given up the last chance of a balance of power in central Europe, whereas Zorro Arelius seemed relatively pleased. Guido Röman sided tentatively with Lindemark, but did so in his usual vague way. Polle Grönroos made his customary contribution, and declared that the world's stock markets would react positively to the Munich Agreement.

And one chair stood empty, as it had done so often in recent years: Yogi Jary's.

The atmosphere was subdued. All of them, including old adversaries Arelius and Lindemark, presented their opinions calmly and reasonably, and there was a general willingness to listen to opposing points of view. It was, Thune thought, as if they had all realised that war – real, large-scale war – had come a step closer, and was now so close that they could hear its rumble.

The only provocative remark made that evening was a tired attempt by Robi Lindemark. He had read about sexual pathology in a psychiatric journal, and in the article, Lindemark claimed, it said that a number of girls in the Bund Deutscher Mädel had brought themselves to ecstasy by standing at attention, fully dressed, and performing the Nazi salute and shouting "Heil Hitler!" until they reached orgasm. But Arelius and Grönroos merely smiled wryly and told Lindemark that he should stop being silly and instead ask the help to fetch more drinks.

Something was nagging at Thune, something that had nothing to do with the anxieties and warnings of contemporary events.

For the first time – although he knew deep down that he had come close to similar thoughts back in the spring, but had suppressed them – it occurred to him that the Wednesday Club had served its purpose and that it would probably be best to let it die.

As the meeting began to wind down, Lindemark took Thune aside and asked if he had time for a short chat. They went into the library, and there Lindemark asked:

"I presume you have a copy of *The Silk Cushion*?"

"I bought it from the Academic Bookshop the day it was published," Thune replied coolly.

Lindemark cleared his throat and looked as if he were going to say something more, but dropped the subject.

"That was a good article in *Svenska Pressen*. Concise and well argued. But I was surprised by your longing for pan-Europeanism. I'm afraid the time for that might have passed, sadly. Have Zorro, Polle or Guido said anything?"

"To be honest, I don't think Zorro or Polle have read it," Thune said. "I daresay I'd have been hauled up for it this evening if they had. And Guido . . . no, he hasn't said anything either. But his head is probably full of football scores and boxing matches, as usual."

"You're probably right on all counts." Lindemark smiled. "That was actually why I didn't want to congratulate you out there. I'd rather not take any risks. One doesn't want to sow discord when one is the host. Next time that will be your responsibility. And may we hope that it will be in your new home?"

Thune felt unsettled by the question, but hoped it did not show on his face.

"Of course," he replied, but realised that he had failed to convey any enthusiasm.

They were standing next to the bookcase containing the multiple copies of *The Silk Cushion*, and the atmosphere was awkward. Thune noticed Lindemark shifting his weight from one foot to the other. Evidently Robi had not said all he wanted to say.

"Was there anything else?" Thune asked.

"Well, you see . . ." Lindemark began hesitantly, then plucked up courage and said: "Well, I was wondering if you'd like to come out to Kopparbäck one day, have lunch and . . ."

"Really?" Thune interrupted. "And what would we be celebrating?"

Lindemark looked both disappointed and embarrassed.

"That was exactly how I hoped you *wouldn't* take it."

And before Thune had time to respond, he went on:

"It's not the lunch that's important this time, Claes. Yogi Jary has been asking after you. I just thought that offering you lunch was the least I could do, if I was going to ask you to come out and help."

"Yogi's been asking after me?" Thune repeated thoughtfully. "And in what way would you like me to help?"

"Yogi isn't at all well, Claes," Lindemark said seriously. "He's suffering from extreme depression, and, to be honest, I don't know what to do. You're the person he trusts most, you always have been. He would probably feel a little calmer simply from seeing you. Will you come?"

"I don't know," Thune said. "I'm too tired to make a decision now. And I'll have to consult my diary together with Rolle and Mrs Wiik. Call me in a few days."

In truth, Thune was feeling more downhearted with each passing day. And his dejection had many causes.

He missed the crowds of people on Stora Robertsgatan and Fredriksgatan, and on Högbergsgatan when families would go for their weekend walk to church or down to the sea on Sundays. Out in the suburbs the streets were empty and silent in the evenings, there were not even many people about on Stora

Allén, just tarmac shimmering in the rain, and discoloured fallen leaves that stuck to the surface of the road like liver spots on ageing skin.

Occasionally a tram would rattle by, and the greasy faces inside would stare out at the autumn darkness. That was all, the only sign of life.

Thune longed for Mrs Leimu's home cooking and her little surprises – the blackcurrant juice and glass jars of dried mushrooms that she would often have with her after visiting her sister. The fact that Thune had never actually dared taste Mrs Leimu's creamy mushroom sauces was another matter: he had been worried that there were pieces of fly agaric among the chanterelles and boletus and saffron milkcap, and feared death by poisoning. But he missed Mrs Leimu nonetheless. His new home help, Miss Gunvor Johansson, made his home miserable. Miss Johansson was difficult and taciturn. She may have been a Swedish-speaker, and relatively young, but that did not compensate for her sour demeanour.

Thune's article in *Svenska Pressen* had been well received. There had been letters from readers, and colleagues and old friends had stopped him on the street to congratulate him.

But he had also met resistance, and the attacks on him were brutal and came from many different directions.

Someone had evidently informed Zorro Arelius of the existence of the article, because two days after the Club meeting at Lindemark's Thune received a postcard from Arelius. It was a photograph of a raging waterfall, and on the back were two sentences: *Among my misguided friends, you are the most deluded. But when I go off to war I shall be doing so for you as well.* Tuus, *Lorens.*

Arelius' message was only the start. A few days later *Hufvudstadsbladet* published an unaccredited leader column which was a veiled polemic against Thune. Behind the customary caveats its message was clear: when constrained by legislation and in the right doses nationalism was a force for good, and any excessive criticism of it weakened Finland's internal integrity and willingness to defend itself, and only served to strengthen the hands of Stalin, the Comintern and other evil forces.

The writer of the column in *Hufvudstadsbladet* had taken exception to Thune's concluding aphorism, which he had spent a long time polishing and himself thought rather elegant: *Nationalism and tribal thinking are tenacious sicknesses. They are best treated with reading and travel.*

Someone writing under the name Timo in *Uusi Suomi* a few days later also drew attention to the same sentences, and condemned them as unpatriotic. In other respects, too, Timo's analysis resembled that of *Hufvudstadsbladet*.

Thune was a well-meaning humanist, but sadly, Timo wrote, he was gullible in his analysis of contemporary Europe. As a result, Thune had hawked about ideas that he would doubtless have shied away from had he simply thought a bit more before composing his article. He also suffered – and this Timo found remarkable given that Thune had worked in two of the country's most important embassies – from the classic hubris of the carefree intellectual, as well as *Besserwisserei*: when a writer knew that his opinions and proposals would never be tested against the harsh realities of the world, he could speculate and shoot from the hip as much as he liked.

The day after Timo's response was published Lindemark called to find out whether or not Thune was going to go out to Kopparbäck to visit Jary. Thune said he would, they agreed a date the following week, and Lindemark concluded the conversation by asking how Thune was dealing with the criticism.

"It has to be good that people are talking," Thune said curtly. "At least that's better than nobody saying anything."

"True enough," Lindemark said. "But you probably don't want to read what the blackshirts are writing about you in *Ajan Suunta*. The Interior Minister really has got to legislate against them soon, they keep crossing the boundary of acceptability."

"Now that you've said that much, you have to tell me the rest," Thune said, trying to keep his voice as calm as he could. "What have they said?"

"The usual, but in slightly coarser terms this time," Lindemark said. "That you're a decadent cosmopolitan who's betraying his country. And they imply that you have impure blood."

"That I'm Jewish, you mean," Thune said.

"Yes. Or rather, as they put it, rumour has it that you have a degree of Semitic ancestry."

One gnawing cause of Thune's discontent was his newly arrived business partner, his nephew Dr Rolf-Åke Hansell.

It was nothing to do with his work. On that point Rolle had exceeded Thune's already high expectations.

Rolle had already managed to handle one complicated court case in a quite brilliant way. Thune & Hansell's client had practically been cleared, merely receiving a fine for a crime for which the maximum penalty was four years' imprisonment.

And the clients Rolle had taken over were full of admiration and confidence in the new star.

One of those clients was Leopold Grönroos. Grönroos was so delighted with Rolle that he had offered an injection of fresh capital to help Thune and Rolle make the firm stronger and better. Grönroos had told Thune that great talents needed to be supported, and Rolf-Åke Hansell was just such a talent.

Thune had felt tempted to take Grönroos up on his offer. He wanted to extract some profit from the company and be in a position to pay off both his bank loan and the money he had borrowed from his mother Esther, as she kept reminding him with painful regularity.

Rolle and Polle. Perhaps that was the future, Thune thought. He felt tired, but also hopeful. If Polle and Rolle stood for the

246

investment and legal glories, maybe old Claes could withdraw into the background, harvesting money from the company and spending all his time writing daring articles, which the country's foreign policy establishment and leading newspaper columnists would in turn have to spend time and energy engaging with and refuting.

Unfortunately there was a fly in the ointment.

Thune had always regarded Rolle Hansell as encouraging proof that the apple could indeed fall a long way from the tree, and that children are not bound by their parents' limitations, and not doomed to repeat their forebears' mistakes. One important component of this – and it was not easy for Thune to admit that this was the case, but in moments of self-criticism he did so – was of course that young Hansell admired his modern, free-thinking uncle.

Rolle had done so as recently as that spring, when he and Thune had eaten lunch together at the Continental in Stockholm.

But no longer.

Rolle's attitude towards Thune had changed. There was now a roughness, a barely perceptible resistance which meant that they disagreed about most things. In a civilised way, naturally, because they were both at least partly descended from the same restrained and taciturn Thunes and Hjorths – Thune's mother and Rolle's grandmother Esther was born a Hjorth – but Thune could still tell that their lack of unity ran deep. And as the weeks passed and one quarrel followed the other, this resistance was becoming increasingly mutual: to his surprise, Thune found himself actively disliking the nephew of whom he had been so fond. But he tried to resolve the conflict by backing away as much as he could, while again and again Rolle went on the attack against his uncle's attitudes and opinions.

They had spent all of September quarrelling about Hitler's demand for the Sudetenland. During their rows Rolle pointed out that the Germans needed *Lebensraum* for their language and culture: they were the people of Goethe, Schiller and Beethoven, a people who had now taken on the task of cleaning out the stinking Augean stable of the Weimar Republic, and then standing as a bulwark against Marxist barbarism. Rolle returned to this time and again, until the double image of the Augean stable and the bulwark became a constant refrain.

When Thune expressed his alarm at a speech in which Hermann Göring called the Czechs a race of pygmies and a shameful stain on Europe, Rolle retorted that Göring may have been guilty of indiscretion, but that had to be seen in the light of the ongoing conflict and was therefore forgivable. Besides, it was a cowardly flight from reality to claim that all races were of equal value, Rolle said, adding that sadly most people were terribly feeble: even a great poet like Schiller had fallen into the treacherous trap of moral nihilism and proclaimed that all people would one day become brothers. The truth, of course, was that the greater, more developed cultures were more profound and had higher absolute value that those that were less developed, and without the help of the greater cultures the more primitive and sadly often ungrateful parts of humanity would have no chance at all of raising themselves to further stages of development. Great cultures, Rolle declared, carried the rest of humanity like the Titan Atlas carried the entire heavens on his shoulders, and anyone who chose not to see that was both blind and stupid.

Rolle was full to bursting with impressions from the trip he had made with his Elin.

He and Elin had talked to Germans the same age as themselves, who loved their *Arbeitsdienst* and sang songs as they marched along the road with their shovels on their shoulders. On the beaches along the Baltic coast Rolle and Elin had seen young people engaging in naked gymnastics in the open air. They had liked the naturists' striving for bodily health, and had admired the joy and simple beauty of their games. Even so, Rolle remained ambivalent about what he had seen, because other Germans had revealed to him that nudism was one of the Marxists' secret weapons: the Bolsheviks were habitually infiltrating *Freikörperkultur* associations, and then conducting their machinations while they pretended to enjoy the gymnastics and sunshine.

Rolle had asked direct questions of the young Germans he had met. And the Germans had replied just as openly: no, the new Germany and its young people did not want war, and nor did their Führer. The only thing the new Germany wanted, according to Rolle, was to be allowed to become more prosperous and to nurture its own culture in peace and freedom. And Rolle had certainly not minced his words: he had also asked about the Jewish laws and work camps and all the rest. One young man whom Rolle and Elin had particularly liked – "Gunnar cut his bread and sausage into three equal parts, and shared everything with us like a brother would share what he had with his siblings," Rolle said, his emotion evident in his face as he said this – had answered their questions in a quiet, almost humble way: surely it was obvious that a nation which had set ambitious goals needed healthy human capital, and of course the strongest and best survive in nature, so why should it be any different for civilisation?

During the first weeks of September Thune sometimes engaged in verbal polemics with Rolle.

He did not want to sound arrogant or domineering, and therefore chose not to reveal to his nephew the ironic observations he made. He remembered a German youth movement which had been popular when he was young, *Wandervogel*, and its grand emblem had been a heron-like bird drawn in the art nouveau style. Thune thought that Rolle resembled the bird on the *Wandervogel* emblem when he puffed himself up and made speeches full of pathos about the grandeur of the old European cultures. Thune also suspected that there had been a deal of sexual energy in Rolle and Elin's delighted meetings with people of their own generation during their trip. Two young people in love, on a shared journey through a country where the young population imagined that it had risen like a phoenix – always these birds! – out of the grey ashes of the past. Rolle and his fiancée had no doubt been erotically attracted by the naked gymnastics they had witnessed on the beaches in the north, but Rolle's innate shame had obliged him to formulate an ideological objection to it based on a fear of Bolshevism and Marxism.

Thune said nothing of all this to Rolle. Instead he said, making a real effort to choose his words carefully, that life and travel and, above all, encounters with other people had taught him that even the most righteous and apparently wise slogans and calls to arms could conceal something else. This something else was at best simply an entirely understandable impatience and anger at the inadequacies of humanity and society. And impatience, Thune conceded, had served many good causes through the course of history, because the young often saw through the hypocrisy and decay in the world built up and guarded so jealously by their elders. But unfortunately there were also pent-up forces which, when expressed without restraint, constituted a threat to the peaceful coexistence of peoples. Sometimes these slogans contain an ecstatic longing for purity, a longing so abstract that its adherents could not explain what this pure life would contain, only what they wanted to be rid of. Or the slogans contained an equally strong longing for unequivocal, total victory, and both these types of longing had, in different ages and circumstances, misled people to abandon their democratic instincts and switch to hating and despising their neighbours.

But Rolle no longer wanted to listen to what Thune had to say. Rolle had become hostile and restless, Thune could not avoid noticing: when they sat opposite each other at the same table having a discussion, he could feel the floor vibrating from the movement of Rolle's foot tapping as his uncle spoke. On one occasion, one afternoon when Thune had been expounding on the authoritarian inheritance of Prussia, Rolle said, placing great emphasis on words he particularly loved and loathed:

"But the Germans really *believe* in their leader now. They feel *love*, Uncle, can't you understand how uplifting that is? I've had to listen to so many café philosophers in my time . . . sitting in Fazer's or Bronda's, *seeing through* all the people who believe in something. In what sense could that be better?"

In the end Thune gave up. He and Rolle spoke to each other less and less, and by the time September turned to October they were both sulking in their separate rooms. The door between the old Cabinet and Thune's office remained closed, and the two lawyers only addressed one another when they had to, for the sake of the firm and their clients.

Their differences of opinion on ideological matters were matched by all sorts of other things: everyday details, little nuances, modes of address.

Thune was now seeing a side of Rolle that he had never noticed in him before.

Rolle repeatedly ate up Thune's biscuits without showing the slightest sign of ever going to the Market Hall to replenish the stocks. Nor did Rolle ask Mrs Wiik to do so. He just ate them.

Rolle gave a mocking smile when, on a warm September day, Thune came to the office wearing a short-sleeved pullover and grey suede shoes. Thune's intention had been to dress youth-fully, in a sporty way, but Rolle pointed out that the tank top was several sizes too small, and that suede shoes were not a mascu-line invention.

Worst of all, in Thune's opinion, was the way Rolle treated the clever and patient Mrs Wiik: he was pompous, patronising, and occasionally downright hostile. Thune did not understand why Rolle behaved like that, there was no justifiable reason, the only explanation was that Rolle was the son of Thune's class-conscious sister Ulla and the royalist Sigurd Hansell, and that this was suddenly coming to light.

Sometimes when Thune saw Rolle behaving inconsiderately or snapping at Mrs Wiik he regretted his decision to take his nephew into the firm as a partner: if Rolle had been an ordinary employee Thune could have dismissed him on the spot.

There were times when Thune suddenly realised that he missed the conversations he and Mrs Wiik had had during the spring and summer more than he cared to admit. They were no longer alone in the office, and Rolle's aggressive presence precluded any confidentiality. Thune and Mrs Wiik's exchanges had hardly been *that* confidential, but Thune occasionally found himself missing their little chats.

He also had a sense that there was something unfinished between them. The holiday period had begun badly with Thune's unfortunate decision to accept Mrs Wiik's invitation to go to a dance. The badly behaved Konni had knocked him down, un-necessarily hard in Thune's opinion. He admitted to himself that he had not behaved in an entirely gentlemanly fashion towards Mrs Ahlbäck, but Konni's reaction was nonetheless a prime example of a defensive overreaction. And then Mrs Wiik had called Thune the following day, with anxiety in her voice, and with a self-assumed, multiple intent: to assure herself that Thune was not planning to report her brother to the police, to reassure herself that she would still have a job to go to after the holiday, and to make sure that Thune did not blame her for what had happened.

Which he had not done. He was perfectly aware of the fact that he was already far too fond of Mrs Wiik to be able to do that.

*

252

This was Thune's mood as he was sitting in his office late one evening when the call from Sergey Gerasimoff came.

Both Rolle and Mrs Wiik had gone home several hours earlier.

Thune felt his usual internal reluctance towards the long tram ride out to Munksnäs, where the dour Miss Johansson would once again serve food that had either been boiled to oblivion or fried to a crisp. He reflected sadly on the ox-blood red armchairs he had sold to Zorro Arelius, who had put them in the waiting room of his surgery: if the armchairs had still been there, Thune would have called home and given Miss Johansson the evening off, and spent the night sleeping in one of the chairs.

It was raining outside, a steady, dismal autumn rain. One window was open for ventilation, and the rear courtyard was so quiet that the light drumming of the raindrops on the roof was clearly audible. Shortly before the telephone burst into life he considered playing "Boléro", but decided against it.

Gerasimoff was surprised to find Thune at the office. He had called Borgvägen first, and when he got no answer there he had reasoned that it would do no harm to try him at work.

"You shouldn't be sitting there brooding," Gerasimoff said with forced sternness in his voice. "You need to get out more, Claes. You need to start meeting women again. It's time to stop thinking about Gabi now."

"Yes, yes," Thune said irritably. "What do you want, Gera?"

"I had a long lunch with Victor Hoffman at the Kämp yesterday," Gerasimoff said. "It was very pleasant, and we had time to talk about all manner of things. It was so pleasant that I dared broach the subject that you wanted to know about."

"What subject was that?" Thune asked vaguely.

"The one you mentioned when we were out at Zorro's in the summer," Gerasimoff said.

Then he related everything that the recently retired Director Victor Hoffman had revealed to him about the reason why

Mrs Wiik had ended her lengthy employment with Hoffman & Laurén.

"But Hoffman was very keen to point out that she had been entirely blameless until then," Gerasimoff concluded. "Extremely competent, and easy to work with."

When Thune hung up he went over to the large oak cupboard that stood in the darkest, dustiest corner of the room. He opened one of the doors, took out a bottle of whisky, fetched a glass from the pantry, poured himself a drink and then put "Boléro" on.

He remained at the office for another hour, playing "Boléro" through twice, listening to the music and taking a lot of small sips of whisky. Every now and then he sighed in resignation and thought:

As if I didn't already have enough unsolved problems and worries.

19

As October drew on it became increasingly clear to Matilda that the situation in the office was critical and that something was going to happen. She fantasised about various scenarios, but remained unsure of how things were going to develop.

The biggest argument between Thune and Hansell arose because of her. But she was also aware that it was wrong of her to think that way. The argument had come about as a result of Hansell's treatment of her, not because of her specifically.

It was in itself insignificant. She was typing out some letters and an appeal for Hansell, according to the timetable they had agreed and according to all pertinent rules. But her mind was on other things – she was thinking about Konni – and she accidentally put the documents on Thune's desk instead of Hansell's.

When the mistake came to light Hansell stormed out into the lobby and gave her a severe telling-off, shouting that not only was she miserable and boring, but also an incompetent and sloppy worker.

Thune got angry in a way that Matilda had not thought him capable of. He rushed out of his room and yelled at Hansell that that was quite enough, Mrs Wiik's mistake was insignificant and did not justify such an outrageous response, Hansell was behaving immaturely and Thune expected him to apologise to Mrs Wiik immediately.

"Like hell I will!" Hansell hissed, and marched back into his office so heavily that the heels of his shoes sounded like an officer's boots as they hit the floor.

Thune went after his nephew, and even though he closed the door behind him Matilda could hear every word as uncle and nephew continued their row.

Thune said in an uncharacteristically hard voice that the atmosphere in the office had to improve, and above all had to become more respectful, otherwise they would not be able to run the business together. And this was not merely a question of Hansell's attitude towards Mrs Wiik, Thune pointed out, but also of his constant questioning of everything Thune stood for.

Hansell asked bitterly if Thune really believed that the atmosphere would be improved by his taking his subordinate's part against his business partner. Thune replied that it was not a matter of who was subordinate or in a position of authority, but about common human decency, regardless of status. Hansell said that he and Thune clearly had differing opinions on that matter, as well as on a number of other issues concerning how to make the firm function in the best and most effective way.

Thune asked in measured tones if Hansell had any suggestions as to how their many problems and differences of opinion might be resolved. Hansell replied coldly that yes, he did, but as yet they were mostly formless impressions. But if his uncle would permit him to, Hansell was prepared to give the matter some consideration and come up with an entirely new strategy for the firm.

Thune said that it might be best if they could draw a line under what had happened first. He still thought that Hansell should apologise to Mrs Wiik, but apart from that it would be to everyone's advantage if they both calmed down, he and

Hansell alike. Once an appropriate amount of time had passed, they could have another discussion and see what positive lessons they could learn from what had happened: at that point Thune would be happy to listen to Hansell's thoughts about the firm's future strategy.

Later that afternoon, when Hansell had gone to the City Court to take care of some business, Matilda told Thune that there was no need for Hansell to apologise to her. The day's events had not hurt or upset her, she said, and she had had considerably sterner and more capricious superiors than Hansell, and that everything would improve once they had got used to each other.

Thune had already calmed down. But he made no attempt to defend his nephew, and shook his head and said:

"I simply don't understand what's happened to Rolle. He's Mr Hyde these days, in every sense. I've been extremely tolerant all autumn, but even I have my limits."

And that was what Matilda saw that afternoon: that even the placid Thune had his limits, and once they were crossed he felt obliged to object, no longer trying to mediate and negotiate peace at any cost.

Matilda felt a degree of pride.

Because she liked Thune, but had also been of the opinion that he was too soft. He had not made the slightest attempt to defend himself or exact revenge when Konni knocked him to the floor. He had not tried to get up and hit back, but had simply lain there moaning as blood poured from his nose. At that moment Matilda had thought that Thune lacked something, that he was not a real man.

She was pleased to see a more decisive side of him now. She could feel herself starting to like him again, properly like him, the way she had done when they used to talk of serious and not so serious things in the weeks preceding the evening at the Mikado.

When Matilda arrived at work the morning after the incident, lawyer Hansell's raincoat was already draped on its hanger in the lobby: he was early.

On her desk was a small bouquet of autumn flowers in a simple vase, and when she pulled out the card tucked inside the envelope leaning against the vase she read: *I regret and apologise for my unjust behaviour. Rolf-Åke Hansell.*

But when Hansell asked her to go to his room to take dictation later that morning he was as stern and uptight as ever. She understood that he had bought the flowers merely to placate his uncle and set the firm on an even keel again, not because he truly regretted his actions.

She was also beginning to suspect that Thune knew something.

Perhaps not knew, exactly, but had an inkling. It made little difference – what mattered was that she thought Thune was looking at her more often, and more thoughtfully than before.

Naturally he tried to do it surreptitiously. But he was a bad actor. She caught him out time after time as he was looking at her with – so she thought – a new, more studied gaze. He looked away quickly each time, but always a fraction of a second too late.

When Thune discussed work matters with her he seemed thoughtful and distracted. He no longer asked any personal questions, and the discord between him and Hansell meant that none of the three people in the office said more than was strictly necessary.

But once he asked her if Konni and Arizona were still playing at the Mikado. He used Konni's surname when he asked: "Your brother, Ahl . . . Ahlbäck?"

Matilda replied that Konni and Arizona now had an engagement at the Lepakko restaurant in the premises of the Hotel Metro.

But she did not tell him that this was a serious demotion, or that Konni could now barely afford to pay for his room in the Imatra hostel, or that she had lent him a considerable amount of money.

Nor did she tell him that Arizona had been forced to leave the Mikado because Konni had been in another fight.

One afternoon when she was taking dictation Thune suddenly said: "But Mrs Wiik, whatever's happened to your hands?"

She started, instinctively lowered her pen and notepad, glanced quickly at her right hand and saw her bitten fingernails and scabby cuticles.

"A new hand-cream . . . unfortunately I'm badly allergic," she mumbled, and felt the lie rise to her cheeks as a blush.

She pulled herself together and thought about Konni's voice – bitter and as taut as wire – when he told her on the telephone about his dismissal from the Mikado. She felt the blush begin to subside and her cheeks become cooler again: she hoped that Thune had not noticed anything.

Fortunately the business of her hands occurred on a Saturday.

Matilda went to the cinema three times that weekend, and kept herself in constant motion so that Miss Milja would stay away, or at least have the sense to stay quiet. On the Saturday evening she saw "The Riding Master of Ruhala" with Santeri Soihtu and Ansa Ikonen, on Sunday afternoon she saw a matinee screening of "Pépé le Moko" at the Adlon, and on Sunday evening Fanny had managed to get tickets to the premiere of a Tyrone Power film, to which Reinhard and Heikki also came.

It worked. Her cuticles stopped hurting on Sunday. On Monday morning they were no longer so swollen, and the scabs were small and dark.

On Monday evening she went to the Salon Roma straight after work. Mrs Tuomisto shook her head when she saw Matilda's hands, but set to work at once. This time Matilda chose a stronger, almost cherry red shade of polish.

She made a mental note that she must be more on her guard around Thune: he was probably not as unworldly and distracted as he sometimes appeared to be.

After the caress on the woodland path in Munksnäs and the abandoned lunchtime meeting, Matilda had received half a dozen letters from the Captain.

She had not replied to a single one.

She left him alone. Left him to worry.

As the weeks passed and the letters mounted up and she responded to them all with silence, she steeled herself against the possibility that he might call her at work.

If he did call her at the office she had her plan ready. When he tried to engage her in conversation she would quickly interrupt him and say, in such a loud voice that it would be heard in Thune's office: "You'll be wanting to talk to either Mr Thune or Mr Hansell!"

Thune was starting to get curious. And this game was also dangerous on a number of other levels. Even so, she did not want to hurry herself too much.

The most important thing was that the Captain had not changed his mind after her reaction out in the woods. And she liked the thought that he felt spurned by her. *Was* spurned by her.

The Captain was still eager. She would allow herself to be persuaded, all in good time.

She guessed that sooner or later he would succumb to the inevitable and ignore her entreaty, and would find out her home telephone number. It would not be difficult, one call to the Telephone Corporation would do.

Nonetheless, she was taken by surprise when he did call.

It was a rainy Monday evening and she was expecting it to be Fanny: they had agreed to talk on the telephone to discuss the cinema repertoire and which films they would go to see next.

The Captain identified himself with his name and professional title, and began to explain the reason for his call – "I'm so unhappy, you haven't replied to . . ." – before she brusquely interrupted him:

"You must have the wrong number."

"Mrs Wiik," the Captain persisted, "I beg you . . ."

"No," Matilda interrupted. "I don't want you to call me. Good evening."

Her first thought had been to ask Konni to help.

But she decided against that, for several reasons.

To begin with, she knew that Konni would start to worry, become protective, ask questions, get involved.

She had of course prepared an explanation. Several, in fact, but they were all based on the fact that a woman living on her own was so vulnerable.

After all, Matilda did actually live in a building where a woman had been murdered six years before. Matilda had a husband who had disappeared seven years ago and had never been heard of again: she had not changed the locks since then – she had never got round to it – and even if Hannes had been a kind and peaceful man, you could never be sure.

Life in Helsinki had got better and, as living standards rose, the number of knife fights and rapes had decreased. But Helsinki remained a raw and untamed city, a big port city in a country which had gone through a civil war just twenty years before, and where the men liked to drink. There was still more violent crime than in the country's Nordic neighbours or the continental countries to the south.

That was what she would say if anyone were to ask.

But that would not have worked with Konni. He knew her far too well, and he cared about her far too much.

And it was not only a question of what was best for her. This was also about Konni, and the fact that she wanted to spare her little brother any more worries.

Konni's latest outburst had had unhappy consequences. This time it was nothing to do with Tuulikki – she was in Åbo with the children. During one of their breaks Konni had got into an argument with one of the restaurant's guests, for no apparent reason. It had started as a light-hearted exchange of insults but quickly developed into something much coarser, until Konni once again lost control. Unfortunately his new victim was not as placid and forgiving as Thune, but a rich man's son named Herbert Balck. Balck had reported the assault to the police at once, and Arizona's contract with the Mikado had been terminated with immediate effect.

When Konni was fourteen years old one of the teachers at the children's home, Mrs Reincke, had discovered how musical he was. Because he was relatively old, and because he was also difficult and unruly, the manager of the home had contacted an acquaintance, a musical major in the Lifeguard battalion. The major had arranged an audition for Konni. At the time Konni only played the piano and a little guitar, but the officers of the Band Corps liked what they heard. One of them patted Konni on the shoulder and said he looked a bit scrawny, but that the mother country would feed him up and turn him into a real brass blower in time: from the age of fifteen Konni would receive board and lodging and musical training, and when he was ready he would start in the Corps.

All this happened during the winter after Matilda found him again.

She was only twenty then, and would never have found Konni without the help of some kind-hearted neighbours in the building on Flemingsgatan, where Zaida and Konni and Matilda had lived in a single draughty room in the years following Adolf's death.

The autumn when she found Konni she was still marked by her time in the camps, and took whatever work she could get – just then she was working in a soap factory – and could not even have dreamed of one day studying at business college. It was their former neighbours, particularly Jokela the tailor, who went to the authorities and made them provide information about Konni, not her.

Ever since then Matilda had been troubled by Konni's volatility. Back at the start she had met the manager of the children's home, Kilpinen, several times, and did not like him. She could not help worrying about what had happened to Konni in the three years during which she did not know where he was: he was eleven years old in May 1918, when the Whites came to Fleminggatan and took her away for questioning.

She had always suspected that the people working in the children's home had beaten and tormented Konni. Maybe they had – Konni was not the sort of person to talk about what he had been through – but that did not explain why Konni had become even more taciturn and moody during his years in the Music Corps.

Only as recently as July, when she spent a few days with Tuulikki and the children while Konni was in Helsinki playing at the Mikado, had she started to work out what had actually happened.

She could not be certain, because Tuulikki had not really said very much at all.

Nonetheless, Matilda had understood that she had probably been wrong all along, and that it was not about the children's home at all, or at least not to the extent she had thought.

She and Tuulikki had talked about that evening at the Mikado, and about Konni assaulting Thune.

Matilda had said that she found Konni's jealousy childish,

and that she did not understand why her brother always had to behave like a cockerel in a henhouse whenever he was in the company of both beautiful women and other men.

"You're wrong," Tuulikki had said, in a serious tone of voice that was unusual for her. "It isn't just jealousy. I think there are things we don't know."

"Like what?" Matilda had asked. She knew it was ridiculous, but she had still felt a little offended. She did not like the feeling that Tuulikki might know more about Konni, her husband, than she, Matilda, knew about her little brother.

"I used to think it was just jealousy," Tuulikki had said. "After all, there was no other explanation. But then one autumn a few years ago, after Konni had been drinking . . ."

"What?" Matilda had asked when Tuulikki tailed off.

"Tilda, I don't know if I can tell you this. I promised him I'd never breathe a word to anyone."

Matilda had used the strongest argument she could think of:
"I'm his sister. The only one he's got."

Tuulikki had looked unsure, then went on:

"Konni was so sad that autumn. He drank a lot, and when he drank he sometimes used to cry. He . . . he hit me, and after he'd done that a few times I told him I was going to leave him and take Raija with me – we only had Raija then. That was one of the times he cried. So I stayed."

She had fallen silent again, and sat there staring at the table and looking embarrassed. Matilda had become irritated:

"Tuuli!"

Tuulikki had looked up and said:

"He didn't say much. It was more that I read between the lines. But I think . . . when he was training to be a musician, that one of the older men, that Konni . . . well, I don't know for sure. Only that his eyes were completely empty when he tried to talk about it."

"No!" Matilda had exclaimed.

Her reaction had come from deep inside – she would have stopped it if she could.

Tuulikki had been upset when she went on:

"The next day he made me promise never to tell anyone. He said he'd been very drunk. Joked and said I knew he always made things up when he was full of drink."

Matilda had shaken her head and said: "Konni has many faults. But he rarely lies. Not when he drinks, and not when he's sober."

She had recalled the March day in 1922 when she arrived at the children's home for the first time.

A harsh, ice-cold wind, her wearing clothes that are far too thin. Wet snow, big, soggy flakes that melt when they hit the ground. Konni standing on the gravel drive in front of the big wooden house waiting for her. His half-length dark coat – a charitable gift from some conscientious citizen – is worn and frayed and far too big for his skinny body. The coat is unbuttoned and the woollen jumper he is wearing underneath is full of moth holes. She looks at Konni and at the snowflakes settling on his hair, and thinks how small and undernourished he is. He looks happy when he says hello to her, but when they start talking about what is going to happen his eyes narrow and become hard, and he says:

"I know why this is happening. It's because they don't want me here anymore. They're scared of me."

Matilda thinks of the evening when she solemnly promised Zaida that she would look after Konni. When Mother Zaida went off to help the Reds in Tampere, Milja Matilda promised to make sure that Konni was alright until Zaida returned.

She did not succeed in keeping that promise. But Zaida never came back either.

There in the slushy snow outside the children's home in March 1922, Matilda thinks that she wants to see Konni every day, that she wants to protect him from all the evil of the world.

She cannot protect him, not then and not later, but she will never stop thinking about it. Over the years she will always see Konni as her skinny little brother, even though he goes on to become so many things that she, Matilda, never becomes: a musician, a band leader, the parent of three children.

She chose Reinhard Ålander instead.

Just like Konni, Reinhard moved in circles where it was possible to get hold of all sorts of things, she was sure he would be able to help.

And he did not know Matilda well enough either to question her explanations, or to really care about her.

But Reinhard wanted her. And that hope usually made men willing to help with all manner of things. In Reinhard's case it was not a question of infatuation or love. Reinhard did not believe in things like that, he used to say that in scientific terms, love was merely a chemical storm inside a person, that love was a bourgeois invention from the 1800s that had no place in the twentieth century. "Love enslaves us!" he used to conclude, looking extremely happy at his ability to come up with slogans.

What Reinhard felt for Matilda was desire. If she said yes to that desire, Reinhard would tire of her within a few weeks, a month, maybe, she knew that. But she could make use of him if she allowed him to live in hope.

Reinhard had been in the war, a Red lookout in Kotka, just fifteen years old. He had escaped the camps, perhaps because he was so young, but he was bitter nonetheless. His side had been soundly beaten, its soldiers and supporters had been tried and locked away, but the war was still going on inside Reinhard's head. There were still plenty of men like that, on the victorious side as well.

It worked just as Matilda had hoped. Reinhard accepted her explanations without batting an eyelid: of course he appreciated

266

that she had to protect herself against bourgeois thugs who were always out to sully the honour of a working-class woman, then leave her alone with a child and the responsibility to look after it.

"Of course I can get you one," he said at their first meeting in the cafeteria of one of Elanto's cooperative stores. "Do you want me to teach you how to use it too?"

Matilda did a quick calculation of advantages and risks, then said:

"Yes, please. Obviously, I'm never going to need it. But show me anyway. Just in case."

The next time they met in a secluded corner up on the Marjatta hills, one chilly evening after ten o'clock.

Her first thought was: how small it is. Can such a tiny thing really work?

20

It happened increasingly often that Thune woke up between five and six o'clock in the morning. He was rarely able to get back to sleep, and his days consequently commenced earlier than before. On Wednesday, 19 October he was up and about early. They had agreed upon half past eight, but by ten past he was already waiting in front of the building of the Helsinki Gymnastic Club on Lilla Robertsgatan. It was an overcast, still morning: when the tram passed Hesperia Park, Tölö Bay had been shrouded in fog and was practically invisible.

Thune could not help thinking of that October morning two years ago. When he had got into Lindemark's car outside the Broberg School, only one block from where he was standing now. The weather had been clear but windy, and during the drive he had revealed to his host that he knew about Lindemark's affair with Gabi. Thune recalled the way he had sat in the dining room of the consultant's fine residence, looking out of the window. The maples in the hospital grounds had trembled in the wind, yellow and red leaves swirling through the air, and Thune had been obsessed with the idea of sticking a knife in Lindemark.

Lindemark was as punctual as ever, and his car rounded the corner of Högbergsgatan at one minute before half past eight and braked in front of Thune. The car was still the same Opel Olympia. They crossed Skillnaden and drove along the South Esplanade, then up through Kronohagen. Thune had always admired Lindemark's driving. Robi was a good driver: he drove calmly and steadily, like a man who was sure of his destination. But there was a slight, uncharacteristic jerkiness in his way of handling the car now, he drove a little too fast, changed gear rather too quickly, and therefore had to brake sharply at a succession of junctions.

Thune had a mean comment on the tip of his tongue – that criticising a man's driving was like suggesting he was impotent – but chose not to draw attention to the jerkiness. He and Robi Lindemark had not been alone together since that lunch two years ago. It was only natural that Lindemark was nervous, frightened, even. As for Thune, he was still stuck in the thoughts he had been thinking as he stood waiting on the pavement of Lilla Robertsgatan, and as they drove up the long slope of Tavastvägen he could not help breaking the tense silence by saying:

"Well, the divorce comes into effect some time in December. Then there's nothing in your way."

Lindemark did not answer, merely stared out through the windscreen with his lips tightly closed. The factory district of Sörnäs was as murky and shrouded in fog as Tölö Bay had been an hour or so earlier. Thune could see that Lindemark's jaw was clenched, and his knuckles were white as they clutched the wheel.

A few workers were crossing the street and Lindemark braked to let them pass, then put the car in first gear, pushed the accelerator pedal so hard that the engine roared noisily, and said:

"You've got that all wrong. Gabi and I are fine as we are, we haven't talked about marriage."

The corrective tone in Lindemark's voice made Thune stay silent unto they had driven some way out of the city along the road leading north to Helsinge, then on towards Tusby and

Kopparbäck. During the long silence he had time to regret his gambit, and when he finally spoke again he said:

"I'm sorry. That was tasteless of me. But I couldn't help thinking that it's exactly two years since . . . well, perhaps you understand."

Lindemark gave Thune a grateful glance, then looked back at the road again. He cleared his throat and said:

"Of course I understand. And I've told you how sorry I am. And ashamed, if I'm honest. I don't deserve to have you sitting here beside me."

Thune was somewhat abashed by Lindemark's words, and wondered if he ought to tell his friend about his fantasy of sticking knives into him. Yet Thune was also well aware that he, and no-one else, had raised the subject of the affair, and that it was therefore up to him to defuse the situation and drop the subject, otherwise the awkward atmosphere could last indefinitely.

He let a couple of minutes pass. During those minutes he considered confiding his concerns about both Rolle and Mrs Wiik in the office to Lindemark. But he refrained, and decided instead to go straight for the main purpose of the day, and said:

"Let's talk about Yogi. What can I expect from today? Should I be worried?"

When Thune was young he had seen two people descend into madness. One was a female cousin, the other a fellow student at the faculty of law, a talented young man from a poor family: his harsh study regime proved too much for his nerves. Thune had seen the start of both breakdowns, they had occurred when he was living the high life and he never dared visit them in hospital once they had been admitted. And on the occasions when he had eaten lunch with Lindemark out at Kopparbäck he had never visited the hospital wards: he had never been inside any of the other buildings in the hospital grounds apart from the consultant's pleasant, airy modernist villa.

Thune was terrified of mental illness, of the very idea of madness: of the fact that the great narrative of mankind's capacity for analysis and planning, which so clearly separated it from the animals, had a contrary narrative that was so merciless. Thune's worldview rested on one single foundation, and that was the principle of rationality. He suffered a severe internal reaction – more than that, he was torn apart by fear and frustration – whenever he was reminded of how abruptly and irreversibly *homo logicus* could disintegrate and be replaced by capricious, treacherous, incapable, apathetic or overactive, randomly associating and unbalanced creatures who were impossible to understand and who not infrequently posed a danger to both themselves and others. But Thune had never thought of Joachim Jary in that way, not as a young man and not later on either. The pair of them knew each other too well for Yogi Jary to become impossible for him to understand, and for years Thune had clung to the idea that Yogi was merely unhappy, possibly a little nervy and highly strung, but no more than that. Only in the past year had Thune been forced to face the facts, and if Lindemark, a psychiatrist, was to be believed, their childhood friend was now walking a path that led rapidly and inexorably into the darkness.

But Thune was not only the ultra-rational lawyer and pragmatist that he so dearly wanted to be. He was also an educated man, interested in culture, who against his will had been equipped with a vivid imagination, and when it came to the hospital at Kopparbäck, his imagination was having a field day.

The entire hospital area – the beautiful park and raked gravel paths, and above all the main building with its white surfaces and regimented rows of windows – exuded hygiene and progress in the most persuasive way. Thune also had a vague notion that Lindemark had made his name by always preferring gentler methods focused upon psychoanalysis and therapy. But because

271

Thune had never been on the wards and had never even lain on a psychoanalyst's couch, his image of the interior of the mental hospital resembled something out of Dante or Dickens. He saw before him a Charenton, full of filthy madmen bathing in cracked tubs full of brown water. Among the patients were the Marquis de Sade and a scab-covered Marat who scratched his body so frenetically that great flakes of skin swirled in the air like snowflakes before slowly floating to the floor. Thune imagined a Salpêtrière where hysterical women fainted in the arms of Dr Charcot in front of a crowd of admiring students, while the other rooms of the hospital echoed with the screams of the other female patients. And he saw images that seemed much older to him, images in which the wreckage of human beings sat chained to stone walls in dark dungeons, chewing or twitching uncontrollably, and he heard wailing and saw wretched creatures dressed in rags that barely covered their genitals. Thune had no idea where the worst images came from, but he instinctively connected them with snow and cold. Perhaps, he thought in an attempt at self-analysis, he had taken them from Dostoevsky or Gogol or one of the other great, dead Russians, or possibly from one of the proletarian Swedish writers whose depictions of the suffering of the poor had become so fashionable.

"There's nothing to be worried about. And there's absolutely no reason for you to be nervous or scared."

Lindemark's words roused Thune from his restless thoughts. He glanced to his left and saw that Lindemark was smiling, a reserved and slightly superior smile. When Thune failed to think of anything to say, Lindemark went on:

"Yogi is in my open ward. You'll definitely recognise him, both his appearance and everything he says."

When Thune remained silent – he suspected that he looked worried, but there was nothing he could do about that, they were fifteen kilometres from Kopparbäck now and he could feel his stomach starting to tighten – Lindemark added:

"I've admitted Yogi as a private patient this time. I've actually done that once before. I'm authorised to have a limited number of my own patients, the sort I judge as being of interest to my own research. I had to make quite a fuss to have that included in my contract, the director was very sceptical. But it was worth the effort."

Thune's curiosity came to life and overcame his fear:

"Does that mean that you look after them at no cost? Because Yogi hasn't got any money, has he?"

Lindemark shook his head thoughtfully:

"No, Yogi certainly hasn't got any money. He'll soon be a case for poor relief. But I don't look after any patients free of charge. I have neither the time nor the resources for that."

Thune let his question hang in the air:

"So . . . ?"

"Polle," Lindemark said.

"*Our* Polle? Polle Grönroos?" Thune asked. He could hear the incredulity in his own voice, and realised that it was not especially appropriate with regard to a fellow Club member.

"Polle does have some redeeming features," Lindemark said mildly. "And last time I admitted Yogi as a private patient, Zorro footed the bill. So we can probably say that the Club does what it can to look after its own."

Thune could not help feeling a pang of envy.

He was the one Yogi Jary regarded as his closest friend, he was the one Yogi asked for, but he had no money to contribute. He longed to be as rich as Polle Grönroos, or at least as comfortably off as Zorro Arelius, so that he was in a position to be able to help those he cared about, people like Yogi Jary, with whatever they needed.

"I can't claim to have succeeded in treating Yogi terribly well," Lindemark said. "If I'm honest, he's something of a mystery to me."

273

"In what way?" Thune wondered.

"He doesn't fit the pattern," Lindemark said, before going on: "How much do you know about the diagnosis of psychiatric illness? About the latest research?"

"Not much," Thune admitted. "I've read about psychoanalysis. And I know that there's mania, and depression. And that you say that they're parts of the same illness."

Lindemark smiled amiably.

"We've got a little further than that. The problem with Jary is that he doesn't really fit any form of diagnosis. Then there are days when I could easily give him several different diagnoses at the same time."

Lindemark had used Yogi's surname in what was perhaps a sad attempt to maintain some sort of professional distance in the case. Thune pretended not to have noticed, and said:

"Try. Tell me your diagnosis."

"He's trapped . . . in himself, if I can put it like that," Lindemark said hesitantly, and went on: "When he manages to perform the everyday functions that he needs to carry out, like eating healthy food, taking restorative walks . . . then he retains his ability to concentrate, as well as some of his former brilliance. At times like that, the old Yogi sometimes shines through."

Lindemark fell silent and turned onto the smaller road that led to Kopparbäck. There were only ten kilometres left, less than that, before they reached the beautiful straight avenue leading to the hospital.

"I can hear a *but*, even though you haven't said it," Thune said.

Lindemark gave a resigned shrug.

"Yogi pays little attention to other people – he doesn't seem to hear what they say. But despite minor relapses when he loses his focus, his own speech remains coherent. And he's actually talking more than ever, it's almost as if speech has become the very foundation of his existence. He talks more, and more

274

quickly, than he used to, and often becomes very agitated at what he says."

Lindemark tailed off again, and cast a troubled glance at his hands as they clutched the wheel. Thune guessed that he was wondering if he could say more, or if he had already broken his oath of confidentiality.

"Please, go on," Thune said. "That was just a description, not a diagnosis."

Lindemark stared ahead in concentration. The road was getting narrower, and the autumnal yellow branches were reaching out across the ditches. Thune felt uneasy: it looked like the forest was getting ready to swallow up the road. Lindemark continued:

"Yogi's associations are usually clear and logical. But he's overactive, he barely sleeps, talks to himself and smiles for no reason. Sometimes he is euphoric but can't explain why, then when the euphoria passes he becomes apathetic for hours. He's quick to take offence and is oversensitive socially. He has delusional thoughts, often about being misunderstood, or even persecuted. And, considering the incidents we have experienced in the Club, I don't know if I should really be saying this, but . . ."

"You really do need to tell me!" Thune said sharply when Lindemark failed to finish his sentence. "You can't leave me on tenterhooks!"

Lindemark sounded perplexed when he said: "Yogi has also started to emphasise his Jewishness with a persistence which . . . well, he wasn't like that before, he always used to be irreligious and was as good as entirely assimilated. He is over-emphatic about his Jewishness now, in a way which feels almost self-destructive in the current climate."

"So what's your diagnosis?" Thune asked. "Paranoia?"

He felt pleased to have remembered a piece of psychiatric terminology, and was disappointed by Lindemark's reply:

"No. In spite of certain paranoid delusions, he is not suffering from a persecution complex. And I don't think it's schizophrenia either. He has autistic and hebephrenic symptoms, but he's too old, I can't understand why they should appear now. He also displays elements of classic artistic hypomania, but I'm more inclined to believe that it all has its roots in depression, a depression which he directs in such a way that its expression is contorted and out of the ordinary."

"I can't claim to have understood everything you just said," Thune admitted, "but what do you mean by him directing his depression? Is that possible?"

"Someone gifted with unusual intelligence and a strong will can do that," Lindemark said. "To some extent, at least. We're almost there. Shall we visit him first and then eat, or vice versa?"

"I don't know," Thune said. "What do you think?"

"I would suggest that we visit him straight away. In the afternoons he gets tired much more quickly. His medication keeps him calm, but also drains him of energy."

The open ward was in the main building of the hospital complex, and during the minute or so when he and Lindemark were waiting in the hall for Jary to arrive from the dormitory, the primitive horror of madness that had tormented Thune throughout his adult life was eradicated.

There was nothing to be afraid of. It was almost ten o'clock, and there, a short distance north of the city, the morning fog had already lifted: it was bright and beautiful, a fresh breeze was blowing, the trees were swaying in the park, but not as hard as they were during Thune's visit two years earlier. Most of the leaves had already fallen and lay in a sparkling yellow and red carpet that hid most of the grass, which still looked vibrant and green beneath them. A whitish sunlight streamed in through the high windows of the corridor of the open ward, which led to an impressively large hall. A few nurses hurried past, but always

276

took the time to curtsy and say hello to Lindemark. The curtsying made Thune think of subordination and terrible regimes, but he maintained his façade and said nothing. Twenty or so patients were seated on the benches set out along the corridor, or were wandering about in the hall. Even the patients all greeted Lindemark, and Thune saw no trace of fear or intimidation in their eyes: on the contrary, several of them lit up when they recognised the consultant. The patients were wearing their own clothes, mostly very modest garments, but clean and intact: it was clear that this was a hospital where people cared about the patients' hygiene.

Thune was struck by the fact that everyone looked so normal. If Lindemark and the other doctors had not been wearing white coats and the nurses their uniforms, it would have been difficult to tell the staff and patients apart. The glances the patients directed at Thune as a stranger might perhaps have been a little more suspicious than usual, but that was all.

"Don't worry about the nurses," Lindemark said breezily to Thune. "I've tried to introduce less rigid working practices, and more informal interaction among the staff, but it hasn't succeeded. We live in a shy, uptight country, Claes. Minimal *esprit*, no inclination for improvisation. Do you think we could learn? Can a whole nation cast off its skin and change?"

"No idea," Thune mumbled. "Dear God, the things you ask . . . Look, there's Yogi!"

Joachim Jary was not accompanied by a nurse as he approached from the direction of the dormitory; he was alone, and was carrying a book under his arm. This was Thune and Jary's first meeting in a hospital environment, but there was nothing scary about that either. Jary walked towards them down the corridor with a firm and fairly rapid stride, but when he was a few metres away from them he did not hold out his hand to take Thune's and shake it like they usually did, but instead held out his arms for an embrace that seemed to encompass both Thune and Lindemark. Even so, he only embraced Thune, as he smiled broadly and exclaimed:

"Claes, you old *makher*! So it's taken you this long to come and visit me at last!"

Thune freed himself from the embrace and smiled as warmly as he could, while simultaneously shaking his head as if to say that the visit was not so much a favour as the natural, decent thing to do. He was happy to see Jary, he always was, but Jary had changed since they last met. He and Thune had not seen each other since that evening in the Stadium which had ended with Jary's stubborn entreaties and the scarcely concealed irritation of the other Wednesday Club members. Four months had passed since then, and Thune noticed that Jary's curly black hair had started to turn grey over the summer: it was most obvious at the back of his neck, where his hair was long and tangled.

Yogi Jary had always been slim. There had long been something feline and lithe about his slight frame, but that was gone now. He looked even skinnier than before: his legs looked almost bird-like in his cheap gabardine trousers, his shoulders were narrow and sloping under the pale brown woollen cardigan that Jary had fastened in such a hurry that the first button was in the wrong hole. The badly buttoned cardigan made the whole of Jary's torso look crooked, and his slovenly appearance was only exacerbated by his coarse woollen socks and the worn, outsized leather slippers he had stuck his feet into.

Thune thought Jary looked like an old heron, a cowed creature who was alarmingly unlike the young man who had been one of the city's great bohemians ten years earlier, admired and loved but also loathed by many, so provocatively talkative and intense that he often took up more space than those around him could actually bear. And perhaps more space than he himself could bear? Was that why his path had led him to this sun-drenched corridor in Kopparbäck Hospital and was that why Jary had made the journey from peacock to lame duck in just ten years?

278

Thune knew that he was unlikely to find any answers to his questions. And in the midst of worrying about Jary, he realised that his sadness at the state of his friend was pushing him towards thinking far too melodramatically about life. *Remember that sentimentality is a form of cruelty*, he told himself sternly. The wisest thing he could do was to forget his worries and simply make do with being a listening ear.

"How are you feeling, Yogi?" he therefore asked simply. "What's that you're reading?"

Jary responded by holding the book out towards Thune.

"Hummelschmitt," Thune said with approval. "I read that this summer. What do you think?"

Jary looked askance at the book he was still holding out in his right hand and said:

"Thought-provoking. Don't you think it's thought-provoking? But a little pretentious, perhaps? I could certainly be feeling better, couldn't I, Robi? I could be feeling better. But I'm being very well looked after! By my dear doctor and miracle-worker, of course, and by my generous patrons! Imagine, they still believe in me! As I do myself! I believe as well! And you, dear Claes, I know you do too! Even Zorro does, even though at night he dreams of forcing me to my knees to scrub Henriksgatan with a toothbrush. No, joking aside, I'm being cared for as if by the adoring mother whom I miss so dearly! Hippocrates Lindemark, unchallenged ruler of us *schlemiels* here at Kopparbäck, he never leaves our side!"

The frenetic nature of Jary's response silenced Thune, who had no idea how to go on. Lindemark noticed his predicament and therefore caught Jary's gaze and said:

"Yogi, would you like us to go to the dining room? It isn't time for lunch yet, but I can ask Mrs Vänttinen if she could brew us a pot of coffee. Or tea – perhaps you'd rather have tea?"

A shrewd expression spread across Jary's face.

"Coffee isn't good for me," he said. "Nor tea. You know

279

that, Robi, don't you? It must say so in my notes?"

"Or we could stay here," Lindemark said gently. "Shall we sit down on one of the benches, perhaps? Or go and sit in the hall?"

They started to walk towards a modest seating area – a round table and some simple white chairs – at the far end of the hall.

"Claes," Jary suddenly said, "have you still got that secretary I met back in the spring when you were away?"

"Mrs Wiik, you mean?" Thune said. "Yes, she's still there. But she isn't my secretary. She's my office assistant."

"A very fine person," Jary mumbled. "A good listener."

He raised his head and looked Thune straight in the eye, his gaze dark and intense: "I wanted to tell her a story about being broken. But I didn't have time. She was very polite, but I could see she had a lot to do."

"What was the story?" Lindemark asked. He had been sitting there quietly, just listening, but now he joined in the conversation, and sounded interested.

"It's a story about Miss Selma," Jary said. "Miss Selma Nobel-Prizewinner. And about a man from these parts, an author called Tavaststjerna."

"Thune and I aren't illiterate," Lindemark said amiably. "We know who Tavaststjerna was."

"I heard it from the poet Gripenberg, many years ago," Jary mumbled. He did not appear to have noticed the interjection, and carried on in the same distracted voice: "Unless it was Mörne? Or Hemmer – I'm not really sure. But they had heard it from Miss Selma's own lips. She came over one winter and gave a lecture at the Literary Society."

"Tell us!" Lindemark prompted. "Tell us the story you didn't have time to tell Mrs Wiik."

"It's quite long," Jary said, looking first at Thune, then Lindemark. "You say I talk far too much myself and listen far too little to other people, Robi. Are you sure you feel like hearing it?"

"We're listening," Lindemark said seriously, giving Thune a quick glance. Thune realised that he was being called upon for support, and added his role:

"Tell us, Yogi."

"It was autumn, a long time ago," Jary began. "Miss Selma had travelled to a small town in Sweden to write her story about the image of Christ in Diamante. I don't know what town it was, but it was by the sea, and it was old, because it was surrounded by a town wall. Miss Selma was travelling with her friend, Mrs Elkan, and they stayed in a boarding house that lay on the edge of a large park, just like Kopparbäck. And staying in that same boarding house was the author from these parts, Tavaststjerna, the one who wrote *Hard Times*."

Jary fell silent and looked at Lindemark again, who gave a nod of encouragement. Jary went on:

"Miss Selma and Mrs Elkan arrived in the town at the end of August, autumn was on its way but the heat was still lingering, the sea had been gathering sunlight all summer, of course. And Tavaststjerna had come to the town to write, and soon there were just the three of them in the boarding house. They became acquainted, they started to talk at dinner and while they were drinking their evening tea on the veranda facing the park and the town wall. They talked about writing, and Miss Selma admitted that she was having trouble with her story about the image of Christ. It was towards the end of the last century and Miss Selma had published her book about Gösta Berling, but she had not yet become the Great Storyteller. She was just one author among many others, and Mrs Elkan was almost as famous as she was. Then it was Tavaststjerna's turn to explain why he was there. He admitted just as openly that he was having trouble with both his health and his writing, he said he loved the sea, and that he had come to the little town to walk along the beach and let the strong winds blow through him, in the hope of regaining the imagination and courage that had given him the strength to write his novels and poems and plays. And, he told Miss Selma and Mrs Elkan, it had already succeeded! He told them that he was actually writing again, that words and images were pouring out of him, and that he felt better physically as well. He said that if he could only manage to bear the coming autumn darkness and the fact that the town was slowly emptying of visitors and would soon close down for winter, if he could bear all that and was able to stay at the boarding house and write, he would have his new story finished in a month or two, ready for publication. Do you follow?"

"Yes," Thune and Lindemark said, almost in chorus: they were leaning forward in their chairs, resing their elbows on their thighs, hands clasped under their chins. One of Jary's fellow patients, a tall, thin man dressed in black trousers and a creased brown jacket, had also stopped to listen. He had not dared to sit down on one of the empty chairs but was leaning against the wall a couple of metres from Thune.

Jary continued:

"The authors stayed at the boarding house as the days shrank and the wind howled and the maw of the sea filled with foam. Miss Selma and Mrs Elkan went for walks down by the sea, they liked strolling through the beautiful park at dusk and watching tree after tree and bush after bush turn yellow, then red, and lose its leaves. With each passing day the sky grew black earlier and the storms grew wilder, soon the wind tore the very last leaves from the trees and chased them along the old cobbled streets, the storms made the windows of the veranda of the boarding house rattle and the ropes on the flagpoles crack like whips in the night. Miss Selma and Mrs Elkan saw less and less of Tavaststjerna, they never met him down at the beach or in the park anymore, if they ever caught a glimpse of him it was inside the boarding house, at the main mealtimes, but never at breakfast or over evening tea. When he came down from his room his face was often white, with a deep carmine blush on his cheeks, he gave the impression of

282

an overwrought youth, even though he was a man approaching forty. But he continued to tell the two ladies how strong his inspiration was, and how it had him firmly in its grasp, and that a constant stream of scenes and chapters was coming to him, and that his manuscript was growing and growing, soon it would be finished and he would send it to his publisher in Helsinki. But Miss Selma was beginning to suspect that something was not right. There is something unhealthy in his enthusiasm, she told Mrs Elkan, he is like an impetuous boy who has gone astray in his passion, and devotes each evening to self-abuse. Here we have a man, Miss Selma went on, who says he loves the sea but never goes down to look at it, he just sits in his room breathing stale air: that man is not well, I don't think he should be writing. But Miss Selma only confided her concerns to Mrs Elkan, she never revealed them to Tavaststjerna. The two ladies and the slightly younger man were, after all, only acquainted as a result of staying in the same boarding house, and in those days one did not readily meddle in another's inner world. Things went on in that vein for several weeks. The two ladies, the walks, the storms, sometimes the clouds would break and light up the evening sky red and purple, then the rain stopped, and soon the first frost arrived. Tavaststjerna sat in his room, and on the rare occasions when he came down to the dining room he was even quieter and paler than before. And then one day he was gone, he had packed in a hurry, ordered a cab to the harbour and taken the first boat, the landlady of the boarding house told them. Then Miss Selma said to Mrs Elkan: 'I don't think there is any book.' And the following spring Miss Selma and Mrs Elkan saw the notice in the Stockholm newspapers announcing the death of the Finnish writer Tavaststjerna."

When Jary had finished his tale none of them spoke for a long while. The tall, thin patient lingered, leaning against the stone wall and picking nervously at one sleeve of his jacket, looking worried. Thune and Lindemark exchanged glances. Thune could see from Lindemark's eyes that he was concerned, and guessed that the same emotion was visible in his own.

"One should know when it's time to stop," Jary mumbled. "That's the whole point, one needs to know when it's time to stop."

"Our age has a Janus face, it forces us to make unpleasant contrasts," Lindemark said when they were sitting in his official residence eating salmon soup.

They had taken their leave of Jary fairly quickly. The story of Miss Selma and the unfortunate Tavaststjerna seemed to have worn him out, because he reacted unpredictably and irrationally to Thune's and Lindemark's attempts to make conversation afterwards. Just as Lindemark had said, Jary did not respond to questions. Instead he made wild associations, to the point where what Thune thought would be an answer to the question of whether Jary was happy at Kopparbäck, or whether his sporting nephews had broken any records recently, could turn into absolutely anything at all – a lament about the persecuted Jews of Austria, or a witticism about bad actors, or a long-winded story about an electronic instrument that could play itself. The closer it got to lunchtime, the muddier and more apocryphal Jary's stories had become. Lindemark had leaned forward and whispered to Thune that it was unfortunately a bad day, Jary was usually better than this in the mornings. Then Lindemark had patted Jary on the shoulder and said that it was probably best that he put on his outdoor coat and made his way to the patients' dining room, where lunch would soon be served. Jary had shaken his head and looked at Thune with eyes so brim-full of loneliness that Thune felt his throat tighten. "It was good of you to come, Claes," Jary had said. "It's been good to see you too, Yogi," Thune managed to say in response. He had put his arm round Jary's shoulders and added: "Now just you get well! You'll soon be out again!"

284

"What sort of contrasts?" Thune asked Lindemark. "You're going to have to elaborate."

"There's a reality that's crueller than ever," Lindemark said. "But at the same time escapism is more enchanting and enticing than before. And more available to the masses! We're dancing the Lambeth walk on piles of rotting corpses from the Spanish Civil War, Dorothy Lamour and Shirley Temple are kissing Stalin on his pockmarked cheeks. There's a lethargy to it all, an unease in the midst of the desire for pleasure."

"Perhaps it's just fear of another war," Thune suggested. "Fear can take many expressions."

"Naturally," Lindemark said. "But I think it's something else as well. I'm revealing my own limited outlook if I take an example from my own profession, but at conferences in recent years, in my meetings with colleagues . . . it's as if there are two distinct movements, heading in almost opposite directions."

Lindemark stopped, put his left hand in his jacket and took a steel pen and small notebook from his inside pocket.

"Do you mind if I make notes as we talk? I'm in the middle of preparing a lecture, and I often get ideas during good conversations. But I've learned that I need to write a few keywords down in order to retain the thoughts."

"By all means," Thune said. "If a conversation with me can be any use, then I'm only too pleased."

He was surprised at how conciliatory he felt. He had thought it would be painful to see Kopparbäck again, but it was not. For the first time he felt a sort of warmth towards both Lindemark and Gabi, and he wondered if he had made it through purgatory now.

"On the one hand," Lindemark said, as he scribbled some words in his pad, "we're on the way to a more reflective way of looking at what was once described in such simplistic and stigmatising terms as *lunacy* and *madness*. There is a degree of humanism in the very act of questioning terms and diagnoses.

When do strange and odd ideas switch from being merely odd to degenerate and sick? When does the ability to see hidden connections and find inventive solutions become a tendency to spout nonsense and incomprehensible gibberish? Most people know instinctively that creativity and mental illness are cousins. But how are we to learn where the boundary between them lies? What if there is no natural boundary? What if it is our responsibility to draw that boundary, how are we to do that? And is it even possible to draw such a boundary?"

"You're thinking of Yogi now," Thune said quietly.

"Yes, I suppose I am," Lindemark admitted. "I'm thinking about Yogi, amongst other things. When you've known him in better times, it's impossible not to be moved by what's happening inside him now. But you have to remember that he has plenty of brothers and sisters in misfortune. And that I also have a purely professional interest in his case."

Thune found himself wondering if Lindemark was so professional that he could read Gabi's erotic stories and appreciate them in an objective way in terms of behavioural science, as interesting examples of how an individual has used her intelligence and imagination to create verbal artefacts which reflect her understanding of reality, but not as anything more. For a brief moment Thune felt like asking, then jealousy and pride popped up again, after all, and he remained silent. Instead he nodded appreciatively at Lindemark, who went on:

"There are a lot of us in the profession who believe that people who are afflicted by mental illness are of higher intelligence than the average person. Unfortunately empirical research is rather lagging behind there. But let us take it as axiomatic that it makes sense. That makes it less of a leap to imagine that images we all see when we fantasise are simply stronger and more vivid in people who fall ill. And that the sick are merely paying the price of their greater mental abilities. And from that we can take a step further. We can claim that people really ought to be allowed to think and believe whatever they like, see whatever images they like, as long as what they think and believe and see does not make them behave in a way that makes the lives of other people, and of the collective, less secure, or simply worse."

"It's a nice idea," Thune said. "But I can see several problems with that reasoning. The problem of definition, to be more exact."

"You're right," Lindemark conceded. "When does my life, and mine specifically, become less secure and worse as a result of the different thoughts and peculiar understanding of reality that other people are harbouring? There's no agreement here, the answer to that question unfortunately only exists inside each individual's head. And, in a way, that takes us off in the other direction I mentioned."

Lindemark stirred his soup without enthusiasm and then let go of his spoon without lifting it to his mouth. He looked simultaneously oppressed and determined, as if he were preparing to say something that he really did not want to say. Then he went on:

"The big dividing line these days is in our view of human beings. Are we merely complicated biological machines that must fulfil certain minimum requirements in order to be allowed to exist? The old rulers may have been toppled, but do human beings now only exist to serve the state and the party? Or do they deserve freedom? Where does their value come from? Is there . . . is there any longer anything inviolable in life itself?"

"There's something troubling you, Robi," Thune said. "You know something that you're not telling me."

"That's just it," Lindemark said, and his voice sounded genuinely tormented. "I know nothing. All I've got is suspicions."

"Suspicions about what?" Thune asked.

"At certain conferences I've attended . . ." Lindemark began, but trailed off.

"Yes?" Thune said encouragingly.

"There's something about the way some of my colleagues talk," Lindemark said quietly. "Colleagues from . . . certain countries. I don't want to tarnish anyone's name, because on this subject no-one dares to be clear. Everyone uses euphemisms, everyone talks in metaphors. It's more about imagining the ultimate consequences of certain ways of reasoning. And I've begun to suspect . . . perhaps you're aware of the practice of medical intervention to ensure that individuals who are regarded as deficient are prevented from passing on their poor genetic features?"

"I've understood that it occurs," Thune said. "But of course it isn't exactly the sort of thing that they announce on the radio."

"There's a strong belief in rationalism among us doctors," Lindemark said. "And occasionally we are criticised for that belief. But you have to understand that a lot of us are forced almost daily to see things that lay people may only have to witness a few times in their lives."

"You're talking about suffering?" Thune said.

"Yes," Lindemark said. "I'm talking about suffering. We're forced to see more of it than we can actually bear. And you'd probably think that some of the conversations we have inside the profession are cold-blooded. But we don't have those conversations because we're evil, but simply to survive as professionals. We have them so that we can remain able to act in the face of . . . Dear God, I've seen fates so terrible, creatures so deformed that they can barely be called human anymore, so that you really are . . . well, tempted to think . . ."

"Tempted to think what?" Thune prompted again. Lindemark looked deeply troubled now, and Thune had a good idea of where his reasoning was leading. Part of Thune did not want to hear Lindemark say those words. But at the same time he felt that he needed to hear them: he needed to know where his childhood friend and fellow Club member stood.

"That life is cruel and merciless," Lindemark said. "That the

288

care of these creatures is merely an excuse, an escape. That . . . that a syringe full of poison would be a mercy."

"So what you're trying to say," Thune said, "is that there are cases in which you think that sterilisation does not go far enough, that there are people who . . ."

He broke off, as unwilling as Lindemark to be the one who said the words.

"Who want to go further, yes," Lindemark said. "Who want to poison the entire art of medicine."

He sounded frightened as he said this, like a child who has been out making mischief with older, tougher boys, and is now tormented by what he has seen them do. Thune felt just as nauseous. Outside in the park the sun was still shining, and the autumn air was doubtless cool and fresh, but inside the once pleasant dining room there was now only decay and shadow.

"It's terrible," Lindemark muttered. "It can never be allowed to happen."

"It *can't* happen," Thune said. "It's too grotesque."

"Yes," Lindemark said. "That's what one would like to think. But I've heard some of my colleagues talk specifically about mercy and deliverance . . . it's as if they were wearing blinkers."

"They believe in their own goodness, and therefore don't see the abyss opening up?" Thune suggested.

Lindemark did not answer. He jotted some more words on his notepad, then lifted his spoon and was about to lower it into the bowl of soup, but changed his mind at the last minute.

Thune could see that Lindemark was claming up, the way he had done ever since they were small. Lindemark had always been impulsive and open, a child of the moment whose moods had been easy to read by more calculating friends like Arelius and Thune. Lindemark had remained the same into middle age, but sometimes he seemed to tire of his own directness and retreated into his thoughts in a way which people who did not know him occasionally interpreted as arrogant. Thune knew that this state could last for several hours, so he said:

"Thank you for lunch, Robi. There's a bus to Helsinki in half an hour, would you mind driving me down to the village?"

"Of course," Lindemark said politely. "Thank you for coming, Claes."

As Thune settled down inside the bus he still felt oppressed. He had a couple of books in his briefcase – a Wodehouse and a new volume of poetry – and had been planning to spend the journey reading.

After a moment's reflection he decided against this: the driver was going far too fast, and the unwieldy vehicle lurched as it went round bends. If Thune tried to read he would end up feeling sick.

And he would not have been able to concentrate anyway.

Their route took the bus through the idyllic Tusby landscape, and Thune tried in vain to anchor himself in sun-drenched reality again. The night and fog that had brushed up against him and Lindemark was still there, and the inner darkness was stronger than the light on the fields and forests outside. When the landscape continued to look like stage scenery, in spite of his efforts, Thune moved on to thinking about the various tasks that lay ahead of him.

He had to talk to Mrs Wiik, and he had to do so at once. He could not postpone the conversation a day longer: it was unpleasant but he knew too much simply to let it all pass.

Mrs Wiik had seemed tired in recent weeks – she had been quieter than usual. Thune knew that she had sharp eyes and ears. Perhaps he had already – inadvertently – given off signs of unhappiness, and now Mrs Wiik was fretting about what was going to happen.

But it was probably more likely that Rolle had told her off

again, shouting at her on some occasion when Thune had been busy in the City Court or having lunch at the Kämp with one of his clients. What if Rolle had taken the opportunity to behave outrageously towards Mrs Wiik today, now that Thune was away all day?

He decided that it was time to talk to Rolle as well.

He would tell it like it was: their partnership was not working, and it would be best if Rolle took a few weeks' paid leave while they both considered how to move on. Perhaps Rolle could continue to own a share of the business while taking up a post in another firm: both Snellman and Roschier had advertised vacant positions during the past week.

21

The western sky was tinted a garish orange as Matilda took
her evening walk down by Edesviken. It was the last Friday
in October, and the clear, cold evening had been preceded by
several days of continuous gentle rain. It looked as though there
was a war raging over where the sun had just gone down: Matilda
imagined a city burning beyond the horizon. She remembered
the sun-drenched summer morning when she had seen Santeri
Soihtu and the other stars recording a film. In the quickly fading
autumn twilight it felt like something that had happened several
years ago. She wondered if the film was already finished and
would soon have its premiere: for the time being *Elokuva-Aitta*
and the other magazines were maintaining a wall of silence.

During the past week Matilda had forgotten her concerns
regarding Thune.

She had forgotten them because so much had happened that
she had been unable to foresee.

First Thune had been ambushed and assaulted when he left
the office just before ten o'clock on the evening of Thursday,
20 October.

Thune had been working late to finish some outstanding
tasks from Wednesday, when he had been off all day because
of a private matter, the nature of which he had not revealed to

Matilda. When he emerged from the stairwell two men were waiting for him in the doorway and immediately set about him. They knocked him to the ground, punching him hard in the face and stomach, then concluded by kicking him in the side and back as he lay on the tarmac. According to Thune, the men had been stocky, and he had a sense that they were fairly young. One of them had been wearing a mid-length black leather coat, the other a jacket. Both had their hats pulled down to hide their faces, and in the gloom of the doorway Thune had been unable to identify any distinguishing features. Besides, he had lost consciousness, he did not know for how long, but when he came to again the men were gone.

It was no robbery: the perpetrators did not take Thune's wallet even though it had been easily accessible in the inner pocket of his raincoat. According to the police, it was unlikely that the men had been in the doorway by chance. The windows of the office lobby faced Kaserngatan, and the lamp in the lobby had been lit all evening: the men had probably been keeping watch, then moved from the street to the doorway as soon as Thune switched the light off and went out into the stairwell.

Besides, one of the men had hissed at Thune while the assault was taking place:

"Swedish bastard! Traitor!"

The police and Thune shared the same theory about the motive: the assault was revenge for the article that he had published in *Svenska Pressen*. His assailants probably did not number among the city's known criminal fraternity, but came from elsewhere. Thune's article had provoked criticism not only within the Patriotic People's Party but more widely, and the police feared that it would be hard to find the perpetrators and bring them to justice.

Thune had called the office from the hospital at half past eight on Friday morning. Matilda had been at her desk, but not lawyer Hansell. Thune had sounded groggy and scared, but had still assured her that there was no reason to be worried about him: he had escaped with little more than a bad fright. He left hospital on the Friday evening and spent Saturday and Sunday at home on Borgvägen.

When he came to the office on Monday morning his right eye was swollen shut, and completely blue. He had four stitches in his upper lip and as a result he spoke more slowly than usual. His left arm was in a sling, and close to his wrist the skin was bare, yellowish and covered in small scratches. Thune tried to make light of the situation and told Matilda with feigned solemnity that under no circumstances was she to say anything funny – he had two cracked ribs, his torso was tightly bandaged, and it hurt to cough or laugh.

When Matilda asked if he ought perhaps to have stayed at home for a few more days, because she and lawyer Hansell could easily take care of the routine tasks, Thune replied that painful ribs in the office were preferable to being at the mercy of Miss Johansson's cooking for one more day. Besides, he added, he had important business to attend to.

With those words he went into his office, and it was only much later that Matilda realised that lawyer Hansell was not in his room. She and Thune were alone in the office, just like they used to be.

Thune played the strange, monotonous piece of music on his gramophone several times that day. Towards the end it was so loud and cacophonous that Matilda had trouble concentrating on her work. When the music was not too loud she could hear Thune muttering on the phone in a voice that sounded irritated and pained, even though he was talking quietly.

He did not want her to take any dictation that day: she guessed he was in pain and wanted to be on his own as much as possible. Only late that afternoon did he ask her to come into his room, where he asked if Director Gerasimoff and Consul Gadd had paid the invoices that the firm had sent out. After Matilda had told him that they had not, she asked Thune if lawyer Hansell was spending the whole day at the City Court, seeing as he had not been in the office.

"Lawyer Hansell and I have agreed that he should remain as a minority shareholder, but that he seek a position elsewhere," Thune had replied in a voice made indistinct by the stitches in his lip. Then he had straightened up in his chair, grimacing with pain, and continued:

"Rolle . . . lawyer Hansell is taking some time off until further notice. In case you were wondering, that was my sister I was talking to a short while ago. It was not a pleasant conversation."

Then Thune and Matilda had worked in their separate rooms from Tuesday to Friday, with a minimum of contact. Thune seemed tired and sad after the assault, and sat in his office, silent and immersed in paperwork. He was still in pain, and needed help with his outdoor clothing before he set off to the Kämp or Gillet for lunch. When Matilda held his overcoat up for him to put on very gingerly, he merely said: "Thank you very much."

That went on until Saturday morning, when the orange sky of Friday evening had been replaced by the usual steady rain. Then he called her, and she picked up her dictation pad and two pens and went into his office, and sat down as usual on the chair by the wall.

Once she had sat down Thune said in a serious voice:

"Mrs Wiik, I have to inform you that I am aware of the circumstances surrounding your departure from Hoffman & Laurén. I have known about it for a while, and I apologise for not raising the subject before."

Matilda felt an icy chill start to spread through her body. It was fortunate that she was already sitting down, so that the sudden weakness in her legs was not visible.

But Thune had apologised to her.

For some peculiar reason he had apologised, and therein lay perhaps a measure of hope. She gathered all the strength she had in her, took a deep breath, and said:

"Of course you have had a great deal to . . . with the assault and lawyer Hansell, and so on."

He could hear the fear and deference in her voice.

"Yes," Thune said. "I have. But now that I am raising the subject, and telling you that I have known about it for a while, it feels as if I have been keeping you on the edge of your seat. You deserve better treatment than that."

Matilda interpreted his words to mean that she was being dismissed. She lowered her gaze to the floor and felt nausea rising. Her skin started to crawl, as often happened in situations in which she was afraid of losing control. Her whole body was crawling, even her hair, tiny, tiny lice everywhere, tickling the roots of her hair as they moved, they were under her arms and on her back and on her thighs and between her legs and even in there. She had started to feel them in the autumn after the camps, the doctor had said it was just her imagination, because she had, after all, been deloused several times, it was merely a mental reaction, a reaction that arose when she was under pressure, the doctor had said, and she had also had attacks during the years with Hannes, she had never got rid of them, not completely, even though she kept her distance from people as well as she could: the attacks still came, the tiny creatures were always there, waiting to strike.

They could be beaten, but only with an immense amount of self-control.

She raised her head, straightened her back, looked Thune in the eye and said as calmly as she could:

"I can clear my desk and return the key at once, if you like."

Thune squirmed in his chair and made that face again, presumably his ribs hurt every time he moved.

296

"Don't let's get ahead of ourselves now, Mrs Wiik. I simply want to talk to you. There's no more to it than that at the moment."

He took a cigarette from the case on his desk, lit it, then asked:

"What happened, exactly?"

Matilda saw in her mind's eye that stuffy August day more than a year ago. She had been standing in the archives of the shipping agency, looking for a book of accounts in one of the cabinets. She had been holding the office scissors in her right hand and was looking for the book with her left. The window had been open, and from down on Lönnrotsgatan came the sound of noisy traffic.

She had not heard Director Hoffman approach, and was entirely unprepared when his hands closed over her breasts.

She could not bring herself to answer Thune.

He looked at her patiently and asked:

"What did Hoffman do?"

"He put his hands on . . . he touched me," Matilda said stiffly. She added hastily:

"I didn't even know he was in the room. It was . . . like a reflex, that's all. I didn't have time to think. Of course I shouldn't have . . . I shouldn't have been holding the scissors in my hand. But I was in the middle of packing some things and was just going to get some string and . . ."

"There are scissors in every office," Thune interrupted. "No-one can criticise you for holding a pair in your hand. And everyone knows that Victor Hoffman is an incorrigible old goat. It was lucky for everyone that nothing worse happened."

"It was a nasty cut," Matilda said quietly.

She wished she could forget that afternoon, forget the terrible moment when she realised that she had not only pulled free of Director Hoffman's grip, but had also waved the scissors at him and hit him on the cheek.

"Let's forget the matter now," Thune said, as if he had been reading her thoughts.

For a fleeting moment Matilda thought she saw sympathy in his eyes. She wanted to say something, wanted to explain herself, make excuses. But she could not find the words, and while she was still searching Thune said:

"In my profession you learn how to find things out. A good lawyer also learns that he should listen to his instincts. Sniff things out. Now I don't wish to claim that I'm a good lawyer. To be honest, I've stagnated and am fairly mediocre. But I'm good at finding things out."

Matilda had a suspicion of what was coming, but was none-theless surprised when Thune got straight to the point:

"You're the daughter of Adolf Ahlbäck, a railway mechanic, and Zaida, née Nikitin, and a cook by profession. And Konni is your only brother?"

"Yes," Matilda said. "All of that is correct."

"And in 1927 you married factory worker Hannes Wiik?"

"Yes," Matilda agreed reluctantly.

"We married in the same year, you and I," Thune said. "Gabi and I were wed in the summer of '27."

"Hannes and I got married in October," Matilda mumbled.

"I'm guessing that you don't live with your husband," Thune said. "But you're not divorced either. What happened? Where is he?"

Matilda looked down at the floor and did not reply.

"Naturally, you don't have to say anything, Mrs Wiik," Thune said amiably. "But isn't it reasonable that I should want to know whom I have employed? Especially when you have been very reticent about your background, which strikes me as a little . . . complicated."

Matilda looked Thune in the eye and nodded:

"Hannes moved out seven years ago. I don't know where he went. For the first few months post would sometimes arrive for him. The occasional letter, a few postcards, a call to military exercises. I tore them up. Then they stopped coming. I was pleased about that."

She saw the surprise in Thune's eyes and guessed that he had thought her tone of voice emotionless and therefore alarming. She added:

"Perhaps this interests you as a matter of principle, as a lawyer. Unless perhaps you're wondering why I'm not curious about where Hannes went. Perhaps you're wondering, *How could a woman react like that?*"

Thune stubbed his cigarette out in the ashtray and said nothing, so she went on:

"If you have any questions, I don't have the answers to them. I presume that Hannes is alive, because I have received no information to suggest otherwise. And because I have not received a request for a divorce, I assume that he has not remarried. If he has, then he is a bigamist. But he doesn't interest me. Not at all."

Thune was looking at her intently. The surprise had vanished from his eyes, to be replaced by curiosity.

"What would you do if Hannes suddenly rang on your door and proposed the resumption of the marriage?" he wondered.

"It's such an unlikely idea that I can't really have an opinion at all," Matilda replied.

She noticed, not without surprise, that she was inclined to tell the truth. Within certain boundaries, of course, but Thune had unlocked her again, getting through her defences just as he had in their conversation before the summer holiday.

But they were talking about more serious matters now. If his questions began to drift in the wrong direction it could jeopardise her plans. It struck her that everything might already be over, that the Captain had grown uncertain, possibly even scared, and had confided in Thune.

"I should like to ask you a few more things," Thune said. "Would that be alright?"

The icy chill again. And the strange powerlessness in her arms and legs: she could barely manage to keep hold of her notepad and pens.

"I don't know," she replied truthfully. "I don't know that I can manage any more today. And if you're thinking of dismissing me, I would rather you did it in a decent way."

Thune leaned forward across his desk and groaned quietly. It was obvious that even the slightest movement was painful.

"Your father died in an industrial accident in 1915?"

It was more a statement than a question, Matilda could tell he knew everything. She said:

"Yes. He wasn't paying attention at work and was run over by a locomotive in the goods yard."

"But your mother thought it was the fault of the railway company?"

"Yes," Matilda said. "And then things went the way that they did. Instead of grieving she just got more and more angry."

"And was radicalised?"

"Yes," Matilda reluctantly conceded. "That was more or less what happened."

"I had a suspicion that you had a Red past even during your job interview," Thune said. "Although nothing about you . . . You don't look like that at all."

"How does someone like *that* look?" Matilda asked. "Can Redness been seen, and if so, how? As red, wrinkled skin, perhaps? Or how do you mean?"

Thune leaned back with an effort until his back hit the chair. He sighed:

"Sorry, I expressed myself poorly. What I meant to say is that it doesn't matter to me. I did employ you, didn't I?"

Matilda did not know how to respond. She was one again seized by the hope that deep down he meant her well. After a few moments of silence she said:

"I'm the one who should apologise. That was unfair of me."

Thune shook his head as if to say that her apology was unnecessary, then asked:

"Your mother . . . she died in the uprising?"

"Yes. In Tampere. During the battle. When she left us she told me she was going to make soup and look after the injured. But the Whites said she had taken to arms."

Matilda fixed her eyes on Thune's as she spoke, and once again thought how odd it was that he sometimes looked like Stan Laurel. She wondered if he had any real understanding of what she was telling him. She added:

"It was all so unnecessary. She was over forty."

"And you," Thune wondered, "what were you then, fifteen, sixteen?"

"I was sixteen," Matilda replied. "I looked after Konni. There was no-one else who . . . That was why I later . . ."

It was starting to feel difficult now. But there was no longer any fear of being uncovered. She was sure that Thune knew nothing about the Captain: if he had known, he would already have let it slip, he really was no good at dissembling. But she was getting tired of talking. The only person whom she had told so much was Hannes. But she had not even told him about the time in the camps.

"It just wasn't possible."

"Oh?" Thune said by way of encouragement.

"I took a job with the guard," she said. "It was the only way to get money for food. I couldn't let Konni . . ."

She broke off and suddenly felt tears trying to break through. She had not cried since the autumn when she found Konni in the children's home, or at least could not remember having done so. She shook her head to rid herself of the memory of the ten-year-old Konni during the winter when Zaida went away.

"I understand," Thune said warmly.

She waited for him to say something else, but he did not. She went on:

301

"I was training to be a teacher, I was quite clever. And of course I could speak both languages fluently. I actually worked for the commissariat for a few weeks. I fetched the post and took messages, that sort of thing."

She was relieved that her voice sounded clear and steady. Her feelings had got the better of her, but they were gone now.

"And afterwards?" Thune wondered, and there was hesitancy in his voice as he continued:

"Were you . . . imprisoned?"

Matilda recognised the choice of words. No-one on the White side had ever asked her about her life. But she had been a subordinate secretary and office worker, an invisible spirit listening in as officers and members of the Defence Corps talked about the war and the summer that followed. And she knew it went no further than words like *prisoner* and *prison*, she knew that not even well-meaning men like Thune used words like *punishment camp* or *death colony*, particularly not now, when other countries had started to lock people away in camps.

And good men like Thune wanted to forget that the camps had ever existed.

She did not know what to reply. It was difficult to start telling untruths when she had just forced herself to speak the truth for the first time in almost ten years. But this was where the boundary ran. She believed that Thune liked her, but if she told him about the camps she had no guarantee that he would not tell her story to others. She knew Thune well enough to know that he would hardly relate her life story to the entire Wednesday Club. But what she did not know was if he was strong enough to bear upsetting stories on his own: what if he were to confide in the Captain?

Despite the gnawing sense of danger she chose to go halfway. She said, in a voice that she made as calm and toneless as she possibly could:

302

"If I say that I have seen a man bend down after a cigarette butt and have his head shot off so that half his skull remained while his brain slid out like grey oatmeal porridge down an outhouse wall? If I say I saw a child born on a dirty tarmac floor and die and be tossed onto the back of a truck like a lump of wood a few hours later? Would you stop asking me questions then?"

Her words made Thune start, and as he jerked the pain in his ribs came back and his face contorted. But Matilda could see that there was another pain as well: her words had hit their target. She saw the panic and revulsion in Thune's eyes, and had some idea of how hard his brain was working to stop her words being transformed into images, so that he would not have to understand what had happened, here, in his own country, just a few kilometres from his beautiful home city, Helsinki.

Thune managed to gain control of his features, but his voice was strained when he spoke:

"If you could give me an outline of next week's meetings, and send reminders of those invoices to Gerasimoff and Gadd, we can finish for the weekend. And you must excuse me if I went too far. I shan't ask any more questions."

Matilda looked at him. Perhaps she should not have been surprised, but she was.

"Are you going to dismiss me or not?"

"Under no circumstances," Thune said. "Of course you have the right to resign, if you so wish, but for my part I appreciate your work and have no thoughts of letting you go."

He had already picked up his reading glasses from his desk and put them in place on his nose. Now he took them off again, looked at her seriously, and said:

"And in case you were wondering, the answer is no: I'm not frightened of you."

*

During the weekend and the working week that followed, Matilda gradually realised that she was relieved and anxious at the same time.

She was relieved that she had told Thune. Relieved that Thune now knew who she was, but without actually knowing everything.

As the days passed it also became increasingly clear that Thune was not thinking of exploiting what he knew about Matilda. He made no allusions to their conversation of Saturday, and she even thought he was treating her with more respect than before.

She was relieved about that as well.

But simultaneously she could not help feeling anxious. How much time did she have? Thune had found out a great deal of information about her, and led her to believe that it had been relatively simple. He had promised not to ask her any more questions, but he had not promised to stop digging in her past. What if he were to drink too much whisky one evening and felt like showing off by telling a dramatic working-class story to his friends? What if the Captain had secretly been conducting his own investigation, just like Thune?

Four days after Matilda's conversation with Thune the Captain was sitting opposite her at her table. They were drinking evening tea, talking about current events, and at first the conversation was very sluggish. She had brewed the tea according to tradition and the teapot was a splendid canary yellow. She offered scones she had bought from Kinnunen's bakery on Fredriksgatan, and the same Ryker's biscuits they had at the office. The Captain talked about Chamberlain and Hitler, and the terrible train accident near Villmanstrand, and as he talked he smiled at her in a way that was probably meant to seem reassuring. Matilda was barely listening. Every now and then she thought the Captain was looking at her intently, that there was some suspicion in his eyes. But she suppressed her anxiety and told herself that it was just her nerves, still on edge after her conversation with Thune.

The door to the bedroom was ajar and she could see a glimpse of the bedside table and red bedspread.

Not now, Miss Milja whispered to her. Not this evening. And you need to find somewhere else. Anyone might get it into their head to open a drawer.

It was Wednesday, 2 November, and it was the first time they had met since the September meeting that had ended so badly. When the Captain had handed over the flowers and she had hung up his overcoat, and he had followed her into the living room, he had said he was relieved and grateful that she wanted to see him, in spite of everything.

Relief. That word again.

Matilda often got stuck on words, it was something of a problem. Sometimes words became almost as obstinate as Miss Milja. For a while last winter it was *mirage*, presumably because of the song Konni had written, and now all of a sudden it was *relief.*

But what did it really mean?

Was there any such thing as relief?

Matilda made an effort to nod and murmur politely as the Captain spoke. When she listened she tilted her head slightly, and towards the end of the evening she could see he had thawed out, that he was longing to reach out his hand and touch her.

She waited until the Captain had finished speaking, then before he had time to grab hold of a new topic of conversation she put her hand to her mouth and yawned slightly, then said:

"You should probably go now, it's already late."

When she served him a second cup of tea he had looked up at her and asked if they could move on to first name terms. Matilda had agreed. The Captain was keen for her to use his nickname, but she had used his Christian name on the few occasions when she was forced to address him.

A little cloud of disappointment slid across the Captain's face as he realised that the evening was over. But then he nodded and looked almost cheerful. The legs of his chair scraped lightly on the floor as he stood up and said:

"Time flies when you're having fun. Thank you for letting me come. But may I come again? You've made your home so cosy."

"I don't know," Matilda said. "Call me next week and we'll see."

When she woke up in the middle of the night she was lying on her left side. She had kicked the covers off, it was dark and cold in the room and she was freezing. For a few moments she did not realise that there were covers to reach for, she was much younger and was lying there staring into a brick wall. Some of the mortar had come away where the bunk was attached to the wall. She could hear the heavy breathing close behind her, hands on her breasts, movements inside her, and the tense voice that whispered *Miss Milja oh Miss Milja* just before.

22

Afterwards, when Thune thought back on those November weeks, he would reproach himself for having been far too passive and uninterested. Perhaps he could blame the fact that he had still been convalescing after the assault, and was still in pain. But it was not only that: he had also allowed himself to be blinded by a feeling he was not used to – the feeling of being a capable man.

He was proud that he had dared to get rid of his nephew, and that he had patiently soaked up all the terrible things his sister Ulla said to him as a result of his decision. He was proud that he had been decisive enough to confront Mrs Wiik and ask her about her remarkable past, and he was very pleased that she was going to remain in the office while Rolle Hansell was a closed chapter.

With this newfound feeling of power Thune was already planning his next dismissal. Miss Johansson had left his Sunday steak in the oven for so long that it had dried up completely, and that same Sunday she had also boiled his Brussels sprouts beyond all recognition. Thune had decided to put up with Miss Johansson over Christmas, but to dismiss her immediately after the holiday.

Thune could also blame his lack of attention on the fact that modern urban life was so eventful. The incidents piled up, and one haphazard meeting followed the other before he had had time to digest and analyse the previous one. In the hubbub of daily life it was so easy to forget that Mrs Wiik was still reserved and quiet. If he thought about her at all, he was prone to thinking that she had not yet recovered from Rolle's appalling behaviour, and perhaps not from Thune's interrogation either, but that in time she would be more like herself again.

Thune was surprised at the superficiality of the traces left on his soul after the assault. The first Monday morning when he locked the door of his home on Borgvägen and walked to the tram stop, and the first evening when he remained at the office long after Mrs Wiik had gone home, he had felt anxious then, glancing over his shoulder as he walked along the street, and starting with fear when he turned a corner and almost collided with an elderly woman walking her dog. But after just a few days he had forgotten his anxieties, even though his ribs were still painful when he coughed, and even though he still had the stitches in his lip and his eye was still bruised and swollen.

As the days passed Thune gradually began to think that his injuries had been a price worth paying for the right and possibility of freely expressing his innermost beliefs in an open forum. He had survived, after all, and would not even be left with any permanent damage from the assault. There were countries in which one would be locked away in a camp or shot and killed for expressing views which the majority, or at least those in power, found uncomfortable. When the pain in his chest eased and the swelling around his eye went down, Thune began to feel a sort of paradoxical gratitude towards his assailants: this was still plain-spoken Finland, where you threw a punch if you got angry, then forgot the whole business, instead of shutting dissenters away in Dachau or shooting them in the back of the head in the basement of the Lubyanka.

Yet even as he felt gratitude at having survived and being able to carry on thinking and writing, Thune also felt oppressed.

He was living in a brutal age. The threat of violence and war was present every day, eating its way into people like a bacterium, making sensitive souls grey and ill, while the less scrupulous were in their element. His friend Zorro Arelius was not the only one enchanted by the age of steel and instinct: the newspapers were full of articles by people praising the military precision of modern life while simultaneously acclaiming innate masculine brute force.

Thune visited his mother Esther and received an unpleasant surprise: after telling him about her latest visit to see "Dr Lorens", and the ailments which Arelius had treated, Esther told him that she had decided to demand repayment of the old loan she had given him to set up his business.

"Without interest, and with no allowance for inflation," she said. "Just the nominal sum. And you can have the whole of next year to get it together. Do you think you can manage that?"

"I don't know," Thune mumbled, somewhat taken aback. "I'll just have to work harder. You know that Rolle has left the firm? He still has his share in the business, but he's no longer working there."

He looked out through the window: the street lamps were already lit, darkness was falling fast.

"Of course I know," Esther Thune said, pursing her lips. "Do you imagine that Ulla hasn't been telephoning me every day to tell me how awful you are? She and Sigurd came to dinner yesterday, and my sense of propriety prevents me from repeating what they said about you. Would you like tea and sandwiches, by the way? I can call Linnea and ask her to make some."

"No, thank you," Thune said. "I've already eaten."

"What was it really about?" Esther asked in a measured voice. "This nasty business between you and Rolf-Åke?"

"We didn't see eye to eye," Thune said. "Rolle . . . Rolf-Åke has changed. We disagreed about most things. How to manage the firm, political issues, everything."

"Pah," Esther snorted. "It's those liberal fancies you've got! We actually discussed them last time, Dr Lorens and I."

Thune could not help smiling:

"Yes, Zorro has let me know that he thinks I'm mistaken."

"I'm inclined to agree with him," Esther said severely. "Naturally, the life of the nation must rest on constitutional foundations, but there are actually more important things than democracy. Is it really worth getting beaten black and blue for such naïve ideals?"

Isn't it precisely naïve ideals for which one is supposed to be willing to be attacked? Thune felt like asking. But he was tired and had little appetite for a political row, and before he could make up his mind whether or not to ask the question, Esther said:

"You know that Dr Lorens has got rid of his lady friend?"

"No, I didn't know that," Thune said with interest, remembering the serious face staring out at him from the photograph in the Russian Villa.

"Oh, yes," Esther said. "Astrid Segersven, history teacher and deputy headmistress of the girls' lyceum. He's been courting her for several years. No doubt she was expecting an engagement ring, but now he's given her the elbow instead."

Two days after that Thune finished work at half past four. He walked down to the main city harbour – his doctor at the hospital had prescribed fresh air – then back into the centre, and took the tram out to Brändö. Sergey Gerasimoff was having a cocktail party at home, and his villa on Silversundsvägen was full of prominent Helsinki citizens. Gera and his wife Maria were performing their duties as host and hostess with great elegance, and the guest list was magnificent: there were serious politicians

310

and journalists, from Ernst von Born to Eljas Erkko, there were important businessmen like Leopold Grönroos and Erik von Frenckell, there were Thune's former diplomatic colleagues Snellman and Nykopp, and there were famous authors and actors, led by Hella Wuolijoki and Tauno Palo.

Thune had been thinking of only staying an hour or two. He still had some difficulty moving about, and the yellowish swelling around his eye meant that he had to reply to curious questions time after time, and absorb the expressions of affronted sympathy that he was already heartily sick of.

There was a large measure of tension in the festive atmosphere that evening. There were plenty of suspicious glances and cool nods, and Thune knew why. The guests represented opinions from all points on the political scale. There were Marxists and men and women from the far right, and Thune thought with amusement that no-one but Gera Gerasimoff would hit upon the absurd idea of inviting representatives from across the political spectrum and expect everyone to have a good time.

Thune spent a while talking to Snellman and Nykopp, and picked up the rumour that Foreign Minister Holsti had started drinking again and had embarrassed himself at a reception in Geneva. Then he slipped his anchor and drifted about for a time, but found a refuge in the form of a group of talkative film people. In the centre of the group stood one of the new stars, Santeri Soihtu. The others were directors, film journalists and actors of lower rank, and they were all exerting themselves to praise Soihtu's performance in the historical drama "The Riding Master of Ruhala".

Santeri Soihtu was a tall, slim man with an almost unbelievably beautiful face: his exquisitely chiselled, masculine chin even had the requisite little dimple for a film star. But Soihtu did not appear to be cheered by the lavish praise bestowed upon him. He seemed almost miserable, and when a red-haired woman in an evening jumpsuit looked round carefully and then predicted

311

that Santeri Soihtu would be a bigger name than Tauno Palo in a few years, Soihtu said:

"I'm not sure it would be worth it. I want to play proper roles, not make sentimental propaganda."

Thune could see that Soihtu's vision was unfocused and his voice was slurred: the star had evidently drunk too much. Thune recalled that Mrs Wiik had said that she admired Soihtu, and that she liked him more than Palo and someone else – Kalske, perhaps? For a few moments Thune wondered whether to break into the conversation and ask Soihtu to send a signed photograph to the office, Mrs Wiik would surely be pleased by a surprise of that sort in the midst of the November darkness. But then he rejected the idea: what if Soihtu did not believe his story about his film-loving office assistant and thought that he, Claes Thune, was homosexual and was asking for a portrait on his own account?

The following evening Thune saw Gabi for the first time since the weeks before his move to Moscow.

It was Wednesday, 9 November, and exactly a week before the Club was going to meet in Thune's apartment. He was on his way to make the first advance purchases for the evening. It was a task he could easily have entrusted to Mrs Wiik or Mrs Leimu, but which he did not believe Miss Johansson would carry out satisfactorily. He did not feel any enthusiasm about the coming Club meeting, merely weariness and irritation. Perhaps it was the fault of the fog and damp, but the only thing he really wanted to do was sit in front of a warm fire and read novels.

So immersed in such thoughts was Thune that he did not see Gabi, and practically walked into her: they were a hair's breadth from colliding on the pavement of Henriksgatan outside Stockmann's department store.

Thune was not surprised that it happened, nor was he surprised that it happened there.

He had handled the divorce negotiations together with Gabi's solicitor, Henrik Hindsberg: Thune and Gabi had not even spoken by telephone or written to each other. But although the city had grown, its core remained surprisingly small and uncosmopolitan, and Thune and Gabi also moved in the same circles. Thune had assumed that they would meet sooner or later, and he had suspected that it would happen in the heart of the city.

Gabi was wearing a pearl-grey autumn coat, and on her head she had a red, Basque-like velvet hat. She was wearing elegant high-heeled shoes – both the hat and the shoes looked unsuitably summery in the November mist – and when she pulled her glove off to shake hands Thune saw that her nails were freshly varnished. After they had shaken hands Thune looked at the blonde curls peeping out from beneath the beret.

Gabi had always been thin, but she seemed to have lost even more weight. She looked oddly young, and Thune's memory played a mean trick on him and took him back to their time together in Stockholm. He saw himself and Gabi travelling on the underground railway between Södra Bantorget and Slussen on one of the first days after the line was opened. Gabi had smiled uncertainly at him as the train sped up and headed into the tunnel, the lighting inside the carriage was dull and weak, and on the other side of the aisle sat a boy idly spinning a yoyo. Gabi had been wearing a pearl-grey coat then too – a different coat, but the colour was exactly the same.

Thune came to his senses and they stood there on the street making small talk for a while.

Gabi looked with sympathy at the yellow bruise around his eye and said:

"I heard about what happened. You're lucky it wasn't worse. It's dreadful, the way barbarity is spreading."

The evening air was chilly and every now and then Gabi coughed slightly. Thune wanted to ask her about *The Silk Cushion*. How had she reacted to the book's reception? Was

313

she not embarrassed by everything that had been said and written about her? But something stopped him, and instead he could not help thinking about her short story, "Little Miss Forlander".

It was the most improper of the stories in *The Silk Cushion*. Young Miss Forlander is burning with a desire to become an actress and work in films, and in the key scene of the story she meets a producer at a cocktail party. She travels in the producer's car "out onto the lonely forest roads beyond Alberga", and there feels "a salty and insipid taste on her tongue", and returns to the party "with her garter clumsily fastened and the promise of a small role in Vaala's next comedy."

Thune looked at the woman who would shortly become his ex-wife, and who had written about clumsily fastened garters and so much else, and he felt his lack of experience rise to the surface yet again: his ears were burning, and he knew they were already red.

He pulled his hat down a little further and hoped that Gabi would not notice the state he was in, while simultaneously thinking about how quickly people become strangers to one another. He did not feel that he knew the elegant woman standing in front of him in the thick Helsinki fog, and he was struck by the thought that perhaps that had always been the case: they had never known one another.

Once again he succumbed and steered the conversation onto precisely the subject he ought to have avoided:

"Well, in December it will all be done. Then you can both do as you like."

Gabi gave him a sad smile and shook her head:

"Please, Claes, don't torment yourself."

She had never used a nickname for him. When they were newly married she had admitted to him that she thought the one his friends sometimes used, "Klabben", was ridiculous, a name for closed gentlemen's clubs in which men pretended to be more

314

stupid than they were. A name on a par with Zorro, Lorre, Polle and Yogi.

During his time in Moscow Thune had passed lonely, jealous nights when he would have liked to ask her if she actually thought that "Gabi" and "Robi" were so much better. But now it no longer mattered. When he did not say anything Gabi went on:

"We've decided to take things a bit more slowly, Robi and I. Things are fine as they are. Besides, I want to try writing a novel now."

Thune felt a mixture of relief and anxiety. The fact that Gabi and Robi were not going to get married presumably meant that Gabi had no plans to make a late attempt to have children: she was thirty-eight now, so time was running out.

But if she was going to write a novel, Thune had no guarantee that she would not use material from their life together. There had already been a lot he recognised in the short stories, and Gabi seemed to be taking her writing seriously.

Why? was the thought that echoed around Thune's head. Why did all this have to happen?

And, for once, he asked the question the moment it popped into his head, saying it quickly, without hesitation.

Gabi looked surprised and awkward. She stared down at the pavement and said nothing for a long time.

"*Le cœur a ses raisons que la raison ne connaît pas,*" she then said quietly.

Thune recognised the quotation. He could not think of a response: nothing sarcastic and sharp, but nothing forgiving and wise either.

"You probably think you were expendable," Gabi said. "That you were there one day, then replaced and forgotten the next. But that's not how it is at all."

Thune shrugged and hoped his facial expression was not revealing what he was thinking.

315

"I only believe in people's actions," he said. "Words mean nothing to me anymore."

"Nothing is unambiguous, Claes. Nothing is simple and clean. I'm . . . very happy with Robi, but I miss you often. I think about you every time I walk down Högbergsgatan."

"I'm sorry, Gabi," Thune said. "I know you want me to say that that's fine. But I can't. What you're saying is no comfort to me."

23

She asked Thune for a Saturday off. She got it, and went to see
Konni and Tuulikki and the children in Åbo that weekend.

She thought she might as well be there as at home. Tuulikki's
good humour was infectious and sometimes she managed to get
Matilda to smile. The eldest child, Raija, would notice and say:
"Look! Aunt Tilda's laughing!"

She had decided to give Konni what was left of her savings.
She would call it a loan, of course: otherwise Konni would refuse
to accept the money.

Miss Milja did not like either Tuulikki or Konni, she was
always sulky and completely silent in their company. It was nice
like that. Not that it really made any difference. Miss Milja had
nothing to say, not anymore.

She told Thune that she would be going away for the weekend,
but not where, or who she was going to see.

Thune was recovering from the assault now, the stitches had
been removed and the swelling round his eye was as good as
gone. He had started to smile at her again, and sometimes said
friendly things.

Like the afternoon when he complimented her on her green

scarf, and said it spread light in the November darkness, and went so well with her hair.

She now knew who Thune's wife was, and that it was his wife who had left him. She had asked around very cautiously, calling some former work colleagues who had contacts in bourgeois circles. She had wanted to prove to herself that her boss was not the only one who knew how to find things out.

And Thune was right, it was easy to get hold of information.

The details were of course surprising. They made her feel even more sympathy for Thune. They made her feel sorry for him, and her empathy for him made her think that under other circumstances, in a different life, she and Thune might have been able to get closer to each other.

Perhaps she might even have been able to console him.

But as things stood now, none of that mattered. It was too late for friendship now.

As the weekend approached Thune's mood sank again. There had been riots all over Germany after the murder of a German diplomat in Paris. The killer was a Jew, and in revenge synagogues had been burned down and Jewish shops and businesses razed to the ground. Jewish men and boys had been assaulted and taken away to camps, and even murdered.

Matilda thought that Thune was on his way to becoming almost obsessed with the news. He read the newspapers over and over again, both *Hufvudstadsbladet* and *Svenska Pressen* as well as *Helsingin Sanomat*, he listened to the news agency bulletins on the radio in his room, and when he had switched the radio off he listened to that noisy, monotonous piece of music time after time.

On Friday she had a small suitcase standing in the entrance hall all day – she was going to the station straight from the office. When she knocked on Thune's door to wish him a good weekend the music was approaching its cacophonous finale and he did not hear her knocking. She did not open the door, and

318

went and sat back down at her desk to write a message on a blank page of an accounts ledger. She left it on top of the provisional list of the following week's meetings, picked up her case and walked out through the door.

In Åbo Konni was in a good mood, almost a different person: he had stopped drinking again.

He had the weekend off as well, he was full of plans and talked non-stop.

It was good that Konni talked a lot, because Matilda did not say much, she just listened. When Tuulikki asked how she was, she said calmly that everything was as it should be, and that she was happy with her work.

Konni was upset about the Jewish pogroms, just like Thune. He was not depressed, though, but utterly furious, saying that fascism was on its way to dragging the whole of Europe to destruction, and that no-one but the Communists dared put up any resistance.

But mostly Konni talked about Arizona and his music.

Arizona's engagement at Lepakko was almost over, and Konni was longing to leave Helsinki and move back to Tuulikki and the children. *Ajan Suunta* had written that Arizona and the other dance bands who mixed jazz songs in amongst their Finnish numbers were responsible for an erotic Bolshevism which was despoiling European youth, body and soul. Konni said it did not matter where you played and lived, the Patriotic People's Party were everywhere, even in Åbo.

Konni was convinced that the band would be able to play at the Hamburger Börs, just like last winter. But while he was waiting for things to improve he had been forced to sell some songs to Klaus Salmi and the Ramblers, among them "Mirage".

That week something peculiar had happened. Pahlman and Laakko from Dallapé had turned up and asked if Konni wanted some extra work, a day job that Dallapé had been offered but could not take on, because everyone in the band was exhausted after their tour of Sweden, which had lasted the whole of October.

"What sort of work?" Konni had asked.

"A Dutch radio company is here doing some experiments," Pahlman had said. "Radio with pictures, 'television'. They arrived from Sweden on the same boat as us. They want some musicians to go to the studio while they do test transmissions. You'd be well paid."

Konni had taken Snurre, the xylophone player, with him. Outside the Radio House on Fabiansgatan a large van had been parked, a transmission van with the name *Philips* painted across the side. Konni and Snurre had played trumpet, piano and xylophone in a cramped studio which only just had room for the instruments, camera, musicians and cameraman.

The radio directors had been sitting in the next room watching them on a screen while they played. Afterwards Konni had heard one of the directors say: "This is the future. We're going to be able to bring moving pictures into every home."

"Snurre thought it was interesting," Konni said. "But I didn't like it at all. It felt like the camera was staring at me."

"You wouldn't like being a film star, then," Matilda said.

"Don't say that," Konni said, and smiled. "But everything's become so strange. Next week there's a concert at the Conservatory in Helsinki. Some sort of electrical instrument. They claim it can play itself."

"I don't believe that," Matilda said.

"It's going to end with machines doing everything," Konni said angrily. "Us musicians won't be needed – we'll all end up on the scrapheap!"

"So you're not thinking of going along to listen?"

"I can't. We're playing our last night at Lepakko then."

"Why didn't you come and see me when you'd been at the Radio House? You know I work on the other side of the square."

320

"I was going to. But then I thought about your boss. I'm ashamed of what I did back in the summer."

"Thune forgave you a long time ago. He's been through worse things since."

Matilda gazed at Konni as he sat there looking down at the table, stirring his coffee with his spoon, and thought how much she liked him.

"It's a shame you didn't come," she said.

On the train to Helsinki on the Sunday evening she spent the whole of the first hour thinking about Konni.

She had had to pester him into accepting the money. He had admitted that he needed it, but said that she had already helped him so much: even if things improved, Konni did not know when he would be able to pay it back.

She had said that was not important, that she had enough to get by, and in the end he gave in.

She saw the yard in front of the children's home again, the slushy snow, the flakes in Konni's hair, the coat that was far too big for him, the moth holes in his sweater, and his eyes, simultaneously hard and sad.

She tried to think good thoughts.

Things had turned out well for Konni and her. That was the way to look at it. There were so many who had starved to death or been shot, but she and Konni had survived and found good jobs, and had been able to live as free, respected individuals.

The good thoughts did not help. The creatures caught up with her in the second-class compartment. They teemed over her, thousands, hundreds of thousands of them, she could feel her neck and cheeks pricking with anxiety and shame as beads of cold sweat broke out all over her body and started trickling downward. Her ears were roaring, but at the same time she could hear quiet rustling as the invisible insects laid their eggs in her and released their excrement on her, they were everywhere, from the top of her head to the balls of her feet, in the past few weeks she had felt them time and time again, marching across her body in their millions, whole armies of them. She mumbled an apology to the person sitting next to her and stood up to leave the compartment and go and stand in the passageway, where the air was cooler and she could get to the toilet if she found herself having to throw up.

24

The Russian scientist and inventor Léon Theremin, who was living in New York, has disappeared without trace. Theremin, who has both a home and an experimental laboratory in central Manhattan, has not been seen for several weeks, and his friends and the authorities are perplexed. "We cannot rule out the possibility that Soviet counter-espionage is responsible," says James Dowd, a senior officer with the New York Police Department. Léon Theremin, whose real name is Lev Termen and who is said to be of Jewish extraction, is best known as the inventor of the famous musical instrument, the theremin. A concert demonstrating the instrument in question will take place this evening at the Helsinki Conservatory.

Article in *Hufvudstadsbladet*,
Tuesday, 15 November, 1938

Yogi Jary was the one who had noticed the forthcoming concert at the Conservatory and asked Robi Lindemark if he could attend, even though he had been admitted to Kopparbäck.

Lindemark spent several days considering the request – he told Thune that Jary was in a depressive phase and that exposing him to stimuli likely to provoke an emotional response was risky – but finally decided to agree to the proposal.

The concert was due to take place the evening before the November meeting of the Wednesday Club, and Lindemark suggested that the entire Club attend the performance. It would not be appropriate for Jary to come to the meeting at Thune's home, Robi said, because there was a danger that Yogi might go to pieces if the meeting became political and heated, but a concert in the company of good friends and a small glass afterwards could actually have a therapeutic effect.

Lindemark said he was very busy at the hospital, and wondered if Thune had time to call the others. Thune agreed to help, and his round of telephone calls on the Saturday before the concert gave good results. Arelius, Grönroos and Röman all asked what sort of peculiar instrument it was, and how come Jary was aware of it, but of the three both Arelius and Röman agreed to come. The only one who was unable to attend was Grönroos, who was catching the boat to Stettin on Monday: a business trip, so he would miss not only the concert but also the Club meeting.

On Monday evening Lindemark telephoned Thune, sounding worried. Not on Jary's account – Yogi's mood was better than it had been for several weeks, and he was looking forward to the concert. Lindemark was concerned for himself and those around him. His workload at Kopparbäck had long been inhuman, he said, and that had led to him seriously neglecting his family and friends.

It's Gabi, Thune thought. You mean Gabi, but you don't want to say that to me.

Several months ago that insight would have felt like a mortal blow. But not anymore. It still hurt a little, but the bitterness was gone.

"Are you trying to say that you can't come, and would like me to take charge?" he asked, without beating about the bush.

"No, I'll come to the concert," Lindemark said. "It's just

that I shall have to leave immediately afterwards, so I was wondering . . ."

"Yes?" Thune said when Lindemark hesitated.

"It's just that Yogi needs to get back to the ward that evening," Lindemark said seriously. "All other alternatives are too risky. So I was wondering if you could borrow my car and drive Yogi to Kopparbäck after the concert?"

"By all means," Thune said, aware that he sounded hesitant. "It's just that I haven't driven for a while. And in the dark, as well . . ."

"I know you've got a lot of work to do as well," Lindemark said. "And that you've got the Club meeting to think about. But of course you'd take the car back to Borgvägen afterwards. And you can keep it all of Wednesday if you like."

"You won't need the car yourself?" Thune wondered.

"Not at all," Lindemark said. "Catching the bus would suit me very well, I've got a lot to read at the moment. If you leave the car on Kaserntorget on Wednesday afternoon, you can give me the keys when we meet at yours that evening. That would be perfect!"

Thune thought how much easier it would be to get the bottles of drink back to his if he had a car. He also realised that this was his chance to help Yogi Jary in such a way that Yogi noticed. It would doubtless feel odd to drive Robi Lindemark's car out to Kopparbäck in the dark when he knew that at the same time Robi was going to bed with Gabi. But for Yogi's sake he wanted to do it.

"Very well," he said. "That's what we'll do."

"Thanks, Claes!" Lindemark said. "I won't forget this."

"If you're trying to make Yogi well again, and Polle and Zorro are paying for his care, this is the very least I can do," Thune said, meaning every word.

*

325

Late on Tuesday afternoon, just a few hours before the concert, one of them cried off. Zorro Arelius called Thune at his office, pleading *force majeure*. Not one, but two of his elderly patients had fallen ill: they were in pain and very anxious, and needed Arelius. He had also been called up for reserve manoeuvres and would be catching the train to the east on Thursday morning. He needed time to pack, and of course Wednesday evening was set aside for the Club meeting.

"That's a shame," Thune said. "That means there'll only be four of us this evening."

"Yes," Arelius said. "I'd like to have been there. But what can you do? This is what happens once you've taken the oath."

The concert was a peculiar experience.

There had been rumours, but they turned out not to be true: the theremin did not play itself, it needed a musician.

The musician in question was a woman, from the U.S.A. But she had a Russian name, Olga Nemchova.

The theremin looked like an unwieldy radio receiver. A piece of metal protruded horizontally from one side of the wooden box, and another stuck out vertically from the other side.

The odd thing was that the musician's fingers never touched the instrument. Olga Nemchova held each of her hands close to the pieces of metal and moved them elegantly and rhythmically closer to and further away from the metal. Thune noticed that her fingers moved the same way as a violinist's or a guitarist's fingers sought out notes on the neck of their instrument, only in the air.

To start with, the members of the meagre audience seemed almost shocked. Then they listened with interest, but Nemchova had to play a number of pieces before anyone dared applaud.

During the interval Thune stood in the foyer smoking.

Three men of a similar age to him were standing some

distance away smoking heavy mahorka tobacco and speaking Russian, but he could not hear what they were saying. He had read in the newspaper that the inventor of the theremin had recently disappeared, and for a few moments he was convinced that two of the men were guarding the third, who looked frightened and unhappy. But then the sad man laughed and slapped one of the others on the back, and Thune smiled at his own imagination. Léon Theremin had disappeared in New York, so what would he be doing in Helsinki?

Before the interval Olga Nemchova had played original compositions by Theremin himself and other modern composers. After the break she played three Russian folk songs, a chanson by Chevalier, and then concluded with Camille Saint-Saëns' "Swan". As she played this last piece Thune saw that Yogi Jary was in tears.

It was not only the way the theremin was played that was peculiar – the sound itself was almost as odd. Thin and clear, yet simultaneously shrill and occasionally almost ghostly. Just before the interval Thune said to Lindemark that the ethereal effect was probably because the theremin was often a few microtones off the note. Thune did not know how the notes were produced, but even though Olga Nemchova was very skilled, it was clear that it was extremely difficult to make the instrument sound perfectly clear.

By the time they emerged from the Conservatory the wind had got up and it had started to rain. The city lay wet and dark, over where the General Post Office was being built the tarpaulins were flapping in the wind, and the gaudy neon lights of the city centre only served to emphasise the sense of desolation.

It was already late and none of them felt like going for a drink. Guido Röman was in a hurry to get home to Kammiogatan: while they were waiting for the concert to start he had told the

327

others that Ghita was expecting again, their fifth child. Thune had felt both envy and sympathy, and wondered how Ghita Röman managed to cope, seeing as the children had all been born so close together.

Once Röman had left, Lindemark gave Thune the car keys and told him that the Olympia was parked behind the National Museum, and that it started and went like clockwork: there was a map on the back seat in case he should need it, but otherwise it was ready to go.

"Don't you want us to drive you home first?" Thune asked. "It's such awful weather."

"No, I'm happy to walk. See you at yours, then, Claes – *à demain!*" Lindemark said cheerily, then stood and adjusted his scarf and put up his umbrella as Thune and Jary started to walk away.

Outside the city the November night seemed even darker, and Thune and Jary spent most of the drive in silence.

That was partly down to Thune. He had not driven for a very long time, and his night vision was not particularly good: given that the weather was poor and gusts of wind were making the car shake, he preferred to concentrate on the task at hand.

At the same time he could see that Lindemark had been right. There was nothing left of the nervous energy Jary had shown when Thune visited him at Kopparbäck a few weeks ago. Jary was deeply depressed, and the strange concert seemed to have left him in a state in which he shut the rest of the world out completely. He simply stared out through the side window without saying a word.

Eventually, when they had already turned off the main road towards the village of Kopparbäck, and had just a few kilometres left to drive, Thune felt he had to come up with something to say.

328

"It will get better, Yogi," he said. "It will get better, you just have to stick it out."

Jary did not reply immediately. Only when Thune cleared his throat as if he were about to say something else did he finally mutter:

"All the borders are being closed now. We're being treated like animals."

Thune realised that Jary was referring to the Jews, and said:

"It can't be quite that bad. Zbaszyn was terrible, and what happened last week even worse, but . . ."

Jary interrupted him:

"You don't understand. You could be beaten up fifty times for something you'd written and you still wouldn't understand how it feels to be a pariah."

Thune felt irritation flare up inside him. His left elbow still ached and he did not appreciate Jary downplaying what he had been through.

He could not help his annoyance growing. Time after time Jary took on the role of sacrificial lamb, and he did so in a self-pitying way. He was nothing like the courageous, lively Yogi Thune had once known. He was aware that he and Jary were similar, insofar as neither of them knew how to defend himself in a fight. But from there it was still a big step to feeling sorry for yourself simply because you were Jewish, or Swedish, or a Mussulman, or whatever it happened to be that was not to the taste of those around you.

Thune thought that Yogi would do better to follow the example of his nephews, Salomon, Reuwen and Elias. They were not only men's men and good at all manner of sports, but were also known for their drinking, fighting and womanising: the young Jary brothers were making the most of life, and made no apology for the fact that they existed.

While Thune was trying to find a friendly, uncritical way to put his thoughts into words, Jary said:

"Do you know what we heard this evening?"

"I heard a peculiar instrument that was not quite in tune," Thune said. He thought it time to lighten the mood a little, and went on: "I think I'd rather hear 'The Swan' performed on the cello. What did *you* hear?"

"Death," Jary said, so quietly it was almost a whisper. "Death, in the form of two kings from Germany and Russia."

Thune sighed silently to himself and put his foot down impatiently on the accelerator as he drove along the avenue towards the hospital. Naked tree trunks appeared as black spectres in the flood of light in front of the car, passing and disappearing into the darkness again. Thune thought of the long drive back to Helsinki and regretted his willingness to be helpful. He saw to his relief that they were expected: the entrance to the main building was lit up and a night nurse was standing outside, and raised her hand in greeting as the car approached.

"Please, Yogi, get better," Thune said, even though he knew it was wrong of him to talk like that. "You've got to get better, it hurts to hear you talk like that."

It was almost one o'clock by the time Thune parked the Olympia on Borgvägen.

It will be a short night, he thought as he went inside his home. Too little sleep, and tomorrow evening I shall have to be witty when the Club meets here.

A few hours later he realised that he was not going to get any sleep at all. He had been tossing and turning from side to side in his bed, trying to sleep on his back and his stomach, he had been up for a pee, had drunk a glass of milk and made himself a liver pâté sandwich.

Nothing helped, and he decided to brew a pot of tea. He moved quietly so as not to wake Miss Johansson, who slept in the maid's room behind the kitchen, and while he waited for the tea to brew he stood at the window looking out at the darkness and smoking a Chesterfield.

He sat through the rest of the night.

Anxiety was tugging and tearing at him, but he could not put his finger on what was causing it.

He thought about Yogi Jary, he thought about the unhappy drive back to Kopparbäck and the fact that he had not been capable of being as friendly to Yogi as he would have liked.

He thought about something that someone – Zorro or Robi, he could not remember who – had said at one of the Club meetings back in the spring.

That one of the strongest motives for wanting to do good was a guilty conscience at having done bad things earlier in life.

Thune had wanted to do something good for Yogi Jary. Did that mean he had let him down in the past, that he had done harm by not being there when Jary started to show the first symptoms of illness?

Could Yogi have been saved if Thune had been a better, more supportive friend?

Thune did not know.

When the clock on the wall struck half past six his eyes were stinging with tiredness, but he got dressed regardless and went for a walk. He had to get through the working day, and he was going to host the Club that evening. It was still dark, but perhaps the fresh air would give him the energy he needed. And he could always sleep for an hour or so in the office.

It occurred to him that if only Rolle would remove his things from the Cabinet, he would be able to buy a chaise longue or camp bed. Then, if necessary, he could spend the night in the office, and take restorative naps whenever he felt he needed to.

He walked over the hill and down towards Fiskartorpet.

The air was raw and chill. For the first time that autumn Thune felt that winter was on its way.

Thoughts were swirling through his weary brain.

He thought about Rolle: had he been wrong not to show him more patience? Ought he to have given Rolle more chances?

He thought about Mrs Wiik, who was getting quieter and quieter, even though her tormentor, Rolle, was gone.

He wondered if he should dare to suggest the unthinkable that evening – that they dissolve the Wednesday Club.

So many things about which to have an opinion. So many decisions to take.

Down at Fiskartorpet work was progressing on the extension, in spite of the early hour. The round banqueting hall was almost ready, and in the vestibule a number of artists – presumably a master and his apprentices – were putting the finishing touches to a fresco.

Thune thought he could see a familiar figure among the painters. At first he could not place her, but then he remembered: the rower who had appeared out of nowhere when he was sunbathing on Synnerstlandet back in August.

He searched his memory. What was it she had said to him . . . that he should not worry so much?

There was something else as well, something he had forgotten.

He searched for her again, but she was gone. He looked from one painter to the next, but she was not there, and Thune was soon convinced he had never seen her.

A mirage.

Like so much else.

Everything about that morning, everything about his life, suddenly felt like a feeble mirage.

As if nothing were properly real, as if everything he undertook remained unfinished.

As if there were not sufficient oxygen in the world for him to go on breathing.

It's probably just tiredness after a sleepless night, he thought.

He needed to pull himself together, he had to go in to the office and get going with the day's work, there was so much to do.

He turned on his heel and walked quickly over the hill and back to Borgvägen, opened the front door of the Olympia and got in.

It struck him that he ought to go inside and tell Miss Johansson that he would not be having any breakfast.

But then he shrugged, started the engine and drove off.

25

It was quiet inside her home, but she knew she had to hurry: she could hear surprised voices from one of the neighbouring flats; she did not know if it was the one next to hers, or downstairs.

At first she had lain awake, sensing that the Captain was doing the same: he was sleeping far too uneasily and lightly.

Then he had woken up properly, and had wanted to do it again.

It was still pitch black in the bedroom, her curtains were thick and did not let in any light until dawn arrived.

She had let it happen, thinking that if everything went as it should, it made no difference if he was careful or not.

He had been careful the second time as well. She had not helped at all, just lay still and felt him pull out and grunt, and then the splash as it hit her thighs and stomach.

After that he had fallen asleep properly, peaceful as a child, apart from the snores, which – although sporadic – were long and deep.

She had waited until dawn: she needed light to see by but did not dare turn a light on.

She had gone out into the kitchen, turned the tap on and let the water run as she stood there waiting.

He could have woken up then, and she would still have been able to back out.

He had gone on sleeping, his snores rumbling through the silent flat. Grey light had filtered in through the curtain in the living room. She had opened the pantry door and fumbled behind the tin of flour.

The previous evening, when she had been sitting waiting for him, Miss Milja had set about her with her ideas. Miss Milja had seen too many films. She was silly and theatrical, thought she should lean over him and whisper "You're only a little lance-corporal" or something else similarly confected immediately beforehand.

She had dismissed Miss Milja. It was too dangerous, there was no time for anything like that.

She had started to shake as she stood in the kitchen.

Had tried to remember everything Reinhard had said and shown her. Had commanded herself to stop shaking.

Had gone into the bedroom, round to his side of the bed, and leaned over.

He had been sleeping on his left side. She was not sure, but believed she had simply held it against his temple and fired.

She had been frightened, of course, the blast was much harder than she remembered and she had jerked back, and her legs had threatened to give way.

The Captain's body had quivered slightly, not for long, but she was beside herself, rushed into the living room, heard herself whimper with terror, turned round and took aim at the doorway in case he came after her.

She sat in her reading chair and could not stop shaking, it was as if she were freezing, she was still aiming at the open doorway even though she knew he would not be coming.

She had been worried that she would start thinking about Konni and Tuulikki and the children and start crying. But it was easy not to – she was alone now.

She did not want to think about Thune either. But the thoughts came anyway, rushing through her head, telling her that she had betrayed him and that he was bound to misunderstand everything.

A door opened out in the stairwell and she heard anxious, agitated voices.

She had to get the shaking to stop, so that she could lift her arm.

She looked away from the doorway and saw Miss Milja standing in the corner to the right of the window. Her eyes were grey and calm, her hair glistened, freshly washed, her fingernails were long and intact and gleamed dark red.

She nodded.

Epilogue

Anxiety took hold of him during the ten-minute duration of the tram ride.

When he got off he was no longer content to jog, and ran the length of the block down to Mechelingatan as fast as he could.

He was still some distance from the building when he saw the crowd of people.

As he got closer he saw the building's inhabitants and other citizens standing in small groups whispering and talking, and he saw the policemen, and he saw the doctor and the ambulancemen vanish through the doorway just as he got there.

Afterwards he would realise that the police and ambulance must have arrived during the fifteen minutes or so it had taken him to get from Kaserntorget to Tölö: otherwise they would have answered the telephone when he had called.

But at the time he understood nothing at all.

He stood on his own a short distance from the whispering crowd. He stood and stared at the closed front door, and when twenty, perhaps thirty minutes had passed and the ambulancemen emerged carrying first one stretcher, then another, he was still standing there motionless, staring.

Only when the covered stretchers were being lifted into the

ambulance did he go up to the policeman he thought might be in charge and ask what had happened, even though he already knew.

He said who he was, and that he had an employee who lived in that stairwell, and was given confirmation that Mrs Wiik was dead. The superintendent asked him in an authoritative voice to remain there, they would speak to him shortly.

He asked who the other body was. The superintendent gave him a suspicious glance, but said that it appeared to be a doctor by the name of Lindemark.

Thoughts began to race through Thune's head, one after the other, all equally quick and empty. He thought he was the victim of a huge conspiracy, he wondered where Gabi was, he wondered how many times he had been deceived in his life, he thought that he might have been able to prevent the whole thing if only he had listened harder, he thought that the Wednesday Club would never meet again, that he had told Mrs Wiik that he appreciated her work but not that he appreciated her, that there was an Opel parked on Kaserntorget and that he, Thune, had the keys in his pocket, and that he had wanted to stick a knife into the man whose dead body had just been carried out from Mrs Wiik's stairwell.

He stood there on that November morning, a morning as cold and transparent as glass, and thought that the world he had known and had such great hopes of had disintegrated into nothingness: perhaps it had never even existed?

Some Observations

This is a novel, and the central characters of the story have no equivalents in real life.

The song "Mirage", written by Konni Ahlbäck, is fictitious. It feels important to point out that the song "Mirage" ("*Kangastus*"), which does exist in the real world, was written by Kauko Käyhkö and was recorded by the dance band Dallapé in 1940. There is no doubt at all that Käyhkö wrote the song.

Connoisseurs of older Finnish popular culture will note that I have compressed time slightly. Anyone who, for instance, recalls that the famous film scene in which Ansa Ikonen leans out from a kiosk and sings was not recorded until the summer of 1939 is entirely correct.

Acknowledgements

My list of acknowledgements is long. Even so, I know that I am bound to forget to mention one or more people, and for this I apologise: it is not intentional, but entirely the result of a poor memory.

Many thanks to my publishers and editors, Tapani Ritamäki, Jaana Koistinen, Stephen Farran-Lee and Sara Ehnholm Hielm: your advice is occasionally contradictory but always wise, and your support is invaluable.

I would also like to thank the Finnish National Council for Literature, the Arts Promotion Centre Finland, the Swedish Cultural Foundation in Finland, the Society of Swedish Authors in Finland, and the Otava Literary Foundation, whose support has made it possible for me to devote many years wholeheartedly to writing novels. I should also like to express my gratitude to the National Library, that silent and cool oasis in the centre of Helsinki.

The following individuals have helped me in various ways during my work on this book. The list contains the names of people I have never met, but whose books or films have been important sources of information and inspiration to me: Peter von Bagh, Johan Bargum, Christina Hedberg, Magdalena

Hedlund, Katariina Heilala, Annika Hällsten, Cita Högnabba, Monika Holmén, Ulla Hörhammer, Mikaela Johansson, Klaus Kaartinen, Eeva Kanerva, Kasper Kronberg (Arch Tech), Jukka Kukkonen, Anna-Lena Laurén, Brita Lindberg, Kjell Lindroos, Lisa Luukkanen, Arto Mansala, Patrik Muskos, Maarit Niiniluoto, Janina Orlov, Lena Pasternak, Tuulikki Pekkalainen, Pekka Railo, Thomas Rosenberg, Liisa Ryömä, Aleksi Salonen (Arch Tech), Ann-Sophie Sandström, Jaana Seppänen, Maria Silfverberg, Maria Slangus, Viljo Sohkanen, Eva Tamm, Margareta Tamm, Peder Tamm, Bengt Thorson, Marko Tikka, Hillel Tokazier, Marina Wallman, Jenny Westergård, John-Eric Westö, Svante Weyler, Göran Wörlund.

For practical help during a long winter: Benjamin, Calle, Helena, Janne, Magda, Mårten.

And, last but not least, thank you to the people with whom I have had the pleasure of making music during the years I was working on the book.

Bandmates: Henrika, Mårten, Bengt, Pede, Tapsa, Silja, Pasi H., Mauri, Juba, Arto, Aku.

Also: Hannu, Sampo, Markku, Johanna, Teijo, Väinö & Totti, Christoffer, Pekka, Michael, Meelis, Kari H., J. P., Joe White alias Tero M., Tero P., Lefty Willie, Johannes, Daniel, the boys in Wentus (thanks for Åbo!).

K.W.
Helsinki, June 2013

KJELL WESTÖ was born in 1961 and lives in Helsinki. He made his literary debut in 1986, and since then has published poetry, collections of short stories, and novels. His novel *Där vi en gang gått* (*Where Once We Walked*) was translated into most major European languages and was awarded the Finlandia Prize, Finland's most prestigious literary award.

NEIL SMITH is a translator from Swedish and Norwegian to English living in Norfolk. His translations include works by Leif G. W. Persson, Liza Marklund, Mons Kallentoft, Anders de la Motte, Lars Kepler, Jonas Karlsson, Jo Nesbo and Erik Axl Sund.